The sequel to White Lake

RETURN HOME

A Novel

Debbie,
Follow your
dream!
SA Todd

SUSAN AMOND TODD

This book is a work of fiction. Names, characters, places, and incidents either are products of the author's imagination or are used fictitiously. Any resemblance to actual events or locales or persons, living or dead, is entirely coincidental.

ISBN: 978-1-7323362-2-3

Edited by: Amy Ashby

Published by Warren Publishing
Charlotte, NC
www.warrenpublishing.net
Printed in the United States

*This book is dedicated to
the memory of my grandmother,
Hazel Pearl Gomber Amond*

CHAPTER 1

"I can't believe half your visit has already passed by," Arthur Westerly said to his sister, Cynthia Lewis. They were enjoying the pleasant July afternoon in the garden behind Arthur's house. The house Arthur lived in was over a hundred years old and looked like something you would find in a movie. A six-foot stone fence surrounded the backyard. Running along the back of the fence was a section planted heavily with flowers in a rainbow of colors.

Arthur, his wife, Ann, and daughter, Samantha, whom they called Sammy, had been living in a little town called Dove's Nest on the outskirts of London for the past several years. He had been sent there by the company he worked for in the US to manage their London accounting department.

"I know, I hate the way time flies when you're having so much fun," Cynthia replied. "Makes me sorry I didn't come visit you sooner."

Cynthia's brother had begged her over the years to bring her family and visit him, Ann, and Sammy in England. Her excuse was always that they had so much going on in addition to the cost for the four of them to fly over there. If she had it to do over again, she would've gone ahead and done it, because now her husband, Philip, had passed away and the kids were busy living their own lives.

"I've taken this whole next week off from work so we can visit some places in the countryside you might not always go to. You know, more of the real England you wouldn't see as a tourist," said Arthur. "Thought we might hop in the car and drive around if that sounds okay."

"I think it sounds perfect." Cynthia loved the idea of seeing the non-touristy parts of England.

"We'll stop at the local pubs and restaurants. Ann and I loved doing that when we first moved here," he said. "People are so warm and friendly, and we found some great places to eat and drink. I think that's what made me fall in love with England and be able to live here as long as we have. We'll start out one morning next week and see where we end up," Arthur said with the sense of adventure in his voice she remembered since they were kids. He was always the instigator, coming up with spur-of-the-moment experiences. Many times, he had gotten her in trouble when he dragged her along on one of his great ideas. Like the time he talked her into chopping down trees to build a log cabin on White Lake, where they went every summer to visit their Granny who had a cottage on the lake.

Ann came out to the garden and put her hand on the back of Arthur's neck, kissing the top of his partially balding head. "You two look like you're enjoying the afternoon. I'm going to drive over to the market and get a few things. Won't take me too long. Anybody want to come along?"

Cynthia enjoyed Ann's company, thinking of her as the sister she never had. Ann and Arthur had met their freshman year in college, marrying the fall after they graduated. Cynthia recalled what a beautiful bride Ann had made. Petite with short blond hair and twinkling blue eyes. She still looked the same and had the same sweet, kind disposition as the day Cynthia had met her.

"I'll pass," Arthur said and looked to Cynthia.

"Sorry, Ann. I pass also. This is heaven out here," Cynthia responded.

"Okay. You both enjoy," Ann said and laughed. "I think Sammy should be home before I get back. Tell her we're probably going to eat dinner at six thirty or seven o'clock." Sammy was attending Hammersmith & Fulham College not far from home. She had her own car and lived the typical life of a college student, not much different than a young person in the United States.

"Okay, dear," Arthur said. "I was telling Cynthia about how we traveled the countryside when we first arrived here and thought we should do the same with her next week."

"Let's. We ought to plan an overnight somewhere so we can cover more territory. I've got the perfect idea. Let's drive to Hampshire and go to Steventon, where Jane Austen lived. I know you love her as much as I do, Cynthia."

"I sure do. That's a great idea. When do we leave?" Cynthia smiled.

"You women and Jane Austen. I can see I'm outnumbered. As long as I can find a pub while we're there, I'll be fine," Arthur said and laughed.

An hour later, Sammy was home and found them still in the garden. "I saw Mom's car gone, so I thought maybe no one was home. Where'd she go?" Except for being about four inches taller, Sammy was told she favored her Aunt Cynthia, with her light-brown hair and hazel eyes.

"Oh hi, sweetheart," said Arthur. "She went to the market. I expected her back a while ago. I guess she needed more than what she thought."

"I think there's something blocking one of the roads," Sammy said, taking a seat. "Someone's cow probably got out again. I took a different route home because cars were backed up. She's probably caught in the mess."

"We love living in the countryside outside of London, even though the roads are mostly two lanes and can be rough at times. They make the ones back home in Wisconsin look good, even after surviving the snow and ice of a long cold winter," Arthur told Cynthia. They'd grown up in a small town called Walden Falls in the Suring, Wisconsin, area, spending summers at a family cottage on White Lake.

"Part of the charm of the area," Cynthia said.

"I guess so," Arthur responded with a laugh.

After an hour and a half, Ann was still not back. *What could be holding her up?* Arthur began to worry, so he called her phone with no answer.

"I think I'm going to drive over to the market and see what's taking Ann so long," he said, unsuccessfully hiding his concern. "I hope she doesn't have car trouble, although I would think she'd have called."

"Okay, I'll stay here in case she shows up. She probably bumped into someone she knew while there and got to talking. You know how that happens," Cynthia assured, but in reality she was concerned also.

About fifteen minutes later, Sammy's phone rang. It was Arthur, and he wanted to talk to Cynthia.

"Ann has been in a car accident," he said flatly. "That's why the road was backed up. It was someone's cow, just like Sammy thought. Ann swerved to miss it and her car went into a thicket of trees. I spoke to some people at the scene. All I know is that she's unconscious and where they took her. I'm on my way to the hospital now." His voice cracked a bit, then he paused before he continued, obviously trying to stay in control of his emotions. "Tell Sammy I'll call when I know something." Arthur paused, his breathing deep. "The men I talked to didn't know if she was alive or dead. Don't tell Sammy."

Cynthia could sense the distress in her brother's voice and didn't want him to be alone at the hospital.

"Sammy and I can jump in her car right now and be there with you. I don't want you to be alone," Cynthia said, remembering how she'd had no one with her the night Philip died.

"No. I'll call and you can come then," he said. "I want to see what the situation is first."

Cynthia understood he was afraid of what might have happened to Ann and didn't want to expose Sammy to it unless he had to.

"Okay, we'll be waiting to hear from you." She hung up and told Sammy what Arthur had shared.

Sammy was upset and wanted to go straight to the hospital, but Cynthia convinced her they should do as her dad wished and wait for his call.

It seemed forever before Arthur phoned. The news was good and bad. Ann was alive but had suffered bad head trauma in the crash. She was still unconscious, so time would tell.

❦

Later that evening Arthur and Cynthia met with the neurologist who was treating Ann. Arthur suggested Sammy stay in the waiting room. Sammy protested at first, but Arthur was adamant and increasingly upset, so Sammy agreed.

"Hi, I'm Dr. Geoffrey Rosen. I'm so sorry about your wife's accident, Mr. Westerly. I've been attending her since she arrived." He put his hand out to shake Arthur's, but Arthur sat down not acknowledging it, obviously in shock.

"I just need some answers," Arthur said and turned to Cynthia. "This is my sister, Cynthia Lewis. She's here visiting from the US and is actually a nurse back home," he said in a flat voice unlike his usual tone.

Dr. Rosen nodded to her and motioned to some chairs for them to sit down and talk.

"Mr. Westerly, Ann suffered a closed head injury when her car hit a tree, as I understand it. With this type of injury, the brain has not penetrated the skull, but it still causes serious damage as the brain is battered and bruised inside the skull. This can result in permanent damage to the nerves of the brain. Right now, Ann is being observed and monitored, so we can determine the extent of that damage. I'll have more to tell you when she starts to become aware of her surroundings. This will help us know how to treat and help her. Right now, it's a waiting game."

Cynthia was familiar with this kind of injury from her experience as an ICU nurse and also knew the results could vary.

Arthur had a blank look on his face and was speechless. Cynthia wasn't sure he'd heard any of what the doctor said, so she took over.

"Thank you, Dr. Rosen. My brother has a lot to digest at the moment, but I'm sure he'll have some questions later. We'll let this all sink in and go from there."

From Cynthia's experience with doctors, she could sense right away Dr. Rosen cared deeply about his patients just by the pained look in his eyes when he delivered the news to them about Ann. Ann was fortunate to have someone like him in her corner.

"Again, Mr. Westerly, I'm so sorry. Please know I'll do all I can to help your wife. A nurse will be in with my information for you and some papers to read about closed brain injuries." He deliberately took Arthur's hand in his, this time prompting Arthur to look him in the eyes. Dr. Rosen nodded and left.

Tears rolled down Arthur's cheeks, but he made no sound.

"How am I going to tell Sammy?" he asked, finally looking at Cynthia.

"Don't worry, Arthur. I'll be with you and explain it to her. The three of us will do it together."

Cynthia wrapped her arms around her only sibling as he sobbed into her shoulder. Arthur was younger, so he'd always looked up to her. Yes, he was the typical annoying brother you hated at times, but he had always been there for her when needed. *He* could tease and say mean things to her, but let someone else do the same and they answered to him. It was good when someone had your back like that.

"Arthur," Cynthia said quietly as she sat back and looked him in the eyes. "Ann has a long road ahead of her. I've cared for people with these injuries and know what to expect. She's strong, so we have to think the best and give her all our positive energy."

"I know, but what am I going to do? If I could, I would come back to the States right now, where all our family is, but I doubt she could be moved. I'm sure the doctors are good here, but I still would like to be home. What do you think?"

"You can ask her doctor, but you're right—probably not at the moment. She needs time and then we can see." Cynthia was being truthful. The last thing Ann needed was a long plane trip to the US impeding her recovery. "It's going to be one day at a time for a good while. She'll need regular doctor visits. Dr. Rosen is a good doctor. I can tell."

Then, Cynthia made a split-second decision.

"Arthur, I'm changing my ticket to stay longer. You need me right now, and that's all there is to it. The people at the hospital where I work will understand." In reality, she wasn't sure if they would understand, since she was told her ICU job may not be available when she came home. She had taken an extended leave of absence not only to come to England and visit her brother, but in hope that the time away would help her resolve a decision she was struggling with. It involved a relationship with a man named Daniel Benton.

"No, Cynthia," Arthur pleaded. "I can't impose on you to sacrifice so much. It's out of the question. I would never ask you to do any such thing."

"You're not asking, I'm offering. The kids have their own busy lives now," she said, handing him a tissue. But she was really thinking of Daniel and the decision she'd been running away from.

"Are you sure, Cynthia? I don't want to keep you from your life, but I'm not going to lie, I need you."

"Let's find Sammy and tell her what's going on together," Cynthia said. "She needs to know, and from now on, you need to include her in any meetings with the doctor. She's an adult, and you'll have to lean on each other in the future."

"You're right. I'll always think of her as my little girl, but she's a young woman now. What would we do without you, Cynthia?"

That question seemed to be one she could not get away from. It seemed, perhaps, it was her plight. Then, something else came to mind. *Daniel Benton was just not meant to be.* Life was making the decision she had avoided. It was a sign she'd been here for Ann's accident. She was needed here, so here she would stay.

CHAPTER 2

Late October

"*D*o you want me to fix your tea now or after you come back, mum?" the woman asked.

"Oh, after I come back, I think," Cynthia responded and added, "Thank you," with a smile.

The woman's name was Margaret. She'd been hired by Arthur to come to the house three times a week to help out.

In the three months since her sister-in-law's car accident, Cynthia had become a caregiver-companion for Ann. Arthur had arranged for Margaret to cook, clean, and stay with Ann a few hours here and there to give Cynthia a break, but other than that, Cynthia was it while Arthur worked and Sammy attended classes.

She was happy Margaret had come today, because there was something she needed to do. Today was the two-year anniversary of her late husband Philip's death. A run was what she *needed*. Cynthia felt like a different person after a run. It allowed her to be alone and clear her mind enough to put things into perspective. There were only three things you could do when you ran: Run, breathe, and think.

Her usual route was from Arthur's house down to the town's only park, around the pond, and back. Just shy of four miles. Her interest in running had begun when she was in high school and continued throughout her adult life. She loved being outside with just herself and the world around her.

Naturally, her thoughts went to Philip. A little over two years ago, they'd decided since the kids were both in college and on their way, it was time to sell their Atlanta home and buy a beach house on St. Simons Island in Southern Georgia. But then … Philip had died on the day they moved in. What were the odds?

Soon after Philip's death, she'd discovered the money she thought they saved was gone with no trace. Philip had been an investment banker by profession and always handled their money, telling her they were well set for the future. There'd been no reason for her not to believe him.

Then one day shortly after Philip's death, a woman had rung Cynthia's doorbell to say he owed her $100,000. At first Cynthia thought Philip had been having an affair with this woman—the likely thing you would suspect—but the woman, Connie Dickson, had turned out to be his bookie. Cynthia would never forget that woman's name or what she looked like. He'd lost a large sum of money on risky investments and high-dollar bets Connie had made for him, or so she said. Unbeknownst to Cynthia, Philip had taken most of the proceeds from their home sale to pay his gambling debts, leaving them—no, leaving *her*—very little.

It was apparent Connie had expected Cynthia to be alone when she'd come to see her that day, but thankfully, friends had been present, taking charge and sending the woman away without a dime. Cynthia remembered the threatening look on the woman's face as she laughed and said, "We'll see." The worst part of it all was poor Christopher. Her son had been there to hear the whole exchange, tarnishing his dad's image.

She wished Philip had shared his gambling problem with her. She would've understood and tried to help him. He had been her life. All this news made her feel as if she'd never really known the man she'd loved since college.

And then, as if this hadn't been enough, she'd found out Philip had a condition called Brugada syndrome that could have been taken care of with a simple surgery, preventing his unexpected death. This *really* bothered her, because she might have been able to help had he just shared it with her. The words Connie had hissed at Cynthia echoed in her head: *Not the fella you thought he was at all.*

It seemed he hadn't been.

Cynthia arrived at the park's iron gate and went in. The park sat at the center of Dove's Nest. Located in the back of the park was a playground for children and a pond circled by benches. The pond was her favorite spot, as it contained a huge tree that overlooked the surrounding area, and a bench so close you could touch the tree while you relaxed. The first time she'd come here, she felt as if the tree were drawing her in like a magnet. She'd sat on the bench to study it. Now, Cynthia stretched her hand out, resting it on the rough, cratered bark that surrounded its trunk, and felt a peace inside her chest. Was she crazy?

The tree reminded her of the Wesley Memorial Garden where she would go many times to be alone and find peace back home on St. Simons. The first time she'd visited the Memorial Garden, she swore she heard the moss-covered trees sing to her as she walked the trail.

One day, with a chuckle, she'd told her friend Betty Franklin about the trees singing at the Wesley Memorial. With the serene look Betty always wore on her face, she told Cynthia she regularly went to the Memorial Garden herself and heard the trees sing. Betty had one of the purest hearts Cynthia ever came across. She would tell Betty about this tree if she ever got back home to St. Simons.

One day some children playing in Dove's Nest Park had told her the tree was called a "conker" tree, though she'd later discovered its true name was "Horse Chestnut." The kids had played a game where they laced a long piece of rope through the chestnuts, or conkers as they called them, swinging them at one another in an attempt to smash the other's conker. The person with the last whole conker was the winner. She read somewhere that the game was a tradition going back to the mid-1800s in England.

Today the pond was so still, it looked like glass. Not a thing to stir it. Cynthia was the only one in the park right now, but school would be getting out soon, changing the peaceful atmosphere. She would head back before then.

Staring at the water, she whispered, "Oh, Philip," and closed her eyes in contemplation, her right hand once again going to the tree. Immediately, her heart was warmed. She was fifty-seven years old, still trying to figure out where she fit in, and not sure she ever would. It seemed as if since Philip's death, her life had been at a standstill not dissimilar to the pond in front of her. The pond was there, but never moved anywhere else, only recirculating within itself.

At the beginning of this year, her best friend, Purvell, a New York Realtor, had suggested, in an attempt to help alleviate Cynthia's money problems, that she might want to rent out her home during the winter months. Her beach-side house would be perfect for people Purvell knew in New York who wanted to get away from the cold weather for a few weeks or longer. Cynthia could live in the little apartment the previous owner had built below the house while the renters were upstairs. It turned out to be a great idea, bringing an income she desperately needed.

Several different people had rented the house in January, February, and March until a man named Daniel Benton rented it for the months of April and May, shaking up her mundane life. He somehow wiggled his way into the places of her heart she didn't think would ever be occupied again. And it frightened her.

After Ann's car accident, Cynthia called and told Daniel she didn't know when she was coming back. She felt helping Ann was what she was called to do at that time, and didn't feel it was right to string him along. Still, she wished him the best. She hadn't had any contact with him since that day.

She stopped herself. Today was a day to remember Philip, not to think of Daniel. What was wrong with her? It was the second anniversary of Philip's death.

It seemed as if everyone had already forgotten. No phone calls, emails, texts from anybody—nothing. She knew Arthur didn't remember, since he had enough on his mind, but what about her mom and Granny—or Purvell? Sure, there was a time difference, but they'd had plenty of opportunity to call. She guessed this was the way it would be from now on. All their lives had gone forward, Philip no longer a part of them, forgotten.

If she were truthful with herself, she had started to remember some of the events in their life together as if she were watching a movie, not a part of them, just watching from a distance. She still missed the warm, engaging husband she'd loved with all her heart. If she could only go back in time—back to the way they'd once been—the way they were supposed to be.

Several kids were running down to the park with skate boards under their arms. Time to head back. Margaret would probably have tea ready for her and Ann.

She closed her eyes and gave the tree one more touch before leaving.

❦

Cynthia's phone rang. "Hi, Millie," she sighed, smiling. Millie didn't forget.

"Hi, Mom. It's so good to hear your voice. I miss you so much. Is Aunt Ann getting any better? We want you to come home." Of course she remembered her dad today.

"Oh sweetheart, it's so good to hear your voice, I only wish I could wrap my arms around you," Cynthia said, holding back tears.

Millie was twenty-four years old and married to a young man by the name of Jimmy Skidmore. They'd married a little over two years ago when Millie had become pregnant. Sadly, however, they had lost the baby the September before her dad died, making it an especially difficult time for a person her age to face. Cynthia hadn't liked Jimmy when she first met him and wasn't crazy about them getting married, but after they'd lost the baby, he started to change. He'd become a man she knew her daughter could count on as she watched their love flourish and grow.

"I've been thinking about Dad and the baby all day today. I wish we could have spent this time together like we did last year," Millie said.

Last year, the first anniversary of Philip's death, at Christopher's suggestion, they had all spent the day together hiking, something Philip would have loved to do with them.

"I know, sweetheart. Last year, who would have ever thought I would be living in England right now, helping with your Aunt Ann."

Ann's condition had improved very little, leading Cynthia to feel she would be in England forever. She missed her family, her friends, and her life on St. Simons Island. It seemed there was no end in sight, though she could never leave Arthur as long as she felt he needed her.

"Maybe if I'm still here in the spring, you and Jimmy can come visit. Maybe Christopher could come also." The thought gave her something to look forward to.

"Do you really think you'll still be there? We need you too, Mom. Have you talked to Uncle Arthur about finding some permanent help or even moving back to the States?"

Millie echoed everything Cynthia had turned over and over in her mind at least a hundred times.

"I think your Uncle Arthur feels more comfortable and safe with me here. I'm happy to be able to do it for him. He would do the same for me. So, tell me what's going on with you," she said, eager to change subjects.

"Not much other than work. Jimmy just got a promotion at the bank. Looks like he's on the way up the corporate ladder."

"Have you seen much of Christopher?" Cynthia asked. Both of her children lived in Charlotte, North Carolina. Millie worked for an accounting firm, Jimmy at a bank, and her son Christopher was a junior at UNC Charlotte, going into their nursing program.

"We got together with Christopher last weekend for dinner. He's doing good. We were wondering if you'll be back for Christmas?"

"I'm not sure, sweetheart," Cynthia said.

"We've talked about going to White Lake to be with Grandma and Granny if you don't come home, so we could be with family. I'm sure Grandma and Granny will be lonely not coming to your house like they usually do."

Cynthia's heart hurt thinking about what she was missing.

"Jimmy and I went down to St. Simons a couple weekends ago and stayed in the apartment. Brad said the house above was rented, but we never saw anyone there. Everything looked fine, though."

Cynthia also missed her beach house. She'd decided to continue renting it out while she was in England. She could use the money. Brad Davies, the same Realtor who sold them the beach house, was managing the rental of the house while she was gone, since he lived on the island. Brad had it rented for every month until the end of the year. Money she sorely needed.

"Well, that's good to hear. Tell that brother of yours to call me sometime—collect if he has to." They both laughed and shortly after said good-bye.

After her call with Millie, Cynthia sat alone in her bedroom and stared at a picture of Philip on her phone for a good while, letting memories of him fill her every thought. His gambling had added an extra sadness to his death; he hadn't trusted her enough to share his problem. She sighed and put her phone away. It was 8:30 p.m. and time to help Ann get ready for bed. The poor thing became so confused and out of touch at times. How could Cynthia leave?

CHAPTER 3

The middle of December

A light dusting of snow fell outside as the cab pulled up to the curb. The occupant really didn't want to get out, having the desire to give his condo address and be taken there instead.

He passed his credit card through the little opening to the cabbie and watched as the card was run through the terminal.

"It's twenty bucks," the cabbie blurted in an accent he couldn't identify.

"Put another fifty dollars on for your tip. Happy Holidays."

"Hey man, you're generous. You going to be here long? Maybe I could hang around and take you somewhere else when you're done? Tell me what time and I can come back later if you're going to be here long," the cabbie said, eager to please.

Daniel Benton took back his card and smiled at the man. "No. Thank you, though. Merry Christmas," he said with finality and exited the cab onto the sidewalk.

He walked a few feet, then stopped before slowly tipping his head back to look up at the facade of the building in front of him, oblivious of the people hurrying past. As his eyes followed the fluffy snow that floated down onto his face, he had the urge to stick out his tongue like he had as a kid to catch as many flakes as possible.

The two doormen outside the building looked at him before turning their heads to the sky to search for whatever Daniel was seeing. Their gazes returned to each other, as one of them shrugged his shoulders and the other shook his head, neither having seen anything.

The holidays were bittersweet for Daniel. His wife had died seven years ago, and they had no children together, so he was alone. Maybe if he had someone to share the season with it might be easier for him. He held no real desire for the women who appeared interested in him at present—his desire was for only one woman, and she had gone away. He wasn't sure when or if he would ever see her again.

After Daniel tipped his head down, he came back to the present. He glanced around at the cars and people moving quickly around him, then finally at the doormen. With his leather-gloved hands, he brushed the snow off the shoulders of his black wool coat and headed toward the heavy glass door of the hotel. The doorman on the right pulled the door open.

The Valley Inn Suites hotel was one of Daniel's favorite places in New York to hold an event. Not only was it conveniently located to his office, but the staff was excellent.

This evening he was hosting an annual event for his staff and the people he worked with throughout the year. As a successful developer in New York City, he partnered with many other developers and Realtors. This was his chance to personally thank them all.

"Mr. Benton. Happy Holidays," said the hotel event planner, Tina. "We have everything ready. If you'll follow me, I'll show you the way."

Because he had used this hotel for many events, he had a great relationship with Tina and the hotel staff. All he had to do was have his assistant pick up the phone, tell them what he wanted, and they took care of it.

The area used for the party was an atrium in the hotel. Daniel loved the way the openness felt as if it were outdoors. This year the hotel had decorated the space in festive gold and silver Christmas trees of varying sizes arranged at one end, with round tables interspersed, decorated in the same colors.

His guests wouldn't start arriving for another hour and a half. He enjoyed the time before an event like this to settle in and take in the surroundings. It also gave him a chance to meet the servers and bartenders, make sure the tables looked nice, and have a drink while he listened to the piano player warm up for the evening. Once his guests started showing up he was on, so this was his quiet time.

One of the bartenders was setting up in the bar area.

"Could I bother you for a glass of whiskey?" Daniel asked.

The man turned around and said, "Yes, sir," quickly grabbing a glass and pouring out two fingers.

"Thank you," Daniel responded and picked a table off to the side, where he sat down, giving him a good view of the whole area.

The piano player started to warm up in the background, prompting Daniel to reminisce about this time two years ago, when he'd met Cynthia Lewis.

She had been standing by the clock in the middle of Grand Central Station the first time he saw her, when he noticed she'd dropped her jacket on the floor. He felt compelled to call her attention to it, when he noticed tears pooled on the lower lids of her eyes. She said she was looking for Starbucks, so he gave her directions and went on his way. Later that night when he was with friends at a restaurant, she walked out of the ladies room and right into him, causing him to spill the drink he was holding. She never looked up.

He'd watched as she sat down at a table with several people, one of whom was a woman by the name of Purvell Whitlock, who just so happened to be a friend and favorite Realtor of his. Much to his surprise and amazement when Purvell had shown up at his holiday party the next night, the woman, Cynthia, was with her. Turned out the two women had been college roommates and lifelong friends, and now Cynthia was in town for a visit. When they were introduced, he'd expected Cynthia to recognize him, but she looked at him as if it were the first time their paths had crossed. He was disappointed.

Later he found out from Purvell that Cynthia's husband had died only a few months prior to her visit. Purvell had convinced her that coming to New York would be a good change of scenery. Having lost his own wife, he knew what she was feeling and didn't pursue any further.

For some crazy reason, he'd thought the next year Cynthia might come visit again and Purvell would bring her to the party, but sadly he'd been wrong. He made a fool of himself asking Purvell questions about Cynthia, revealing his feelings, when Purvell shared with him an opportunity he couldn't pass up.

Cynthia lived on St. Simons Island, Georgia, in a house on the beach. Because of some financial circumstances, she was renting out the upstairs of the house while she occupied an apartment below it.

Without hesitation, he'd rented the beach house for April and May, allowing him a chance to get to know her better. After he'd been there several weeks, he'd sensed she had begun to like him and in his excitement, went overboard, asking her to move to New York so they could be together. His eagerness caused her to panic and run, first to where she grew up in White Lake, Wisconsin, and then to England, where her brother lived. She was only supposed to have been in England a few weeks, but because of a tragedy in her brother's family, she'd stayed to help. It had now been almost six months.

"Excuse me, Mr. Benton. I don't want to disturb you ... you seem a million miles away. But we'll be setting up the buffet soon and thought you might like to check it out to make sure it's the way you want it," Tina the event planner said, breaking his trance.

He glanced at her and took a long drink of his whiskey before asking, "A million miles?" He tipped the glass to drain the last drop. "More like 3,500."

The young woman smiled, having no idea what he meant but possessing enough sense to pretend she did.

Daniel rose to follow her, and she guided him through the room to make sure everything was to his liking.

After making a trip to the men's room, he came out to the first group of guests arriving.

The one guest he was anxiously waiting for was Purvell, once again dreaming Cynthia might be with her.

He looked past his guests to see who was next. No Purvell. Perhaps she wasn't coming tonight. Although he wore a happy face, his heart felt heavy.

Finally after he'd thought everyone was there, Purvell showed up. Alone. She slipped over to where he was talking to several Realtors. He politely finished his conversation and took Purvell aside.

"I was beginning to think we wouldn't see you tonight. So glad you made it," he said, with a friendly embrace.

"Had a late client today who wanted to see just one more. It paid off since that 'one more' became a sale." Purvell smiled, grabbed a glass of wine from a passing waiter's tray, and took a sip.

Reluctantly, Daniel said, "I can't believe I'm admitting this to you, but I'd hoped you would walk in with Cynthia." He felt a flush of red crawl up his neck to his face, like a high school boy.

"I'm sorry." Purvell laid her right hand on his left arm and gave him a sad look. He didn't want her pity, only what she knew about Cynthia.

"Do you hear much from her?" he asked.

"I've started to hear more lately. You know, she was a little mad at me in the beginning, thinking I was playing matchmaker. I was, actually ... but it was for her own good." Purvell didn't have to convince him.

Daniel took Purvell's arm and walked her to a table away from the other guests.

"Please tell me what you know. Is she doing okay? Is she happy there?"

"She won't talk about you at all with me. *I've tried.* You know her brother's wife was injured badly in a car accident. Cynthia feels obligated to stay because of her niece, and her nursing skills make her presence there very helpful. They feel her sister-in-law shouldn't be moved from England yet. It's a bad situation. Who knows when she'll be back."

Daniel couldn't believe what he was hearing. He thought for sure she would have been back by Christmas. What about her family here? She spent every Christmas with her mother, Granny, and kids.

"So she's not coming back for Christmas for sure?" he had to ask.

"Nope. The kids are flying up to White Lake, Wisconsin, to be with their grandmothers. I'm visiting my family this year also and driving up there for a few days. Already have my reservation at the Kelly Lake Motel since Cynthia's mom's cottage is small. You would love it. Hey, why don't you come with me? We can spend Christmas with my family and then go to White Lake. Or maybe you need to spend time with your sister and brother?"

"You've forgotten I've been to White Lake once already and stayed at the Kelly Lake Motel." They both laughed, even though he felt a slight pang in his heart.

"I don't think my sister and brother would mind if I told them I wanted to go somewhere else for Christmas."

"Well, you think about it. Cynthia's mother and her Granny would probably love to see you again."

He would love it also. He knew the two older women liked him after the one time they'd met. Cynthia's son, Christopher, was in his corner also. He had never met Millie and her husband. Why not go?

"Shouldn't you check with your family first? You're sure they won't mind?" he asked. "I mean, they've never met me before."

"I come from a farm family and in Wisconsin, nobody has ever met a stranger."

"Okay, you have a companion for your trip. But maybe you should check it out with Cynthia's family?"

"Nah. They love surprises."

CHAPTER 4

*L*aGuardia Airport was usually a zoo, but four days before Christmas—it was ridiculous. When Daniel's cab dropped him at the airport, he vowed to never travel at this time of year again. Slowly he made his way through security and to the standing-room-only gate so he could connect with Purvell for their trip to Wisconsin.

"Daniel." He heard his name and turned to see Purvell waving in a corner. He made his way through the crowd to her smiling face.

"I was getting worried about you. Thought you chickened out," she laughed and gave him a hug.

"This mob of humanity almost did have me turning around," he chuckled, hugging her back and giving her a little peck on the cheek. "Thanks for inviting me to come with you. I'm really looking forward to it."

"Well, I'm happy to have the company. Wait until you meet my family and then let me know if you're still happy you came." She laughed again.

They soon boarded the plane. Daniel upgraded their tickets to first class—they might as well be comfortable, he told Purvell.

"I usually fly coach, so this is a treat for me," Purvell told him.

This is going to be fun, Daniel thought. When he'd visited White Lake this past summer, he had other things on his mind, only spending one night at the Kelly Lake Motel. It didn't give him a chance to experience the friendliness he had heard about the people who lived in Wisconsin.

After a short delay, they were in the air heading west to Chicago, where they would change planes before heading north to Appleton, their final destination. The flight attendant came around with the drink cart. He and Purvell both ordered wine and visited a bit before Purvell dove into her book and he fell asleep.

❧

Purvell looked over at Daniel sound asleep in the seat next to her. Such a nice guy—and he was rich, to boot. Not a bad combination.

Although she was sure they were both aware of it, she would never admit it to Daniel, or Cynthia for that matter, she was committed to getting the two of them together. They were perfect for each other, even if one of them didn't know it just yet. Daniel knew and also knew Cynthia needed to figure this out on her own. It didn't mean Purvell wouldn't give it a little nudge when she saw an opportunity here and there though.

She looked at Daniel again and sighed. Why didn't she ever find someone like him? She had resigned herself to being a career woman and found satisfaction in what she did, but at times thought it would be nice to have someone to grow old with.

Having Daniel come home with her this Christmas would make her mom less likely to pump her with questions about her love life. To make sure there were no speculations about Daniel, she'd already informed her parents that Daniel liked Cynthia and he was just a friend of hers. She would probably still hear about what a nice guy he was, and how it was too bad she couldn't find someone like that. Did he have a brother available, by chance?

Parents never change.

The last time she had been to Neenah, her hometown, was two-and-a-half years earlier. She normally avoided coming in the winter, opting for the summer, when the weather was beautiful.

Neenah was located on Lake Winnebago, the largest inland lake in the state. As a kid she and her friends would have fun on the lake during summer and winter—in the summer, boating, fishing, and swimming and in the winter, snowmobiling, skating, and driving on the frozen lake. Neenah was a great place to grow up, but she hadn't realized it until after she graduated from business school in Madison.

That's where she met Cynthia and Philip. She was with Cynthia the night the two met at a frat party. Philip was also in the business school, Cynthia in the nursing school. Such a long time ago, and so much had happened since then.

Purvell's parents were dairy farmers. She was the youngest of five and the only girl. Her four older brothers, Bertie, Bobby, Bennie, and Earl ran the farm now, since her parents had retired about four years ago, or so they said. You never really retire from farming. They were still as involved as ever, her dad getting up every morning to help with the milking. Purvell felt it's what kept her parents going. They were third generation Germans, having been raised on hard work and farming. Purvell knew she was successful in her career as a Realtor because this same work ethic had been instilled in her growing up.

"So what has you so deep in thought?" It was Daniel, now awake from his nap. "Boy, I really passed out. I'm sorry."

He sat straight up, stretching. "I'm not very good company. Guess I needed it because I feel great now."

"Oh, don't worry. We're on vacation, so that means relax. I honestly think once a person gets out of the city, life slows down anyway. You're just rebooting for the Midwest."

"Yeah, it's like that for me when I visit my family back home in Saratoga Springs. I go there when time permits to reboot. You know, I come from very humble beginnings. My dad worked in a brewery. Didn't even graduate from high school. He never understood why I had to go to college and then New York City after I graduated. Even when I started doing well, he didn't want to hear about it and would never take any help from me. Was like that until the day he died, but I love him for all he did for our family. He worked very hard to give us a home, food to eat, and a roof over our head. I don't think he ever missed a day of work."

"My life on the farm was very similar," she responded and then changed the subject. "Anything special you want to do while in the Badger State?"

"Well, I don't know much about the state other than people are Packer crazy, like cheese, and drink a lot of beer," he said with a smile.

"You've got to be kidding," Purvell said with a stunned look on her face. "I hope to widen your view by the time we return to New York."

After the plane landed in Chicago, they headed to their next terminal, where they walked out on the tarmac and up portable stairs to board the smaller jet they would take to Appleton. No first class option on this one.

Purvell took the window seat and watched the ground below as they continued on to Wisconsin. It was late in the afternoon, and the sun sinking in the west provided a picture perfect view for someone who hadn't set eyes on this beautiful land in a long time. Even with snow covering everything, she could see the grid of patchwork patterned roads, houses, and farm fields that only meant she was home. When they flew over Lake Winnebago and the plane descended, she felt a little excitement in her heart but kept it to herself.

When they pulled into the Whitlock farmyard, it was already dark, although the farmhouse was lit up with white Christmas lights on the outside, and a multi-colored tree radiated in a big bay window, giving the home a Norman Rockwell look from days gone by.

Daniel had thought he might feel awkward staying with Purvell's parents, but that only lasted a few seconds, for once he met them, he felt he had known them for years. Purvell was right: nobody in Wisconsin had ever met a stranger.

The first thing Purvell's mother did was give him a big hug and a peck on the cheek, and then ask if he was hungry. Her dad grabbed his hand and shook it until Daniel felt it might fall off and then handed him a can of beer, a brand of which he had never heard of before. Chilled to the perfect temperature, it went down smoothly after his long day of traveling.

Purvell favored both her parents in different ways. Her blond hair and blue eyes were like her mother, yet she was tall like her dad and had many of his facial features.

"Listen, you two kids come in here to sit down and have some of my special cheese ball I made. Bet'cha never had one like this, Daniel," Purvell's mother said as she pulled a glass dish out of the refrigerator, containing what he assumed to be the cheese ball and placing it next to a bowl of crackers. He didn't think he'd ever had a cheese ball before. "I want you to tell me what you think of it. I bet'cha can't guess what I make it with," she said, looking at him with great anticipation.

God, I hope it's good, he thought as he took a small butter knife and spread a chunk of the mixture on a cracker, quickly popping it in his mouth while Purvell's mother stood beside him in anticipation. It was good, but he had no idea what it was made of.

"This is great, Mrs. Whitlock … what's in it?" His response obviously made her happy, because she laughed, throwing her head back.

"It's just softened cream cheese, Worcestershire sauce, minced onion, and garlic, mixed together with some chopped dried beef. I mix half the beef in the cheese and make it into a ball, then roll the ball in the rest of the beef. Then you just chill. Nobody ever guesses. Oh, and please don't call me Mrs. Whitlock. I'm Jane and he's Ronnie."

"That's right, Danny. We don't need formalities around here," Ronnie said, reinforcing his wife's request.

"Okay," Daniel said. "Works for me." Just then he caught a look of Purvell off to the side, red faced from laughter.

"Dad, it's Daniel, not Danny," Purvell said, still pink.

"What the hell. Daniel, Danny—they're both the same. Right, son?"

"Sure," Daniel said.

"Ronnie, leave the boy alone. He just got here, you're going to frighten him," Jane scolded her husband.

"Listen, woman, you're overreacting as usual. Have I frightened you, son?"

"No, sir. Not in the least," Daniel said.

In all his travels, with all the people he met, he'd never come across anyone like Purvell's parents.

Daniel and Ronnie went into the living room, where there was a fire burning in the fireplace, and sat by the Christmas tree. Ronnie said to leave the women to their talking and let the men do theirs. The room had a comfortable feel to it.

"So, what the hell do you do for a living, Danny?" Ronnie asked.

"I'm a developer."

"So, what is it you develop?"

"Real estate. That's how Purvell and I know each other. She's one of my star Realtors. Very talented in sales. You should be proud of her."

"So, you build houses? That's a good living, I guess." Ronnie looked doubtful.

"No, more like offices, and I renovate places to repurpose them in New York."

"Oh yeah, I watch those shows on TV where they renovate and flip houses. I like watching them, but farming is for me."

"Right," Daniel said, and knew it was a waste of time to get Ronnie to understand what he really did for a living. Ronnie proceeded to expound on farming as Daniel nodded and smiled.

"Purvell's always trying to get us to come visit her," Ronnie explained. "I'm not sure I would like all the noise and goofy stuff going on where she lives, though. Jane has gone, but not me. I worry about Purvell, but she says she's in a good part of town."

"Yes, she is. You don't need to worry."

"Do you like hunting and fishing, Danny?"

"Well, I do like to fish. I've never gone hunting."

"You're shittin' me. You haven't lived then! Have you ever shot a gun?" Ronnie asked.

"Why, yes," Daniel responded. "Not a shotgun but a handgun at a shooting range."

"Tell you what, next year you come back around Thanksgiving and my boys and I will take you deer hunting. Never been hunting, ya say. I can't believe it. Nothing like a bunch of guys out in the woods doing what a man does."

The conversation went on about hunting and fishing, Daniel nodding and drinking another beer and then another until he began to doze off. Daniel was unaware of what time it was when Jane eventually came in and told Ronnie to stop monopolizing the conversation. She proceeded to show a groggy Daniel to his room, where he saw it was 10:30 p.m. *What a day.* He stripped down to his underwear and was asleep before his head touched the pillow.

❦

It was morning now. Daniel had slept well, possibly because of the last several beers—not sure how many—he'd drunk with Ronnie before turning in for the night. He went in the bathroom to relieve himself, splash a little water on his face, and brush his teeth before heading downstairs to find Ronnie, Jane, and four men dressed in overalls eating breakfast. He wondered where Purvell was, guessing she must still be asleep. Before he could ask, Jane jumped up and started fussing over him.

"So, Daniel, how do you like your eggs? I have some bacon and sausage over here. Can I pop some bread in the toaster? I even have homemade strawberry jam for your toast," she said with a big smile on her face.

"For cripe's sake, Jane! Leave the boy alone. You're scaring the hell out of him. He's a city boy. Be easy on him," Ronnie said, addressing his wife.

"Ronnie, M-Y-O-B. Now Daniel, I want you to meet our sons. This is Bertie, Bobby, Bennie, and Earl."

"Pleased to meet you," Daniel responded, offering his hand. The four men took turns shaking it.

"We've already milked the cows, but maybe you'd like to hang out with us the rest of the morning," Ronnie suggested. "Let the girls to themselves. I've got some overalls you can use along with some boots you might want to wear. So, what do you think?"

"Sure. I'd love to."

"Great! You eat your breakfast and come find us in the barn."

"Okay," said Daniel in as positive a tone as he could muster. How hard could farming be?

He spent the rest of the day helping Ronnie and his sons feed the cows, fix the milking machine, and shovel manure. When they finished, he was exhausted and hungry from a good day's work. It occurred to him, he'd never realized all that went into farming and how important it was. He had a new appreciation for the profession.

❦

The next morning was beautiful. Snow on the ground, the sun shining strong and clear.

"I thought I might take you into town this morning so you could see the more metropolitan part of Neenah," Purvell laughed. "It's really a nice place."

Purvell drove Daniel by her elementary, middle, and high school, all on the same road, and then they went to downtown Neenah. It was very similar looking to downtown Saratoga Springs, New York, where he'd grown up, except smaller. They drove to Riverside Park and decided to go for a walk.

"See that over there, across the water next to the bridge? That's the hospital where I was born and had my tonsils out when I was five," Purvell explained. "I've been told a story my whole life about how the nurses chased me around the room before my tonsil surgery when I overheard they were going to give me a shot. Took three of them to hold me down. The nurses referred me as 'Tiger' until I went home."

"That doesn't surprise me at all. I've heard other Realtors in New York call you Tiger," Daniel laughed.

Not laughing but surprised, Purvell asked, "Do they really?"

Daniel was laughing so hard at her response, he could only manage to shake his head up and down.

"I didn't know that. Really? Huh," Purvell said with a look of satisfaction on her face.

They found a park bench and sat down. "It doesn't look like it now, but this is a little harbor tied with boats in the summer. I used to come here with my friends and family when I was a kid for picnics and to play. The best things in the summer were the Park Dances in that pavilion when I was in high school, and the play they put on there every July. Neenah is known for the picnic held in this park on the Fourth of July and their fireworks. I remember a couple of times I watched them from the bridge with my friends." Purvell kept her hands in her pockets and nudged her head in the direction of the bridge. They sat in silence for a while, enjoying each other's company and the peaceful snow that covered the park. They returned to the car when they started to get cold.

"I'm going to treat you to lunch, but first I want to show you where we went to make out when I was a kid."

They drove a short distance to the Point, where a light house sat all alone.

"So, how many times did you come here?" Daniel asked.

"Me? Never," Purvell laughed and her blue eyes twinkled. "I'm taking you for a hamburger at Mihm's for lunch. You'll never forget it," she said.

And she was right. Best burger he'd ever had. Perfectly done beef with all the right condiments, bathed in butter that ran down his hands.

After the sightseeing tour, they went back to the farm to help Jane decorate cookies and get things ready for the next day, when Purvell's brothers would come with their families to celebrate Christmas Eve.

Purvell went off to wrap some presents, leaving Jane and Daniel alone to finish the cookies.

"Jane, I was wondering. Is Purvell a family name?"

"No, Daniel. When I found out I was pregnant again, I was sure it would be another boy. I decided if it was a girl I would give her a name so special she would have to do great things to live up to it. I played around with letters and came up with Purvell. It suits her, I think."

"It does," said Daniel. "She looks like a Purvell and she *has* become something. I don't know if you knew this, but she is very well-known in New York. One of the best Realtors I know, and I know a lot of them. You should be very proud of her."

"I am," Jane said, getting teary eyed. "My only regret is she has never found anyone to marry. It breaks my heart. You don't have any brothers or a friend you could set her up with, do you?" Jane asked.

"Well, my brother is married and not really her type, and I'm not sure about my friends. Let me say that Purvell lives a full life even though she's not married."

"Purvell tells me you have a thing for Cynthia. You couldn't find a nicer person. That girl has a good heart—it's what makes her an excellent nurse. Philip was a nice fella also, rest his soul." She hung her head.

"So, what were Purvell and Cynthia like in college?" Daniel asked to steer the conversation in a different direction.

"Why, those two girls were friends from the git'go. They lived across the hall from each other in the dorm at Madison and didn't like their roommates, so somehow they switched at the semester. They've had lots of fun together."

"I'm sure they weren't perfect angels, though."

"No, they were not. Back when they were young, the drinking age was eighteen years old here in Wisconsin. One summer, Cynthia came down to visit us for a few days—you know this is the big city compared to where she lived. The girls went to this bar in downtown Appleton called Cleo's all the kids talked about. That place has every gaudy decoration possible hanging from the ceiling and every wall. Lit up like a Christmas tree all year round. They're also known for their generous drinks. Purvell didn't want us to know they went there and got stinkin' drunk, but thank God they had enough sense not to drive. Purvell called one of her brothers to pick them up. It was a dead giveaway the next day when they finally got up at three in the afternoon and walked around like they might break. Ronnie put me up to making kielbasa, sauerkraut, and fried potatoes for supper. You should have seen the look on their faces." Jane started laughing so hard it brought tears to her eyes, causing Daniel to join in, when Purvell walked into the room silencing them both.

"I didn't know cookie decorating was so funny," she said. Just then Jane started laughing hard again and so did Daniel.

"Mom, what are you two talking about?"

"Oh, nothing, dear. Telling Daniel about how I make kielbasa and sauerkraut," she said, and they started laughing again.

"Are we having that tonight? You know, for some reason I can't stomach it."

"No, I've got a pot roast, honey. Don't worry." She winked at Daniel.

The next day was Christmas Eve. Purvell's brothers and their families would be over in the evening for the annual Whitlock gift exchange. Daniel looked forward to meeting all of Purvell's family and wondered what it was like to be related to so many people.

Christmas day they'd go to Purvell's brother, Bertie's for dinner. The day after Christmas, they would say good-bye to the Whitlocks and head to visit Cynthia's family at White Lake before catching their return flight to New York. Daniel had been looking forward to seeing White Lake at this time of year, although he was especially looking forward to visiting with Cynthia's mom and grandmother again. He was sure he wouldn't be disappointed.

CHAPTER 5

The warm, cozy kitchen made it easy for the women to forget about the snow falling outside. Cynthia thought her, Ann, and Sammy making cookies together would be fun and something Ann might enjoy. Ann's emotions and desires went up and down like a rollercoaster, Cynthia never knowing what she may want or be thinking. For the moment, Ann seemed to be interested in the cookies.

Even though this was not the cookie baking Cynthia was used to doing back home with her mom and Granny, it filled the void she felt. Her mom and Granny's baking was serious cookieology, involving discussion and a list made of old favorites and new possibilities that resulted in dozens of cookies they would give away to friends. This may not be the same, but she was carrying on the tradition in her own way, and even though her mom and Granny weren't in the kitchen with them, she felt them in her heart.

They all had cups of tea next to them. Cynthia had always liked tea, but during her stay in England, she'd grown to love it. The English tea tasted better and the serving of it was an art she would miss when she went home—if she ever went home.

While she was forming some dough into balls for Samantha and Ann to roll in sugar, she thought about the Christmas two years ago, when she and Philip were to celebrate the holiday in their new home along with their first grandchild. *So much has changed*, she thought.

And then Daniel came to mind. She did miss him. This was crazy, because she hadn't known him long. Still, something inside her missed him. It was too late, though. She chose her family over him, and their lives had moved on in different directions. She was sure with his busy life, he'd easily put her out of his mind.

Just then, Ann started crying. These drastic emotional changes came out of nowhere, a side effect from the head injury she'd suffered. Poor, sweet Ann. Cynthia turned to her.

"What's wrong, Ann? Are you getting tired?"

"When's Arthur coming home? Where is he?" Ann whimpered.

This was something she asked constantly, and even if Cynthia gave her an answer, she would ask again a few minutes later. Ann's whole personality had changed after the car accident. Cynthia kissed her forehead.

"He's at work, but will be home in a few hours. I bet you're getting tired. How about I take you to your room for a nap? Arthur should be home when you wake up."

Ann looked confused, though she always had some degree of confusion on her face. The cookie baking must have tired her out.

"Come with me, Ann. Sammy, can you handle this while I go tuck your mom in bed?" Cynthia took her hand and led Ann to her room before Sammy could answer.

When she came back to the kitchen, Sammy spoke.

"Aunt Cynthia, how much longer are you going to stay here? You must be getting homesick for Millie, Christopher, Grandma, and Granny."

Cynthia *was* homesick for them, but didn't want to say so. She missed St. Simons Island and her friends there also. She missed her work at the hospital, runs on the beach, the beautiful weather ... her list could go on.

"It wasn't mere coincidence I was here when the car accident happened," Cynthia said, trying to sound positive. "Look how much I can help you and your dad."

"You do help so much. I just feel a little guilty about how long you've been here."

Just then they heard a cry. Ann did this occasionally when she slept, however, Cynthia felt she should check on her to make sure she was okay.

"I'll be right back." She rose from her chair and crept to the master bedroom. Ann was only dreaming.

Cynthia looked at Ann sleeping. Ann had only slightly improved since the day of the accident, leading the doctor to believe this was the best she was ever going to become.

After Cynthia closed the door, tears began to roll down her cheeks. She wanted to go home so badly, but what kind of person would leave her brother and niece in this situation when she had the skills to help out? Still, she longed to get as far away from here as she could. She stopped in the bathroom, wiped her eyes, and looked at herself in the mirror. What was she going to do?

❧

Cynthia's daughter, Millie, and mother, Grace Westerly, sat in the living room of the house on White Lake, watching the snow outside.

"It sure doesn't feel right without Mom being here," Millie said to her grandmother. "Have we ever come up here for Christmas before? I always remembered you and Granny coming to our house."

"When you were very young, you came. Granny and I like to come south, though, to get away from the weather. Helps shorten the winter for us," Grace said.

Just then, the door flew open and a gust of frigid air came in along with Christopher, Cynthia's son, and Jimmy Skidmore, Millie's husband.

"For Pete's sake, you two boys have to remember this is not Charlotte and you can't let the door swing open like that," Grace cried.

"Hey Grandma, Jimmy and I were checking the lake to see if it was frozen yet, and it looks like it's pretty solid. So, is it okay if we get the tip-ups from the shed and put them out there to catch fish?"

"Yeah, I can't wait to tell everyone when I get back home. I never heard of fishing like this before," Jimmy added.

Tip-ups were a contraption involving a fishing line, fastened to a red flag on a spring attached to a board. The line would then be dropped through a hole in the ice, as the flag was pushed down to a hook that allowed the flag to "tip up" when a fish was caught. The person fishing could then stay warm inside and only go out when a red flag went up. Christopher had been dying for an opportunity to try the tip-ups after finding them in the shed when they were visiting one summer. Now was his chance.

Grace laughed at her grandson and Jimmy's enthusiasm. "Sure, boys, go for it," she smiled. In a flash, the two young men were out the door again, letting in the cold air.

"I swear, guys never grow up, Grandma," said Millie. "When Jimmy gets with Christopher, both of them are like little boys again. I'm happy the two of them get along, especially since Jimmy is an only child. Christopher's like the brother he never had."

"Yes, I think it's good also. You never know, I may be frying us some fish for supper tonight," Grace said, and they both laughed.

Grace was happy to have her grandchildren and Jimmy visiting for Christmas, though she missed her daughter terribly. Still, she understood what a big help Cynthia was for Arthur. The last two years had been the most difficult in Cynthia's life, and it gave Grace concern as she wondered how hard it must be for Cynthia to care for her sister-in-law on a daily basis. Cynthia's weekly phone calls were always happy and upbeat. Being a mother who knew her daughter well, however, Grace was still concerned.

Grace turned her attention again to Millie. "So, Millie. When's the baby due?"

Millie looked up with surprise on her face. "How did you know, Grandma? I'm not really showing that much."

"I can see it your face, my dear child. You have the beauty of an expectant mother. Saw it when you first walked through the door when you arrived."

"I've been wearing baggie clothes to hide it," said Millie, tugging at the hem of her baggy sweatshirt. "After what happened last time, I wanted to wait until I was further along before I told anyone. Jimmy and I have kept it to ourselves." Grace nodded with understanding, knowing Millie had suffered a late-term miscarriage two years previously. The baby was a little girl, and Millie had delivered her as if she were full-term.

Millie lifted her sweatshirt to expose the protruding baby bump that was tightly covered by a T-shirt. Like all women do, as if by instinct, Grace placed her hand on the bump, and closed her eyes for a moment, with a prayer for this great-grandchild of hers growing in Millie's belly. She smiled at her granddaughter.

"This is wonderful, Millie. So, I guess your mother doesn't know? You should have told us so we can all be there to help support you through it. I know what happened last time, but this needs to be celebrated."

"I know you're right, Grandma. I'm going to tell Mom after the first of the year. I honestly thought I would be able to tell her in person, thinking she would come home for Christmas. It doesn't look like it will happen, though."

"This may bring her home to us. I know it would do it for me. When's the last time you spoke to your mom?" Grace asked.

"Just before we flew up here. I told her we would call Christmas morning so we could all visit. I really miss her a lot and wish she would come home. Uncle Arthur needs to find some other help. Especially now. When I talked to her the on the anniversary of Dad's death, she suggested maybe this spring we could come visit her. You could have a talk with Uncle Arthur, Grandma; he would listen to you. Mom can't stay there forever. She has us and she's missing out on a lot."

Millie was right. "I'll speak to him after the first of the year, dear," Grace said, patting Millie's belly.

Just then the phone rang. It was Granny. Granny lived in a little house up the hill from Grace. No one ever believed she was ninety-five years old. The petite woman was active and sharp as could be.

"Granny was wondering if someone could walk her down here," Grace relayed. "I told her one of the boys would be up after they were done with their fishing. We certainly don't want you taking a chance at slipping on the ice."

In the winter, Granny was cautious. A slip or fall on the ice could be disastrous for her active lifestyle.

"I agree. I've been very careful, and the doctor has kept an eye on me because of last time."

"I'm going to put a kettle on so we can have a cup of tea. Let's sit over by the window and watch your husband and brother out on the lake."

Grace headed into the kitchen, put the kettle on, and took two mugs out of the cupboard. Talking with Millie about Cynthia made Grace think about the man who had showed up on her doorstep last summer in search of Cynthia. Grace liked the little bit she'd seen of him and wondered what happened. She didn't ask, because she wanted Cynthia to tell her on her own. The relationship must have ended or never really been anything since nothing more came up. *Too bad*, she thought. Grace had been sure something was going on between the two of them and thought he would have been good for her daughter.

❦

Much to everyone's surprise, Christopher and Jimmy caught four medium-sized fish, and Grace fried them up for their supper.

"You know, the two of you are lucky Mrs. Deen goes into Walden Falls to live in the winter," Granny informed the boys as they were taking the first bite of their fish. "She would have called the Department of Natural Resources on you, because you don't have a fishing license."

Mrs. Deen, who was about Granny's age, owned the cottage a few doors down. She kept an eye on everything that happened on White Lake.

"Years ago when Mrs. Deen used to stay on the lake year round, some fellas about the age of you two thought it would be fun to drive their car on the frozen lake," Granny told them. "If it hadn't been for Mrs. Deen, they probably would have died. You see, the ice wasn't quite thick enough for a car yet, and they fell through. Mrs. Deen saw it happen and called for help. The boys were saved, but the car sank to the bottom."

"There's a car on the bottom of the lake? Are you serious?" Christopher asked.

Granny was known for the stories she told. Most of them seemed to stretch the truth a bit, though no one ever challenged her.

"Yes, a 1975 Ford Pinto. I think it was considered to be one of the worst cars ever manufactured, so no great loss," Granny interjected, laughing.

"It'd be cool to rent some scuba gear and try to find it next summer," Jimmy said, reading Christopher's mind.

"Yeah, just what I was thinking. We'd have to make sure we took pictures of it for proof," Christopher said.

"I think you need to stick to fishing," Grace said and then looked at Granny. "Granny doesn't need to be putting ideas in your head."

"Oh, alright, Grace," Granny responded, waving a hand at Grace. "What day does Purvell come, and where will we put her?" she asked. Christopher was staying with Granny in her cottage, and Millie and Jimmy were in Grace's cottage.

"She's coming two days after Christmas," Grace answered. "I offered to let her stay here, but she's got a room at the Kelly Lake Motel. Says she's bringing someone with her."

"Interesting," Granny said, raising her eyebrows. "Probably one of her New York boyfriends."

⚜

It was evening when Cynthia's phone rang on Christmas Day. There was a seven-hour difference between herself and White Lake, where her family was. She had been waiting all day for their call.

"Hello! You all sound as if you're in the next room," Cynthia said as she pressed the phone to her ear and heard the conversation in the background.

"We miss you, Mom." It was Millie. Cynthia almost lost it.

"I miss you too," she finally was able to say.

They all took a turn talking to her, even Jimmy. She missed them all. After she hung up, she sat in a rocking chair in her bedroom looking out the window. It was dusk and snowing lightly. So pretty and peaceful.

At that moment, the decision was made. She wanted to go home. This was not the place for her. She had backed herself into a corner pleasing everyone *again*, and she didn't know how to get out of it without hurting someone's feelings.

She even forgot about how she at one time planned to get her master's in nursing. Would it ever happen? It seemed like a distant dream now.

Now was the time to tell Arthur she was going home. St. Simons Island was where she belonged, and it was calling her back. She would never leave there again.

The tears started and wouldn't stop. Arthur and Sammy were waiting for her, so she looked in the mirror to check her face and saw it was a little flushed. She would say it was due to sitting close the fireplace if anyone asked.

But how could she tell Arthur she was ready to leave? Her life was in limbo here, and she was missing her family and life in the States. She'd helped Arthur as far as she could and would stay until he found someone suitable to help him—not any longer.

After making this decision, she felt better and went back out to the parlor, where Sammy and Arthur were waiting to hear about her phone call. Cynthia, however, had only one thing on her mind.

She was going to return home.

CHAPTER 6

"Hey, you two kids, I got some cookies and my special party mix for you to give Grace and Hazel. Do you think you should maybe take some snacks along in the car so you don't have to stop?" Purvell's mom suggested.

"It's only a little over an hour drive, so I think we'll be okay, Mom," Purvell said as she turned to face Daniel and roll her eyes.

"Well okay, but you better call when you get there so I know you're safe."

"Of course I will," Purvell said, turning back to her mom with a smile and wrapping her arms around her tight. Jane started crying.

"I just miss you, sweetheart, and I don't know when I'll see you again."

"Let's plan a trip for you to come to New York in the spring," Purvell suggested. This seemed to perk Jane up a bit.

"Bye, Dad. You and Mom take care of each other, okay?"

"What the heck, sweetie. No one else would have me but your mom," said Ronnie, who started to tear up himself.

Jane went over to Daniel and gave him a hug and peck on the cheek and said in a whisper, "Remember what we talked about. You know, about finding her a husband."

"Yes, ma'am, I'll keep it in mind," Daniel responded. "Thank you so much for your hospitality. It was a treat to spend Christmas with your family. I'll never forget it."

Next, Ronnie walked over and shook Daniel's hand. "It sure has been a pleasure meeting you, young man. You're not too bad for a city guy," he said, laughing a little too hard at his own comment. "I hope that house-flipping business of yours does well. I'm sure there's some money to be made in it."

"Yes, sir, I'll try my best," Daniel responded as he caught the puzzled look on Purvell's face.

Soon, they were in the rental car and Daniel was asking Purvell for directions to White Lake as he pulled out of the driveway.

"Who are Grace and Hazel?" Daniel asked.

"Grace is Cynthia's mom and Hazel is Granny."

"Ah. I never got that far with them last summer when we briefly met," Daniel said.

"Oh yeah. What was that comment my dad made about your house-flipping business?" Purvell asked.

"I explained to him what I did for a living and he assumed I flipped houses. It wasn't worth explaining to him what I really did." He shrugged and they both laughed.

"Your family is great, Purvell. I've really enjoyed meeting them. They're real people."

"So, *that's* what you call them," she smiled. "I wish I could see them more often though. Mom asks me all the time what my plans are for my future—you know, retirement— since I don't have a husband. They have no idea how well I've done for myself. I'd like to consider slowing down, but

I don't think I would ever be able to come back here to live. I don't fit in anymore."

"It's interesting you bring that up. Can I tell you a secret? You can't tell anyone. Promise?"

She turned to Daniel, intrigued. "Of course you can. I promise."

"You know I've been grooming my nephew, Stephen, so he can eventually take over the business someday. He's the closest thing I have to a son, and the kid is good and has more on the ball than I did at his age. He's a natural."

"So, you're retiring? I can't believe you can just walk way like that."

"No, I'm not retiring. Not yet. I'm very involved still, only stepping down a little so Stephen can spread his wings. I'll be around, just not as visible. I'm pursuing something else." He smiled and briefly glanced at Purvell.

"Like what?" Purvell asked.

"I'm not ready to say. I have to see how things work with Stephen."

"Does it involve Cynthia?" Purvell had a sly look on her face.

He turned to look at Purvell and then turned back. "Cynthia isn't here, as I'm sure you noticed, and no one seems to know if and when she will come back. Life moves on without you when you're not present. Cynthia's biggest problem is she needs to make a commitment and stop running away, allowing everyone else to decide her life for her."

"Yikes. Tell me how you really feel, Daniel."

"I'm done talking about this. It's best you don't know everything," he said abruptly.

"Now I *am* curious," Purvell said, smiling. Daniel gave her an *I wouldn't if I were you* look. "Okay, I'll not ask another question," she said. And she didn't, which was unusual for her.

What Daniel didn't want Purvell or anyone else to know was that he'd fallen in love with the St. Simons area when he rented Cynthia's place in the spring. So much so, he had been flying his plane down there to get away now and then. Cynthia's friend. Ian and he had become good friends and would go fishing, out for drinks and dinner sometimes, and ride Ian's motorcycles around Jekyll Island.

In a conversation with Ian, he had found out Cynthia was renting out her house while she was gone, so he thought, *Why not?* He called Brad Davies, the man who was managing the property while she was gone. After Brad and Daniel got to talking, he realized they could work together on some projects, the first of which was to help Cynthia's friend Betty Franklin develop a property where she'd once had a barbeque restaurant that burned down.

Daniel had then decided to stay permanently in the area, prompting him to buy a place on Jekyll Island and start a new company developing property down there. On December thirty-first, he would close on a home and start the new year as a resident of Jekyll Island.

Cynthia hadn't wanted to come to New York to get to know him better. *Well, now New York is coming to her,* he thought. *That is, if she ever comes back.* When she did come back, she'd *have* to get to know him better, and then he'd see what happened.

❧

Daniel and Purvell decided to take the scenic route to White Lake through all the small towns instead of driving the highway. Purvell thought it would be more fun. Before they knew it, they were at Hickory Corners and turned to the left down White Lake Road.

The lake area looked so different to Daniel, covered in snow. Magical. Maybe he could buy a place here, also.

Wonder how Cynthia would like that, he thought and laughed to himself.

Daniel stayed behind Purvell as they went to the door of Grace Westerly's cottage.

"Purvell! I am so happy to see you and who is this you brought with you?" Grace asked as she peeked around to see who Purvell's friend was.

"Why, Daniel, I never expected to see you, but I couldn't be happier," Grace responded when she saw him. "Wait till Granny finds out. We've been speculating on who Purvell was bringing with her, but never thought it would be you. Your name comes up occasionally in our conversations, though. We enjoyed meeting you this past summer."

Daniel liked that. "Thank you. I've thought of you ladies myself now and then," he replied, wearing a big smile as Grace first hugged Purvell and then him.

"Well, come in out of the cold. I'm here by myself right now. Granny and Millie are upstairs taking a nap, and Christopher and Jimmy are out on the lake fishing, believe it or not. Take your jackets off and come sit by the fireplace to get warm. How about some tea?"

"We'd love to have some tea," Purvell answered for both of them, and Grace went to the kitchen.

Millie walked down the stairs.

"Purvell. I heard your car pull in and couldn't get up from my nap fast enough." The last time the two had seen each other was at Millie's wedding two-and-a-half years earlier. "You look great, as always. Who's your friend?"

"Millie, I want you to meet Daniel Benton. Daniel, this is Millie Skidmore, Cynthia's daughter."

"You know my mom, Daniel?"

"Why, yes. It's so nice to meet you, Millie," he said.

Grace entered with the tea on a tray.

"Oh, good, Millie. Glad you're up, and you've met Daniel. We're so happy you're here again and can see the place in the winter too, Daniel," she said, and realized she might have spoken too soon when Millie raised an eyebrow.

"You've met before?" Millie asked.

"Why yes, dear, this past summer," Grace said, saving face. She quickly went into conversation, not looking at Millie and speaking to Purvell. "Now, here's your tea, and tell me about your visit in Neenah, and your trip up here to our little place. It must feel good to get away from New York."

Purvell jumped in and didn't give Millie a chance to ask more questions as she and Grace kept the conversation rolling.

A voice came from the stairs, "Purvell! It's so good to see you." It was Granny, finished with her nap. "I heard your voice upstairs. Why, Daniel! It's so good to see you again. Purvell never told us it was you she was bringing along."

Millie looked from person to person as they spoke, mostly concentrating on Daniel, but didn't say a word. She continued her silence while they all visited. Then in a flash, the door to the outside flew open and in walked Jimmy and Christopher, very excited with a string of six fish.

"Grandma, we caught more fish," Christopher exclaimed, and then realized the company had arrived.

"Purvell!" He went to give her a hug, then seeing who was behind her, said nonchalantly, "Hey, Daniel. I didn't know you were going to be here. How come you didn't tell me when I saw you last month?"

Millie couldn't stand it. "How is it you all know Daniel and I don't?"

"I thought you always knew everything, sis. Guess you're slipping," said Christopher, enjoying the moment. "I know Daniel through Mom. He rented the beach house this past spring. Ian knows him too. I see him when I'm down there and he's hanging out with Ian. He's kind of like … Mom's boyfriend."

"Now wait a minute, Christopher …" Daniel jumped in. "Your mom and I are friends." Daniel could see the distressed look on Millie's face. He wanted to win her over and Christopher's conversation was alienating her.

"No. She likes you, Daniel. I know my mom. She would act all funny whenever I asked her questions about you," Christopher said, as if he were an expert on women and relationships.

Grace took over. "That's enough, Christopher! Millie, your brother doesn't know what he's talking about. We can discuss this later, both of you. Purvell, maybe you and Daniel want to get checked in at the Kelly Lake Motel and then come back here for supper so we can visit more."

Daniel quickly stood up. "Yes, let's get checked in, Purvell. Well, thank you for the tea, Mrs. Westerly," he blurted, and Purvell followed him to get their coats.

"Please call me Grace, Daniel."

And the unusually silent Granny finally said, "Please call me Granny."

"Okay, Grace and Granny," he smiled and, with a wave, they left.

"Well, you were no help, Mother," Grace said to Granny after they left. "Why didn't you jump in?"

"You seemed to be doing fine. I can't handle everything for this family. I mean, I'm going to be ninety-six next year. Give me a break, Grace," Granny said, rolling her eyes, and she went to sit down by the fire.

❦

Grace asked Millie to come help her in the kitchen, but what she really wanted to do was talk to her about Cynthia and Daniel. She sat down at the table with Millie.

"Millie, I want to share with you the little bit I've been able to piece together about your mom and Daniel. Most of it has come from Purvell and a little from your mom." She continued to fill Millie in on what details she knew about how her mom had met Daniel.

"Well, that doesn't sound like much, Grandma. What was Christopher going on about?"

"Remember how your mom disappeared prior to her trip to visit Uncle Arthur, and she ended up coming here? She was very secretive, not telling Granny or me anything. Granny and I decided she needed to work something out, and we were happy she came here, thinking she would eventually tell us … but she never did. Then, she received a package from Ian. We thought it was odd, and when Granny asked her what it was, she got a non-answer. So, we let it be. We still don't know what it was. She went out in the rowboat by herself a few days before she was to go back home, and lo and behold, Daniel showed up looking for her.

"I was cautious at first, and while Granny was talking to him, I went in the house and called Purvell. Purvell said he was okay and she had been playing matchmaker a bit. She knew they had some kind of relationship brewing.

"Being widowed myself, I can understand what may have happened to your mom. I wasn't as young as she when your grandpa died, but you're suddenly alone and you wish you had someone to be with. Yet, on the other hand, you feel as if you're doing something wrong if you want someone else. I think your mom may have felt guilty. Also, she had been doing pretty good on her own. She was proud of that, and I don't blame her. I'm proud of the way I've done since your grandpa died, so I get it. Now she's stuck in England, and I bet she thinks her fate has been decided for her." Grace sighed and waved a hand, indicating she was done with the subject.

"Sweetheart, be nice to this man," she continued. "I have a good feeling about him. No man is going to replace your dad—ever. Your mom's had a tough life the past few years, and if she can find someone to love her, who are we to say 'no?'" She's young and has a long life still ahead of her. Why she should she be alone? I never had someone interested in me after your grandpa died, but I think it would have been nice. Let's just see what happens and let your mom figure it out."

"I feel like she should be honest with us," Millie said.

"I guess it's a matter of perspective, Millie. You're keeping your pregnancy a secret. You have your reasons, your mom has her reasons, and we need to respect that."

"When will I ever be as smart as you, Grandma?" Millie smiled and took Grace's hand.

Cynthia had asked Grace the exact same thing a little over six months ago right there on White Lake. She gave the same answer. "Oh, sweetheart, I don't know about that. I've just lived longer. Learned most of it the hard way."

※

Daniel and Purvell came back, and after supper, they visited for a while until Millie suggested they play Monopoly. Millie, Jimmy, Christopher, Purvell, and Daniel laughed and played until about ten o'clock, when Purvell said they needed to go. The next morning they had to return to the airport in Appleton and fly back to New York.

Before they left, Granny got Daniel alone where nobody could hear what she asked him.

"I'm too old to beat around the bush, young man. I want to know, do you love my granddaughter, and are you going to marry her?"

"You *don't* beat around the bush, Granny," Daniel chuckled. "I do love her, but let me ask you this. Do I have your permission to ask her to marry me?"

"Yes, you do. That was a good answer, son," Granny replied, patting his cheek. "I think you'll fit into our family just fine."

CHAPTER 7

Once her mind was made up, Cynthia decided she wouldn't wait to tell Arthur it was time for her to go back to her life on St. Simons Island. Before she left, however, she'd help him find skilled care for Ann.

It was two days after Christmas. She dreaded telling him her decision, but she wasn't going to put it off like things she had in her past. She would tell him tomorrow evening.

Her heart ached a little, thinking about how much she missed her life. The first thing she would do when she was back on St. Simons would be to head to the beach for a walk or run. Then she'd sit on the deck with a glass of wine while she enjoyed the salty wind blowing her hair every which way as she watched the waves break.

After she told Arthur her decision, she would get in touch with Jackson Irwin, her supervisor at the hospital where she'd worked before she came to England, and beg for her job back. She'd need the money now that she wouldn't be renting her home out. Since she'd been gone so long, she would probably have to reapply as if she were a new employee, knowing the process would take some time.

Also, she needed to call Brad Davies, the Realtor managing the rental of her house while she'd been gone, and tell him she was coming back to live there. She still couldn't get over how he'd been able to rent it every month while she was in England. The rent money all went in the bank. If she were careful and invested it well, she may not have to rent her house out ever again.

Life would return as it had been before she left. Nothing would change. Back to her twelve hour shifts at the hospital, the kids, her mom, and Granny visiting occasionally. Fishing with Ian, time with Betty, dinner at Barbara Jean's, runs on the beach—it sounded good.

Now that she'd decided to go home, her head was humming with thoughts. She told herself to relax, be patient, and allow everything to fall in place.

Ann was sleeping at the moment, so Cynthia fixed a cup of tea and went into the parlor, making herself comfortable in a rocking chair by the fireplace. She immediately began overthinking, the past three years playing out in her head repeatedly as the fire hypnotized her. Soon, her eyelids dropped and her head bobbed back as she fell asleep in the warm, cozy room, when the dream started.

A light touch woke her up. It was Ann, looking much as she was before the accident, an old familiar smile on her face. She held out her hand, and as Cynthia responded, the room turned magically into a beautiful spring garden, a stark contrast to the winter weather that had blown by the window just moments before.

They walked to the middle of the garden, hand-in-hand. A crowd of mumbling people wandered about, interspersed around the perimeter of the area, their faces and bodies as unrecognizable as what they mumbled.

Music began to play and soon, more people joined them in the garden, talking and laughing as if it were a party. She didn't know who these people were at first, but then she recognized them one by one. Millie, Christopher, the rest of her family, and all her new friends on St. Simons were there. She was excited and tried to talk to them, though they didn't seem to see or hear her. It was as if she were invisible.

She saw Ian and Betty. Surely they would be happy to see her. She ran over and started talking, but they looked through her, across the room, and laughed before walking away. She began to feel panicked. What was going on? Ann came to her. She seemed to be the only one who saw Cynthia.

And then she saw Daniel.

Her heart fluttered. He looked straight into her eyes as he walked closer, holding his hand out. Ann stepped in between them and said, "It's time to go home, Cynthia—all of us." There was a flash and then everyone disappeared. It became dark.

She woke up with a start, disorientated, not knowing where she was, and struggling until her whereabouts came back to her. She'd frequently had odd dreams in the past, but the last one she recalled had been over six months ago on the plane trip coming to England. She must have worked herself up over telling Arthur about leaving. She needed to go check on Ann and start dinner. Arthur and Sammy would be home soon.

❦

Today was the day. After dinner she would tell all three of them—Arthur, Ann, and Sammy—at the same time, so she would only have to say it once.

Margaret was there making dinner. It was cold but sunny outside, unusual for an English winter, so Cynthia decided a walk to the park might be nice. Margaret could be there for Ann. Cynthia bundled up and put her boots on before she headed out.

As she walked, she went over in her mind again and again how to tell them about her leaving. She needed to just say how she felt and stop rehearsing. They would understand why she wanted to go home. She missed her family and friends. It wasn't as if she even had a life here in England. She went to Ann's doctor visits and the market occasionally. Other than that, Margaret was the only person outside of Arthur, Ann, or Sammy with whom she had any contact. She had no friends. This was not a life. She was a skilled nurse who should be taking care of many people.

The path in the park had been cleared of the light snow they'd received overnight. There were still patches of ice present, so Cynthia slowly maneuvered her way to the back of the park and her tree. Pulling her jacket down to cover herself, she sat on the cold seat of the bench next to the tree.

The peace she felt was welcome and the silence so profound she could have heard a falling snowflake touch the ground. After pulling her hat down more securely and folding her arms, she closed her eyes and emptied her mind. Unconsciously, she breathed the cool, crisp air deeply as her questions and concerns came tumbling out.

God, why are you taking me on this crazy ride? she thought. *What the heck do you want from me? I'm a simple woman who needs some answers. Am I doing the right thing by leaving? Should I stay? Am I a selfish person to leave my brother like this? What about my family? Don't they need me?*

And then.

Will I ever see Daniel again? Does he ever think of me?

No answers.

She began to think about her old life, imagining not for the first time or the last, *What if Philip hadn't died?* They would have worked in their new jobs and created a life on St. Simons, but it still would have fallen apart, only in a different way. Philip's gambling would have eventually come out later instead of sooner, and she would have found out anyway. Connie Dickson, Philip's bookie, still would have shown up at their door one day wanting her money. Philip wouldn't have ever stopped, because apparently he didn't think he had a problem. Or maybe if they hadn't moved away from Atlanta, things would have been okay and he wouldn't have died.

She missed her life before all this mess. It was such a good life.

A chill ran through her. She should get moving again to warm herself. Automatically, without thinking, she took the glove off her right hand and placed it on the tree. She laughed at herself when she realized her only real friend in England was a conker tree.

Her trip back felt lighter. Walking down to the park had been a good idea. The time alone sorting through her thoughts gave her the unfailing focus to approach Arthur and his family. By making everything so easy for Arthur, she had been interfering and postponing what he needed to face and conquer himself. She looked up to the sky and said to herself, *I guess this is your answer.* Then she thought of her dream from yesterday. It was the right time.

❧

At about 4:30 p.m., Margaret left. Sammy came home from her classes thirty minutes later to find Cynthia in the kitchen.

"Hi, Aunt Cynthia. How's your day been? Mom doing okay?"

"Oh, hi, Sammy. Yes, I got out for a walk—your mom's been fine. Rather quiet, really. I peeked in on her about an hour ago and she was watching an old movie in her chair. Poor thing was pretty agitated earlier. It's good the old movies seem to soothe her."

"I wish we could all go back to the States," Sammy said. "I know the doctors said moving could be traumatic for Mom, but so much time has passed and she hasn't gotten better. I was thinking maybe we can talk Dad into moving back. I think Mom is stable enough to travel now, don't you? It would be better for us to be around family."

"You know, that would be a good question for you and your dad to ask at your mom's next doctor visit." Cynthia agreed this would be the best solution for them. *It's been six months since the head injury,* she thought, *and surely by now Ann would have found her way back to her old self again if she were ever going to.* A move back to Milwaukee, where Ann was from and Arthur's company was located, would give them the family support they needed.

"I'm going to say 'hi' to Mom, okay?"

"Okay," said Cynthia. But soon Sammy was calling for her.

"What, Sammy?"

"Aunt Cynthia, something is wrong. Mom won't wake up!"

Cynthia ran to Ann's side and touched her hand. Ann's face held the peaceful look Cynthia had seen many times as a nurse. Then, the words Ann had uttered in the dream came to mind. *"It's time to go home Cynthia—all of us."* Is this what she had meant?

Cynthia checked what vitals she could, but there was no sign of life. Ann had passed away sometime after Cynthia checked on her about an hour ago.

She turned to see Sammy, who was standing as far away as she could in the room, with tears streaming down her face. Cynthia began to cry herself.

"Is she dead, Aunt Cynthia?" Sammy managed to ask.

Cynthia shook her head up and down, managing only a "Yes." She knew in her heart it was a blessing for the tormented Ann.

"Let me call your dad and then the doctor." This was way too close to what Cynthia had gone through when Philip died, and she was barely hanging on by a thread.

She did it, though. Arthur came home about the same time the ambulance arrived and fell apart. Sammy was surprisingly strong and comforted her father so Cynthia could handle the rest.

They took Ann away. Arthur wanted to be alone, so he went to his room and closed the door. We all have to handle things in our own way.

Sammy sat with Cynthia on the sofa, first talking and then with her head buried in Cynthia's shoulder, the both of them crying. Cynthia knew all too well how a day could change from morning until night and wished she could make the experience easier for Sammy. But she couldn't. Some things can only be gone through the hard way.

How strange this should happen on the same day she'd planned to tell Arthur she wanted to go home. Now what was she to do? It would be cruel to abandon them at this time. How did she get herself into these situations?

"Sammy, I need to call the family. I'll call your mom's sister and let her know to tell your mom's family. I also need to call Grandma, Granny, and everyone else," she said, wiping away tears.

"Okay. I'm going see how Dad's doing," she said and left Cynthia alone.

Cynthia got her phone out.

"Hello, Mom. I really need you right now," she said, and between her sobs, she told Grace everything. About Ann dying, how much she wanted to come home, how she had planned to tell Arthur that night, how she missed all of them and her life on St. Simons, and how she was tired of being alone. Her mom listened and told her to get a good night's sleep and they would talk more tomorrow. She would take care of calling everyone else. Cynthia should go to bed.

❦

The next afternoon Arthur sat in a passive state at the kitchen table with Sammy, Cynthia, and an untouched cup of coffee. Cynthia kept trying to include him in the conversation, but he wasn't listening. All he heard was *wah wah wah* as her voice went on. He wished she would leave him alone. Why wouldn't she be quiet?

He abruptly stood up. "I'm going to my room for a while and want to be left alone," he said with finality, leaving the two women.

Once alone in his room, he lay on the bed and rolled to his side. He didn't cry. He was empty after all the tears he'd cried over the last six months since Ann's accident. He had wept many days over Ann's condition, praying she would by a miracle get better; it never happened. The doctors had told him without coming right out and saying the words that Ann would never get better. In spite of what they tried to tell him, he had chosen to have hope that the woman he loved would come back to him someday.

In truth, he was feeling a little guilty for the relief he felt now her spirit was free to be the vibrant woman she once was. She was free of the pain and frustration he'd seen in her face every day as she struggled with confusion and anger in her attempt to make sense of a world she didn't understand.

His phone rang and he saw it was his mother.

"Mom. Hi." He was so happy she'd called.

"Arthur, darling. How are you, my boy? I've had nothing but you on my mind. I wish I were there with you, and so does Granny."

"I wish you were here also. I'm so confused, Mom. I'm not sure what to do next." Hearing his mother's voice had brought him to tears.

"I'm sure Cynthia will help you with whatever you need," Grace reassured her son.

Oh, and then the guilt he felt from keeping Cynthia with them all this time came to him.

"Mom, I have so much I need to share with someone."

"You know I've always been a good listener, Arthur. I have all the time you need."

"Well," Arthur started, " a few days before Ann's stroke, my company told me they wanted to move me back to the States. I was going to tell Ann and Sammy after Cynthia's visit, and then the accident happened. The company graciously has let me stay here because the doctors felt the stress of moving would be too hard on Ann at the time. I've been concerned about how long they would let this go on. I guess there's no reason why I can't come back home now."

"It seems the answer to your future has been taken care of for you, son. I think it's a good idea that you're coming back here, actually. Will you return to Milwaukee?"

"Yes. It's going to be so good to see you and Granny more," he said; then there was a long pause.

"What is it, son?" his mother asked.

"Mom, a part of me is happy Ann has gone on. She's no longer suffering. I could tell how unhappy she was. I feel guilty about that and about keeping Cynthia here so long." He managed his words between sobs.

"Arthur, you shouldn't beat yourself up over that. Ann went peacefully on her own. All our lives have a plan, and this was hers. We should celebrate who she was and the difference she made because we knew her. It was her time, son. Now you need to have Cynthia come home as soon as you can manage. She has things in her own life to take care of."

"Is everything okay? She could go tomorrow if she needs to."

"No, no nothing serious. Just her family needs her, and I think she needs them. You'll be fine, dear. Rely on Sammy. She'll be a source of strength if you let her," Grace said, always the voice of wisdom.

"Do you think Cynthia will go? I know she feels obligated to help us, and I don't want to hurt her feelings," said Arthur.

"Don't worry about Cynthia. Tell her and start to make arrangements to come back to us. Will you have a funeral there?"

"Yes, something simple here with the friends we've made. We'll have a memorial service in Milwaukee with everyone else. I suppose now it will be after we move back."

"Sounds good, Arthur. Darling, all will be okay. Take it one minute at a time if you have to. Granny wanted me to make sure I gave you her love also. We're both always here for you and we love you so much. Give Sammy and Cynthia a kiss for us, sweetheart, won't you? Call me any time day or night. A mother is always on-call, you remember that."

"Thanks, Mom." And after saying good-bye, he broke down.

His mother was such a wonderful woman. Grace was always there for him and Cynthia; in fact, Cynthia was a lot like their mom. A mother's love was a gift for all to cherish. Even as a grown man, he still leaned on her—and then he thought of Sammy. *She'll never know this as she goes through adulthood. No mom when she gets married, has children, faces life events, and just to talk to.* Arthur would have to make sure he was always there for her and make up for the hole that would now be at the center of her life. He and Sammy would stick together.

Arthur managed to get himself together and decided not to delay moving their lives forward. They'd all been in limbo since the day of Ann's accident. He would tell Cynthia she needed to start making her plans to leave, and he and Sammy would also begin their return home.

CHAPTER 8

The flight attendant announced Cynthia's plane would touch down in fifteen minutes.

Everything had moved so fast after Ann's death. Arthur had finally shared with her that his company actually wanted him to move back to the States, but had been letting him stay in England because of Ann. He wanted to start moving plans for him and Sammy immediately, and told Cynthia he didn't expect her to stay to help them. She had gone above and beyond, and now it was time to go back to her life. It was a relief to Cynthia that the company would take care of moving Arthur and Sammy back to Milwaukee. She would be able to leave as she planned and slip back into her life on St. Simons Island.

Arthur's biggest concern had been that Sammy wouldn't be happy about the move since they had lived in England so long. Much to his surprise, when he'd told her about the move, she said she wanted to be closer to family and really always wanted to go to college at the University of Wisconsin in Madison just like her dad and Aunt Cynthia had.

Once the decision was made, Cynthia emailed her former manager at the Southeast Georgia Health System hospital in Brunswick to tell him she was finally returning and hoped to go back to work in the ICU—if he would have her. He quickly responded, saying he would love to have her back, but there wasn't an ICU position available at the moment, and she would have to reapply. He urged her to get her application in as soon as she could, since people were always moving around to different departments in the hospital and something could develop. That night, she'd submitted her application online, anticipating by the time she was back on St. Simons, she would have news of a job.

She had next called Brad Davies to tell him she would be returning. Someone was renting her house for January, but he would see if they really wanted it for the whole month. He had gotten back to her after a couple of days and said the renters would make other plans. Everything had fallen together, and soon she was on her way home.

She could have flown into Jacksonville, knowing Ian or Betty would have been happy to pick her up, but she couldn't wait to see her children. Both lived in Charlotte, so she booked her return flight to the Charlotte-Douglas Airport. After staying with them for a few days, she would rent a car and drive back to her island.

Saying good-bye to Arthur and Sammy had been hard, but she said she would visit them this summer in Milwaukee—and promised not to stay more than a few days. This brought out a laugh, easing the difficult departure for her.

In Charlotte the kids were going to wait for her in baggage pick up, where customs was located. After getting the okay, she headed down the long customs hallway to the area where people waited for their returning friends and loved ones. Scanning the crowd, she saw the three faces she was looking for. Christopher, Millie, and Jimmy in a row.

They all came rushing toward her, when Cynthia saw it—Millie was pregnant!

"Millie, why didn't you tell me?" Cynthia said, before breaking down into full-blown tears.

"Oh, Mom. I know, but, well—we can talk about it later. It's a little girl, and she'll be here in late April or early May!"

Cynthia first hugged her daughter and then looked down and put her hands on Millie's protruding belly. The little soul inside began to kick. Cynthia looked up at Millie and began to cry all over again.

"Hey, Mom. Remember me?" It was Christopher with his arms open and a dejected look on his face.

"Yes, of course I do, sweetheart." They all laughed as she turned, wrapped her arms around him, and gave him a big kiss, next going to Jimmy and doing the same.

"Jimmy, you're sure being quiet," Cynthia said to the young man.

"I'm just so happy to have you back here in time for the baby, Cynthia. That's all," Jimmy said. "Millie's missed you so much, and so have I." He turned and looked at his wife and Christopher. "We all have."

Cynthia hadn't always been fond of Jimmy, but since he and Millie had lost their baby, Jimmy had evolved from a goofy, clueless kid to a responsible man and husband. She was happy to have him as part of their family.

"Well, let's go," she said with a grin. "It's so good to be back."

The guys grabbed her suitcases, and the four of them headed to the parking deck and then to Millie and Jimmy's house.

꧁꧂

Millie and Jimmy had bought a house in the Ballantyne area of Charlotte. With a baby coming, they decided it was time to have their own home instead of renting.

While they ate dinner, Cynthia told them about England and the whole situation with Ann.

"Poor Uncle Arthur," Millie said. "And you too, Mom, to have to deal with what you did every day. Maybe I shouldn't say this, but I think it's a blessing she passed away. Aunt Ann was always an active woman. I'm glad I didn't have to see her that way."

"I know, it was hard. I'm happy I was there with them, though. You know birth and death are so similar, really. I envision when a new soul comes into this world, there's a band of fellow souls to give them a grand send off until their time is done here. When they leave this world, I'm sure the same souls are waiting to welcome them back with a party like they've never seen before," Cynthia said, smiling at Millie as she watched her unconsciously lay her hands across her belly. Cynthia felt a flush of well-being in her chest.

After dinner, Christopher and Jimmy went to watch TV while Millie excitedly escorted her mom down the hallway to the baby's nursery.

Millie glowed while she showed her mom the crib and accessories they'd already purchased for the baby. In the corner was a rocking chair, and against the wall next to it, a changing table. A bookcase held some stuffed animals and a few books.

"Looks like a good start, Millie. I can't wait to begin spoiling her rotten. Have you picked a name yet?"

"Yes, but we want to keep it a surprise. Jimmy and I both decided on it together. You'll have to wait," Millie said, with a teary-eyed smile on her face that made Cynthia curious.

"I understand, sweetheart. We have to have some surprises."

"Mom, I'm sorry I didn't tell you sooner about the baby. Honestly, I didn't tell anyone, after what happened last time. I also didn't want you to worry about me while you were in England. It wasn't as if I was trying to keep a secret or something. I did tell Christopher before we went to Wisconsin for Christmas, but he's the only one who knew."

"I know that. You went through something no woman ever wants to go through, and I understand."

"Yes. It's been hard buying the baby furniture and things, but doing it helps me set the intention in my heart that all will be fine this time. My doctor specializes in high-risk pregnancies and has assured me everything is going well and as it should," she said, sighing.

"Wait until your grandma and Granny find out. I think you better tell them soon."

"Well, I never fooled Grandma. She called me on it right away at Christmas while we were there. She said she saw it in my face as soon as I walked in the door."

Cynthia laughed. "I'm not surprised. Your grandma is one special woman. Not surprised at all," she said and took Millie's hand in hers. "Maybe we could call her and Granny later to tell them I made it back safe and let Granny know about her great-great-grandchild."

"That's a good idea," Millie said. "We haven't told Jimmy's mom and dad yet, either. So, I guess we better do it soon. They'll be so excited."

They went out and joined Christopher and Jimmy.

"So, how was Christmas with Grandma and Granny? Did you like having real snow?" Cynthia asked.

"It was pretty cool," Jimmy responded. "Christopher and I went ice fishing and actually caught enough fish for a meal. I never thought a Southern boy like me would go ice fishing," he said, and they all laughed.

"Yeah, and it was great seeing Purvell," Christopher interjected.

"Where did you see Purvell?" Cynthia asked.

"She spent Christmas with her family in Neenah and decided to drive up to White Lake so she could see all of us," Millie said.

"Yeah, and it was great seeing Daniel too," Christopher shared.

Cynthia thought she heard wrong. "Who did you see?"

"Daniel. He came with Purvell to Grandma's. I think Grandma and Granny were happy to see him too. I didn't know they had met before."

Cynthia's throat felt as if it had closed up, and she couldn't utter a word.

"He seems to be doing okay," Christopher added.

Cynthia still couldn't speak.

Millie looked at Jimmy and quickly changed the subject, seeing her mother's distress.

"Mom, I've taken some days off so we could spend time together before you go back to St. Simons. Maybe we can go to SouthPark Mall and look at some things for the baby and then to lunch. I think you'll like shopping there. What do you think?"

"What? Oh, sure, I'd love to do that," she said flatly, but her mind was on what Christopher had just shared. Daniel at her mother's house on White Lake? Why would Purvell do that? Her head was spinning.

Daniel and Purvell *were* good friends. Cynthia hadn't shared with Purvell or anyone else what had happened with Daniel, so she needed to calm down. Purvell had probably thought he might enjoy getting away to her parents' farm in Neenah and a slower pace over Christmas. But Cynthia had made her decision about Daniel six months ago. His life obviously had gone on without her, and in a few days,

Cynthia's same old life would go on as it had been before Daniel Benton showed up and rented her beach house on St. Simons Island.

"Hey, let's call Grandma and Granny before it gets too late and let them know you've arrived safely," Millie said in an effort to further alleviate her mother's distress and touched the number on her phone. "Hi, Grandma. Yes, Mom made it here safe and sound. Is Granny there too? Oh, good. I'm going to put you on speaker so we can all talk," she said, and she proceeded to do so.

"Cynthia, darling, I'm so happy you're back home again," said Grace. We've missed you so much. I think Granny and I are going to come visit real soon. We're so sick of the snow."

And then Granny piped in. "So happy now both you and your brother will be back here in the States, and I'll second what Grace just said about the snow. I could use some warmth in these old bones of mine."

"Before we go any further, Granny, I want to share some good news with you," Millie said.

"So, you're finally going to tell me about the baby?" Granny asked.

"How did you know? Did Grandma or Christopher tell you?" she looked over at Christopher who had a reputation for saying things when he wasn't supposed to. Christopher had his *I'm innocent* look on his face, which was very similar to his *I didn't eat the last one* look.

"No, my child. I saw it in your face the moment you walked through the door at Christmas. I can't tell you how happy I am for you and Jimmy."

"Grandma knew then, also," Millie laughed. "We can't keep any secrets from the two of you."

"And don't you forget that, dear," Granny said and laughed as well.

"I heard Purvell came to see you over Christmas," Cynthia said.

"Yes, she did. It was so good to see that girl. We can talk more about it later, sweetheart, when you get back to your place, and not bore everyone else," her mother responded.

The rest of the conversation was centered around Cynthia's plans to go back to her life on St. Simons.

"I mean it when I say we're coming to visit," Grace reaffirmed.

"I can't wait, Mom," was all Cynthia could get out. She was filled with emotion talking to her mother. She wanted a hug and to be told everything was going to work out and be fine again.

They all said their good-byes.

"So, Mom, how about you and I go to breakfast together tomorrow morning so I can have some time with you?" Christopher asked.

"That would be nice, but couldn't we all go?" Cynthia asked, her mind still on the phone conversation and Daniel visiting White Lake. She totally missed the look exchanged between Christopher and Millie.

"Millie's been monopolizing you," he said. "I wanted to have some of my own time with you before you go back."

"I would never turn that down," she said with a smile. "Let's make it more like brunch though, if that's okay?" Cynthia yawned. "I know it's not quite nine yet, but if you all don't mind, I'm ready to go to bed."

It had been a long day. Cynthia felt the jet lag catching up with her, but what she needed even more was to be alone and think. As she lay in bed, her mind went one hundred miles per hour, eventually calming enough so she could drift into sleep.

❧

At about ten thirty the next morning, Cynthia was in Christopher's car on their way to a favorite all-day breakfast place of his.

"So, Mom, I've got something to tell you," Christopher said in way too cheery a voice as their food arrived. *Now what?* she thought.

"I'm not going back to college," he blurted out quickly and then finished with, "I may not ever go back."

"What are you talking about, Christopher? Your father and I planned on both our children getting college educations. You're going to college," she said dismissively.

"I don't think I'm made for college," he said firmly. "I sorta *can't* go back," he added, looking down.

"What does 'sorta' mean?" She was so upset with him. He had done well enough his first two years to get into the nursing program, which wasn't easy.

"I already told them I wouldn't be back this next semester. I feel so burned out, Mom. I'm sick of books and studying. I like the medical stuff, but I don't want to study. It's a waste of your money if I'm not wholeheartedly into it."

"I can't believe you did this without talking to me first. You should have discussed it with me," she said, clenching a fist.

"I'm not a kid, Mom, so don't treat me that way. I'm not the kind of student Millie is, and maybe I'll go back. I just need a break to decide what I really want to do. It's just … so much has happened in the past two years. I want to get it together so I do the right thing. I've had to grow up a lot since Dad died, and I've done pretty good, I think. I didn't want to bother you because of all you were doing for Uncle Arthur, so I talked with Millie and Jimmy. Jimmy and I have become close, and he gave me good advice. I have a plan for my future," he said, sounding so self-assured.

She remained silent, waiting to hear what he and Jimmy had come up with.

"I got a job working at the Jekyll Island Club Resort and at one of the golf courses on Jekyll Island. I would like to be able to live with you—if you will have me—otherwise Ian would probably let me stay with him."

Cynthia hadn't been expecting this at all. A college education was so important to her and Philip. What would Philip have told him? Probably, *Get your butt back to school.* But things weren't the same as they were then. Christopher *had* obviously put some thought into the plan he laid before her. He did have two jobs lined up, after all.

"Where have you been since the semester ended?" she asked. "I imagine you had to get out of the dorm."

"I've been living with Millie and Jimmy. All my stuff is in the garage. I'm sure she's ready to get rid of me, though—especially with the baby coming. I thought I could move down to your house on St. Simons after Christmas, and then I found out you were coming home, so I knew I needed to tell you right away."

"So, you weren't going to tell me at all?" Cynthia asked, shaking her head. "Your dad and I have always been there and available for you and your sister through everything. Just because he's gone doesn't mean that's changed. Why didn't you tell me and get my opinion before you made this decision?"

"I know I can always talk to you. I just didn't want to add any more to what you were already dealing with. I was going to get settled in and start doing well before I told you." He paused and looked down at his hands a moment. "So ... can I move in with you?"

She couldn't believe this. They had saved money so both the kids could get a start in life with a college degree. Christopher never was a straight-A student; she was always having to keep after him, but he did okay. She looked at him. He wasn't a kid anymore but a man; she needed to recognize this in him.

"You've totally taken me by surprise, son. You've already made your decision, and it is your life. Of course you can live with me," she said, sighing. "This will be like the real world, though. You can live as a renter in the apartment below the beach house. I won't be cooking, cleaning, or washing your clothes. I want to see how much money you'll be making, and we'll work out a monthly payment. You'll be my renter. Life is not always free," she said, making the best of it.

"Okay, Mom. That's fair enough. Thanks for being understanding. I'll be the best renter ever," he said, and as he smiled at her, she saw the little boy who always knew the way to her heart.

❦

After his trip to Wisconsin, Daniel had returned to New York for a few days before flying his plane down to Jekyll Island for the closing of his new townhome on December 31. Ian had kindly offered to let him stay at his house until Daniel got his new place ready to move in. Daniel had hired a local decorator who promised to have the townhome tastefully furnished and move-in ready by the end of January.

Most home closings have a bit of drama, but Daniel's had gone off without a hitch, making him feel the decision to move down here was the right one.

Daniel had found out through Ian about Ann's death and that Cynthia would be coming back to St. Simons for good during the second weekend of January. Cynthia's brother and niece were moving back to the States, so she now had no reason to stay in England.

Not ready to bump into her just yet, Daniel felt it was fortunate he was needed back in New York for several weeks, postponing the inevitable. He knew he was taking a bold risk in moving to Jekyll, but then he was used to taking risks. After all, that's how his business had become so successful.

That brought him to his latest risk. He had started a new business call DB Properties. The plan was to go back to his roots and how he'd run things when he started right out of college by doing small jobs. He'd bid on several projects proposed for Jekyll and St. Simons Islands, one of which was for Cynthia's friend Betty, who owned a piece of property on St. Simons Island where she wanted to build a small retail plaza.

He planned to go back up to New York the Friday before Cynthia would be home to check on his main company, Benton Enterprises, and his nephew, Stephen. This was all part of his plan to groom Stephen to take over the company. The boy was doing well, but Daniel wasn't ready to put Stephen totally in charge just yet.

His mind wandered back to Cynthia's phone call from England six months ago, when she'd told him she would have to say "no" to his offer for her to move to New York. She felt called to take care of her sister-in-law and wasn't sure when she'd be back in the States. When she did come back, she told him, she wanted to live nowhere else but St. Simons Island. She was sorry and wished him the best in all he did.

And that was it.

What she didn't know was that her dedication to her brother's family only made him love her more. She was a rare woman in his eyes.

He knew he'd messed things up when he foolishly asked her to uproot her life and move to New York. How much more selfish could he get, not thinking of her but only himself? He now realized this, and was a little ashamed of himself. No, he would instead show her he could become part of her life. She meant that much to him. With her by his side, he'd be ready to slow down and enjoy life more, instead of filling it with the next deal and project, as he'd done since his wife, Julie, died. He felt certain that deep down Cynthia loved him, but he wanted it to be her decision. He'd learned his lesson and wouldn't rush anything this time.

✤

When Cynthia passed the Darien exit on I-95, she knew it wouldn't be long. She'd been enjoying the drive from Charlotte to St. Simons Island, feeling so grateful she would soon be home. The traffic was light that day, she guessed because it was a Sunday.

Normally she would have taken exit 38 to the island, but she was willing to add a few extra miles and go down to exit 29 so she could drive over the bridge before heading home.

Home.

"I'm going home," she said aloud, and a few spontaneous tears stung her eyes. She would cook in *her* kitchen, eat at *her* table, walk on *her* beach, shower in *her* bathroom, have a glass of *her* wine on *her* deck, sit on *her* couch in *her* pajamas, and sleep in *her own* bed tonight. Life was good.

Soon the sign indicating exit 29 was before her, and she veered off the interstate down the incline, turning left onto Ocean Highway toward Jekyll Island and the bridge that connected her to the way home.

She took her time driving over the bridge, not caring how many cars passed her. She wanted to take it all in, remembering the first time she and Philip had driven over the bridge when they visited the area almost three years ago. The trip had been a surprise for her fifty-fifth birthday. Three years ago—really?

Unexpectedly, they'd fallen in love with the area, prompting them to sell their house in Atlanta and move to the island. She'd never anticipated the series of events before her, leading to the life she was living now.

After driving down the Torres Causeway, she took Kings Way to Ocean Boulevard, then to Ocean Road and the road which would lead her to home.

Cynthia stopped at the entrance of her driveway for a brief moment. Brad had taken good care of things while she was gone. The place looked good.

She parked and went up the twelve steps to the front door and inserted her key. As always, she jiggled the key in the familiar way to coax it to turn after being inserted in the slot. The door opened and she was home.

Before getting her things from the car, she walked from room to room, taking it all in, and then slid open the glass door leading to the deck and the view of the beach. She couldn't believe how much she'd missed the sounds and smells of this place. This was where she was supposed to be. She closed her eyes as the salty wind hit her face and knew she would never take this place for granted. This was her home.

☙

Once Cynthia took her suitcases upstairs, she decided she had the rest of the evening to put things away. What she really needed to do was get some groceries, so she went to the kitchen and made a list before heading over to the grocery store. She couldn't wait to cook for herself tonight and open a bottle of wine.

She got in her car and headed to the grocery store in the Shops of Sea Island shopping plaza, thinking about Christopher becoming her renter.

He'd be moving into the apartment below her house at the end of the week, so she had a little time to get used to the thought. She wondered if he might have done better in school if she hadn't been in England the past few months. She would've been there to support him. Could it have made a difference? Had she let him down?

One thing was for certain—there was never a dull moment when he was around, and it might be nice to have some company, she decided. Her life wouldn't be so boring.

Cynthia told Christopher she was going to charge him rent. Her plan, however, was to open a savings account at the bank and deposit the rent money for someday when he wanted to buy a house for himself. She wasn't going to make it too easy for him, though. He would be looking for something to eat every chance he got like usual, so she would probably feed him frequently, but there were not going to be any free rides otherwise.

As she drove to the store, she saw not much had changed on the island since she left. It was as if she had never been gone. Now to get her job back and slip back into her life of six months ago.

CHAPTER 9

*T*o think, a few weeks ago Cynthia had been in cold England, and now she was walking the beach on a pleasant coastal-Georgia day. She wore a jacket because of the wind, but no shoes so she could feel the sand on her feet and between her toes as she walked and drank her morning coffee.

It was nine in the morning, so the sun was already making its trek in the cloudless sky overhead. Cynthia had brought some pieces of bread along with her to toss at the gulls looking for breakfast as the tide came in and out. She enjoyed throwing the bread in the air and watching them snap it up before it touched the ground. *This is the life,* she thought.

No one knew she was back yet except Brad Davies and Christopher. She wasn't sure why, but she wanted more time to settle in before jumping back into her world on the island.

Christopher had moved into the apartment over the weekend. His job at the Jekyll Island Club Resort would start on the upcoming Monday and at the golf course the following week. So far he'd eaten every meal with her. Even though she was still annoyed with him for dropping out of college, she kinda liked having him around. The energy he radiated was good medicine, causing her to smile and laugh back into life.

She was going to give the hospital another call when she finished her walk and make sure they knew she was available anytime. It kind of bothered her that she hadn't gotten a call from HR yet. Of course they would want her back; she only needed to be patient and wait for them to go through the process. After all, when she'd first gone to work for the hospital two years ago, it was well over a month before they offered her a job.

She closed her eyes and lifted her face to the sun to say a thank-you to God for the beautiful day. All in all, she was a fortunate woman. She then wondered how her tree was doing in England and laughed to herself. A *conker* tree. She laughed again.

Back in the house, she was getting ready to pour herself another cup of coffee when the doorbell rang. There stood the first friend she'd made on the island, Betty Franklin.

Cynthia had happened to wander into a barbeque restaurant on the island the night Philip died. It was owned by Betty and her late husband, Jack. Betty had extended Cynthia heartfelt compassion that night, resulting in a strong friendship between the two women thereafter.

Almost exactly a year later, Cynthia was able to return the kindness shared with her when Jack died after being trapped in the restaurant when it caught fire and burned to the ground. Jack survived but suffered a heart attack and burns during the fire, ultimately dying when he suffered another heart attack in the ICU where Cynthia worked. The tragedy cemented an even stronger bond between the two women.

"How did you know I was back? Let me guess, you sensed it," Cynthia said as she embraced her friend. Betty had always had a gift since she was a child of knowing things before they happened, and the ability to sense the way people felt.

Betty laughed. "I would like to tell you I did, but I saw Brad and he told me. Why didn't you let me know?"

"It all happened so fast, Betty. I guess I needed some time to ease back into life here. Listen, I was just getting ready to pour myself another cup of coffee. Why don't you join me and we can get caught up?"

The last time the two women had talked on the phone was before Christmas.

"Tell me about you and the boys," Cynthia prompted her.

"Well, you know John graduated in December with his business degree and Luke will this May," Betty started. "So much has happened, I don't know where to begin. Brad has introduced me to this man who is helping me to build a little shopping center on the old restaurant property. His business is called DB Properties. I'm going to have a restaurant and bakery in it where I'll serve breakfast and lunch and do a little catering. Not sure what I'm going to call the place yet, but we'll also have about six other shops for rent in the complex. It should bring me in enough money to live rather comfortably. This man I'm working with is so nice and knowledgeable. He kind of dropped in my lap."

"If Brad recommended him, you can't go wrong. So what do John and Luke think about all this?" Cynthia asked.

"Believe it or not, they're very interested. You know how they wanted nothing to do with the restaurant. I don't say anything, but it just about broke Jack's heart they didn't want to take it over. They're going to run the shopping center and help with my place. I guess Jack's kind of getting what he wanted, only in a different way. Jack wanted to give them a legacy and he has. They're working with the developer and learning a lot along the way. Developing and investing is more of what they would like to do, and I like that we're working together."

"I think it sounds great, Betty. Nothing could ever replace their dad, but at least they can feel connected to him doing this with you."

"Enough about me. What about you?" Betty wanted to know.

"Crazy as it sounds, the day Ann passed away I had intended to tell Arthur and Ann I was going to start making plans to come back here. Now Arthur is moving back also, making my mom and Granny very happy."

"Isn't it amazing how things can happen? That's how we know there's a force bigger than us in charge guiding our life," Betty said with a smile on her face. "Now, what about you and the kids?"

"So, I'm going to save the best news for last," Cynthia said, taking a sip of coffee. "Christopher wasn't happy in college and has dropped out. I don't have to tell you I'm not pleased, and if his dad were still alive, there would have been raised voices over this. But, he did it all before I could even talk to him about it. Maybe working he'll see he needs a college degree. I can tell you I feel a little bit of guilt, because maybe if I'd been here I could have been a bigger support for him."

"Cynthia, don't you dare beat yourself up over this. The best we can do is provide a foundation for our kids; the rest is up to them."

"I guess you're right," said Cynthia. "He's gotten one job at the Jekyll Club Resort and another at one of the golf courses. I've agreed to let him live below me in the apartment—but not rent-free. He needs to know what it's really like."

"I couldn't agree with you more," Betty said.

"I've also considered the fact both my children have been through a lot the past two years," Cynthia added. "Millie has Jimmy, but Christopher only has me, and I've been dealing with my own problems—and then helping Arthur. I hope to be more of a present source for him from now on, and having him here is a good start." She looked down and then up at Betty with a sad smile.

Betty reached over and took Cynthia's hand. Cynthia squeezed it, knowing Betty was the one person who understood everything.

"I'm hoping to get my job back at the hospital," she continued, "but I haven't heard a word from them. As soon as I knew I was coming back, I sent them an email. I'm going to call them today to see what's going on.

"So, here's the big news. When the kids met me at the airport in Charlotte, the first thing I saw was Millie's rounded tummy. She's expecting a baby girl in late spring. Can you believe she kept it from me all that time? I understand and forgive her, though. She wanted to make sure everything was okay—and it is. I'm going to be a grandma!" Cynthia said, with tears in her eyes.

"Oh, Cynthia, that is great news," Betty said, tearing up herself. "And now you'll be here when the child is born."

"I know. A baby is the best news for all of us."

"It sure is." Betty looked at her watch. "I hate to run, but I have to meet some people about my new restaurant in thirty minutes. Hey, if you think of a catchy name for the place, let me know. I'm at a loss. Does Ian know you're back?"

"No, but I'm sure Christopher will see him when he starts his job and let him know. Is he doing okay?"

"He's doing fine, but I'll let him tell you about his news," said Betty.

Now Cynthia was curious.

❧

After Betty left, Cynthia called the contact number Jackson Irwin, her former nurse manager at the hospital, had given her.

"Southeast Georgia Health System human resources, this is Pam Woulf; what may I help you with?"

"Hi, Pam. I was given your name by Jackson Irwin. I'm a former employee of the hospital looking to come back. I had a family situation that caused me to leave about six months ago, but I'd like to get my job back in the ICU. Can you help me with that?" Cynthia asked.

"Normally I could, but right now the hospital has a hiring freeze due to a company they've hired to help reevaluate staffing. They'll determine where we'll be hiring once the freeze is off," Pam explained. "We can only hire in departments with a shortage of employees that cause a potential liability risk for the hospital. I don't foresee any openings for about a month or more—unless a liability position comes up. Have you thought of checking with some of the doctors' offices in the area? I have access to those postings also and could check them out. They would love someone with your experience," she said, trying to sound hopeful.

"I've always worked in a hospital, so naturally that's where my love of nursing is. It may have to be an option, though, I guess." The disappointment was noticeable in Cynthia's voice.

"The thing is, I'm not sure I'll even be able to hire anyone after this reevaluation is done, so you might want to pursue it. If a liability position becomes available anywhere in the hospital, not just ICU, do you want me to consider you?"

"Yes, I do. I loved working at the hospital and want to get back again," said Cynthia.

"Okay. Jackson has nothing but great things to say about you, and from what I see of your record, you're the kind of nurse we want to keep. I would suggest you find something else in the system, and maybe sometime in the next six months to a year we'll have an ICU position open," Pam said.

Six months to a year? Cynthia felt a churn in the pit of her stomach.

"Really, that long? Well, I guess I have no choice. Please keep me in mind. Is it okay if I call you occasionally to check on positions?" Cynthia felt dejected.

"Sure, I don't mind. If I have something, though, I'll call you," Pam replied. "There are plenty of nursing jobs out there in other places. You may surprise yourself and like one of them."

"Yes, I might. Thank you, Pam. I'm going to still hope for the ICU," she said, and they said good-bye.

Cynthia hadn't been prepared for this. She honestly thought she would get her job back with no problem. Now, what to do? She started pacing the room and didn't notice Christopher walk in the house.

"What's up, Mom?" he asked, not looking at her, and went straight to the refrigerator for a bottle of Gatorade. Then he came and sat next to her on the couch, noticing the look on her face. "Are you okay?"

"I just found out it looks like I'm not going to be able to get a job at the hospital due to a hiring freeze. I'm kind of shocked and not sure what to do," she said, taking a seat at the table and staring straight ahead.

"Mom—really? You've always told me to have a plan B. So, what's yours?"

"I don't have one," she responded with a shrug.

Christopher shook his head as if he were the parent disappointed in his child.

"So, let's make one. Get your résumé together—in fact, I'll help you, and maybe you can get a job with a doctor that does cool stuff."

Cynthia laughed at Christopher. He was right. This wasn't the end of the world. She had a skill and experience that could be used in so many different places.

"Thank you, son. I think I'm going to be very happy with you as my tenant." She gave him a big hug and kiss.

"I knew college wasn't the place for me right now," he said with satisfaction.

❦

On Monday morning after Christopher left for his first day at the hotel, Cynthia dialed Ian's number.

"Well, hello, lass!" he said. "I was wondering how long it would be before I heard from you. I knew you wouldn't forget your old pal."

"It's so good to hear your voice, Ian. Please don't take any offense: I enjoyed England, but I'm so happy to be home." Ian was from a town in England called Berwick on Tweed, located near the Scottish border. "So, who told you I was back?"

"No offense taken about England darlin'. It's much warmer here. Christopher told me about your sister-in-law passing and that you would be back. So, how did you take his news about school?"

"I'm not thrilled, and if his father were alive, I'm sure he would have gone ballistic. However, I'm supporting his decision. Did he tell you I'm charging him rent?"

"Yes, and I think you should. Don't baby him, Cynthia. The world is hard, and he needs to know that."

"Yes, it is at times, isn't it?" said Cynthia, and there was a pause.

"How about you come meet me on the Jekyll pier in the late afternoon on Thursday and I'll cook up whatever I end up catching?" Ian suggested.

"I would love that. Betty made me feel something's going on with you. What's up?"

"Who, me? I guess you'll have to wait till Thursday."

"It's not bad Ian, is it?"

"No, not at all. See you Thursday."

⚜

Cynthia received a phone call Wednesday morning from Pam Woulf telling her about a doctor she knew who needed a nurse in his office on St. Simons. The position was part-time, but a great place to start. She hoped Cynthia didn't mind, but she had set up an interview for her on Friday morning.

"Thanks, Pam. It's great to have people looking out for me. Just happens I'm available." The truth was, she had nowhere else to go and was starting to become bored.

"Well, good," said Pam. "I have your email address here, so I'll send you the particulars. I'm so happy to have found something for you. I'll be honest, I just don't think there'll be something in the ICU for a while. Many of the other departments are being pared down, so quite a few nurses are also looking for positions. If I were you, I would grab this one."

"I appreciate the advice, Pam. Thanks for keeping me in mind. Bye," Cynthia said, realizing as she hung up, she'd never asked what area of medicine the doctor practiced.

When the email came later, she was taken by surprise. The doctor's name was Henry Underwood, and he was a podiatrist. *Seriously?* She'd never seen that one coming.

❦

Late in the afternoon Thursday, Cynthia went to the North Pier on Jekyll Island, where she found Ian fishing just like he'd been the first time they met. The buggy-looking contraption he used to haul all his gear, a cooler, and collapsible chairs onto the pier was next to the six fishing poles he had set up along the railing while he waited for a bite.

Ian must have seen her approach, since he met her as she turned left at the end of the pier.

"Hello, darlin'. Don't you look grand today?"

Ian hadn't changed a bit. He was just as handsomely rugged and his warm brown eyes just as kind as the day he'd befriended her on that very pier.

"Hello, my friend. I can't tell you how good it is to see you," she said and gave him a lingering hug. Ian had repeatedly gone the extra mile for her as a friend. She'd never forget when she'd called him from her mother's home on White Lake in Wisconsin, where she had gone to make a decision about Daniel. While there, she'd decided to spread her deceased husband's ashes over White Lake, a place where they'd had fond memories, in an attempt to move on. She'd called Ian to retrieve the ashes from the urn in her house and mail them to her. Reluctantly, he did so out of pure friendship.

"So, I'm dying to find out what you have to tell me. Please. It's good news, right?" she begged.

"Well, I was going to tell you at dinner, but I can't wait myself. I asked Collette for her hand in marriage, and she said 'yes.'" Ian was beaming.

"Oh, Ian! I'm so happy for you. When is the wedding?"

"The last weekend in March over yonder on Driftwood Beach. We'll have a little reception at the Jekyll Resort after, just a wee affair," he said beaming from ear to ear.

The two friends hugged again, Cynthia with tears in her eyes.

"You women," said Ian, tearing up. "Now, stop it. Look what you've done to me," he sighed, and they both laughed.

"I have some news, also," said Cynthia. "I have a job interview on Friday. It's not what I really want to do, though. Nothing's available in the hospital ICU, so I'm going to hang in there for a while, hoping eventually for an opening I can fill."

"Well, that's not bad. I'm sure it's a matter of time and you'll get your wish." Ian smiled at his friend.

"I think I'm ready to call it a day," Ian said. "The fish haven't been biting, so I'm going to take you to Driftwood Bistro for dinner instead. I just need to run back to my place and get cleaned up. How about you help haul my gear up to the bait shop and then follow me over to my place?"

"Sounds good," she said.

Since Ian was manager of the campground across the street from the pier entrance, the bait shop allowed him to keep his fishing gear in a storage shed attached to the building. They stepped in the shop so Ian could talk to the owner before they left.

"Vernon!" Ian hollered when he entered the shop. A tall, thin man with shoulder length hair about Ian's age came out of a back room. Cynthia thought he had a welcoming face. "Naught a bloody thing worth keeping today. Had to throw all the wee ones back in to grow a bit more. I'll be back in a few days. Want you to meet my friend, Cynthia Lewis, back from an extended trip to my homeland," he told Vernon.

"Hey, it's a pleasure to meet you, ma'am," Vernon said in a heavy Southern accent and extended his hand to shake Cynthia's with a big smile. "You said 'extended' trip? Did ya have a good time?"

"Yes and no. Let's say I'm happy to get back," she replied. "I don't plan on going anywhere for a while."

"Do you live here on Jekyll?" he asked.

"No, I'm on St. Simons. A little over two years now. How about you?"

"Oh, me, I live here on Jekyll. Family's been here for years," Vernon said.

"We have to be going, friend," Ian said. "Taking this lovely lass to dinner. Have yourself a pleasant evening." He nodded, and they were out the door and on their way to Ian's.

Vernon watched out the window as they pulled away. *Seemed like a nice lady.* He pulled his cell phone out of his pocket and touched the screen.

"Hey, it's me," he said. "I should be home the usual time ... Ian and a friend were about the only ones fishing today ... No, not Collette but a friend of his named Cynthia ... Her last name? Let me think a minute—it started with an L, I think ... Stop yelling at me! ... Yeah, that was it—Lewis. How'd you know? ... I don't know. She's been abroad or something and says she's happy to get back ... I only talked to her a minute, but yeah she seemed nice ... I dunno, ask Ian about her next time you see him. You're asking me questions here I can't answer ... Okay, I'll see if I can find out more next time I talk to him, just stop yelling at me. ... Geez. I got to go." Vernon hung up, shaking his head.

CHAPTER 10

*D*aniel was flying his plane back to Jekyll Island, ready to start this new chapter of his life. He loved New York; however, since his first visit to St. Simons and Jekyll Island, he had begun to also love the sandy shores of coastal Georgia.

In New York he was a well-known developer with an excellent reputation. Many projects he bid on were awarded to Benton Enterprises on merit and reputation alone. It was rather nice, though he did miss flexing the skills and talent he possessed as a salesman and negotiator when closing a deal. The projects he was finding in Georgia were new and different. Nobody knew him, and he was the new kid on the block again. He kind of liked having the opportunity to use his knowledge to chart new territories at this time in his life.

When he'd returned to New York after closing on his new townhome, he found his company was doing well with Stephen in charge. It was evident Daniel had trained him well over the years.

As he approached the island, he heard the okay to land his plane, but not before a glance out the window to admire the beautiful coastline below. He was going to be living here. Last year when he'd rented Cynthia's beach house, he would have laughed at the idea, and now here he was. What more could he ask for?

Cynthia.

He wanted to knock on her door and say, *This is enough. You know we belong together, so tell me you love me and let's get on with it.* Probably not a good idea. No, he would start a life on her turf and let her come to him, and if it didn't happen … he wasn't going to think about it. It *would* happen.

After landing at the Jekyll Island Airport, he rented an electric vehicle approved for use on the roads of Jekyll Island. These kinds of vehicles were fancy golf carts that came in a variety of sizes to accommodate up to six people. They were used to get around by many visitors while vacationing on the island. His plan was to buy a car eventually, but until then, the electric car would be fine. If he needed to go off the island, Ian's car was available for Daniel to use since Ian preferred getting around by motorcycle.

Daniel now owned one of the new townhomes in The Cottages on the northeast side of the island. It was brand new and spacious compared to his New York condo. Tonight would be the first time he stayed there. He couldn't wait to see it decorated and furnished. After parking the electric car in the garage and plugging it in, he went to the front door, turned the key, and entered. It was beautiful.

He walked from room to room upstairs and down. How he wished he could share it with someone. His eyes stung for a moment or two. *Stop it,* he told himself.

He went back downstairs. It was too quiet. It was never this quiet in his New York condo, but he'd get used to it.

He wanted to fix something to eat, pour himself a drink, turn on the fire, and stare at the flames, but his cupboards were empty. The island had no grocery store, only a little convenience-type store called The Jekyll Market. Good thing he had the electric vehicle to drive over there to pick up a few things he might need and some beer until he could get to a grocery store. A wave of butterflies fluttered in his stomach. *Everything will be just fine,* he told himself.

Daniel brought his luggage in and started to put his things in the closet and drawers. He pulled a handgun locked in a case out of one suitcase. The gun had belonged to his dad at one time and was passed on to him when Daniel moved to the city "for safety," his dad said. Daniel took it with him wherever he lived. He got a chair and put it high up on a closet shelf in the corner where no one could see or get at it.

Now to get something to eat and drink and then watch some sports before he went to bed. He might try a run on the beach in the morning to welcome in his new life. He told himself again, *Everything will be just fine.*

❧

When Dr. Underwood asked Cynthia at her interview on Friday if she could start on Monday, she said "yes," but wanted him to be aware of the fact she really was looking for a full-time job at the hospital, and if one became available, she would take it. He said he understood, though he still wanted to hire her. Her hours were 8 a.m. until 3:30 p.m., Monday through Wednesday, with thirty minutes for lunch.

Before she started her car to leave Dr. Underwood's office, her phone rang, and she noticed it was a number from the hospital ICU.

"Hi, Cynthia. This is Callie from the ICU. I just heard you were back in the area. Hasn't been the same here without you," Callie said pleasantly.

"Hi, yes, I'm back, and I would love to be working with all of you. I've been told there aren't any openings right now," Cynthia said, wondering if Callie knew something she didn't.

"There aren't any I know of, but I'll keep a lookout for you. The reason I'm calling is my dad's visiting me from California, and being a single parent with three kids and working, I'm not going to be home the whole time he's visiting. I hate he's going to be sitting around doing nothing. When I heard you were back and hadn't started working yet, I was wondering if you might show him around a couple of days. It's his first time visiting the area. You're both about the same age," Callie said in an attempt to convince her.

Really, Cynthia thought—a blind date? She had never been on one before. How was she going to say "no"?

"Well, I don't know, Callie. I start a part-time position Monday. I mean, does your dad know you're calling me about this?" Cynthia asked, hoping to point out her dad may not be willing to be stuck with her.

"Oh, yes. He's fine with it. He's a really nice guy. Owns a marketing company in California and is *very* successful. It would only be for a couple days while I'm at work. Please?" Callie pleaded. Cynthia had liked working with Callie and found her to be an excellent nurse. Maybe doing this favor would put Callie in Cynthia's corner, reminding the ICU nurse manager about her when a position opened up.

"Sure, I'll be happy to spend some time with your dad," she said, caving. "When's he coming?"

"This Wednesday. Maybe you could do something with him Thursday or Friday? I'll call you later in the day Wednesday after he gets here so you can make plans."

"Okay," Cynthia said reluctantly. " I don't work either of those days. What's your dad's name?

"Calhoun Parker."

"I guess I'll talk to you Wednesday then. I work till three thirty."

"Great. I can't tell you how much I appreciate this. Talk with you soon."

"Yes, soon," Cynthia said, and wished she knew how she might be able to get out of this. Maybe she would catch something from one of the patients at work and get sick so she could back out. Unfortunately, not too many viruses came into a podiatrist practice.

When she got home, she found Christopher standing in front of the refrigerator with the door open just like old times.

"Hey," she startled him.

"Oh, hi, Mom. Hope you don't mind. I was kind of hungry and nothing looked good in my refrigerator." He smiled a little sheepishly.

"No, son, I don't mind. So, I got the job. I start Monday," she said, trying to muster some enthusiasm.

"That's great. Taking care of feet should be a nice change for you." He grinned a little and then laughed.

"I know it's not what I want, but it'll do. Just hope I get a full-time job at the hospital soon so I don't have to raise your rent," she told him.

"You wouldn't do that to your own kid, would you?"

"Maybe," she said with a wink. "How about I take you out to dinner tonight at Barbara Jean's so we can celebrate my new job?"

"You know I never turn down a free meal."

"Be ready by six. I'm going for a run on the beach." And she went upstairs to change. A run was what she needed to clear her head. *Everything will be just fine,* she told herself.

❦

That weekend, Cynthia called Purvell. She didn't think her friend even knew she was back. Somehow during their conversation, she wanted to find out why Purvell had brought Daniel to her mother's at Christmas but didn't want to be too obvious. Cynthia touched the number on her phone and Purvell picked up right away.

"Hello, stranger. How's it going now you're back?" Purvell queried right away.

"How did you know I was back?" Cynthia asked.

"I gave Millie a call and she told me. I've kept in touch with both the kids while you've been gone," she responded.

"Yes, I heard they saw you over Christmas. I didn't know when I would be back at that point." She was going to ask about Daniel, but then hesitated too long and Purvell changed the subject.

"So, tell me about what happened. Poor Ann. It almost seems a blessing after what the she was going through."

Cynthia told her all about how she had already decided she was coming back to St. Simons when Ann died. Sad as it was, it had made her departure easier.

"Arthur and Sammy have moved back to Milwaukee, also," Cynthia explained. "Sammy's taken this semester off, but will start at UW Madison in the fall just my like my dad, Arthur, and I did. Carrying on the family tradition. Hope I get a chance to visit while she's there, maybe go to a football game or something."

"Life sure can change in a heartbeat," Purvell said.

"Don't I know it," Cynthia responded. "I'm ready for things to calm down—it just keeps coming. I couldn't get my job back, or any job for that matter, at the hospital, so Monday I start working for a podiatrist—and my new tenant living in the apartment under my house is Christopher," she announced, waiting for Purvell's surprise.

"What? Is he going to school down there now, and what's this about a podiatrist?"

"Oh no, Christopher decided to drop out of school, never even discussing it with me. He is working, so I'm even charging him rent, and other than him raiding my refrigerator on a regular basis, he's not getting a dime from me," Cynthia said.

"Sometimes I miss not ever having children, but other times I don't," Purvell laughed, causing Cynthia to do the same.

"The podiatrist job will get me through till something comes up at the hospital, but enough about Christopher and me; I have some good news. Millie's having a baby! She's kept it a secret because of what happened last time, but it's a girl due in late April or early May. I'll be so happy when the sweet child is born alive and healthy."

"Cynthia, I'm so happy for you. That little stinker never said a word at Christmas. I know how you all must be holding your breath until the child is born," Purvell said.

"We are. Just a few more months to go, though."

"Have you gotten in touch with all your old friends?"

"Yes, I've seen Betty and Ian. Betty is going full-steam ahead on a little shopping plaza being built on the site where their barbeque restaurant burned down, and Ian and Collette are getting married next month."

"How nice. Sounds to me you've been thrown right back into life."

"Yes I have and I know I complain, but I wouldn't have it any other way," Cynthia said, and she meant it.

"How would it be if I came to visit you the end of March?" Purvell asked.

"I would love it, just tell me when and I'll be at the airport."

"I need to get away from here for a while. It's not as much fun doing what I do anymore. Maybe visiting you will give me a break and jump my battery."

"There's nothing wrong, is there?" Cynthia asked her dearest friend in the world.

"Oh no, I'm as healthy as a horse and business is great, just wanting a change of scenery, that's all. I'll let you know when I have a firm date."

Here was Cynthia's opening.

"By the way, I heard you took Daniel to my mother's at Christmas," she mentioned. "You're not trying to mess with my life again, are you, Purvell?"

"Cynthia, I'm hurt you even think that," Purvell said. "I was going to Neenah for Christmas and Daniel wanted to get away, so I invited him to join us on the farm. I already had it planned to visit your mom and Granny, so he had to come along. I didn't think you would mind, since he said you told him things weren't going to work out between you. I'll admit, I was trying to set the both of you up at one time, but I seemed to cause a lot more problems than good. Lesson learned by me."

"Yes, it didn't work," she said with a pain in her heart. Then it just came out of her mouth, "Is he doing okay?"

Purvell smiled. "As far as I know he is. Don't see much of him, really. He's been grooming his nephew Stephen to take over the company, so he's been MIA quite a bit. I'm not sure what he's doing, but heard he's involved in something new that keeps him away from New York. I could ask Stephen the next time I see him for you."

"No, that's okay—just curious. Please don't ask. It doesn't matter."

"Well, okay. I'll let you know as soon as I have a date for when I can come visit. Say 'hi' to the kids, and good luck with the new job."

"Thanks. Sure was good to hear your voice. Bye."

She put her phone on the table and looked around the family room before going out to the deck. She lay back in one of the lounge chairs and, after briefly staring at the ocean horizon, she closed her eyes. Although she hadn't lived in this house long, the home had played a big part in her life. When her husband had died here the day they moved in, she felt she'd lost a part of her life. When Daniel Benton had rented her house, she began to find her way back to a life she thought she'd lost. Now she was right back where she started. Life was full of surprises and disappointments, she decided. She hoped the road ahead would have more surprises than disappointments.

CHAPTER 11

Working for Dr. Underwood was much different from what Cynthia had previously done as a nurse. Her career had always been in a hospital setting with twelve-hour shifts and unpredictable days. This new job had a set schedule and regular appointments without many surprises.

It was Wednesday afternoon, and the first week of work was behind her. She was thinking about what to do the next two days, when her phone rang and she saw it was Callie. She had forgotten about her agreement to show Callie's dad around the island.

"Hi, Callie," Cynthia said.

"Hi, Cynthia, how was your first week of work?" Callie inquired.

"It was fine. Different for me. A definite slower pace. So, did your dad arrive?"

"Yes, he did this afternoon. I really appreciate you spending some time with him since I work tomorrow and Friday. I have five days off starting Saturday, and the kids have Monday off school, so I decided to keep them out Tuesday and Wednesday so we could go to Disney with

Dad. Dad goes back on the next Saturday. You haven't changed your mind about showing him the historic sites around here, have you? I told him all about you," she said, her tone anxious.

"No, I haven't," she lied. "Give me your address and I'll pick him up at ten tomorrow morning," Cynthia said.

"Great, Cynthia. I think you two will hit it off," Callie said.

Right, Cynthia thought.

The next morning, Cynthia pulled into Callie's driveway, walked to the front door, and rang the bell. An attractive man about Cynthia's age answered the door. *This could be interesting*, she thought.

"Hi, Calhoun. I'm Cynthia Lewis." She extended her hand. "I'm pleased to meet you."

"Hi, Cynthia, but please call me Cal. I sure hope that daughter of mine didn't put you out today? I told her I would be fine, but she insisted."

"I have two children myself, and I know just what you mean. I'm not put out at all, though, and happy to show you around our beautiful island. I thought we could go to the lighthouse first and then the pier, since they're close by each other."

"Sounds great," Cal said. "I enjoy sightseeing."

"Well then, let's get started," Cynthia said.

It was a windy day, so they were only able to tour the inside of the lighthouse where the keeper and his family had lived. The top of the lighthouse was closed because of the wind.

They then took a stroll down the pier, where the wind was a little less intense, before heading to Palmer's Village Café for lunch.

Cal was such a gentleman, going as far as to pull out her chair when she sat down.

"Now, I'm kind of old-fashioned, Cynthia. I insist on taking you to lunch," he said, raising his brows.

"Well, I'm not old-fashioned," she said and laughed. "You're company and I'm treating," she said, slapping a hand on the table. She changed the subject. "After lunch I thought I would drive you through Epworth by the Sea, a retreat center, before going to Christ Church and Fort Frederica. Wait till you see the graveyard at the church. The oldest grave dates back to 1802."

"It all sounds great. I was wondering if tomorrow you and I could go to Jekyll Island?" Cal asked. "Callie gave me some brochures about it, and I really would like to see it. What do you say?"

She didn't have anything planned, and she was enjoying Cal's company. "Sure, I love it over there. Very different from this island, though."

"And I want to take you to dinner as a thank-you. I insist."

"Okay," Cynthia said and laughed.

They finished lunch and left the restaurant for their next stop.

While at Palmer's, Cynthia hadn't noticed Vernon, the man to whom Ian had introduced her at the bait shop on Jekyll Island the week before. He was sitting at a table with a woman who had her back to Cynthia and Cal.

"Hey, you know that woman I met the other day, Cynthia Lewis?" Vernon asked the woman.

"Yeah, what about her?" the woman replied as she buttered a piece of bread and took a big bite.

"She's sitting at the table behind you and down two."

The woman put her bread and knife down as she turned slightly, pretending to be looking at something else. There was Cynthia in the flesh. She couldn't believe it.

"I need to go to the ladies' room, Vernon. I'll be back," the woman said and walked by Cynthia's table, taking a quick glance. It *was* her.

The woman went into the ladies' room and looked at herself in the mirror as she fixed her hair. She applied another coat of lipstick, pressed her lips together, and gave a little chuckle.

When she left the ladies' room, she walked by the table slowly. Cynthia Lewis looked up at her and smiled; the woman smiled back and said "hi," and Cynthia did the same. People were way too friendly here, the woman thought.

"I saw you say 'hi' to Cynthia; do you know her?" Vernon asked.

"Are you keeping tabs on my every move, Vernon?" she responded.

"Well, no, but I saw you say 'hi.'"

"That's what people do around here, Vernon. You should know that," the woman said rather meanly.

Vernon went back to his food and didn't speak. She could tell his feelings were hurt.

"Okay, I'm sorry, baby. I was just kidding. I love you and plan on showing you just how much later tonight," she added, and gave Vernon a sly little smile.

"Sometimes I'm not sure if you're kidding or not. Just don't say that stuff, okay?"

"Okay," she said, and then she had an idea. "Hey, can we trade chairs? The fan is blowing right on me."

They switched chairs so the woman could watch Cynthia Lewis until she and her date left.

The next day felt a little warmer since the wind wasn't as strong. Cynthia picked Cal up at noon.

As they drove over the bridge, Cynthia said, "I ran this bridge once. Started out on the Jekyll side and by the time I turned around on the other side and was heading back, a rainstorm came in off the water and drenched me." She fell silent in thought about that life-changing day a little over a year ago. It was the day Jack, Betty's husband, had died.

Cal brought her back. "I used to run in my younger days, but started having knee problems, so I gave it up. I miss it now and then. I'm impressed you ran the bridge," he said, but she didn't answer and changed the subject.

"Let's stop at Tortuga Jacks for lunch first. It's close to the water, so I think you'll enjoy the view," she said, and she headed down the causeway to Jekyll Island.

Cynthia hadn't been back to the Historic District on Jekyll Island since she and Philip stayed there a few days before they closed on and moved into their beach house. After she and Cal went on the tour and looked around the hotel, they stopped by Horton House and the North Pier, finishing the day at Beach Village.

"I've enjoyed this afternoon," Cal said, "but I want to take you to dinner for your kind hospitality on your days off work."

"I was happy to do it, but dinner would be nice. I've been wanting to go to Beach House Restaurant. Do you like seafood?"

"I love it. Let's go," Cal said, and they headed to the restaurant.

❦

After going to the grocery store to fill his pantry, Daniel decided since he now had a fully equipped kitchen, he was going to cook more for himself. In New York, he only cooked occasionally, usually going out, but here he wanted it to be different. He'd had a grill delivered on Wednesday, so he got brave and invited a few of his new neighbors over to break it in that Saturday night with a steak.

His first week back had been busy. He'd spent a good deal of time with Betty's sons, working on the shopping plaza he was helping them develop. The young men reminded him of himself when he was their age. He was hoping to be a mentor, steering them down a career path similar to his own. Daniel had all the money and experience he ever needed; now it was time to give back.

He'd also met with Brad Davies. Brad was starting a company with a woman from his office and wanted Daniel to work on property development in the surrounding area with them. Daniel was looking forward to this new endeavor.

So far, Cynthia hadn't crossed his path, but the day was coming. It made him a little nervous thinking about when it might occur, since both islands were too small to keep the inevitable from happening. Earlier in the day, he'd called Ian to see if he and Collette would like to have dinner at Beach House Restaurant on Jekyll at around six thirty. He told them to get a table if they got there before him, since Fridays were busy at the restaurant.

Just as Daniel was getting ready to pull into the restaurant parking lot, his phone rang. It was Ian. "Hey, mate. Don't know if you want to come in here, but I just talked to Cynthia. She's having dinner with a fella and it's not a relative. Looks like a date. I talked to her for a minute and she introduced us. Told her I didn't know if we would wait for a table and she offered to let us sit with her. I said we had wedding stuff to talk about."

"Who's the guy? Did she say?" Daniel felt a knot in his stomach.

"I'll tell you all about it. How about we meet you at Driftwood Bistro instead? Just relax, friend."

Daniel hadn't thought she would get involved with another man, but then again, why not?

They were able to get a table right away at Driftwood Bistro. Collette spoke first. "Daniel, if you care about Cynthia, you should tell her."

"It's more complicated than that," he said.

Collette continued, "I've gotten to know you pretty well and honestly, you couldn't be a nicer guy. I like Cynthia a lot too. You would make a nice couple, in my opinion."

Ian sighed. "Darlin', there's more to it than that, and actually, I don't know the full story." He turned to Daniel with an intense stare. "And I don't want to know."

"Well, I don't care what you say, Ian. If I can help in any way, Daniel, let me know," Collette said and smiled sweetly.

"Okay, let me tell you what happened when we walked in the restaurant," Ian said. "Cynthia saw us immediately and called us over to her table, introducing her date, as he appeared to be. His name is Cal, I think she said. They had been seeing the sights on Jekyll and decided to end their day with some seafood. They invited us to share their table, as I told you. I didn't know what to say."

"He did great, Daniel," Collette interjected. "She never thought anything of it."

"So, do you think this guy could be a boyfriend? Were they holding hands or acting all lovey?" Daniel said, as he put his hand to his forehead.

"I don't know, mate," Ian said, shrugging his shoulders and fidgeting a bit in his chair. He was clearly uncomfortable with Daniel's questioning.

"Oh my God, Ian," Collette interjected. "No, they weren't holding hands. Honestly, I think Cynthia was more than happy to see us and wanted us to join them. I'm wondering if it was a first date to be honest. I'm not going to lie, the man was very polite and handsome. Looked to be close to her age."

"I'm sorry, you two," Daniel said, shaking his head. "This was supposed to be a nice dinner together. No more talk of Cynthia." He knew his mind would be on her all evening, though.

"I agree," Ian said, raising his eyebrows. "Let's order and then we can tell you all about the wedding."

Daniel didn't bring Cynthia's name up again during dinner and listened to the wedding plans. It was six weeks away, and he could tell how much the couple in front of him were in love. He was a little jealous, he had to admit.

"So, now we want to ask you something," Ian started. "Both of Collette's parents are no longer with us and she has no brothers, so would you, as our dear friend, give her away at the wedding?"

Daniel was touched. Over the past months while Cynthia was gone, he had grown close to Ian and Collette, spending many a dinner with them and fishing with Ian.

"I would love to. Not having any kids, I never thought I would have the pleasure of giving a bride away. Life is sure full of surprises. Thank you. I'm honored." He patted his chest and smiled.

"That's grand," Ian said and planted a kiss on Collette's hand, which he had been holding under the table.

The love and happiness was emanating from them. Daniel thought of Cynthia. He loved her that way and was sure she felt the same about him—she just needed time to discover it. That's why he was there, to be part of her world. She'd told him, "I like you, but I don't love you, because I don't know you, and I'm not sure I'm ready for a committed relationship just yet," when he'd finally found her on White Lake last summer. He'd so foolishly assumed she would want to move to New York—to his world. She had said this was the first time in her life she was on her own, and she liked it. He could understand all of that.

Well it's time for us to get to know each other, Daniel thought. *I'm here and if it's meant to be, the rest will fall into place. If not, at least I've found a beautiful place to live and great new friends.*

Life would still be good.

❦

"Cynthia, I want to thank you for such a wonderful day," Cal said, taking in the atmosphere at Beach House Restaurant. "This is truly a beautiful place. There's something special about it, and of course my grandkids are here, so that helps."

"I know just what you mean, Cal," she said. "My late husband and I felt the same way when we came for a vacation ourselves and then decided to move down here."

"Did you get to spend a good bit of time here before he died?" Cal asked.

"No, not enough," was all she said.

"So, will I get a chance to see you again before I go back?" Cal asked.

"I'm afraid not," Cynthia told him. "My daughter is expecting a baby, and I'm planning to go visit her next Thursday through the weekend in Charlotte. It's my first grandchild, a little girl."

"That's great," Cal said. "Well then, maybe the next time I come to visit, we can do this again. And if you're ever in California, you better come see me."

"Yes, that would be nice," she said.

Cal leaned over and kissed her on the cheek.

As she drove home, Cynthia thought about Cal and what a nice guy he was. He was definitely her type. She began to smile, and then there it was. Daniel's face before her. She wasn't able to stop these periodic thoughts of him. Maybe over time, it would become easier.

CHAPTER 12

*H*er phone rang and Cynthia saw it was the Southeast Georgia Health System. Could this be what she'd been waiting for? It was already the beginning of March, which meant she had been working for Dr. Underwood a whole month and was more than ready to get back in the saddle of the ICU.

"Hello?" she said, her heart beating a bit faster.

"Hi, is this Cynthia Lewis?"

"Yes, it is."

"Cynthia, it's Pam Woulf from HR at the Southeast Georgia Health System. We talked about a month ago about employment at the hospital in Brunswick."

"Yes, of course." Cynthia sat down and grabbed a pen and paper. *They must have a job for me finally*, she thought. "What can I do for you?"

"Well, I knew how much you wanted to be at the hospital, and your reference from Jackson Irwin, your former nurse manager, was excellent, so I have something I think I may be interested in."

Oh my God, Cynthia thought, *I'm back in ICU. I'm back in ICU.*

"It's not in the area you wanted," Pam continued, "but it would be a good move for you to get yourself eventually in the ICU."

"I don't care, Pam. I want to get back to the hospital so badly, I'll take it."

"Well great, it's in the emergency room."

Silence.

"Hello? Cynthia, are you there?"

The emergency room? The ER? That's where Philip had died. She'd been okay working in the hospital's ICU, because she didn't have to go to the ER, but now to actually work there. Could she do it?

"Pam, you've taken me by surprise. I've never worked in the ER before."

"Well, I know, but I think your ICU skills would help many people who show up in the ER. It's all I've got, Cynthia. You said you wanted to be back in the hospital, unless you've decided you like the job you're at right now. So, how's it going with the podiatrist?"

"It's okay." *Just okay.* "Can you give me a day or two to think about it, Pam?"

"Why sure, but I have three other people who I know will jump at this job. I just felt your desperation the first time we talked and wanted to give you the chance."

"I appreciate that and don't mean to sound ungrateful, but I have something personal to take into consideration first," Cynthia said, being perfectly honest. "I don't mean to sound dramatic, but can I have a day or two?"

"Okay, but two days is all I can give you. I need to fill the position. You understand?" Pam said firmly.

"Yes, I do, and thank you so much for thinking of me first. I'm really so appreciative," Cynthia said and they hung up.

The ER, really? Could she do it? She put her running clothes on and headed to the beach.

Cynthia started out her run like she always did, until her breathing and body movement became in sync. Some days it took the full first mile, but today was low humidity and the sky was full of fluffy clouds, shading her path. By the end of a half mile she was in the zone and felt she could run forever.

What was she going to do? The whole time she worked at the hospital before, she'd managed to avoid the ER as if it didn't exist.

Her mind went back to when she'd tried to wake Philip the day they'd moved into their beach house. He'd just wanted a little power nap. But he'd been like a rag doll when she shook him to wake up thirty minutes later; something was very wrong. He wasn't breathing, so she pulled him to the floor, performing CPR until the paramedics showed up and took over.

The paramedics had taken Philip to the hospital, she following behind them. Her mind went to the little room she was taken to where a Dr. Carroll—she'd never forget his name—delivered the news no woman wants to hear. Her husband could not be revived.

Cynthia came back to the present and asked herself some questions. Could she do this, work in the place where he'd died? How had she managed to live in the same house she and Philip were to share together? She hadn't thought of this before. She'd had nowhere else to go at the time, and then she began to love this special place; it became home. The fact that there had been no other memories yet could have helped.

How had she been able to take the ICU job at the same hospital where Philip was pronounced dead? She remembered the day she'd walked down the hall behind Jackson Irwin for her interview, when she noticed the tiles on the floor were the same as the ones she had focused on in the ER. She told herself it was just tile on a floor, nothing more.

How had she been able to go on by herself without Philip? Then, it came to her. Mom, Granny, Arthur, Purvell, the kids, and her new friends Betty, Ian, Brad, her coworkers she had worked with at the hospital, and the people she interacted with in this beautiful island setting who opened their hearts to her.

The sun came out from behind the clouds, making the sand and water sparkle as the tide came in and out.

She loved being a nurse. Knowing she made a difference is what fueled her.

The sweat trickled down her face mixed with the tears that flowed from the corners of her eyes. She'd once heard tears that flowed from the inside of your eyes were sad and painful tears, but tears that flowed from the outside corners were healing.

Her decision was made. She would take the ER job and never look back. Nursing was her calling in life—wherever she was called. As soon as she came back in from her run, she would call Pam Woulf and tell her she'd take the job.

***

Daniel went back to New York the first of March to see how things were going for Stephen. After he'd come back to Jekyll at the beginning of February, he'd felt it wasn't necessary to go back as frequently. He would occasionally go when his expertise was needed, but overall, Stephen seemed to manage things quite well on his own. For this particular visit, he had decided it was important to help transition one of the company's larger clients to Stephen's leadership.

Daniel was enjoying the new business he'd started in Georgia. All he'd thought about since he arrived in New York was when he could fly back to his new home on Jekyll Island.

One of the things he wanted to do while here in New York was catch up with Purvell. He hadn't seen or talked to her since their trip to Wisconsin at Christmas. After having lunch at a nearby restaurant, he walked back to the office and decided to give Purvell a call before he let the afternoon get away from him. He touched her number on his phone.

"Purvell, how have you been? I'm here in New York for a few days."

"I don't believe it. It's as if you've fallen off the face of the earth. How have you been? *Where* have you been?" Purvell responded, genuinely happy to hear his voice.

"In Georgia. I'm living there now."

"I knew you were up to something," Purvell said with satisfaction. "I know Cynthia hasn't seen you yet, because she would have called me immediately and accused me of being your partner in crime."

"No, I haven't seen her yet. Speaking of Cynthia ... do you know if she's," he hesitated, hating but wanting to ask at the same time, "Well, I heard she might be going out with someone?"

"No. She never mentioned anything." Purvell was surprised.

"When was the last time you talked to her?" he asked.

"The beginning of February. We just talked about the kids and her new job. She did ask me why I took you home with me for Christmas. I covered it well. Nothing was mentioned about her seeing someone, though. Huh. I can't believe she would hold out on me."

"Ian bumped into her when she was out to dinner with some guy. She introduced him."

"Well, now I am curious," Purvell said, biting one of her nails. "I was going to call her anyway. I'm visiting the islands the end of the month to get away, so I may have to wait to find out then."

"Please don't say anything to make her suspicious." Daniel was beginning to regret calling Purvell.

"Oh, you don't have to worry. This is one situation I don't want to get involved in. I'll plead the fifth if I'm ever implicated, but I might ask some leading questions when I talk to her next."

"Did she get her job back at the hospital?" Daniel asked, attempting to change the direction on their conversation.

"Ah, no, they didn't have an opening, so she's working for a podiatrist on the island part-time. She seemed very unhappy about it," Purvell told him.

He felt bad for Cynthia. He knew how much she'd loved working in the ICU.

"I really hate to hear that. A podiatrist is a big difference. Do you think she'll be okay financially?" he wondered.

"She'll be fine. So when do you go back south?"

"I'll be here two more days. How about dinner or lunch before I go back?"

"I'm tied up with clients. Maybe I'll see you when I visit Cynthia or your next visit up here." She could feel his anxiety. "Hang in there with Cynthia. I'm sure your paths will cross soon."

"Yes, I'm sure they will. Anything new in your love life?"

"Dry as a bone. I think all the good men in my age range are either dead or already married," she said with a laugh.

"Keep in touch and make sure you let me know when you're visiting Cynthia, okay?" Daniel said.

"I will, Daniel. I wish you the best. I really do."

"I know you do. Thanks."

They said their good-byes and Daniel put his phone down on his desk. He closed his eyes and began to reminisce about when he'd first rented Cynthia's beach house almost a year ago and the one time he'd made love to her. She wouldn't have done that if she hadn't cared for him. The love was there and couldn't just disappear. He was so foolish to have pushed her and wished he could turn back the clock, so the relationship could develop further on its own.

When he got back to Georgia, he would go about his business, and then one day, he'd bump into her. If it were six months, so be it. But then he thought of Ian's wedding the last weekend in March. Surely she would be there. In a few weeks, he may get what he'd been waiting for. He would be ready.

❦

After she'd called to accept the ER position, Cynthia had gone to see Dr. Underwood and give him a two-week notice. She felt a little guilty—even more so after he was so nice and offered her a position back if she ever changed her mind.

Two days later, Millie and Jimmy came down from Charlotte for the weekend. Millie was a beautiful pregnant woman. A couple months to go and then they'd all breathe easier. Cynthia couldn't wait to hold the little baby girl in her arms. Then she thought of the stillborn baby girl she'd held two-and-a-half years ago and gave a silent prayer. The sadness in her heart was replaced with a feeling all would be okay.

After Jimmy brought in all their things, Millie suggested a walk on the beach would feel good after the long car ride. Jimmy told them to go ahead, he would rather watch some sports on TV. So, mother and daughter headed out to the beach.

"Sweetheart, I have some news to tell you," Cynthia started. "Someone called about a job for me at the hospital."

"Oh, Mom. I'm so happy for you. You'll feel so good being back in the ICU," Millie said, excited.

"It's in the hospital, but not the ICU—it's the ER," Cynthia said, hoping there wasn't any distress in her voice.

"Well, that's okay. I think you'll be happier in the hospital, and when an ICU job comes up, you'll know about it right away so you can apply."

"Yes, that's what I'm telling myself." Cynthia decided she didn't want Millie to sense her concern over the fact Philip had died in the same ER she would be working in. Millie had enough on her plate without worrying about Cynthia.

"Mom, I wanted to ask you something you might not want to answer, but I'm still going to ask. When you were at our house after you came home from Uncle Arthur's, Christopher brought up Daniel being at Grandma's while we were there. Grandma said you would tell us about him in time, but you've said nothing."

"That's because there's nothing to tell," Cynthia said with a sigh. "He's a friend of Purvell's who I met. He ended up renting out the beach house last year. That's all there is to it."

"Too bad. I liked him," Millie said, surprising Cynthia.

"It's been nine months since I've seen him last. I doubt I'll bump into him again unless I visit Purvell, but I don't have any plans to leave this island for a while—unless it's to see my new granddaughter," Cynthia said, and she put her arm around Millie as they walked back up the stairs to the beach house. "I really don't want to talk about him anymore if that's okay."

"Sure, Mom. Sorry, I was just curious," Millie said, and they went in to find Jimmy.

Cynthia couldn't have been happier to have the three kids with her. Yes, even Jimmy. She considered him to be hers also.

Millie had gone upstairs to take a nap and Christopher was working at the hotel, so that left Cynthia and Jimmy alone one afternoon. What was she to do with him?

"Cynthia, I was wondering if you know how to play poker?" Jimmy asked.

"Yes, I haven't played for a while, though. My dad taught Arthur and me, but I was never very good. Why do you ask?"

"It's a nice day, so I thought it might be fun to go out on the deck and play a few hands. I'm not that great either," he said.

"Sure. Do you want a beer or glass of wine?"

"Sure, I'll take a beer. Where do you have some cards?" Jimmy asked.

"Ah, I think in that desk drawer over there. I'll grab your beer and a glass of wine for me and meet you out there." She was looking forward to the game.

Jimmy was very good at poker, but it didn't matter. For the first time, Cynthia talked with the boy alone and she actually enjoyed his company. He told her how excited he was about the baby, being a father, and his job.

"I think Millie and I are better prepared to be parents this time than we were before," said Jimmy. "In fact, I was hoping I could employ your help. I'm doing very well financially, so Millie and I have talked about her staying home with the baby. She feels she needs to work to help contribute, but when I think about the baby we lost and the one that will be here soon, I know what a precious gift we're receiving. My mom never worked outside the home, and I was wondering if you stayed home with Millie and Christopher at all?"

"I did until Christopher was in first grade, and then I only worked on-call. I never regretted it. You're right, Jimmy. Children are a special gift. I think this is something you and Millie have to work out on your own. Let me make a suggestion. Wait till after the baby is born and see how Millie feels then. You may be surprised."

"Okay, Cynthia," Jimmy said and smiled.

"What are you two doing out here?" It was Millie up from her nap.

"Your mom and I were involved in a high-stakes poker game," Jimmy said and gave a wicked laugh.

"Okay." Millie looked oddly at them both as she took a seat at the table.

"And your husband is a card shark!" Cynthia laughed.

"Just got lucky today, Cynthia," Jimmy chuckled as he gathered the cards together and shuffled them like a pro.

"I was thinking Christopher should be home late this afternoon, so I'm planning a family dinner around six thirty," Cynthia said. "I picked up some steaks at the grocery store yesterday. Let's go inside and Jimmy can help me fix a salad and get some potatoes ready for the oven while you put your feet up, Millie."

"I'm not going to argue with you, Mom," Millie said and patted her belly.

"How good are you with grilling, Jimmy?" Cynthia asked.

"He's a grill master, Mom. You should see what he fixes us at home," Millie boasted.

"It's settled, then," Cynthia announced. "You've got the job, Jimmy."

"Yes, ma'am," Jimmy said, standing up and walking over to Millie.

He picked up Millie's hand and planted a kiss on it as he looked lovingly into her eyes. It was the same thing Philip used to do so often for Cynthia. He helped Millie up and put his arm around her as they walked into the house.

Cynthia's eyes stung with tears.

CHAPTER 13

T he Sunday after Millie and Jimmy visited, Betty
dropped by to go for a walk on the beach and have
dinner with Cynthia.

"I think it's great you're back at the hospital," she said.
"You'll be busier since it's full-time, but your hours will
be more flexible, allowing you to visit that new little baby
more often. I look forward to the day the boys make me
a grandma. Luke's pretty serious about a girl, so I've got
my fingers crossed. So, are you excited about getting back?
When's your last day at the doctor's office?"

"This past Wednesday was my last day, and I start at the
hospital this Wednesday," Cynthia said. "You're probably
the only person I know who could understand how I feel,
Betty. Where I'll be working is the same ER Philip was
taken to on the day he died. I'll probably have to go to the
same room he was in when I care for patients. I took the job
because I really want to get back at the hospital, but I keep
asking myself, *can I do it?* Can I work there and not let all
this affect me?"

Betty stopped walking and looked at her friend.

"Cynthia, you have to be one of the strongest women I know."

Cynthia also stopped. *She* strong? No one knew what was constantly going through her head: the doubts, uncertainties, and fears. She was barely holding it all together some days—but *strong?*

"You're the strong one, Betty," Cynthia said. "You never complain but keep going. Why, look at how you're developing the site where the restaurant was. That takes guts."

Betty laughed. "I feel the same about you."

Now, Cynthia laughed. "I guess we have a mutual admiration for each other. Our own support group."

"Well I say, 'thank God' for that." Betty raised her hands, looked up in the sky, and gave a little laugh.

"We're a mess, Betty. Let's head back and I'll pour us a glass of wine and fix dinner."

"I'm all for that," Betty said, and they walked back arm in arm.

The two friends enjoyed their evening together, getting caught up with what was going on in each other's lives. Cynthia knew the day they met was meant to be. It was getting late, so Betty announced she better head home.

"Hey, I've got an idea," Betty said. "I'm going to be at my new shopping center tomorrow morning. Why don't you stop by? I'll show you around. You'll have to use a little imagination, but I really want you to see it."

"Okay," Cynthia said. "Honestly, I've been kind of curious. So, how about ten o'clock, does that sound good?"

"Just what I was thinking. See you tomorrow." Betty said and left.

❦

The next morning, Cynthia pulled into what used to be the parking lot of Jack's Barbeque, the restaurant Betty and her late husband had started together. Every remnant of the former burnt-out establishment was gone and replaced by an L-shaped structure of metal framing on a cement base. Cynthia got out of her car and saw Betty walking toward her.

"So, what do you think?" Betty asked. "I know it may take a little imagination, but straight ahead there's where my place will be, and all along there will be little shops. I already have someone wanting a space to open a book shop and another person, a clothing boutique. My restaurant will be the first thing you see when you pull in. Did I tell you Collette is going to be working for me? I never forgot that cake she made for your birthday last year. Do you know she has years of experience as an assistant manager of a bakery? She's going to manage mine. There'll be an old-time bakery, and I'll serve sandwiches along with some catering. So, tell me, what do you think?" Betty could hardly catch her breath.

Cynthia loved to see Betty's excitement. "I think it's great and I can't wait for the grand opening."

"Come on and I'll show you around."

Cynthia nodded her head and smiled but in reality had a hard time envisioning all Betty was telling her—though she never let on.

An SUV pulled in and parked next to their cars.

"Oh, that's the man who's helping the boys and me build this. He's such a nice guy. Has taken John and Luke under his wing, teaching them as we go along. He kind of fell into our laps just when we needed him. Brad Davies knows him," Betty went on. "Hey, we're over here. Daniel! Over here."

Cynthia turned and almost fell over. It was Daniel. What was he doing here?

"Cynthia, I'd like you to meet Daniel Benton, the man helping us build all this. Daniel, this is my dearest friend, Cynthia Lewis."

She couldn't speak. She couldn't move. Daniel extended his hand, and Cynthia just stared at him. He gave her a huge smile, and after a few seconds when she didn't take his hand, he put both hands out at the same time and said, "Hi, Cynthia. Surprise!"

"What are you doing here?" Cynthia asked, finally able to speak.

"I'm working for Betty, helping her build this property, like she said."

"No, I mean what are you doing *here*?" Cynthia repeated.

Betty's forehead was furrowed as she looked from one to the other. "Do you two know each other? I'm confused. I thought you were new down here, Daniel. How do you know Cynthia?"

"Oh, we have a mutual friend in New York—Purvell."

"Well, I know Purvell also. What a small world," Betty said, and then realized there was something more going on.

"Again, Daniel, what are you doing here?" Cynthia asked rather firmly, not hearing or seeing Betty at all.

"I work here," he said with nonchalance. "There are some great opportunities down here for a guy like me who likes to build stuff, that's all. Hey, Betty, I have some new drawings of the restaurant layout. When's a good time to come by so you and the boys can see it? I think you're going to be very happy," he said, and continued to talk business with Betty, ignoring Cynthia.

"I think later today if you're available," Betty said, not sure why her friend was so distressed.

"I'll give you a call after lunch and we'll set a time," he said, then abruptly turning to Cynthia, he pointed a finger at her. "And it's *so* good to see you, Cynthia. I *really* mean that," he said, giving her a huge smile again before he jumped in his car and drove away.

Cynthia stood speechless and watched his car until it vanished down the road. What had just happened? Was this one of her dreams? It must be, she thought, but then Betty spoke.

"You don't have to tell me if you don't want to, but what was that about, Cynthia?"

"I'm not sure myself, Betty. Listen, I need to go home, I'm not feeling well," Cynthia said, then got in her car and left.

What was Daniel doing on St. Simons? Purvell would know and may have even had a hand in this. After all, she did bring him to Wisconsin over Christmas and then visited Cynthia's mom and Granny on White Lake while there. Was there more going on?

Cynthia called Purvell as soon as she got home and got her voicemail. *Hmm.* She'd try again later. For now, she went out to the beach for a walk.

❧

The rest of the day, Cynthia's mind was occupied with Daniel's appearance on St. Simons. His words bounced around her head like tennis balls: *There are some great opportunities for a guy like me who likes to build stuff, that's all.* He was a successful New York developer, at least that's what she'd been told. Maybe his business hadn't been doing well and he had to find something else, or maybe he was over-extended and needed to get out of New York, or maybe he didn't pay his taxes or something, so he'd come down here for a new start.

She dialed Purvell's number again, and it went straight to voicemail. *Where the heck is she?* Cynthia thought.

Cynthia gave Christopher a call. "Hi, are you going to be home tonight?" She was hoping for his company to get her mind off Daniel.

"Hi, Mom, no. After I get done here at the golf course, I'm going over to Red Bug Pizza with some of the guys and then there's some kind of party at the club. They needed some of us to valet, so I volunteered since I get paid and tipped. Could be a good night for me."

"Okay, well good. I was just wondering," Cynthia said, trying not to sound disappointed.

"Everything okay? Did you need me for something?"

"I'm fine, just haven't seen you in a while. Seems like you're either running to work or hang out with your friends."

"Aww, Mom. I didn't think you would like me living so close to you that much," Christopher said and laughed.

"Stop it. I love having you here. Just pop your head up to my place once in a while so I know you're alive."

"Okay. See you later."

"One more thing." Cynthia hesitated before asking him, "Have you seen Daniel?"

"Yeah, I told you—at Christmas," Christopher responded.

"No, I mean lately here on St. Simons?"

"On St. Simons? Nope. Why?"

"No reason, just asking. You haven't seen him recently?" she asked one more time.

"No, ma'am, not on St. Simons," Christopher said with certainty.

"Okay, hope you make lots of money tonight."

"Me too. Love you, Mom."

"Love you too, son."

❦

It was almost dusk, and Cynthia hadn't heard from Purvell yet. *Why didn't she call?* Then Cynthia got the idea to go over to Jekyll and see Ian. He may know something about Daniel. Why didn't she think of that earlier? She changed and drove over to Ian's.

The sun began setting over the west horizon as she crossed the bridge. The warm colors reflecting off the clouds took her breath away as she turned onto the causeway that led to Jekyll Island. She was happy to be back home again, even if her life was a bit up and down at the moment.

Ian had a cute, one-story ranch-style house with a single-car garage. His car sat outside so the two motorcycles he owned could be kept in the garage. She wondered if he and Collette would live there after they were married. A light was on inside, so Cynthia was sure he must be home.

There was no response after she rang the front doorbell. As she walked to the car, she heard voices coming from the backyard, so she headed down the path on the side of the house. Ian was sitting around a fire pit with a huge fire blazing. The noise she'd heard was Ian singing, the song barely recognizable. He was wearing some kind of headband flashlight, so when he looked at her, the light hit her directly in the eyes, blinding her for several moments.

"Well, looky who's here. One of the loveliest lasses I know," said Ian, and he broke into song again. He'd obviously been drinking.

"What's with the flashlight?" Cynthia asked. This prompted him to look up, blinding her again.

"The better to see you with, my dear," he said, and broke into a fitful laugh along with another person she hadn't noticed when she walked up.

She put her hands to her eyes and let them adjust to the darkness before she looked to Ian's drinking buddy to see who was sitting there. She couldn't believe it. There was Daniel. He was just as drunk as Ian and also wearing a flashlight on his head. The two were laughing so hard they were almost falling on the ground. Ian started wiping tears from his eyes and got in control for a moment, only to lose it again when he and Daniel made eye contact, blinding each other with their flashlights.

Cynthia wasn't sure what to do. She didn't see what was so funny. In fact, she was beginning to feel angry.

"Ian, I'm sorry to interrupt your ... little ... boys' night. Call me when you have time," she said and walked away.

"No, no, lass. We'll behave," he said with a sincerity that lasted two seconds before they were laughing again. Daniel stood up.

"I was getting ready to go home anyway. Ian, it was a pleasure," he said, and bowed deeply, causing himself to fall over. This incited more hysterics as he eventually righted himself.

"You can't drive in your condition," Cynthia said, frowning at him.

"No problem, Cynthia. I walked here and I can walk home. I have a flashlight to find my way," Daniel said as he pointed to his forehead and tipped his head in a smaller bow. Then he left down the same path she'd come down.

Cynthia shook her head. "What does he mean 'walk home,' Ian? How long have you known he's been here? What's going on?" But when she turned to Ian, he was leaning over in his chair, sound asleep.

She was tempted to leave, but with her luck he would get up and stumble into the fire and she would never forgive herself. Cynthia gave him a shake and he roused enough to walk into the house, where she sat him on the couch.

"You stay right here while I go put out that bonfire," Cynthia said, and she headed out to the back to find a hose and douse the fire. When she came back, Ian was passed out and snoring on the couch in a fetal position.

"Oh no, you're not getting off that easy. I want some answers," she said, shaking him again.

"No, no, I didn't do it, Mum," Ian said, slightly delusional. She shook him again and started asking questions.

"What did Daniel mean by walking home, Ian?"

"I don't want to get involved with this. Please."

"You're involved whether you like it or not, Ian. Guilt by association."

"He has one of the cottages down the road. Please let me sleep," Ian whined.

"He lives on Jekyll? He lives here?" Cynthia was shocked.

That was all she could get out of Ian. He was out for the night. Cynthia covered him with a blanket, then checked to be sure the fire was no longer burning and went home. She was sure Purvell would know more, so she would wait for her call. Until she could speak to Purvell, the best thing Cynthia could do was keep her mind on the new job she would start this Wednesday—only two days away.

CHAPTER 14

*I*t wasn't until the evening of the next day when Purvell finally called Cynthia. By then Cynthia had calmed down and decided not to jump into her inquiry about Daniel.

"Hey, sorry I missed all your calls," Purvell apologized, "but I've been out of town at a real estate convention. So, is everything okay down there? You called several times," she asked.

"Yeah, I'm fine," Cynthia said. "I just wanted to find out exactly when you were coming to visit, because guess what? I'm going to start back at the hospital tomorrow full-time."

"Well, that's great! I know how happy you are to be back in the ICU. It'll be almost like you were never gone."

"Not really; I'm back at the hospital, just not in the ICU. Nothing can be that easy for me. I'm going to be in the ER, in fact the same ER I went to the night Philip died. I hesitated at first, but then I thought, 'I'm going to take the job' because I love what I do and it's all I have. It's my purpose in life."

"Wow, Cynthia. You are one tough girl. Don't think I could do it."

"I need to work, that's all."

"You're one of the strongest women I know," Purvell said.

Cynthia hesitated, "Betty said that to me several days ago, and I'm going to give you the same response I gave her: I think you're also one of the strongest women I know."

"Well, thanks," Purvell said, smiling. "We're all in good company, aren't we?"

Cynthia changed the subject back to Purvell's visit. "So, when do you think you might come? I'll be working twelve-hour shifts a few days, then I'll be off a few, so I should be able to have some free time when you come. I want to make sure I'll be off to pick you up at the Jacksonville airport too."

"How does two weeks from tomorrow sound?"

"Sounds great. Can't wait to see you. How long can you stay?"

"I was thinking ten days if that's okay? I *really* need a break from New York. I hope that's not too long."

"No, I think it's just right. I would love your company, to be honest," said Cynthia.

"So, I was wondering, have you made any new friends since you got back? Gone on any dates?" Purvell asked.

"Like who?" Cynthia led her on, figuring she meant Daniel.

"Oh, I don't know. One of the locals, maybe."

"One of my former ICU coworkers asked me to show her father around a few days when he visited. Nice polite man, but I have no interest; I'm telling you, Purvell, don't start playing matchmaker with my life. I don't want any more hurt. Do you hear me?"

"I hear you," Purvell said, then asked, "So, you haven't gotten together with anyone else?"

She just gave herself away, Cynthia thought. "I've seen Betty and Ian. Oh, and I've seen Daniel. Did you know he was here?"

"Well, kinda, sort of. I don't know the details, because I told him I didn't want to get involved. I heard he's down there and he's started some kind of company. That's it."

"You heard, huh?" *Great.* "Why didn't you tell me he was here?" Cynthia said.

"Because he asked me not to and he's my friend, also. You two have to work it out on your own," Purvell said, sighing.

"There's nothing to work out. I told him that back in July. When I saw him a few days ago, he was polite but acted like he didn't have any interest. We can talk about it while you're here, but not now. I have enough going through my mind about tomorrow without adding Daniel Benton to it."

"I hear you. Well, good luck on your first day," Purvell said.

"Thanks. You know, it's really too bad you're not coming next week. Ian's getting married next Saturday on Driftwood Beach and then having a reception at the Jekyll Island Club Resort, where Christopher works. I could bring you as my date," she said and laughed.

"That would be fun, but I can't get away any earlier. I'll email you my flight information after I buy my ticket, okay? Give me a call tomorrow if you need a friend to talk to after your first day. Love you," Purvell said.

"Love you too," Cynthia said, and they said good-bye.

⚜

Daniel couldn't believe how effortless his first encounter with Cynthia had been. Poor Betty was puzzled, but yet she never asked about the exchange between him and Cynthia when he'd come by Betty's house later with some restaurant plans.

And then in the evening he'd walked over to Ian's house for a bonfire and a few drinks and who should show up? Cynthia. He and Ian were both fairly drunk. What did he say to her? He couldn't quite remember. Ian's wedding was coming up, which should make things more interesting. Cynthia would certainly be there.

Cynthia had looked so beautiful when he saw her at Betty's site. Her face was a giveaway when she'd looked at him. She cared, but was confused. That's okay; he would let her figure it out.

The ER was busy, with people everywhere. Cynthia was not a participant, but an observer in a corner. From where she stood, she could look out the wide double automatic doors at a long line of ambulances waiting to bring their patients in for medical help. A chorus of mumbling voices came from blurred-out people who mingled with the injured and sick in the ER. Whatever brought all these people in must have been a massive tragedy.

Gurneys continued to flow through the doors. Cynthia recognized Dr. Carroll, the doctor who'd spoken to her the night Philip died, and now he was in her face. "What are you standing there for, nurse? Can't you see people need help? Are you blind? Get some gloves and put a gown on, then get to work on that patient over there," he said, then hurried into a room, slamming the door. She was taken aback. Never had a doctor spoken to her like that before.

Cynthia started looking for the gloves and gowns and couldn't find anything. She asked the others working in the ER for help, but they ignored her. At last, she found them in a drawer and put them on.

The patient Dr. Carroll had pointed to was still in the same place, lying on his side with his back to her. When she spoke, the person turned over. It was Philip. He looked at her, a little bewildered at first, but then smiled. He reached out to touch her, but his hand was bloody and mangled. She screamed just before he touched her.

Cynthia woke in a sweat. What had happened? Where was she? The clock said 2:00 a.m. She turned the light on next to her and sat on the side of the bed for several minutes before going downstairs to the kitchen. After pouring herself a glass of milk, she grabbed a few cookies and a blanket and decided to go out on the deck. It was windy, so she pulled a lounge chair over to a sheltered area of the deck and focused her attention on the hypnotic movement of the tide as it glided in and out over and over, allowing the rolling waves to calm her mind.

She was letting the anticipation of this job get the best of her. After eating a couple cookies and drinking some milk, Cynthia put her head back on the chair and pulled the blanket up to her neck.

The moon and stars above made her feel so small as she looked up. *I'm only a speck in this vast universe,* she thought, *a grain of sand on its beach.* Did her concerns and fears matter in the grand scheme of things? Probably not. We all live in our own little world, dwelling on the past or the future instead of occupying the present.

The past had already happened and couldn't be changed. Philip and Ann were both gone, along with Millie's first baby. The money she and Philip had worked hard to save was gone too. Daniel had wanted her to give up life on St. Simons to be with him, but she felt this was where she belonged, and then the situation with Ann had happened. Christopher had dropped out of school. None of this could be changed.

Her future couldn't be orchestrated, either, but her actions in the present could steer her path. So, how would she support herself? Would she ever get her master's in nursing? What if she got sick and needed to be cared for? Would Millie's baby be healthy? What would Christopher do with his life? Why had Daniel decided to move to Jekyll

Island? Would she spend the rest of her life alone? Why was she here? These were only a few of the questions going through her head.

She ate the last cookie and finished the milk.

The present. She had a place to live, a job, and people who cared about and supported her. She ate well and took care of herself to stay healthy. Millie's doctor said the baby was fine. Christopher was working two jobs. And then there was Daniel. She did care for him more than she would admit to anyone. She knew she'd like to share the rest of her life with the right someone, but still valued her independence and didn't want to feel like she couldn't survive on her own.

This is way too deep for the middle of the night, she concluded. The morning would be there before she knew it, so she went inside and crawled back into her bed. *All will be fine and as it should be in the morning,* she thought as she drifted back to sleep.

⁂

The first day of work, Cynthia had managed to avoid the ER because she had orientation. This was good because it gave her a chance to ease back into the hospital. Now orientation was over, however, and this morning was her first day in the ER.

Hesitant, she stood outside the door and glanced down at her feet and the tile she remembered so well. *You can do anything,* she told herself, turned the door handle, took a deep breath, and walked in.

The first person she met was Dr. Carroll. "Hi, are you the new nurse?" he asked, extending his hand. "I'm Dr. Carroll. They told me you have good ICU experience. I'm going to love having you here."

"Yes, I'm Cynthia Lewis. Actually my whole nursing career has been spent in ICU."

"Well, it's great to meet you. The nurse manager is down that way. You'll want to check in with her," he said and pointed down the hall as he entered a patient's room.

Cynthia found the nurse manager, who introduced her to an ER nurse named Nicky for Cynthia to shadow the next several days until she felt comfortable.

The day went quickly, and soon she was on her way home. It had gone much better than she thought.

Ian was spending some much-needed time on the fishing pier. His and Collette's wedding was one week from today. *All the fuss.* Why couldn't they just go and get married somewhere by themselves? No, Collette wanted a wedding with all their friends present, so he'd said he understood.

Not many people were on the pier fishing, but as the day progressed, more would show up. There was a woman walking down the pier. As she got closer, he could see it was Cynthia. He was dreading the inevitable conversation about Daniel and the other night. He ran his hand over the stubble on his face and turned her way.

"Hello, lass, to what do I owe the pleasure?" he greeted her, sounding as happy and upbeat as he could muster.

"I knew I would eventually hunt you down," said Cynthia. "I went by your house first, next the campground, and then I stopped by the bait shop and asked Vernon if he had seen you, and he told me you were here. How are the fish biting?"

"Not that great yet. Have caught a few wee ones, but tossed them back to grow more. Been watching the dolphins play over yonder. See them? It's a good sign there's some fish meandering around."

The two friends watched from the railing as a pod of beautiful dolphins played in the water about twenty feet from them. Neither of them spoke; they knew it may scare them away and spoil the experience.

After about ten minutes, the dolphins headed out to sea.

"Does this happen often while you're out here?" Cynthia asked.

"I see them surface way out, but only rarely this close. These must have trusted us. You know, they're very smart creatures. It's said they have self-awareness and can teach, learn, and grieve. When one in their pod is ill, the whole lot stick with them, and if one dies, they've been known to carry the body around like they're saying good-bye before they let it go. Humans can learn a lot from animals," said Ian.

She didn't respond to him and kept staring out at the water, watching the animals glide in and out of the water, clicking and squealing in a language only they understood.

"They are beautiful," she finally said and turned to him. "You know why I've hunted you down. Why didn't you tell me Daniel was here?"

"Cynthia, neither you nor Daniel has ever shared with me what your relationship is or was. I only suspected something through conversations I've had with each of you individually. When I dropped you at the airport to visit White Lake last year, I felt you were running away from something. Maybe you need to ask yourself if you're still running."

"I'm not running," Cynthia blurted. "Daniel and I had a brief involvement when he was here, but I broke it off. He's done nothing to indicate he wants to start again. Otherwise, he would have let me know he was moving down here and starting a business. I'm not going to avoid him or look for him. It's a big enough place down here for us both to live."

"I feel like I'm back in high school again. So, you don't have feelings for him?" Ian asked, and he laughed slightly.

Cynthia hesitated long enough for him to know whatever she said would not be her true feelings. He hated being caught in the middle of things like this, and no matter how hard he tried, he seemed to get in deeper.

"I have no feelings either way," she responded and looked back out to the water. Dead giveaway.

"Well, good. I might as well let you know then that Collette has asked Daniel to give her away at the wedding. We've come to be good friends with him, and Collette has no family to fulfill the task, so she asked him and he agreed."

"Well, that's great," was all she could say.

"Hey, Ian." It was Vernon approaching them. "They need you at the campground. The ladies' room is having some plumbing problems."

"So much for my fishing. Will you help me drag my stuff in, Cynthia?" asked Ian.

"Sure," she responded, and she and Vernon silently helped him gather his gear.

Once at the bait shop, Cynthia spoke. "Ian, please let me know if there's anything I can help you with next week before the wedding." She smiled the smile Ian loved in his friend. "And thanks for talking to me about Daniel. I'll try not to put you in the middle of my problems anymore. Your friendship means too much to me. I've been selfish and I'm sorry."

"No apologies, please. It has nothing to do with being selfish," he paused. "Just … Please ask yourself if you're still running from something."

"I'm not. I'm actually moving forward with my life. Now go on and take care of that ladies' room," she said with a wink and left.

Vernon was still standing there. "Does she have a thing for your friend, Daniel?"

"She says 'no,' but I say 'yes.' It's a long story, and I don't know all the bits and pieces. I'm going to put my fishing gear in the shed. Plumbing is never a quick fix at the campground.

Maybe I'll be back tomorrow. Hey, are you and that girlfriend of yours going to be at the wedding next Saturday?"

"We wouldn't miss it," Vernon said. When he'd told his girlfriend, Carrie, about the wedding, she was the happiest he'd seen her in a long time and even went down to Jacksonville to buy a new dress. She was a strange one. Vernon never knew what to expect from her.

"See you later," Ian said and got on his motorcycle, heading across the street to the campground.

CHAPTER 15

*C*onnie Dickson looked at her image in the bathroom mirror. Her hair was now dark brown, short, and curly, which she hated, missing her long, straight, light-brown highlighted hair she'd been able to pull into a ponytail. She'd even worked on changing her Southern accent so it sounded different than before and had lost about twenty-five pounds. Why, she should be an actress in Hollywood, deserving an Oscar after she pulled this one off. Connie's own mother wouldn't recognize her, if her mother were still alive.

There were several reasons she didn't want to be recognized. The biggest being she was wanted in three states, including the one she was in right now, for crimes related to gambling. There also were some guys looking for her, saying she owed them money. But she didn't, at least not directly. It was the money from Philip Lewis's gambling debt she'd never been able to collect after the jerk went and died on her. She'd tried to explain this to her bosses, but they didn't want to hear it. This had forced her to go underground.

Phil, as she called him, had owed $100,000 when he died unexpectedly from—what was it?— she didn't know or care. If only she'd had the money before he moved to St. Simons Island and died. She'd thought a visit to his widow might get her the money, but Connie had hit an unexpected brick wall. A posse of the wife's friends happened to be there at the time and threatened to call the cops, which she surely didn't want.

After that encounter, she'd made the decision to lay low and not rush into anything. She had just begun to put together a plan when she found out Cynthia Lewis, Phil's wife, had left the country, not to return for over six months. Connie hadn't expected to wait that long. But now Cynthia was back and the time for action was upon her. Connie was determined to get the money and move on.

She figured for her time and suffering, she would demand $200,000 from Cynthia Lewis. That'd fix the bitch. Connie could then give the guys their money and still have enough for herself to go somewhere and start over.

Connie really felt sorry for herself. After all, she was just a poor little country girl from a small town in Florida. The middle child of five kids in her family. Her dad was a guard at the prison in Raiford, and her mom had cleaned houses and businesses in the area where they lived until she died when Connie was just fourteen years old. Connie had been on her own since then.

There was a knock on the bathroom door. It was that idiot, Vernon.

"Hey, Carrie. Would you like me to fix you a cup of coffee, darlin'?" he asked.

"No. I like to fix my own. I've told you that before. Leave me alone," she replied.

"I know, sweetie, but I'm just trying to be nice," he replied back.

What was wrong with him? Always so sweet and nice. It was like a mental problem. Not natural at all.

Connie smiled at herself in the mirror before she spoke again. Vernon had no idea who she really was. As far as he knew, she was Carrie Dawson from North Carolina.

"I'll get some coffee when I'm done in here. Don't bother me again unless the house is burning down." That was one her father used to say to them as kids.

Now back to her thoughts.

It'd been over two years since Connie, or "Carrie" as some now knew her, had last seen Cynthia and her friends. A long time, but she'd had to disappear for a while, or else she would have been killed right away by the organization she'd been working for. She hadn't planned on waiting this long for her money, but that's just how it was. Her strategy was to learn enough about Cynthia to coerce the money out of her. Connie liked the word "coerce" better than "extort." The guys looking for her would be paid off, and she could go far away from all of this by herself and start over. Maybe she'd even educate herself in something and get a real job.

Meeting Vernon had been like a gift from heaven. She'd gone to a night spot on St. Simons Island, and there he was, ready for the picking. He really was a nice guy; too bad for him he'd gotten messed up with her.

She'd given him her number, and after a few dates, she was spending the night with him and eventually moved in. Most men couldn't resist once they went to bed with her. Living with him saved her a lot of money too. She'd told him a story about how she was down on her luck, which wasn't far from the truth, and being the nice guy he was, he'd immediately taken pity on her. He was a fool.

She left the bathroom, went to the kitchen for her coffee, and right away Vernon started babbling.

"I'm looking forward to Ian's wedding this afternoon, aren't you? Those two are so in love. Can't wait to show you off as my girl."

How old is this guy and is he for real? she thought.

"Yeah, I'm looking forward to it. What time does it start?" she asked, only caring if she would see Cynthia Lewis.

"The wedding's at four o'clock on Driftwood Beach with the reception right after at the club. You'll love it. I need to take you to dinner there sometime. It's a fancy place. Ian said they were having dancing too. Should be a fun time."

"Yes, a fun time," Connie said. She took a sip of her coffee to see how hot it was as she walked out onto the deck. It would be her test to see if she was recognized and would put her plan into motion. The wedding couldn't come at a better time for her. She smiled and took another sip of coffee.

❧

Cynthia woke up to the smell of something cooking. She went downstairs to find Christopher cooking over her stove.

"Hey, what are you doing up here? Is your stove not working?" she asked.

"Happy birthday, Mom," he said and turned around, causing Cynthia's heart to miss a beat. He looked just like his dad the morning of Philip's fifty-fifth birthday when he'd cooked breakfast for the two of them. She started to cry.

"I'm sorry, Mom. I know fifty-eight must be a rough year, but you look like thirty-eight, really," Christopher said.

"It's not that, sweetheart. You look just like your dad right now. I miss him so much sometimes, that's all."

Christopher came over and put his arms around his mom and just held her while she cried. "I love you, Mom."

Cynthia got herself together and smiled at Christopher.

"Guess what? I forgot it was my birthday," she said, and they both laughed.

"And today is Ian's wedding too."

"Now that I remembered," she said.

"I figured I would be your date today. Hey, you know it's going to be kind of cool for me to be a guest at the hotel today instead of having to work. I'm going to make those guys wait on me," Christopher said.

"Now, be nice. They may return the favor sometime," she responded.

"I'm just kidding, I'll behave. What time do you want to leave? It starts at four. Ian said he wants us to sit in the reserved section. You know Daniel's going to be there, don't you?" Christopher continued cooking.

"Yes, I know Daniel's going to be there," she said as if it were no big deal to her. "How about we leave by three? That gives us plenty of time to get there and park, okay?"

"Okay. Here's breakfast," he said, smiling.

It looked good. Scrambled eggs, bacon, toast, and cut-up strawberries. The two sat for a good thirty minutes after they were done and talked. *What a great start to my birthday,* she thought.

"Hey, I'm going for a run before it starts getting warm," Cynthia said. "You, my dear, can clean up since it's my birthday. I love you for remembering," she added and went over and kissed him on the head.

"Mom, we all remembered except you. I've talked to Millie, Grandma, and Granny this week about it. I'm sure you'll even hear from Purvell and Uncle Arthur today."

"You're right, son, I probably will," she said and went upstairs to change.

❦

After her run and shower, Cynthia headed over to the grocery store. Now that she was a full-time working girl again, she had to plan ahead to avoid running to the store every time she needed something.

While driving, she thought about how her first full week in the ER was now behind her, and she felt rather proud. She'd done it. What made it a little less painful was that the whole ER department was so welcoming. Even though she had much to learn, she still brought a lot to the department from her experience in the ICU. Many of the patients she saw in the ER ultimately ended up in the ICU, so she hoped her care better prepared them for when they got there.

Dr. Carroll seemed not to recognize her at all, and she was happy he didn't. It could've made work awkward otherwise. He was head of the ER and an excellent doctor. She guessed he was close to her age and found out from the other nurses that his wife had died some years ago. His children were grown and on their own, which made Cynthia think his life must be rather similar to hers.

"The room," as she thought of it, was where Philip had lay after his death. It was down the hall in an out-of-the-way place, not used unless they were at overflow limits. She saw this as a good thing for her. Out of sight, out of mind.

She was looking forward to Wednesday, when Purvell would come for her visit. Cynthia wished she didn't have to work while her friend was visiting, but she had to save what days she could for when her granddaughter was born. Even though Millie's due date was about six weeks away, you never knew when a baby was ready.

Millie and the baby were doing well. The little baby girl was past the point when Millie's first baby died, so they all felt very encouraged as they waited for the day.

Although Cynthia had kept pushing the thought out of her mind, she kept going back to how she was going to handle seeing Daniel today. In truth, she thought about him more than she should.

After getting her groceries, she headed home. While she was putting them away, her phone rang. It was Millie.

"Happy birthday, Mom. Are you having a good day?"

"Thank you. Yes. I'm more concerned about you, though. Everything good with you and the baby?"

"Yes, but I feel like I might explode. How in the world can we stretch this much? I can't imagine what it's like having twins," Millie groaned.

"I remember thinking the same thing," Cynthia said. "How's Jimmy?"

"He's fine. His mom and dad came last week for a short visit to see how we're doing. His mom is going to spoil this little girl rotten. Jimmy's taking second place for the first time in his life with her," she said, and they both laughed.

"That's how it is with grandmas," Cynthia said.

"What do you want the baby to call you? Have you thought about it?"

"No." She thought it would be "grandma," but she didn't really feel like a grandma—that was her mom. "Let me think about it. What does Melanie want to be called?" she asked.

"She wants to be 'Mimi.' She looks like a Mimi to me. Ashley wants to be 'Granddaddy.'"

"I'll take it under consideration. You know today is also Ian's wedding? I'm so happy for him and Collette. You remember meeting her at Betty's when we went there for Thanksgiving, don't you?"

"I do. She seemed nice. Send me a picture from the wedding and give them my best."

"I will. So, my first week went okay at my new job. Lots to learn, but I can do it. I've got some nice coworkers, so that makes it all the better. How's work been for you? Do you think you're going to be able to work right up to your due date?" Cynthia asked.

"I am as long as the doctor says everything is alright. I feel real good, and the baby keeps moving constantly. I can't wait to hold her in my arms."

"Me too," Cynthia said with tears behind her eyes. "Sweetheart, thank you for your birthday wishes. I'm sure Christopher will tell you, but I forgot it was my birthday. I guess that happens when you get old," she laughed.

"You're not old, Mom. Why, look at Granny. You're going to be just like her," Millie said.

"That would be fine with me. It's been so nice talking with you, sweetheart, but I've got to get going now so I'll be ready when your brother escorts me to the wedding. He's my date. Give Jimmy my love."

And they said good-bye.

⚜

Cynthia and Christopher arrived at Driftwood Beach about 3:30 p.m. The wedding was on the beach, but the reception would be at the Jekyll Island Club Resort—a little more formal.

Driftwood Beach was scattered with the most amazing pieces of weathered wood from small branches to full-size trees. Ian and Collette had chosen one of the full trees embedded in the sand as a beautiful backdrop for their ceremony. White wood folding chairs were arranged to provide an aisle for Collette to walk to the tree where Ian would be waiting for her.

A girl greeted Cynthia and Christopher with a program and said to sit wherever they wished, also suggesting they might want to go barefoot in the sand. Cynthia immediately kicked off her sandals and Christopher removed his shoes and socks before they took their seats. A few minutes later, Betty showed up and sat next to them.

Soon, the chairs were full. Cynthia guessed about forty or fifty people were there. She didn't see anyone else she knew, except Ian's friend Vernon, who ran the bait shop at the pier. No sign of Daniel yet.

Betty spoke. "I know Jack would've loved being here to see this. Ian has had several girlfriends over the years, but never was very serious until Collette came along. We both speculated if they would get married. I'm so happy to see we were right."

"I know, Betty. They both seem so happy," said Cynthia.

"I was wondering how your first week of work has been?" Betty asked.

"Better than I imagined. I'm so busy, all I can think about is how to take care of the people who come in. It's not as bad as I thought it would be, and Dr. Carroll, the head of the ER, is a good doctor. I still want to get back to the ICU, but I'll be fine where I am," she said and meant it.

"I'm so happy, Cynthia. You know, we have all the power in us to conquer anything we desire," said Betty, and she took Cynthia's hand and squeezed it. "Oh, it looks like they're starting," she noticed.

Ian walked down the aisle, happy and relaxed, with the minister, shaking hands and giving an occasional kiss to someone here and there as he passed by. His hair was combed, face clean shaven, and he wore a kilt of his family tartan. Cynthia had never seen him dressed up like this before. He was so handsome.

After a few minutes a violin started playing "Here Comes the Bride" from the back. Everyone stood and turned as the bride made her entrance. Collette was stunning in a strapless white dress, with a flowing full-length skirt. Her long, golden brown hair was done up with flowers adorning it, and she carried a bouquet of what looked like wildflowers in all different colors. Cynthia's eyes filled with tears as she remembered her wedding day. Then her gaze went to Daniel, who was looking straight at her. She quickly looked down and then back up at Collette. There were no other attendants.

The two proceeded to where Ian was standing. Daniel took Collette's hand and placed it in Ian's before sitting in a chair on the front row. The whole ceremony took about fifteen minutes. After the violin played the recessional song, they all formed a line to congratulate the new bride and groom.

Ian gave Cynthia a big hug and kiss on the cheek when it was her turn.

"Ian, it was lovely. I'm so happy to be here to share this day," Cynthia said, and then she turned to Collette and gave her a hug. "Such a beautiful day and lovely bride. You're stunning, Collette," she said as she choked up a bit.

Betty was next and then Christopher.

"We're going to have a few pictures made, and then we'll see you at the club," Ian said. "And thanks so much for being here."

"We wouldn't have missed it," Betty said, and gave him another kiss.

Cynthia looked around for Daniel, but she didn't see him. Vernon walked up to say "hi."

"Nice to see you again, Cynthia," he said and nodded his head at Betty and Christopher.

"Well, hi, Vernon. Do you know Betty Franklin? And this is my son, Christopher."

"Pleased to make your acquaintance, Betty. I knew Jack from when he came out here fishing. So sorry about what happened to him," said Vernon, shaking her hand.

"Well, thank you, Vernon," Betty said.

"Hey, Christopher," Vernon said as he shook Christopher's hand. "Haven't seen you fishing lately."

"I'm busy working and don't have much time," Christopher said.

Vernon nodded his head and then turned to the woman standing next to him. "Let me introduce you to my girlfriend, Carrie Dawson. This is Cynthia and Betty, Carrie."

"So nice to meet all of you," Carrie said. "Do you live around here?"

"Over on St. Simons," Betty said.

"I love it over there," said Carrie with a weak smile. "Vernon and I go over there frequently for dinner, don't we, darling?"

"Yes. Carrie loves fancy places to eat." Vernon kind of giggled and nodded his head some more.

"Nice to meet you, Carrie," Cynthia said. "We're going to head on over to the club. See you later," she said, and the three turned to leave.

Cynthia looked around again, but no sign of Daniel. As they walked to their cars, Betty spoke.

"Have you ever seen that woman before?"

"What woman?" Cynthia asked.

"Vernon's girlfriend. I don't know about her."

"No, it's the first time I've met her, but Ian introduced me to Vernon recently when I was with him on the pier. He seems like a nice enough guy," Cynthia responded.

"Oh, I know Vernon is as good as gold. Jack always spoke of him so fondly. Something about her—I don't know. I'll see you at the club," Betty said, and they each left in their own cars.

CHAPTER 16

When they arrived at the Jekyll Island Club Resort, they learned the wedding reception was to be held in the hotel's Federal Reserve and Aldrich rooms. Inside the sun-shiny yellow and white rooms, they found a small bar set up with wine and beer, along with servers holding trays of appetizers. On the other end of the room was a small dance floor and a DJ playing some pleasant dinner music. Cynthia and Betty found the table containing their names on place cards. Vernon and Carrie were also at their table.

Cynthia looked around but saw no sign of Daniel. Surely he was coming.

Soon the bride and groom showed up, and everyone applauded their entrance. Ian and Collette couldn't have had bigger smiles on their faces. The DJ played a song for their first dance as husband and wife. Shortly after the dance, dinner was served. During dinner, Cynthia turned to talk to Betty. That's when she spotted Daniel. He must have been watching her, because he lifted his wine glass, took a sip, and smiled. She quickly smiled and looked away, not wanting him to think she was looking for him.

At the appropriate time, Daniel gave a toast to the new couple. Cynthia was very impressed with how eloquent and articulate he was with his speech. *Rather charming,* she thought. Then the dance floor was open to all. Christopher asked her to join him on the floor, which Cynthia gladly accepted. She'd always enjoyed dancing, especially at a wedding, because it didn't matter how good you were. The DJ began playing "Fly Me to the Moon," by Frank Sinatra, and as Cynthia walked back to her table, someone tapped her shoulder.

"May I have this dance?" It was Daniel.

"Okay," was all she could muster.

He led her by the hand to the dance floor, where there were a few other couples, and pulled her body close to his. She couldn't lie, it felt good to have a man's arms around her. Daniel proved to be quite the dancer, gliding her around the floor with no effort. She never wanted it to end, but before she knew it, the dance was over.

"Thank you for the dance," he said and walked her back to the table, where she sat down.

After he was a safe distance away, Betty spoke softly so no one else could hear. "Are you going to tell me what's going on with him? My *Lawd,* the whole room could feel the energy from the pair of you."

"What? I don't know what you're talking about," said Cynthia, fanning herself for a moment.

"Cynthia! That man has feelings for you. Grab him, because you won't find another like him. Trust me. I've been working very closely with Daniel on my shopping plaza. He's a gentleman."

"Okay, we had a little something going on last year," Cynthia admitted, "but he wanted me to give up too much. He wanted me to leave here and move to New York. He wanted me to give up every step I've made since Philip died, and I don't want to do that. I'm proud of how I've been able to support myself through working and renting the beach house. I invested all the money I made renting the house while I was in England, so it should hold me through for a good while if I live modestly. Philip left me no money. I'll rent the upstairs of my house again if I have to, but I'm not going to marry someone just because he can bail me out."

"He asked you to marry him?" Betty's eyes opened wide.

"He wanted me to move to New York and pay for me to live there to 'see what would happen.' I couldn't do that. I don't really know him, Betty. He rented my house last year for two months." She paused and took a deep breath. "That's all I'm going to say. I don't want to discuss this anymore tonight."

"You said Purvell comes next week? What does she say about this? We're having a girls' night when she gets here," Betty said.

"Whatever. No more tonight. I'm going to the ladies' room." She wanted the conversation to end.

As she came out of the ladies' room, she saw Daniel and Christopher talking and laughing together. It was nice seeing the two enjoying each other's company. Daniel was a great role model for Christopher.

"Hey, Mom. Guess what? Daniel and I are going up in his plane tomorrow morning. He keeps it at the Jekyll Island Airport."

"That's nice. It should be a beautiful day." What else could she say?

"I've got a great idea. Why doesn't Mom come too, Daniel? We're going to fly over Cumberland Island, you know, where the wild horses are? How cool is that?"

"Christopher, you can't just go inviting people along," she said, a little annoyed at him putting both her and Daniel on the spot. "Besides, I need to get ready for Purvell coming."

"Mom, you live alone, you're always ready for company. She can come, right Daniel?"

"Yes, I'd love to have you join us. Have you ever been in a small plane before? You're not afraid, are you?"

"No. I mean, I've never been, but I'm not afraid," she said, biting her lip nervously.

"Then it's settled," Daniel said. "I'll see you tomorrow morning. It's a great feeling being up there; I think you'll enjoy it." He smiled.

How do I manage to get myself into these situations? Cynthia thought.

The wedding reception began to wind down by ten o'clock, so Cynthia and Christopher gave Ian and Collette their best wishes again before departing. It had been a nice evening. The wedding couple was going on a honeymoon later in the summer so Ian could take Collette to Berwick on Tweed, his home located on the English-Scottish border, to meet his family and friends.

"It was so nice meeting you ladies," said a voice behind them. It was Carrie Dawson.

"It was nice meeting you too, Carrie, and seeing Vernon again," Cynthia responded.

"Yes," Betty said. "I'm curious Carrie, are you from around here?"

"No, I'm from the mountains of North Carolina. You know where Elkin and Sparta are? That area," she said. The lies were just too easy.

"Then you must have been to Stone Mountain?" Betty asked.

Carrie looked puzzled, "Oh, yes. I wonder how they ever carved that on the side of the mountain," Carrie replied. "Must have taken a lot of dynamite in the right place."

"Yes," Betty replied. "Nice meeting you," she said, and they walked out to their cars.

When they were a safe distance away, Cynthia asked Betty a question.

"Betty, why did you ask Carrie about Stone Mountain?"

"There's a Stone Mountain between Elkin and Sparta, North Carolina. You'd think she would have assumed that's what I meant, and not the carved-out landmark in Georgia. There's something about that woman. I can't put my finger on it ...."

"I thought she seemed okay," said Cynthia. "Vernon seems to like her, and he's a nice guy."

"You two are funny," Christopher said and shook his head. "Let's go home."

❧

Vernon and Connie didn't have to go far before they were home. There was a lot of information going through Connie's head she'd overheard at the wedding. Tonight had been a goldmine for her.

"You were the prettiest girl there tonight, Carrie. I'm a lucky man," Vernon said as he put his arms around her and started to unzip her dress and kiss her neck. She didn't even notice and slid out of the dress and into the walk-in closet. Vernon wasn't going to give up. She was in the closet taking off the rest of her clothes, when he came in naked. She sighed. She would have to go have sex with him and deal with her thoughts when they were done. He always passed out when they finished, but first she had a few questions to ask him.

"I was wondering if you know how many kids Cynthia has?" she asked, walking back into the bedroom, now undressed.

"I just know of her son 'cause he comes and fishes with Ian. Why are you so interested in her?" Vernon asked as he followed her out of the closet and sat on the bed.

"I thought she was someone I knew, but she's not. Is that guy her boyfriend she was dancing with? The one who gave Collette away."

"Why? Are you interested in him?" Vernon asked in a slightly whiny voice.

You're pathetic, she thought.

"No, Vernon, you're the only one for me. I was just curious. Who is he?"

"Daniel Benton. Likes to fish with Ian, and I think he just bought a place here on Jekyll. Ian said he's from New York and owns a company there."

"What's he doing here?" she asked.

"Not sure. Guess he likes it," Vernon said. Obviously done with answering questions, he ran his hands up and down her body.

They made love and soon he was snoring. *Good,* Connie thought. She wanted to look some things up on the Internet.

At the wedding she'd listened in on every word Cynthia said. It sounded like good old Phil had really screwed things up with his gambling, and she was just making it. Not good for Connie. She'd assumed Cynthia had lots of money from Phil, and now felt a little panicked. How was she going to get the money she needed?

She got her laptop and typed in Daniel Benton's name on her Internet search. *Whoa!* He was president and owner of Benton Enterprises, a multimillion dollar corporation. The guy must be filthy rich. It sure seemed like there was a relationship there between him and Cynthia, even if Cynthia denied it. Connie's instinct told her they were in love. She needed to rethink her strategy before moving forward.

That Betty could be a troublemaker, Connie could just feel it. Why the hell did she ask her about Stone Mountain? *Kind of off the wall,* Connie thought, and she didn't like it. She remembered Betty being at Cynthia's house the day she'd paid her a visit after Phil's untimely death and wondered where the other woman was who had also been there.

Connie had to make a decision about this quickly and not make a mistake. She needed that money before the people she was hiding from found her; if they did, she'd be dead.

❧

Christopher and Cynthia were to meet Daniel at the Jekyll Island Airport at 9 a.m. Daniel had gotten there early so he could have the plane ready to go.

He thought about last night and the dance floor. It felt good to hold Cynthia in his arms again. He missed holding a woman, wrapping his arms around her small frame, pulling her against him. He loved the smell of Cynthia's light perfume and the softness of her dress; he hadn't wanted to let go when the song was over.

He would take it slow. She would get to know him like she said she wanted to. Today's plane trip would be a perfect opportunity for just that.

When Christopher invited his mom to come along, Daniel had wanted to jumped for joy. He couldn't have planned it better himself and was pretty certain Christopher was on his side.

Daniel liked Christopher and had gotten to know him better through Ian, who was like a substitute father for the young man. Daniel figured Christopher knew he had been renting Cynthia's house while she was gone, but if he did, he'd never said a word. Cynthia might not be too happy about that. Christopher had always stayed with Ian whenever he came down to the islands to get away from school. Daniel had met them both regularly to go fishing, but was never asked where he was staying, so he never felt the need to volunteer the information.

He remembered the day Christopher told him he was going to drop out of school, and had asked for advice. Daniel understood Christopher's reasons and told him it was his life and his mom would support whatever decision he made. Daniel figured that advice might get him into a little trouble with Cynthia also, but he felt certain Christopher would go back to school eventually. The poor kid had been through a lot the past few years. He'd been thrust into adulthood, whether ready or not, and was doing pretty good, all things considered. He just needed some space to mature.

Christopher's car pulled into a parking spot, and Daniel watched to see if Cynthia stepped out. He thought she might back out last minute, but she didn't. He waved to them.

"Hey, looks like a great day to go flying. Come on around here. Who wants to sit in front with me?" Daniel asked. He was hoping Cynthia would.

"I think you ought to let Christopher be your copilot since he's flown with you before," Cynthia said. "I'll be the backseat driver." She smiled at him.

Daniel was proud of his Cessna 177 Cardinal airplane. Learning to fly and buying a plane were some of the first things he'd done when he became successful. It had been a dream of his to do so since he was a kid. After telling Cynthia and Christopher about the headsets and what to expect on takeoff and landing, they were soon in the air.

"I thought it might be fun to fly over Cumberland Island, south of us. Did you know they have wild horses living there?" asked Daniel.

"I've heard that," Cynthia said. "I would love to go there sometime. I think there's a ferry in St. Marys you can take over. Purvell comes this week; maybe we should check it out. I think she would like that."

"Yes, she probably would. Speaking of Purvell, maybe I could take you ladies to lunch or dinner one day while she's here? I missed her last time I was in New York," Daniel suggested.

"Sure, that would be nice," Cynthia responded.

Daniel wished he could have seen the look on her face when he asked, but he had his eyes on the sky in front of him.

"She's staying ten days, so I'm sure there'll be time," Cynthia added. "I'm not sure if you knew, but I'm working in the ER at the hospital in Brunswick now. My schedule is somewhat flexible."

"Yes, Ian mentioned you were back at the hospital," Daniel said, then changed the subject. "I'm going to head south over to Cumberland Island. If you look over to the right, you can see Kings Bay, where the Navy submarine base is … I won't be flying directly over that," he said, and they all laughed.

This was the first time Cynthia had ever been in a small plane. Other than a few clouds in the sky, they could see for what looked like miles to her. She rather liked the feeling of being able to see the world from a new angle and wouldn't have minded doing it again.

Cumberland Island was covered by a forest of trees with an outline of sand on its eastern shore. Daniel flew close enough to see a few horses running in the sand, but not too close to scare them away. Other than a lighthouse on the north side, the island looked untouched. Cynthia had heard somewhere a visitor could camp on the island or stay in the one-and-only hotel there.

Daniel surprised Cynthia by flying by her house on St. Simons Island before the end of their flight.

"My place looks so different from up here. So small," Cynthia observed.

It had been a fun morning and Daniel didn't want it to end, but it was time. He brought the plane down with a perfect landing.

"How about I treat you both to lunch over at the club?" he asked.

"I need to go home and change for work at the golf course for the afternoon," Christopher said. "But, Mom, you could stay. Daniel would just have to bring you home."

"I can do that," Daniel said, maybe too quickly. He hoped he didn't sound too eager.

Cynthia hesitated. "Oh ... Okay, I'd like that," she said, and smiled at him.

"Well, it's settled then," Daniel said. "Sorry you have to go to work, Christopher," he added, but he wasn't really sorry.

They talked a little longer, and then Christopher had to leave.

"I'll see you when I see you, Mom," said Christopher. "You two kids have fun," he winked and laughed as he departed to his car.

※

The brunch at the hotel was a buffet of just about any breakfast item you might want. After they fixed their plates, Cynthia told Daniel she would like to sit at a table in the sunroom off the main dining room, and she led the way.

Daniel told Cynthia about how he was working toward semi-retirement. He had bought one of the Cottages on Jekyll and planned on staying there, flying back to New York to help his nephew Stephen only when he needed it. His plan was to do projects like he was doing with Betty and her boys. He was tired of New York and wanted a change.

They talked about Christopher and his dropping out of college, Millie's baby, Ann and her death, and Cynthia's return home.

After lunch, they traveled down the causeway off Jekyll Island to the bridge toward Cynthia's house.

She spoke as they approached the bridge. "I ran this bridge once," she said. "I decided the first thing I wanted to do when I moved here was run the bridge, but then Philip died and I lost all desire to run at all. Every time I saw the bridge, I would wonder what was wrong with me."

Daniel understood; after all, he had lost his own wife to cancer and had wondered many times after her death what was wrong with him.

"Then," she continued, "almost exactly a year later, Betty's husband, Jack, died in my ICU from a heart attack after the fire that burned down their barbeque restaurant. I was caring for him," Cynthia explained as she looked straight ahead and up at the towering bridge. "When my shift was done, I drove home in a daze until I saw the bridge on the right. I knew at that moment I was going to run the bridge that day before the sun set."

Neither spoke until they were at the end of the bridge, and then she turned to look at him.

"And I'm guessing you did?" he asked.

She smiled. "I did."

"So, how was it? You should be proud of yourself. I heard bridges were harder to run than they look; the incline is a killer."

"I'm not going to lie, it was tough, but I want to do it again. There's a 5K bridge run sponsored by the hospital in February every year. I think I'm going to do it next year. I used to do races occasionally when I lived in Atlanta, but I haven't done one in years. I always felt a sense of accomplishment when I finished," she said, smiling.

"You know, I think that would be kind of fun to do. Tell you what. I used to run myself; maybe I can whip this old body into shape and run the race with you? What do you think?" Daniel asked.

"Okay. That would be fun," she responded with a smile and a little enthusiasm.

They arrived at Cynthia's house and sat in the car, neither knowing what to do next. There was that awkward moment when two people don't know how to say good-bye, even though it's time to go their separate ways.

"This was fun today. I'd love to take you up in my plane again," Daniel said, breaking the silence.

"Yes, I'd love to go another day. Keep me in mind if you need a copilot. I think I could handle the job next time," she said and got out of the car, walking over to the open window on his side of the car.

"I'll definitely keep it in mind. Don't forget to talk to Purvell when she gets here about lunch or dinner. Do you still have my number?"

"Yes, I do," Cynthia said, pursing her lips. She looked down, then back at him before she gave a little giggle, pulled her hair behind one shoulder, and leaned over so she could see his face better. Was she flirting with him? He loved it. "Thank you again for a lovely morning and lunch, Daniel. I really enjoyed myself. Bye."

"Me too. Bye," he said and watched her walk to the stairs and up to her front door. He couldn't wait until Purvell was there so the three of them could go to lunch and he could see her again.

CHAPTER 17

Cynthia had only made one loop around the Jacksonville airport baggage area with her car when she saw Purvell at the curb with her suitcase. Cynthia pulled up in front of her friend and jumped out to give her a hug.

"It's so good to have you here," Cynthia said. "I've missed you. Let's get your bag in the trunk before that airport guard begins to fuss at me."

"Sounds good. I can't wait to get some beach sand between my toes," Purvell responded, and they were on their way.

On the way home the women went back and forth, talking about their lives in a way no friends are able to on the phone. The car ride between the airport and exit 29 provided a good opportunity to make a dent in catching up.

"All I've been thinking about this past week is how many more days until St. Simons Island," Purvell smiled. "Do you have any idea how lucky you are to live here? I must be getting old, because I'm so tired of my job and life in New York. Please tell me I'm not getting old, Cynthia."

"If you're old, so am I, and I'm not giving in to the thought. You've been doing the same job your entire life. Maybe it's time to do something different," Cynthia suggested.

"I don't hear you whining about being a nurse your whole life."

"Nursing is different. After all, I'm doing something different right now," Cynthia said.

"How's that going?"

"Easier than I thought it would be, really. It helps that I like the staff I'm working with. The head doctor in the ER, Dr. Carroll, doesn't remember me from the night Philip died, and if any of the rest of them know about my history, they haven't mentioned it. We're so busy all the time, I don't think of anything but the patient in front of me. I like it better than I thought I would," Cynthia said. It was satisfying to be able to say those words aloud.

"I'm so happy to hear that. So, how much time will you have off while I'm here?"

"Not much. I have to save most of it for when Millie has her baby. Fortunately when they hired me back, the hospital decided to count the time I took care of Ann in England as family leave, and I was able to keep my time worked and not have to start over," Cynthia explained.

"That's good. How's Millie doing? I loved seeing both the kids over Christmas. I guess she was pregnant then. That little stinker didn't let on at all."

"I know, but both Mom and Granny knew; no surprise there—they always know everything," Cynthia laughed. "Never could hide anything from them. I talk to Millie every day to see how she's doing. We have about six weeks to go. She's not showing any signs of being ready to deliver yet, and the baby is very active. Everything we want to hear. I can't wait for this next chapter of my life."

"That's so great. I don't mind you'll have to work, since I'm looking forward to some downtime. I can go for walks on the beach and do some reading while you're at work," Purvell said.

"… And you can always do something with Daniel." There. She'd brought it up.

Purvell hesitated. "Well … I guess I could. You're not mad at me because I never said anything about him, are you?"

"Oh, maybe just a little, but I can never stay mad at you. You're my best friend, and I know your heart's in the right place," Cynthia said and half smiled at her. "I actually had a nice time with him this past weekend. He took Christopher and me up in his plane and then took me to brunch at the Jekyll Island Club, where Christopher works. It was lovely. A nice start, not like last year. I felt like we were starting over."

"Well that sounds good." Purvell eagerly sat up and turned facing Cynthia in her car seat, showing interest. "Tell me more. Don't hold back."

"There's nothing more to tell." Cynthia looked at Purvell briefly before she laughed and looked back at the road in front of her. "We had a nice time and he mentioned wanting to take you and me out for lunch or dinner while you're here, since he said he hasn't seen you for a while."

"Great. Would love to find out what he's been up to. What day would be good to get together with him? Do you have your work schedule?" Purvell asked.

"I work tomorrow and I'm on call for Friday and Saturday, but work Sunday and Monday, then I'm off for three days, work Friday, and I'm off for the weekend," Cynthia said, without missing a beat.

"Okay, I think I've got that," Purvell said and laughed. "Maybe you could write it down for me. How about I call Daniel tomorrow while you're at work and see if he can meet with us Friday unless you get called in?"

"I'm sure I won't be called, so Friday sounds good," Cynthia said as she pulled into her driveway. "Let's get your stuff in and then go sit on the deck. I made sure to put a couple of bottles of wine in the refrigerator for us," she said and laughed.

"You read my mind," Purvell said as she grabbed her suitcase.

When Purvell got up the next morning, Cynthia had already left for work. Purvell didn't mind being alone all day and actually looked forward to it. She was very rarely alone like this in New York.

After a cup of coffee and a piece of toast, she went for what she'd been waiting for, a walk on the beach.

No one was on the beach except her and the birds who followed as she made her trek along the shoreline. She took deep breaths of the salt air that whipped her long blonde hair around her face. The tide was low, leaving a wide open space to walk. The ocean breeze felt as if it blew right through her, exposing the feelings of unrest she held within. She knew it was time to make a change in her life. *But what?* She wouldn't stress over it but hoped life would decide for her.

Although she wasn't rich, she wanted for nothing, monetarily that is. Still, she envied Cynthia and Daniel. Even though they struggled with their relationship, she knew they were made for each other. *They'll eventually figure it out,* she thought.

Purvell didn't regret not having children, but what she did regret was not having someone to grow old with to share what she had accomplished. Finding a date or a man's interest was never the problem, it was just she never found the *right* man. And now here she was—alone.

The birds soon figured out she had nothing for them to eat, leaving her to herself. She wasn't sure how long she'd been walking and thought maybe it was time to turn around and go back.

On the walk back, Purvell saw an older couple power walking and a man running. A new group of birds began squawking behind her as if they were saying "hurry up," but she took her time.

When she got back, she made herself a cup of tea and called Daniel.

"Purvell! You made it safe and sound, I hope," Daniel greeted her.

"I sure did and already went on my morning beach walk. Now I'm enjoying a cup of tea. So, how's your life been?"

"Not bad. Did Cynthia tell you I took her in my plane and for brunch? I think she had a good time. I know I did," he volunteered.

"Yes, I believe she did, and I'm happy the two of you have had a little date; can we call it that? I've felt you were meant to be together from the beginning."

"Well I guess it was a date, but not really," said Daniel, feigning modesty. "I'm not going to push anything. So, did Cynthia tell you I want to take you both out while you're here? I told her lunch or dinner. Is there a time that might work?"

"As a matter of fact, that's why I'm calling. How about tomorrow night? She's on call at the hospital, but is sure she won't have to go in."

"Sounds good to me. I want to take you to a place I've found called Halyards. Great seafood. Say, how about you and I go to lunch today since Cynthia's not home?" he asked.

"Oh no. I'm enjoying the solitude today, if that's alright. I can wait until tomorrow when we're all three together. Maybe next week when Cynthia's working we can go to lunch and you can show me your place. Do you like it?" she asked.

"I love it," he said. "I'm not missing New York at all."

"Sounds good. I can hear the peace in your voice."

"Island time can do that to you. Speaking of time, I have to run. So, I'll pick you ladies up at 6:30 p.m., okay?"

"Sounds great. See you then," Purvell said and hung up.

⚜

"I'm so happy you want to do some sightseeing while you're here. I know you missed so much last time," Cynthia told Purvell as they drove down Ocean Boulevard. The last time Purvell had been to St. Simons was right after Philip died, and she had spent the trip tending to Cynthia. "This time I want you to see what made me fall in love with this island."

"I can't wait. Your well-being was my primary concern last time; this time I want to have fun," she said, with a laugh and a raise of her eyebrows.

"We're going to start out down in the lighthouse area. I thought I would park on Mallery Street so we can walk down to the lighthouse and take the tour and then come back to the pier, look through the shops, and end with lunch at Barbara Jean's. After that if we have time, we can go to Christ Church since they don't open to the public till the afternoon. There's still much more to see, but we can space it out during your visit."

"I want to see it all." Purvell smiled.

After Cynthia parked, they walked down a path that ran along the shoreline to the lighthouse. Purvell stayed outside while Cynthia bought their tickets.

"Do you want to go to the top?" Cynthia asked when she returned.

"Of course," Purvell answered.

After looking around the office and museum, they took the winding, steep stairs to the top.

"Going up and down these stairs several times every day sure would keep you in shape," Cynthia said, "but wait till you see the view. It's worth it."

They stepped from the dim stairwell into the sunny day, and Purvell sighed. "You weren't kidding." The water sparkled from the morning sun's reflection. Off in the distance there were three shrimps boats bobbing along the horizon and a cargo ship almost under the bridge. Purvell closed her eyes for a moment, imprinting what she saw in her mind, and then spoke. "What a beautiful panoramic view, and the water goes forever—I love it. I see why you and Philip decided to move here. This alone would sell me."

Cynthia didn't say anything but walked to the other side to be alone. Purvell was busy looking around and didn't notice she'd walked away. Purvell's comment had struck a chord. Cynthia remembered asking Philip the day they'd visited the lighthouse what he thought it would take to live on St. Simons. She had planted the seed in his mind to relocate. What would have happened had she not asked? Philip would have died anyway—he was a walking time bomb—and Cynthia would be living a very different life in Atlanta instead of this beautiful place. At the time he died, she'd wondered how she was going to be able to stay here, but all in all, things had worked out well.

Purvell came around and found her. "The view is unbelievable from up here. You can see for miles. So, that's Brunswick over there?" she asked, pointing inland. "The bridge looks like a toy from this distance, and I'm guessing that's Jekyll Island?"

"Yes. We'll go over there next week when I'm off," Cynthia said, mustering a smile.

"I think Daniel is going to pick me up and take me to see his new place over there one day while you're working."

"That's great," Cynthia said. Purvell walked back to where she had been, and Cynthia gazed over to Jekyll. Being up so high made her see things differently. Seeing the beauty of the world she lived in day to day from this level made her mind clearer. She wished she could stay up here where she could observe the world without having to be a part of it. Life on the ground could be so difficult, so complicated.

"Cynthia ... Cynthia." Cynthia was so deep in thought, she didn't see or hear Purvell. Purvell touched her arm gently. "Are you okay? What's up?"

Cynthia looked at her friend and put her hand over the one Purvell rested on her arm. "I'm fine. You make me think of Philip. It's so peaceful here, I can't help but think. I'm good, really," she said, and she squeezed her friend's hand. "You ready to go down? Let's head over to the pier, where you get a different view of Jekyll, and go through the shops before we grab lunch."

The pier was busy with people fishing, so after a walk to the end and back, they went into the shops. They were in a cute little clothing shop when someone said, "Hi, Cynthia. Remember me? We met at Ian's wedding. Carrie Dawson."

"Oh, hi, Carrie. How are you? Good to see you again," Cynthia said, smiling.

"Well, hi," Carrie repeated, doing her best to make small talk. "I think I remember you saying you lived here on St. Simons, didn't you? I love a couple of the little clothing shops, so I come over to see what's new," Carrie said and looked at Purvell.

"Yes, I live here. Carrie, I'd like you to meet my friend Purvell Whitlock, visiting me from New York. Purvell this is Carrie Dawson."

"Nice to meet you," Purvell said and extended her hand.

"Wow, New York. How did the two of you ever meet?" Carrie asked as she shook Purvell's hand.

"In college," Purvell responded.

"Really, where did you go?"

"We're both from Wisconsin and went to college there. Well, it was great to see you again, Carrie. Please say "hi" to Vernon for me. We're headed to have some lunch," Cynthia said, wanting to move on.

"Oh really, where are you going?" Carrie asked.

"Not really sure," Purvell responded quickly. She was looking forward to a lunch alone with Cynthia and didn't want this woman intruding. "We want to look around first."

"Oh, I thought maybe we could have lunch together," Carrie said.

"I don't know how much fun we'd be today," Cynthia said, exchanging a glance with Purvell. *She does not want to give up*, Cynthia thought. "Purvell just got here and we have a lot of catching up to do."

"Well, let me know if you girls would like to get together sometime," Carrie persisted.

"Sure," Cynthia said. "We'll let you know."

"Who *was* that woman?" Purvell asked when they were outside out of earshot.

"Someone I met at Ian's wedding. She dates this sweet guy who owns the bait shop at the Jekyll Island Pier. He and Ian are good friends, so they were both invited to his wedding."

"She makes me uncomfortable. Stay away from her; I don't care how sweet this Vernon is," Purvell said with sincerity.

"You sound like Betty. She felt uncomfortable with her also."

"I just know I'm a fairly good judge of people and I don't trust her. Hey, I'm getting hungry. Let's get a table at Barbra Jean's," said Purvell.

They headed down the street to the restaurant, ordered lunch, and visited.

"Let's go for a beach walk when we get back to your place since we're going out with Daniel tonight," said Purvell as they enjoyed their lunch. They both ordered crab cakes, a dish Barbara Jean's was known for. "I'm so happy you didn't get called into work, aren't you?" Purvell added as she took another bite of crab cake.

"Yes, I am," Cynthia nodded as she sipped her tea. "There's another nurse on call also, so since she knew I had company, she volunteered to be first on the list. Unless some natural disaster happens, I feel I'm safe. Hey, we'll have to get together with Betty while you're here. And you've never met Ian, have you?"

"No, I've only talked to him on the phone when you were MIA last year at your mother's. I think I drove him a little crazy," Purvell said, smiling.

Cynthia laughed. "He did mention that, but I think I won the prize for driving him crazy. I had him mail me Philip's ashes while I was at Mom's on White Lake last summer."

Purvell looked shocked. "You did *what?*"

"I had him send me Philip's ashes. I think Betty helped him with it."

"That's what I call a good friend. What possessed you to do that?"

"I had a dream while at Mom's about Philip. In it I felt he was urging me to move on, but I thought as long as I had that urn of ashes, I would never be able to. Ian sent the ashes to me. A few days after I received them, I went out in a rowboat to a secluded part of White Lake and let them go. It was the most amazing experience. As I started to spread the ashes, it was as if a mini tornado, like a big dust devil, came up, dispersing Philip's ashes around the lake, then dying away as quickly as it started."

"What made you want to spread his ashes there?" Purvell asked, amazed.

"Well, I know White Lake didn't have the same importance to Philip as to me, but I'm the one still living and could go there knowing this was the place where he rested. It made sense to me."

"It makes sense now you've explained it. Who knows, maybe you'll move back up there."

"No, I'll never leave here. This is where I want to spend the rest of my days," Cynthia said with certainty.

"I can understand why," Purvell agreed.

"After I rowed myself back from spreading his ashes, I found Daniel on the porch talking to Mom and Granny. It was not good timing."

"I beg to differ," Purvell said. "In my opinion it sounds like perfect timing. Life does send us messages at times, you know."

Cynthia stared at her friend, never having thought of Daniel's appearance that way. Maybe she'd made a mistake at the time. Maybe life had been telling her something. And maybe life was now giving her a second chance.

"Let's change the subject," she said suddenly. "I've had enough nostalgia for one day. After lunch let's head over to Christ Church, and if we have time, I want to show you one of my favorite places on the island, the Wesley Memorial Garden. It's where I go to feel peace. I know you'll love it too."

"Okay," Purvell responded. "Wherever you want to go, but I still want to get that walk in on the beach."

❦

Connie Dickson sat in her car and waited for Cynthia and her friend so she could follow them. Purvell was the same woman who was with Betty the time Connie visited

Cynthia after Phil had died. At first she couldn't believe her luck bumping into them, but it was obvious they didn't want to have lunch with her. That was okay. Sometimes things took time to come together. She'd waited this long; she could wait a little longer.

She'd dealt with bitches like that her whole life—women who thought they were better than her. Cynthia Lewis and her friend were the type who always got whatever they wanted in life, easy street for everything. So, they met each other in college. If Connie had gotten a college education, no telling what she could have done. But no, of course not; there were no breaks for her like these women had received.

Connie was just thinking of leaving when the two women came out of Barbara Jean's laughing and smiling. She hated them for it.

She waited until she saw them leave before backing out and following. They turned left off of Mallery Street onto Kings Way. So, they weren't going back to Cynthia's house. *Maybe they're leaving the island,* Connie wondered, but then they turned right on Frederica Road. Curious, Connie followed them since she had nothing better to do. They went through the first roundabout and continued on down Frederica through the second one. She hated those damn roundabouts. Cynthia then pulled off into the parking lot across from some little white church. *Why would she stop here? It figures those two would be religious on top of it all. Goody two shoes, bitches.*

Connie wasn't about to stick around while they prayed. She pulled over in the next parking area where there were two stone pillars that read "Wesley Memorial." It looked like there was a garden beyond. Connie put her car in park and got out—for what reason, she wasn't sure. She walked down a gravel path that lead to a circle around a huge, cross-like stone structure with four curved benches around it. A forest of trees surrounded the area with several paths leading off from the circle. Connie sat down, taking in her surroundings. A peace came over her as she watched the moss that hung from the trees sway hypnotically in the breeze. It seemed to hum.

She liked this place, and soon, there were tears coming from her eyes. The tears kept flowing as if turned on by a switch. She wiped her eyes and nose on her sleeve. For a brief moment, Connie felt there was hope for her, she was loved, and all would be okay. Then, just as quickly, the moment passed. *Enough of this crap and sissy crying,* she thought as she wiped her eyes again and began to leave. When she got to the two pillars, she looked back at the circle. She might come back one day, but wasn't sure why she felt that way.

As Connie drove home, her tears continued and didn't stop until she reached the bridge back to Jekyll Island.

CHAPTER 18

When Daniel arrived at Cynthia's house, there was a landscape-service truck parked in the driveway with several guys trimming bushes and edging the grass.

Purvell opened the door. "I have to come all the way to St. Simons to see you now," she said. They hugged, and Daniel gave her a kiss on the cheek.

Daniel stepped back and looked at her.

"You know, you're ageless. I swear you look younger than the last time I saw you. I really do miss you, but I'm not missing New York," he said.

"Why, thank you, Daniel. You look pretty dashing yourself. I know what you mean. I'm loving what they call 'island time' myself. Have a seat. Cynthia should be down in a minute. So, next week you can show me your new place, and maybe I can get Cynthia to come with me," Purvell said, and she smiled.

"Only if she wants to," Daniel replied.

"Only if who wants to do what?" Cynthia asked from the stairs. His heart did a flip-flop he hadn't felt in decades when he heard her voice. He turned around. She was in a royal-blue skirt and white blouse with her hair loose about her shoulders.

"Hi," he said. "Purvell just mentioned the two of you might like to come see my new place next week. How about if we have a cookout and I invite Ian and Collette? I have a rather nice grill," he said with pride, puffing out his chest a little.

"*You* grill? I have to see this," Purvell laughed.

"Sure, why not?" Cynthia said. "And how about Betty also?"

"Great idea. You ladies let me know what day, and I'll make it happen." He sounded more confident than he really was, but he could pull it off. He would call his sister and get some advice on what to make for them. "I'm taking you ladies to Halyards tonight, a great place I've discovered here on St. Simons. Their menu is all fresh and delicious," Daniel said excitedly. He opened the door and they went to his car.

Dinner couldn't have been any nicer. He loved hearing about Cynthia and Purvell's college days together. They all laughed until they cried. Daniel was seeing another side of Cynthia and Purvell and could imagine how much fun—and trouble—they were in college. Too soon, dinner was over, and he drove them home and had to say good-night. Cynthia did tell him she'd had a wonderful time and took his hand in hers, but he wanted more than her hand; he wanted her heart. He felt encouraged.

As he left her house, he thought of a day when he wouldn't have to leave her and they would have a life together. That day couldn't be too soon. He took a deep breath and smiled.

When Daniel reached the middle of the bridge, he smiled to himself as he viewed the beauty of the night skyline. He was happy he'd made this move. He exited left off the bridge, taking him to his home on Jekyll. There was not a streetlight in sight on the causeway that lead to the island. A sprinkling of stars was visible in the darkness, like nothing he would see in New York City, and he thought about how small everyone was compared to the vastness out there. He was surprised at some of the things he thought about these days. Must be his new life. He loved it here.

❧

The next day rain, thunder, and lightning greeted Purvell and Cynthia as they poured their morning cup of coffee.

"Darn, I really wanted to go for a walk on the beach," Purvell said, disappointed as they ate breakfast. "I ate too much at dinner last night. Speaking of dinner, I think you're a fool if you don't see how much Daniel cares about you."

"I see it and I care about him," said Cynthia, feeling a little giddy inside. It was like in middle school when you liked that first guy, but didn't know what to do with him. "I'm looking forward to his cookout next week. I like the fact he's in *my* world. It upset me last summer when his solution to our relationship was for me to pick up and move to New York. Now tell me you wouldn't mind if a guy asked you to pack up your life. It's a big deal, right? You know enough of my history with Philip to understand I don't ever want to feel I can't take care of myself again. I'm proud of the fact I'm floating on top of the water."

"You're right, I wouldn't like it either, but I like you both and hope things work out, that's all," Purvell said and squeezed her friend's hand. "Hey, let's go to a movie this afternoon since it's raining and maybe out for a glass of wine and dinner. Sounds good, doesn't it? I don't want you feeling like you have to cook for me."

"Okay, you don't have to talk me into it. There's a movie theater over by where we had dinner last night and a small Italian restaurant. I'm sure we can get a glass of wine there, or we could do takeout and come back here," Cynthia suggested.

"Good idea, let's just play it by ear," Purvell agreed.

The sun came out around noontime, so the women went for a walk.

"See that off in the distance? Another storm is on its way. Many times storms will rain themselves out before they come to shore, but I don't know about this one. Let's head back," Cynthia suggested.

They made it into the house just in time. Soon, the wind blew heavy and the rain pelted the windows again, when the electricity went out.

"This happens all the time when it rains," Cynthia sighed, and she thought of the first time the lights had gone out— the night she'd come back from the hospital after Philip died. And then the last time—when she'd made love to Daniel. "The lights should be back on shortly, and if not, I have some candles," she said abruptly, but no sooner spoke the words than the lights came back on and the storm passed.

"This gloomy weather is making me want to stay in. Let's get takeout instead and rent a movie on the TV. Will Christopher be around? I want to see that sweet boy," Purvell said.

"I'll text him and tell him we want to hang out tonight. We better not pick too girly a movie though, or he'll find something better to do," said Cynthia.

"Agreed."

Another storm came through, bringing several more hours of rain. Christopher would indeed be home and suggested Southern Soul Barbeque. At five o'clock there was a break in the storm, so Cynthia and Purvell went to pick up dinner. By the time they were back, Christopher was home and greeted them at the door.

"Purvell," he said and gave her a big hug. "I'm so happy you're here. Maybe we can go fishing next week."

Purvell had a doubtful look on her face. "Maybe," she said, and then remembered something. "Cynthia, I left my purse in your car. Can I have the keys?"

"Sure, why don't I send Christopher?"

"I can get it," she said and went out the door. A split second later, there was a scream.

Cynthia and Christopher rushed to the door. Purvell was lying at the bottom of the long flight of stairs that led to the driveway. Cynthia rushed to her.

"Purvell ... Purvell," Cynthia repeated, "where does it hurt?"

"All over," she cried, "but my foot and leg hurt the worst. I'm fine. Let me get up," Purvell winced, but the pain was too much and she was unable to put any pressure on her leg. She sat on the steps in obvious pain.

Christopher pulled his mom aside. "What should we do?"

"Go get my car. I think we should take her to the hospital and get it checked out."

Christopher soon had the car pulled up. He and Cynthia got on either side and slid Purvell into the back seat, then the three headed to the ER at the Southeast Georgia Health System hospital where Cynthia worked.

"I really don't think this is all necessary, Cynthia," Purvell said.

"We need to get this checked out. You're unable to put weight on your foot. Humor me with an X-ray, okay?"

"Looks like I don't have a choice," Purvell answered.

Dr. Carroll happened to be the doctor assigned to Purvell. "What are you doing here, Cynthia? I thought you were off?" he said when he entered the examining room they were placed in.

"I am, but my friend Purvell fell down the stairs at my house. I guess they were slick from the rain. I think there may be a chance she has really hurt herself."

Dr. Carroll gently examined Purvell's leg and foot. "In a lot of pain?" Purvell just nodded her head up and down.

"We need an X-ray to confirm it, but I think you possibly might have broken something. The X-ray will let us know for certain. I'll be back after we get the results," he explained, and he left the three alone.

"I'm so sorry, Cynthia. Not the way we planned our evening to be, is it?" Purvell said as someone from the radiology department wheeled her away to x-ray.

"Don't feel sorry, you slipped on my steps," said Cynthia. "You'll be fine, we just have to see the X-rays like Dr. Carroll said."

Dr. Carroll came back with the X-rays. He looked at Christopher and asked Purvell, "Is this your son?"

"No, I'm so sorry," Cynthia answered. "I should have introduced you; this is my son Christopher."

"Nice to meet you. You have a great mom," he said, and then Dr. Carroll was back to business. "Do you live around here, Purvell?"

"No, New York City," Purvell responded.

"When do you go back?" Dr. Carroll asked as he pulled something up on the computer in the room.

"Next weekend," Purvell said, looking at him inquisitively.

"I suggest you change your ticket. You have two pretty bad breaks in your ankle and leg. Look here," he said, and he turned the computer to face her. "Your ankle would be bad enough by itself but this leg, if not healed properly, will give you trouble the rest of your life. Do you have anyone to help you when you get back to New York?"

"No, I'm alone." Purvell's forehead was furrowed and her voice flat.

"I suggest you stay here. Right, Cynthia?" said Dr. Carroll.

"Yes, I agree," Cynthia said.

"For the next two weeks, no pressure whatsoever on this leg. We're going to have to put you in a cast from below your knee to your toes. I'm going to send you home with crutches and a wheelchair if you want," Dr. Carroll explained. "The nurse will give you the name of an orthopedic doctor I want you to see in a few days. Cynthia, you need to take the day off tomorrow to care for Purvell. Maybe you can work Monday instead. Do you have anyone you can get to stop in and check on her while you're at work?"

"Yes, I do, several people, and Christopher lives at home also."

"Great. The nurse will also give you some more information on bone breaks, a prescription for some pain pills, and take you to get your cast," said the doctor. "Any more questions?"

"Not at the moment," Purvell said. You could tell by her expressionless face she was in shock.

Dr. Carroll extended his hand and shook hers. "I hope all goes well for you. I would do what Cynthia says, because she's a very good nurse. Have a safe rest of the evening," he said and left the room.

It was almost 11 p.m. when they got back to Cynthia's house. *What a night,* Cynthia thought. She was exhausted, but happy she wouldn't have to work tomorrow.

With the help of the crutches, Purvell was able to maneuver herself up the same stairs she had slipped on earlier. Fortunately there was a bedroom on the first floor for her to settle into.

It was midnight by the time Cynthia slipped into her nightgown and fell into bed.

✤

Cynthia was up by seven the next morning. She had gotten up once during the night to help Purvell to the bathroom, but otherwise slept soundly, as had Purvell. She went downstairs and peeked in on Purvell, who was still asleep. After making a pot of coffee, she poured herself a cup and went out on the deck for a moment of alone time.

She emptied her mind and occupied it with the tide rolling in and out. So many times she had done this since moving into this beach house. The water always seemed to heal her. White Lake came to mind, and she remembered as a kid sitting on the end of the dock, watching the movement of the water. Sometimes she would gather pebbles that lay along the shore and toss them one by one in the calm lake to watch the ripples as they traveled outward until she couldn't see them anymore. She was hypnotized, watching as each ripple intersected with the others.

People and life events were like stones tossed in the lake of life. Some stones were like the pebbles she found along White Lake and others were like boulders, causing waves instead of ripples in varying intensities, affecting those around them in both positive and negative ways. She wanted to believe all her ripples were always positive, but regretfully accepted the fact they probably were the opposite at times.

Philip came to mind and so did Ann. Although she felt sadness from missing them, she saw how they both had affected her, even after death. Their ripples still rolled through her life, especially Philip's. Almost two-and-a-half years had passed since Philip died, but she still seemed in the same disarray. When would she feel complete again?

She finished her coffee, and contemplated her revelation, forgetting about Purvell for a few minutes. Then she remembered with a start and went back into the house to find her sitting on the sofa with her leg propped up and holding a cup of coffee in her hand.

"Hey, you shouldn't be moving around by yourself. I'm so sorry I went outside and deserted you," Cynthia admitted.

Purvell laughed. "I'm not an invalid. I have to figure out how to get around, don't I?"

"Eventually, but not the morning after you broke several bones! I've had patients like you. I tell them, 'Don't get out of bed without me,' and I come in and find them sitting in a chair, and then they tell me they just used the bathroom. You need to take it slow."

"I was careful … and I did go to the bathroom also," Purvell chuckled. "I promise I won't do anything I can't do, okay?"

"You're a mess," Cynthia said and laughed also.

"Cynthia, I'm so sorry this happened," Purvell said, apologetic. "I hate that you'll be stuck with me for a while. I really think I'll have trouble getting around in New York and would prefer to see the doctors here, you know, where it happened."

"Of course you'll stay here, but what about your business? What will you do?" Cynthia queried.

"I have two assistants and a partner who can run the office while I'm gone. I'll just use my phone," she said and held her cell phone up. "It'll work out fine."

"The first thing I'm going to do is get something put on those steps to prevent anyone else from slipping like you did. I'm the one who's sorry."

"It's probably a good idea, but this was an accident," said Purvell. "I hurt and may be a little cumbersome, but I still want to have some fun while I'm here. I'll be doing better in a few days."

"I was thinking of running to the grocery store after lunch to make sure you have some things to eat while I'm at work," Cynthia suggested.

"That's probably a good idea. I think I'll take a nap while you're gone. Those pain pills they gave me last night have me feeling sleepy." Purvell yawned, then laughed.

"I never thought I would see the day something slowed you down," Cynthia said, shaking her head with a little chuckle.

After lunch, Cynthia's doorbell rang. It was Denny from Cynthia's landscape service.

"Hi, Denny."

"Hi, Ms. Lewis. I hope it's okay, I've come by today to take that dead tree down I told you about that's leaning over the driveway. It looks like it's ready to fall. I know it's Sunday, but I'm so busy this time of year, it's the only way I can squeeze it in," he explained.

"Sure, Denny, I understand. I don't want it falling on one of our cars or someone visiting us, so get it down. How long do you think you'll be? I was just going to run to the store."

"A couple hours for sure, maybe a little longer."

"Okay. I should be gone and hour at the most," Cynthia informed him and closed the door.

"Sorry, Purvell, but they're taking down a tree outside in the yard. You might not get a nap till they finish."

"I don't think it'll even bother me," Purvell said. "Why don't you help me get situated in bed and go to the store now?" Cynthia did so and was on her way.

Cynthia was back home an hour later and putting the groceries away when Denny rang the bell. "Why don't you come out and take a look to make sure you don't want us to do anything else while we're here?" he suggested.

Cynthia obliged. "It looks great. I'm happy to have someone like you keep up with all this so I don't have to."

"So, I guess that guy who stayed here while you were gone is a friend of yours?" Denny asked.

"What guy?" Cynthia asked, confused.

"The guy who was here the other day while we were working."

"You must be mistaken," she said. "That man lives here now, but lived in New York at that time. Are you sure you saw him here?"

"Yeah, I saw him several times when I came to do the lawn. I never talked to him, but I'm sure it's the same guy. He's a friend, isn't he?"

"Why yes, but he must just look like the man who rented my house. They say we all have a twin," she told him.

"I'm pretty sure it's the same guy, but if you say so. Well, we've got to run to the next place, so call me if you need anything else in the meantime. Otherwise, see you in two weeks."

Could it have been Daniel who rented her place all those months? She'd never felt the need to ask Brad who was renting it. The only way to put her questions to rest would be to call Brad. She got her phone and dialed his number.

"Hello, Sandy Shores Realty, this is Sherrye Gibson. How can I help you today?

"Hi Sherrye, this is Cynthia Lewis. I was wondering if I could speak to Brad?"

"Oh, I'm sorry, Cynthia, but Brad and his family are out of town for several days. Perhaps I could help you? Brad and I are partners. Did you want to lease your house out again?" Sherrye asked.

"No, I was just curious if you could tell me who rented my house the months I was out of town last year."

"Well, I should be able to find out, just give me a second to pull it up on the computer. Let's see now...." Sherrye was silent for a few painstaking moments. "Here it is. It was one company that rented it all the months by the name of Sky Associates, LLC. Is everything okay? There wasn't a problem, was there?" Sherrye was concerned.

"No, no, only wondering. No problem. Thank you so much. I wish you and Brad the best with your new company. Tell him I said, 'hi.'" She hung up. A company? She was still curious, so she brought it up later when she and Purvell were eating dinner.

"Denny my yard guy mentioned this afternoon that Daniel looked like the man who rented my house while I was in England. Out of curiosity, I called Brad's office and his partner told me it was a company that rented it the whole time."

"What was the name of the company?" Purvell asked, putting a fork of food in her mouth.

"Sky Associates, LLC. I've never heard of it."

Purvell looked up from her plate and put her fork down. "I have."

"What do you mean?" Cynthia asked.

"It's a subsidiary of Daniel's company. It's the one I get my commission checks from," Purvell said.

"I can't believe it," said Cynthia, shaking her head. "Did he think I would never find out? Why would he do it in secret? Now that I know all that money came from him, I don't know what to do."

"I'm sure his heart was in the right place, he just didn't think about it rationally. Listen, sweetheart, you just need to talk to him. Don't jump to any conclusions until you talk to him."

"I can't lie; the money for the rental has helped me out greatly. I invested it all. I may now have to give it back," Cynthia said.

"You'll do no such thing! It was a business deal as far as I see it. Yes, talk to him about it, but the money is yours. He rented this house instead of any other one he could have on the island. Why shouldn't you have it?"

"I guess you're right, but it bothers me. He never told me, as if he were hiding it from me."

"Cynthia, be realistic. He was not going to call after you parted ways last summer. Ask him about it if it bothers you that much—or let it drop."

Purvell was right. She would ask him.

CHAPTER 19

*C*ynthia went to work the next morning, making sure
Purvell's phone was programmed with numbers for
the hospital ER, Betty, Christopher, Ian, Collette,
and, of course, Daniel. Purvell promised not to go up and
down the stairs while she was alone and swore she would
carry her phone everywhere. Christopher didn't work until
the afternoon, so he was going to check up on her until then.

The ER was not too busy. They tended to have more
patients usually on the weekend. Dr. Carroll inquired
about Purvell as soon as Cynthia arrived, and she assured
him everything was fine. The day progressed like a
normal Monday.

At about 8:30 a.m., she felt her phone vibrate in her
pocket, so she told one of the other nurses she needed to step
into the ladies' room, expecting a call from Purvell. It was
from Jimmy. Concerned about Millie, she called him back.

"Cynthia, I'm so glad you called right back. Are you
working?" Jimmy asked, excited.

"Yes, I am, Jimmy. What's going on?" Her heart beat
hard with concern about Millie and the baby.

"Millie's water broke. Oh my God, Cynthia, the baby's coming. I'm so scared, but I told Millie everything's fine."

"Jimmy, calm down. Everything will be fine. Have you called the doctor?" Cynthia asked the obvious.

"Yes, she said things are fine and even though contractions haven't started, we should still come right away because of the past history. Millie's getting her stuff together since she didn't think she needed to do so for several weeks yet. When can you get here?"

Cynthia was speechless and overwhelmed. What should she do about Purvell?

"Okay, Jimmy, I have to tell them here at work and then I'll let you know, but right now your job is to get Millie safely to the hospital. You have to stay calm for Millie, okay?" she said, equal parts excited and anxious.

"Yeah, yeah, I know, I know you're right. I'm just kinda scared because of what happened before. We're going to be at the Novant Hospital in Matthews. When do you think you'll leave?" he asked.

"It's like I said, I have to tell them here at work and I'll call you. Why don't you let me talk to Millie?" Cynthia said.

"Oh sure, yeah, what was I thinking?" Jimmy found Millie.

"Hi, Mom. I guess the baby's ready to come. Do you think it's too early? I hope everything is okay. I don't have any contractions at all. Do you think that's normal? Shouldn't I have contractions?" Millie asked, obviously nervous.

"You're going to be fine, sweetheart. It's not uncommon for your water to break and contractions to start a little later. They'll be coming soon enough. The best thing is to get to the hospital so they can check you out and put your mind at ease." Cynthia tried to speak in as calm a voice as she could. "Just rely on Jimmy."

Millie started to cry. "I'm scared, Mom."

"Darling, you and the baby are going to be fine. Just get your bag together and get to the hospital. I told Jimmy I would call as soon as I leave, so you'll know I'm on my way. Now go on and I'll talk to you soon, sweetheart."

"Okay. I love you, Mom."

"I love you too, Millie. Everything is going to be fine," she assured and hung up.

Dr. Carroll was a few feet down the hall as Cynthia exited the ladies' room.

"Dr. Carroll, I just received a call from my daughter and her husband. I told you I was going to be taking some time off several weeks from now when she had her baby, but I just got a call that her water broke. The baby is on the way and she needs me."

Dr. Carroll calmly looked over his glasses at Cynthia. "A little girl, huh? Does your life ever get boring, Cynthia?"

"I can assure you, Dr. Carroll, it's usually as mundane as can be."

"Of course, you should go. I'll pull someone from the nurses' pool. What about Purvell?"

She had forgotten about Purvell.

"I'll figure something out," she said, trying to sound convincing.

"I think you mentioned living on St. Simons, right? I live there also. Give me your address and tell Purvell I'll make a house call on my way home. I get off at three today."

"That's very kind of you," she said, taken by surprise. "Are you sure?"

"I wouldn't have offered if I wasn't sure. You have enough to worry about, and someone should look at her leg, anyway. Do you want to check with her first?" he asked.

"No, I'm sure it's fine. Thank you for being so helpful. I'm going to clock out, and when I know more, I'll give you a call."

"Drive carefully and congratulations, Cynthia."

She smiled as the reality sank in. She was going to be a grandma. "Thank you, Dr. Carroll."

❦

Daniel's car was parked in her driveway when Cynthia arrived home. The first thing she thought of was how he'd rented her house and not said anything, but this was not the time to bring it up. She'd talk to him about it later. Today, she needed a quick getaway. She walked in, surprising the both of them.

"Are you okay?" Purvell asked when she walked through the front door. "I thought you were scheduled all day?"

"I received a phone call from Jimmy; the baby's coming. Millie's water broke, and they're on the way to the hospital. When I spoke to them, contractions hadn't started yet, but because of last time, they wanted her at the hospital right away. I need to be with her."

"That's so exciting! I'm coming along, right?" Purvell started up from her chair using one of her crutches.

"The last thing you need to be doing is going for a long car ride. Right now the best thing for you to do is to keep that leg elevated and rest as much as you can. I need to figure out what I'm going to do about you before I leave. I'll call Betty and Ian. Christopher's still home, isn't he?" Cynthia said, as if she were Purvell's mother.

She then looked to Daniel, who hadn't said a word. "Sorry, didn't mean to ignore you, Daniel. How are you? What do you think of this one here?" she exhaled heavily and tossed her head Purvell's way.

"She's a handful for sure," he said looking at Purvell. "You must be so excited, Millie having a baby. I called Purvell about coming over for the cookout I promised and she told me about her misfortune. Yeah, there's never a dull moment with her around. Thought I would stop by and keep her company, maybe take her to lunch."

"That's nice of you, but she really shouldn't go anywhere at least until the weekend," Cynthia said, distracted with her mind on Millie. "You'll have to excuse me, Daniel, my mind is spinning," she said and headed upstairs.

A few minutes later, Purvell called her name, so she went back downstairs.

"Cynthia, listen. I'll be fine by myself; I've got everyone's phone number, and I'm getting around better. I promise I won't take any chances. Daniel has a great idea I think you should consider. While you're packing, he'll go over to the Jekyll Island Airport and get his plane out of the hangar, fueled and ready to go so he can fly you to Millie. He says it takes about two hours to get to Charlotte. What do you think?"

"Gee, I don't know." She had so much going through her mind at the moment. "How would I get to the hospital from the airport? I need my car."

"I can have a car waiting for you," Daniel replied. "I do this stuff all the time. I only have to make a phone call. You can use the car while you're there and then drive back with it, or I'll come and pick you up when you want to come home. It's really very simple."

"Simple," he says? Huh! Would she feel more indebted to him? It didn't matter; Millie and the baby were more important than anything else. *I should be grateful for the offer,* she told herself.

"Okay. Have the car ready, but after I get there, I'll figure out what I'm going to do. How long does it take you to get the plane ready to fly?"

"Don't worry about what I have to do to get the plane ready, just get yourself packed and over to the airport. I'll get the guys at the airport to help me," Daniel assured her.

"Christopher will be leaving to go to work soon, so if you hurry, he can drop you off at the airport. It's as if it was meant to be, sweetheart. Now get going," Purvell encouraged her.

Cynthia headed back upstairs but stopped at the bottom step. She knew this was a godsend for her. Turning back she said, "Thank you, Daniel. I appreciate this."

He smiled and bowed his head.

"Oh, and Purvell, I almost forgot to tell you. Dr. Carroll doesn't live far from here, so he offered to stop by and check up on you after his shift later today. Very nice of him."

"He doesn't have to do that. I'm fine. I have plenty of people keeping an eye on me," Purvell said, waving a hand as if swatting a fly.

"I know, but he feels someone should look at your leg, and since I'm not here, he volunteered. He's only trying to help me out. Be nice to him, you hear?"

"Okay, you know I will," she laughed. "Now get going and I'll give Christopher a call to let him know what's going on."

❦

When Cynthia and Christopher arrived at the small Jekyll Island airport, Daniel was ready to go.

"Are you sure you want to do this?" she asked Daniel. "It's going to take up your whole day."

"Remember, I've met Millie and Jimmy at your mom's place. They're great kids, and anything I can do to help them and you is my pleasure." He leaned toward her, his breath warm on her neck, but then went for her suitcase. Was he about to kiss her, or did she imagine it?

She got into the plane, strapped herself in, and put on a headset. Last time she'd sat in the back, but this time she was the copilot. Soon they were off. It couldn't have been a more beautiful, clear day.

Once they were on a steady course, Daniel's voice came through the headset.

"I stopped by Red Bug Pizza and had them make a couple sandwiches before I came to the airport. I was hungry, so I figured you would be also. They're behind the seat in a bag. I got one turkey and one ham sandwich, so pick the one you'd like. I'll eat either one. There's some bottles of water also."

She grabbed them each a bottle of water and the bag containing the sandwiches.

"If you don't mind, I'd like the turkey," she said.

"Fine with me," he said, and she handed him the other. They still hadn't gotten into any conversation, other than a little chitchat.

"Has Millie had an easy pregnancy? How long have she and Jimmy been married?" he asked.

"She has, but she's considered high risk," Cynthia said. "Millie was pregnant when she and Jimmy got married three years ago this summer. I never really liked Jimmy, and when that happened, I didn't like him any better, but I tolerated him. Between their wedding and Philip's death, Millie lost the baby. A baby girl—stillborn. We were all heartbroken, but it did something to Jimmy. He became a man, and the goofy kid I tolerated seemed to grow up. I genuinely like him now."

"I like him also," Daniel said. "We talked about business when I met him at your mom's place. He seems smart, and he's on a successful path. It was obvious he loves your daughter and gets along well with Christopher. Did they find the reason why Millie lost the baby?"

"No, it was never determined. I didn't know she was pregnant this time till I came home from England. She didn't want me to worry, and I think keeping it to just herself and Jimmy made it safe. She didn't fool my mom and Granny, though. They knew when they saw her at

Christmas, and Mom called her on it. The whole pregnancy has gone perfect so far. I'm sure the little girl is just ready to make her appearance," said Cynthia, smiling inside.

"A little girl, just like the first one. I know I've told you Julie couldn't have children," said Daniel, thinking of his late wife. "The only regret I've had in life. You're a blessed woman, Cynthia. What's the baby's name going to be?"

"I am blessed. Millie and Jimmy are keeping the name a secret. That's okay. I can wait to find out."

After they finished their sandwiches, Cynthia put the wrappings in the bag and placed it back behind the seat. They talked a little about Purvell and about Daniel's business on the islands and how he was getting calls from Jacksonville to Savannah for projects. He told her a few funny fishing stories involving Ian, who Cynthia mentioned had been very low-profile since his wedding.

"They're going this summer, I think, to visit his family in England, but have taken a few weekend trips on Ian's motorcycle. I haven't seen much of him either, but they are newlyweds," Daniel said, keeping his eyes on the open sky before them. "You know, I'm never going to live full-time in New York anymore," he added, out of the blue. "I love it on Jekyll Island and plan on staying." With that comment he turned and looked directly into Cynthia's face, smiling momentarily before he turned back to the sky in front of them.

The rest of the way, she kept the conversation on safe subjects until they began approaching Charlotte. Then Daniel broached the subject she hadn't wanted to deal with.

"I have to be honest with you, Cynthia. I would like to see you on a regular basis. I think since you've been back, more than a friendship has been slowly developing between us. Last year I was wrong to push you, and I see that now. I wasn't trying to flash my money at you or control your life, nothing like that. I only wanted us to know each other better, and I thought that was the answer. I'm trying to be truthful with you," he said.

She hesitated, but couldn't stop herself as she blurted it out, "But if you're being truthful like you say, why did you rent my beach house while I was in England and keep it from me?" Her tone was not so much angry, but to the point.

He looked stunned. "How do you know that?"

"It doesn't matter how, but that I do. I feel I need to pay you the money back," she said.

"I won't take it. Don't be ridiculous. I needed a place to stay and figured, why not yours? You had it for rent and I had been your renter before, so it seemed the logical place to stay."

Cynthia saw his point and then, as if a crack had opened inside her, she knew this wasn't his problem at all, but hers. Why was she being this way? Her insecurity was chasing away what might be one of the best things that could happen to her at this time in her life. She felt awkward and embarrassed, unable to speak after this revelation, and turned to looked out the window until they landed, not sure what to do or say next.

True to his word, Daniel had a car waiting for her to use when they landed. They didn't say much to each other until she was about to get into the car.

"Thank you again, Daniel. You were very kind to run me up here. I don't know how to repay you," she said, looking down at her hands.

"That's the thing, Cynthia: you don't have to repay me. Everything I do is because I love you. And I know you love me, but you have to stop running. I know your life with Philip didn't turn out to be what you thought, but I'm not him. Life is never what you dream or plan, so accept what's before you—and live it. I think you've been running from things for such a long time, you're not even aware you're doing it."

She was speechless and started to feel emotional, not because she was upset with him. Instead, she began to wonder if he may be right.

"I think it might be best if you drive back to St. Simons when you decide to come home," said Daniel. "I'm done trying to woo you. You know how I stand and where to find me if you want to work things out. Please tell Millie and Jimmy I send them my best wishes and I'll be thinking about them." With that, he got into his plane and flew away.

☙❧

The ride to the hospital gave Cynthia time to regroup. Not only were her emotions on overload about Millie, now Daniel's words kept playing over and over, *you've been running from things for such a long time, you're not even aware you're doing it.* She now began to feel some anger the more she thought about what he'd said. His wife hadn't been living a lie like Philip had when she died. How would he have reacted if she had?

That was enough. He was ruining this special day for her. She forced thoughts of Daniel out of her mind and focused on Millie.

The hospital was easy to find. Once she arrived, a patient representative escorted her to labor and delivery, where she found a tired but smiling Millie, holding a baby in her arms. Cynthia rushed to her side, all thoughts of what had happened earlier obliterated from her mind.

"I'm so happy you're here, Mom. She was born at 11:45 a.m. and weighs six pounds, eight ounces. A good size for being born four weeks early. The doctor says she's perfect. Do you want to hold her?" Millie asked.

"Do I want to hold her? More than you can imagine, sweetheart."

Cynthia bent down to Millie and lifted the precious bundle, instantly feeling the warmth of the baby in her arms, and looked at her little face. The baby's eyes were open, surveying her new world, and then she fixed onto Cynthia's face. Next to Millie was a rocking chair Cynthia sat in, bringing back memories of the first time she'd held Millie and Christopher in her arms. She kissed the top of her grandchild's head and then took in a deep breath of newborn baby. The child smelled like heaven.

Cynthia looked at Millie. "What's her name? You can't keep me in suspense any longer."

Millie looked at Jimmy and took his hand before speaking. Her voice cracked, "Philipa Ann," she said and began to cry, "for Dad and Aunt Ann. We're going to call her Pippa."

Cynthia looked back down at the little princess she held in her arms. Philipa Ann. Pippa. She looked like a Pippa. Now Cynthia had tears of joy running down her cheeks. Holding little Pippa was what she had been waiting for her whole life. Her baby had a baby. Life was good.

CHAPTER 20

Grace Westerly stared out the window above her kitchen sink at the familiar lake. This winter White Lake had frozen fairly solid, allowing many of her neighbors to ice fish up until the end of March. Now that it was the beginning of April, she could see a few wet spots on the lake here and there as spring was attempting to make an appearance. Several shaded spots around the cottage were hanging on to the snow as long as possible, while one snow-covered flower garden on the side of the house provided a beautiful backdrop, accenting the brave purple crocuses that defied those last remnants of winter.

This winter had been a rather long and lonely one for Grace and her mother, Granny. They hadn't visited Cynthia in the South this past holiday as they usually did, but stayed put on White Lake since Cynthia was in England. It was a nice break for them though that Millie, Jimmy, and Christopher had managed to visit for Christmas.

Granny and Grace decided that during the winter, Granny should temporarily move from her cottage to where Grace lived down the hill 500 feet away. That way, they could keep each other company. They also felt they should be under one roof for safety reasons. At their ages, neither one of them needed to be traipsing back and forth between their cottages in the winter snow and ice. Although the mother and daughter were very compatible, Grace liked her space, and she knew Granny did also. Granny was going to move back up the little hill to her place during the upcoming weekend.

"Grace, what are you staring at?" Granny asked, breaking the silence when she entered the kitchen.

"Oh, nothing, Mother. Just wondering when this snow will be gone for good. I'm ready for spring."

"I'm with you. I sure did miss going to see Cynthia this past year. Helps make the winter more tolerable. Let's stay longer this next winter to make up for it; what do you say about that?"

"I'm all for it," Grace responded. "How about I fix us a cup of tea with a couple of cookies?" Grace asked.

Just as the ladies were sitting down at the table with their tea, Grace's phone rang and she saw it was Cynthia.

"Oh look, it's Cynthia. You know Purvell's visiting her right now. I didn't think we would hear from her since she has company." She touched her phone screen. "Hello, dear, you and Purvell having fun? What? Let me put you on speaker so Granny can hear."

"I left Purvell alone on St. Simons because I had to make a trip to Charlotte," Cynthia said. "The baby was born at 11:45 a.m. today! A healthy baby girl. She's beautiful."

"Oh, thank God," Grace said. "Granny and I have had them in our prayers daily. And Millie, how's she?"

"Couldn't be better," said Cynthia. "She had a short labor. I guess the baby was ready to come! She's six pounds, eight ounces, a good healthy weight, full head of dark-brown hair, and it looks like brown eyes. Started nursing right away like a pro." Then Cynthia choked up a bit as she added, "They've named her Philipa Ann; we're going to call her Pippa."

"Oh, how lovely," Granny said. "I can't believe I've been given the gift of a great-great grandchild. When can we see her?"

"I'm not sure, Granny," Cynthia said, "but we'll work something out soon. Even though little Pippa was early, she's at a good weight and in perfect health, so their little family will go home tomorrow."

"Dear, we couldn't have better news today," Cynthia's mother responded. "And I'm with Granny—I want to see and hold her."

"We'll let them get settled and take it from there."

"I'm surprised you didn't bring Purvell with you, Cynthia. The poor thing left alone on the island," her mother said, concerned.

"She wasn't able to come, Mom. I've got some bad news. Purvell fell down the steps outside my front door and broke her ankle and leg. She's in good hands though. I have all my friends checking up on her, and Christopher's there when he's not working."

"Oh, my goodness. That poor girl. What in the world, Cynthia? Is she alright?"

"As good as can be. She's going to have to stay awhile longer though, which I don't mind. I'll tell you more about it later and email you some pictures of Pippa," said Cynthia.

"Dear, Granny and I text now, so send them that way. It's easier for us to share pictures with our friends and post them on Facebook."

"Well, okay. I'll text some as soon as I can," Cynthia laughed a little.

"Please give Millie and Jimmy our love, and kiss Pippa for us," Granny said.

"I will. First chance I can, I'll talk to Millie about you two visiting. Plan on staying awhile with me when you come. Love you both."

"We love you also, Cynthia," said Grace, and they said good-bye.

※

During his flight home, Daniel kept overthinking his conversation with Cynthia. Had he been too harsh? *Women.*

He knew there could be trouble if Cynthia found out he'd rented her house, but he'd never thought she would, since he used a subsidiary company and not his name or Benton Enterprises. He'd been a little sneaky about it; his intention was to help her out without her knowing, although he'd never admit to it. What was her problem, though? She obviously wanted to rent her place to someone. *She's so stubborn and bull-headed, wanting to do everything alone,* he thought, but then again, these qualities were also ones that attracted him to her.

He was too old for this.

Even as Daniel concentrated on his flight, his thoughts went back to times spent with Cynthia. He thought about the first time he'd seen her in Grand Central Station, then how she'd bumped into him at a restaurant, and finally how she'd shown up with Purvell at his Christmas party. He believed people met for a reason—to help one another's lives along or to become a part of them. He felt certain Cynthia was to be a part of his, although it didn't seem to be going in that direction at the moment.

To get his mind off Cynthia, Daniel focused on the other topic that filled most of his thoughts—work. He was doing very well. No high-rises like he'd developed in New York, but little shopping centers like Betty's and repurposing buildings for stores and restaurants. The fun stuff, in his opinion. Last week he'd received a call from someone in Savannah to bid on a project, so his work was getting noticed.

He saw the Jekyll Island coast in the distance and prepared to land.

Later that evening he was getting together with Ian and Collette for a beer at Tortuga Jacks and see a local band play. *Should take my mind off Cynthia,* he thought.

❦

"Hello, Cynthia. Yes, I'm fine and no, you don't need to rush back," Purvell told Cynthia later in the afternoon when Cynthia called to tell her about the baby and check up on her.

"I hate to think of you all alone like that at my house like a prisoner. I mean you can't even go for a walk on the beach," Cynthia replied.

"No, but I sat out on the deck this afternoon with Dr. Carroll when he came over. He's a nice guy. Says I'm doing well. He showed my X-rays to the orthopedic doctor he wants me to see. She said I may need some surgery with the emphasis on 'may'. I'm going to see her next week and get another X-ray. They're just being overly cautious, I think."

"It was nice of Dr. Carroll to come by. Did he give an opinion on the possibility of surgery?"

"No, he did not, and that's enough about me. I want to hear about the baby."

Cynthia filled her in on the details.

"I'm not sure what day I'll be coming back," Cynthia told Purvell with a concerned tone in her voice.

"Please, take as long as you want," Purvell said. "I'm fine. By any chance did you call Betty and tell her what happened? She showed up today with some homemade soup and muffins. Acted like she knew what was going on."

"That's Betty. I'm not surprised. I don't try to figure it out, but she always seems to know everything. I planned to give her a call later and tell her about the baby. What about Christopher, is he around? I called his phone and it went straight to his voicemail," Cynthia said.

"He called and asked if I'd heard anything yet. Try his phone again; I think he gets off work soon. You said 'drive back'? I thought Daniel would stay and wait or fly back for you." Purvell had been dying to find out how things went.

"Don't ask," Cynthia said. "I don't want to talk about it."

"What happened?"

"I don't want to talk about it," Cynthia said again, with more force, so Purvell knew she would have to wait for details.

"Okay, I won't say another word," Purvell said, but hoped Daniel would stop by to see her so she might get some details.

"I'll check up on you later. Maybe Christopher can pick you up something for dinner? Call him," Cynthia suggested.

"That's not necessary. I'm going to have Betty's soup. You run along and don't worry; I have enough people here to keep me out of trouble until you get back. Give Millie and Jimmy my love and congratulations, and Pippa a kiss from her Great Aunt Purvell."

"I will. Talk to you later," Cynthia said, and they hung up.

Thirty minutes later, Christopher called Purvell and told her he had just gotten off the phone with his mom and heard about the baby. He was so excited. He asked what Purvell wanted to eat for dinner.

"Don't worry about me. Betty dropped some soup off today, so why don't you go do something with your friends?" Purvell suggested.

"Well, I really would like to meet some of the guys I work with at Tortuga Jacks since there's a band playing tonight. The lead's a guy I know through Ian. He and Collette are going to be there also. I won't be late, 'cause I have to work tomorrow."

"Stay as long as you want," said Purvell. "I've got a movie to watch tonight and a good book I've started on. I'm used to being home alone, so you have fun."

"Are you sure you don't want me to stay with you?" he asked. "Mom might get mad at me if I don't stay." He chuckled, only half joking.

"No need, sweetheart. I'm insisting. You run along and have fun with your friends. I would feel bad if I kept you from them. After all, I was young once and you don't want to miss a thing."

"Well, okay, if you insist."

"I do," she said, "and you can tell your mother I was adamant."

Thirty minutes later the doorbell rang. She hobbled over and looked out the side window transom.

"You are so sweet to do this," said Purvell when she answered the door. "I can't tell you how much I appreciate it."

"Well, it's my pleasure," said her visitor, as they headed to the kitchen with bags of Chinese takeout.

CHAPTER 21

*D*aniel found Ian and Collette at a table inside Tortuga Jacks. Normally a Monday night would be quiet, but tonight they were letting a local young man and his band play, because a talent agent was in the area to hear them. Ian knew the kid from fishing on the pier and was there to support the boy. Daniel was looking forward to the evening after his long day.

"Hey, mate," Ian called out to Daniel. "What's new?"

"Well, I flew to Charlotte and back today."

Ian looked at him funny and said, "What?"

"You heard right. Cynthia's daughter, Millie, went into labor today. I just happened to be at her house when she came home from work with the news."

"What were you doing at her house?"

"Since you got married, you've been out of the loop my friend," Daniel laughed and briefly put his hand on Ian's back. "Purvell is visiting. She fell down Cynthia's front steps on Saturday and is now in a cast, getting around with crutches. I don't think it's too bad, but it's enough that she's going to have to stay awhile longer."

"Do you know I've only talked to the lass on the phone and never met her? I can tell you, she's a persistent woman," he chuckled and shook his head. "About drove me out of my mind when Cynthia went to White Lake last summer and everyone was trying to find her."

"That was partially my fault," Daniel admitted. "I kind of put her up to calling you, but in reality, she is a persistent woman."

"I forgive you, mate. It was all for love. I would do the same," Ian said, and he leaned over and kissed his wife.

"Hey, Ian." Vernon and Carrie had just arrived. "Didn't know y'all would be here. Kind of nice to see one of our island boys getting a break."

"I agree. Why don't you join us?" Ian suggested. "We've got room."

The guys started talking about fishing, and Carrie and Collette talked about how beautiful the wedding was, plans for the trip to England when Collette would meet Ian's family, and what they were doing now.

"I've moved into Ian's house," Collette explained, "so we're going to sell my place in Brunswick, and I just started working for Betty Franklin. Do you know Betty? She's building a shopping plaza."

"I met her for the first time at your wedding," Carrie lied.

"She's going to have a little restaurant in the plaza she's building, and I'm going to work for her as a pastry chef when it opens. It's one of my hidden talents," Collette shared.

"How nice for you. Seems you all are interconnected in everything you do," Carrie observed.

"I guess we are. It's a small area, so I suppose you can't help it. Everybody kind of knows everybody," said Collette.

Then Carrie had an idea. "I wonder if Betty needs any other help. I'm looking for a little something to do."

"I can mention it if you'd like next time I talk to her, or maybe we could go to lunch one day and I'll take you by so you can see the new building. I'm sure Betty will be there and you can talk to her."

"That would be great," Carrie responded enthusiastically.

Christopher came over to the table.

"Well, look at this. The new uncle. How does it feel?" Ian asked.

"Kinda cool. Can't wait to see her. I don't know much about babies, so it'll be a new experience for me," he said, and then he saw Daniel. "You're back. I thought you would stay up there and bring Mom home. How's she going to get back? If you're flying back to get her, maybe I can go with you."

"No, I dropped her off at the airport and came right home. Your mother is driving back in a rental car," Daniel explained, and then he changed the subject. "Everything okay with Millie and the baby?"

"Yeah, I talked to Mom before coming here and it's all great."

"What's the bairn's name?" Ian asked.

"She's Philipa Ann after my dad and Aunt Ann, but they're going to call her Pippa."

"A lovely English name, Philipa is. It means lover of horses. Your mum will have to buy her a horse," Ian laughed. "Pippa. Beautiful."

"So, you have a plane, Daniel?" asked Carrie.

"Yes. A Cessna 177 Cardinal. I keep it at the airport here on the island. I've had my pilot's license for about twenty-five years."

"And you flew Cynthia up there? How nice. I was surprised not to see her here with you tonight, so that explains it," Carrie said.

Daniel was taken off-guard. "We're just close friends," he insisted.

"I thought you two were dating?" she said, surprised.

There was an awkward silence, and then Christopher spoke. "See you all later. I think they're going to start soon. In case anyone wants to know, Mom will be home Friday." He looked at Daniel and smiled. "Call me if any of you want any other information," he said and went back to his friends.

"Daniel." It was Carrie again.

Now what? Daniel thought. "Yes, Carrie?"

"Do you ever just go up in your plane for fun? If you ever do, maybe Vernon and I can ride along. I've never been up in a small plane before; have you, Vernon?"

"I don't go up for fun too often, but I'll let you know if I do. I can fit three passengers in with me, so if I decide to go one nice day, I can take you and Vernon with me."

"Sorry, I pass," said Vernon. "I'll fly in a big commercial plane, but not a little one."

"Collette and I will go," Ian said, and Collette nodded her head.

"Maybe sometime if the weather is nice," Daniel said to put her off. Carrie sure was annoyingly persistent.

"Why don't I give you my phone number and you give me yours, Daniel, so I know it's you when you call me," Carrie suggested.

"Sure," he said, and they exchanged numbers.

❦

"Geez, Vernon, you almost screwed that one up for me," Carrie said when they were home. "At least Ian isn't chicken to fly in a plane."

"I'm just afraid of heights, that's all. I can fly in a commercial plane as long as I can sit on the aisle," Vernon said. "We all have our phobias."

"Woo hoo, 'phobia.' A big word for you," she responded. Carrie—or rather, Connie—wasn't afraid of anything.

"You seemed to have a nice time visiting with Collette tonight," Vernon said, changing the subject. "Maybe the two of you could have a girls' day together sometime."

"She mentioned having lunch," said Carrie.

"Great. I just want you to have some girlfriends to hang out with. Maybe go for a drink sometime. Cynthia would be nice to do that with, also. She seemed to like you."

Vernon went on talking, but she tuned him out.

When they got home, Vernon went to watch some TV in bed. He was probably waiting for her, hoping for sex, but she wasn't in the mood.

She stuck her head into the room. "I'm not coming to bed for a while," she said, but there was no response. She guessed he was already asleep.

After getting ready for bed and fixing a glass of water, Connie found her laptop and made herself comfortable in an overstuffed chair. She signed on with a password so no one else could access her computer. That was the last thing she needed, someone stumbling on the truth.

While waiting for her computer to come up, she thought about the evening. Collette was going to talk to Betty about a job for her. If it weren't for her situation, Connie knew she and Collette would become real friends. Collette and Ian were always nice whenever they bumped into her, like tonight. Right away, Ian had invited them to sit at their table. Connie must be getting soft, because she was thinking about how much she liked them. She had business to take care of, however, and shouldn't allow herself to be swayed.

Tonight Connie had found out information that could be helpful. Some of Cynthia's closest friends were sitting at the table at Tortuga Jacks, in addition to a family member. She didn't care what Daniel said, there was a love connection between him and Cynthia. What was wrong with Cynthia? The man was filthy rich. And all the information about

Cynthia's friend Pur ... whatever her name was, and then her daughter having a baby that day. Oh, and about that friend Betty. There were a lot of people Connie could threaten in an effort to get the money owed to her.

Connie did a web search for Betty's name and an old newspaper article came up about the restaurant fire and her husband's obituary. She wondered how much insurance money Betty had received. Looked like she had two grown boys.

Daniel was the one with all the money, and Connie was sure he was in love with Cynthia. Even if they were "just friends," he still had enough money to help her out and never miss it. That's where Connie needed to focus her efforts.

She was getting tired. After making sure her computer was securely turned off, she rinsed her glass out and put it in the dishwasher.

It had been a good evening. A part of her was beginning to like these people though. She needed to get rid of that feeling, or it could ruin everything. They were the enemy, the ones with the money and good lives. She needed some of that money so she could be free to start her own good life, somewhere far from here, where no one knew her.

CHAPTER 22

*I*t was already Friday, and a reluctant Cynthia was in the rental car on her way back to St. Simons.

Millie and Pippa were all she could think about. Before her eyes, Millie had transformed into a mother, holding her baby as if she'd been doing it her whole life. Jimmy was a bit awkward, but dedicated to learning what to do with the priceless little soul who now made them a family.

Cynthia supported Millie as best she could in the short time she was there to help change diapers, bathe Pippa, swaddle her, and answer the hundreds of questions Millie had. Of course both Millie and Jimmy had read all the books out there about babies, but were soon finding out how each baby was different and no owner's manual came with them.

Jimmy's company gave paternity leave benefits, so he had three months off just like Millie. The two of them together would figure it all out just like everyone did. They were both smart kids.

Cynthia passed the outlet mall just outside Savannah where she loved to stop, but not today. She was ready to get home and check on Purvell. She felt she had deserted the poor girl. How boring it must be for her.

Once she was home, she would call Daniel and find out what to do about turning in the car she was driving, knowing it was going to be awkward. She couldn't stop thinking about what he'd said to her. The day she scattered Philip's ashes on White Lake, she'd thought her life would move forward, but she was still carrying baggage she couldn't rid herself of.

Soon, the sign for exit 38 was in front of her. This was a shorter way home than exit 29, which would have taken her over the bridge.

It was almost 4:30 p.m., so she stopped at Southern Soul Barbeque to pick up some pulled pork since she wasn't sure what she had at home and was tired. If they didn't eat it that night, they could have it tomorrow, she figured. She made sure there was plenty since she knew Christopher would sniff it out and want to join them.

She parked the rental car next to her own car and went straight in without getting her suitcase, barbeque in hand. In front of the TV sat Purvell and Christopher, playing a video game so involved they didn't even hear her come in. She took a moment to watch the hilarious scene in front of her. Purvell, obviously a novice, next to the cool, calm, and collect pro, Christopher. They finished the game, and Christopher spoke to Purvell. "Hey, do you smell barbeque?"

"Is this what you're talking about?" Cynthia asked, holding up the bag.

"Mom, glad you made it home safe and brought barbeque. Awesome," Christopher said, taking the bag from her. He had his priorities.

"Cynthia, I didn't think you would be back this early. I want to see pictures right now. You only sent me a few," Purvell chimed in.

"I have to go back and get my suitcase and then I can show you," Cynthia said.

"Christopher, go get your mom's suitcase," Purvell directed Christopher, and he hopped to it. "Now, tell me about the baby."

Cynthia took a deep breath and started, "It's like nothing I've ever experienced before. She's perfect in every way. Her eyes and hair are dark, but that can change, and for being a little early, she's really the size of many full-term babies. I'm in heaven, Purvell. I had no idea how wonderful this would be." She pulled out her phone. "Here are some pictures."

"Hey, I want to see them too," said Christopher, back in with her suitcase.

"Come sit over on this side of me so we can all see." Cynthia patted the sofa cushion where she wanted him to sit. All three of them, including Christopher, oohed and aahed over Pippa.

After seeing all the pictures, Christopher suggested they eat the barbeque, so they went into the kitchen.

"Oh, I need to get in touch with Daniel about the car," Cynthia said.

"Don't worry about it, Mom," said Christopher. "Daniel told me what to do. He said to let him know when you're back and I'll drive it to him and then he'll give me a ride back here. He said something about not wanting you to feel burdened."

Cynthia felt a flush go up the back of her neck.

"Well, okay. Tell him to come in when he drops you off so I can thank him."

"Okay, let's eat," said Christopher, and he opened the bag with barbeque. "Oh great, you got mac and cheese and fried green beans too. You're awesome, Mom. Let me get some plates," he added, rushing to the cupboard.

Purvell looked at Cynthia and spoke in a soft voice so Christopher wouldn't hear. "I thought this little flight would be good for you and Daniel. What happened?"

"I can't seem to get it together, Purvell. I don't know. Maybe I'm not ready for a serious relationship yet. Daniel pointed some things out to me I've had time to think about. I know what a nice guy he is, but I'm still dealing with something inside me. Until I can get past that, I can't be with anyone." She shook her head.

"I guess I understand. You know I'm always here for you; in fact, according to the doctor I saw this week, I'll be here for you several more weeks. I won't need surgery as long as I take it easy, which means no traveling."

"I hate that this happened to you. What about work?" Cynthia asked.

"If Daniel can run his business from down here, why can't I? This accident has got me thinking about what I want to do in the future. I like it down here—and that's all I'm saying."

"Well, I think that's good," Cynthia said. "We should always think about our future."

"I'm just thinking about things. I don't want to talk about it now until I work it out in my head," Purvell added.

"Me neither," said Christopher, back with the plates and silverware. "Let's eat."

When Christopher was done, he left to take the car back to Daniel. Cynthia was going over in her mind what she would say to him. Maybe a good start was to just thank him for his thoughtfulness and all he did in flying her up so see Millie, but when Christopher came home, he was alone.

"Didn't you invite Daniel in?" Cynthia asked.

"Yeah, I did, but he said it was better he didn't come in. Did you guys have a fight when you went up to Charlotte? I saw him Monday night at Tortuga Jacks and he didn't seem to want to talk about your trip," Christopher said, concerned.

"I'm sure he just has a lot of work to do," Cynthia responded, but she felt a sadness that he didn't want to come in.

"Hey, Purvell, do you want to play another video game?" Christopher asked.

"Sure, why not, kid? I'm getting good at this stuff."

"While you two battle it out, I'm going to call Mom and Granny," Cynthia said, and she went upstairs.

She decided to get ready for bed before she made the call. It had been a long week, and she was tired after the drive today. She washed her face and after she dried it, slowly took the towel away and looked at herself. She was fifty-eight years old. Maybe it was time to make some life changes of her own. Some *she* chose to change, and not the ones forced on her.

The last time Cynthia had felt like this was after Betty's husband, Jack, died and she'd finally run the bridge. Cynthia thought she had moved her life forward after running the bridge, but now felt she was back where she started. Maybe the fact that her life had been put on hold while she cared for Ann until her subsequent death had affected Cynthia more than she thought. It didn't matter what it was that had set her back, only that now she was aware.

But where to begin? She thought about baby Pippa and this new kind of love she felt for her. The child was the closest thing to heaven Cynthia had in her life. She would take that love she felt for Pippa and let it seep into every part of her. The light from this love surely would show her the way out of whatever was holding her back. She had nothing to lose and everything to gain.

Daniel. She wouldn't blame him if he never spoke to her again. She had returned his honest and sincere kindness with ungratefulness. It was like he'd said. She had been running from things for so long she didn't even know she was doing it. Philip also came to mind. She'd never wanted to make waves during their marriage—and then the gambling situation right under her nose. The clues were there, but she'd never wanted to rock the boat. And why hadn't Philip seen the doctor? He would be alive right now if he had gone. It was all past history she had to learn to let go. But how? She had so many questions only Philip could answer.

After she brushed her teeth and got her nightgown on, she lay on her bed and closed her eyes. *God be with me. I can't go on alone. Thank you for this gift of Pippa You have given us. She reminds us where we came from and the possibilities of how we change the world as we go. Her presence has already changed mine.*

She lay for a few more minutes and then decided she needed to talk to her mom. If she could only be half as smart as her mom was when it came to life. She got her phone and touched the number on the screen.

"Hi, Mom ... Yes, I made it home safe and sound ... Let's start planning a trip for you and Granny to come down here to see that baby. She's the most beautiful thing I've ever seen."

❧

Daniel had really wanted to go in and see Cynthia after he dropped off Christopher, but no, he would have to wait. He began to think about what he'd said to Cynthia. He was hard on her and felt bad, although it was the truth.

Having gone through the death of a spouse himself, he knew you didn't jump back into life overnight. It took time. In his case his wife had been sick for a while and he knew the possibility of her death was there, but for Cynthia, there was no warning. Philip had been a healthy person and his death was like a candle snuffed out in a windowless room. No warning. And then to find out he wasn't quite what she thought he was, well, Daniel couldn't imagine that.

He knew Cynthia still had some grieving to do, but she didn't know it herself. Until she figured it out, he would wait for the day she said she loved him.

When Daniel reached his house, he pushed the garage door opener, parked, and went inside to his empty, dark home.

It was so quiet, he flipped on the TV and found a basketball game before he went into the kitchen to see what he could fix for his supper. He didn't much care about the basketball game, only that it filled the silence.

After fixing some scrambled eggs, a couple slices of bacon, and toast, he made himself comfortable in front of the TV. Feeling a little chilly, he picked up the remote for the gas logs and pressed the button that ignited the flames. Soon the night he'd spent in front of the fire at Cynthia's house came to mind.

He turned the TV and gas logs off, grabbed a jacket, and headed out to the beach for a walk.

The moon was full, and the salty air whipped across his face as he walked into the wind. He loved being able to do this.

The lights of Beach House Restaurant were shining ahead. A beer was what he needed, so he headed up the steps to the restaurant and went in to the bar.

After situating himself on a bar stool, he ordered a beer and struck up conversation with some of the people around him. Then, he heard his name and saw Vernon's girlfriend, Carrie, standing next to him.

"I thought that was you," she said. "I met Vernon over here for dinner after he closed up the bait shop tonight. Had to use the ladies' room before I drove my car home, and saw you sitting here alone. So, what's new?" she asked, as she plopped herself down on the chair next to him and ordered a beer.

"Isn't Vernon going to wonder where you are?" Daniel asked, wanting her to go away. He was enjoying his newfound friends at the bar.

"I texted him when I saw you sitting here and said I forgot I had to make a couple stops before I came home. He doesn't care," she said, waving away the thought as if it were a fly.

"Well, okay. I'm not staying much longer anyway," he said, hoping this might motivate her to leave. No such luck.

After a few more beers, Daniel was beginning to feel the effects of the alcohol and decided he better start walking home before he couldn't do so. He addressed his new friends at the bar.

"It was very nice to meet all of you tonight, but I need to go home," he said and slid off the stool a little unsteady.

"I don't think you should be driving home, Daniel," Carrie said.

"Oh, I didn't drive. I walked, so I'll be fine," he said and headed to the door.

"I don't think that's such a great idea, either," Carrie persisted. "I can drop you off on my way. I insist. If I heard you were washed away by the tide, I could never forgive myself. I'm ready to go right now anyway, so come on," she said and walked beside him out to the parking lot.

Daniel was feeling a little unsteady, so he thought, *What the heck?* "Okay, Carrie. I guess you're right. I'm in The Cottages."

Carrie jabbered on as they headed north down Beach Drive to his house. When they got there, she turned off the car and hopped out.

"I'm fine now," he told her, but she continued to his front door. "Thanks for the ride," he said with a wave, but she stood next to him smiling.

"I want to make sure you get in okay," she said, but he didn't want her in. Carrie took his keys from his hand, opened the door, and let herself in. What was he going to do?

"Wow, you have a nice place here," she said as she looked around. "Pretty fancy."

"Yes. Well, I don't want to seem rude, but I need to call it a night, so thanks again," Daniel said, this time more firm. He stood by the door outside until she came back over by him.

"Now don't forget I want to go up in your airplane sometime," she said with a grin.

"Right, I won't forget. Thanks again," he said, and without a word, Carrie went out to her car.

Daniel locked the door and thought, *What a strange woman*. Then again, Vernon was a bit strange himself—only in a good way. Daniel would take her up in his plane, but only if Ian and Collette could go also. Something inside told him never to be alone with this woman.

CHAPTER 23

$\mathcal{B}$etty called the next morning, Saturday, and invited Cynthia, Purvell, and Christopher over for dinner that night so they could all visit and she could tell them something important. Cynthia hadn't seen Betty since Ian's wedding two weeks previous and was looking forward to the evening.

John, Betty's son, answered the door when they arrived.

"Hi, John. This is my friend Purvell," Cynthia said.

"Nice to meet you, ma'am," John said to Purvell, shaking her hand. "Luke's here too."

"What've you boys been up to?" Cynthia asked.

"We've been learning a lot about how to develop our property. You know, helping Mom. Kind of on-the-job training. We're learning from a guy by the name of Daniel Benton who moved down here from New York. He's a great guy," said John as he saw them in.

Christopher spoke up. "Yeah, trust me, we know *all* about him," he said and walked into Betty's family room with John, where they found Luke watching TV. "Hey, man, it's been a long time since I've seen the two of you together," he added and they plopped themselves in front of the TV.

"Hi, Luke," Cynthia said. "I want you to meet my friend Purvell."

Luke jumped up immediately and extended his had to Purvell. "Nice to meet you, ma'am. Mom's in the kitchen, if y'all are wondering."

"Great, we'll go find her," Cynthia said and led the way to the kitchen, where they found Betty, putting the finishing touches on dinner.

"Hi, there. What can we do to help?" Cynthia asked.

"Oh, it's so good to see y'all," said Betty, first hugging Cynthia and then Purvell. "You just set yourself in that chair, Purvell, and put your leg up."

"I'm fine, Betty," she said. "You know, I really enjoyed the soup and muffins you brought by the other day. I appreciated it. I have to admit, I did hide the muffins on Christopher so I could have them all. Will they both be on the menu of your new shop?"

"The muffins for sure, but I haven't decided about the soup yet," Betty said. "I want to start out with a simple menu and go from there. Just the bakery, sandwiches, and some catering on a small scale until I get my bearings."

"Well I can't wait," said Cynthia. "When do you think you'll open?"

"That's what I wanted to tell you and kind of celebrate tonight. I'm opening for business the first Saturday in May, but having a grand opening party the Friday night before. I hope all y'all can come. It's just four weeks away. I've struggled with what I was going to name the place, but I've settled on something: Heaven Sent. I'm so excited."

"You should be," Cynthia said. "I love the name. I'll make sure to get the day off so I can be there." The two women hugged again, but Betty had tears rolling down her face when they pulled away.

"I'm trying hard, but I miss Jack so much," she said.

Cynthia started tearing up also. "I know what you mean."

"Alright, ladies, that's enough. Betty, you said you wanted to celebrate. Do you have any wine around here?" Purvell intervened.

"I do have a bottle of white wine in the garage refrigerator," said Betty.

"I'll do the honor of making a toast," Purvell said, "but you'll have to go get the bottle, Cynthia, and you get the cork screw and glasses, Betty."

Cynthia gave the bottle to Purvell, who removed the cork and poured three glasses of the wine, handing one to each of the other women, and then raised her glass high. "To new beginnings."

Cynthia and Betty followed suit and raised their glasses. "To new beginnings," they chimed, then all three took a drink and laughed.

Dinner was in Betty's dining room at a beautifully set table. She'd made both a roasted and fried chicken, peas and rice, green beans, corn bread, and for dessert, pound cake with strawberries. A delicious Southern meal.

After dinner, the boys went outside to play basketball, so the women were alone. They sat together in the family room, talking about the grand opening of Heaven Sent. Such a perfect name for Betty's restaurant because to Cynthia, Betty *was* heaven sent since the first night they'd met.

"I guess you'll be back in New York by then, Purvell. Sure do wish you would be able to come also," Betty said.

"I have a feeling I'll still be here from what the doctor has told me," said Purvell. "Getting around in New York with a broken leg and ankle will be difficult, so I'm going to stay here until I get released. I'll be in this cast for a while and doing everything they tell me to. Don't want to jeopardize being able to wearing my high heels again," she said and laughed.

"I don't know, Betty, but I think this place is softening my friend here," said Cynthia, and she turned her head slightly to glance at Purvell out of the corner of her eye. "She's enjoying the slower pace of life far better than I ever thought she would."

"We'll see how she's doing by the time of my grand opening, Cynthia. That'll be the true test. What do you say, Purvell?" Betty asked. "I sense there's something more going on here."

"Betty, I have no idea what you're talking about," Purvell said, raising her eyebrows. "I just feel fortunate to attend your grand opening. Now I want to hear more about the bakery." She smiled as she changed the subject.

"I feel so blessed to know Collette," said Betty, taking a sip of wine. "Do you know that girl went to culinary school and can bake up a storm? As soon as the kitchen is approved by the county, we're going to start testing our menu. Hey, y'all should come by and be our taste-testers. I'll give you a call when I need you, how's that?"

"I'm sure I'll be available," Purvell said.

"You know that girlfriend of Vernon's?" Betty asked. "She told Collette she wanted to come work for me. I already have my staff hired, so I don't need anyone else, but I don't feel good about that girl. What do you think of her?"

"I don't really know her, Betty, but I think she's trying real hard to fit. I'm nice to her because I have no reason not to be. I would say if you don't feel good about her, go with what you sense," Cynthia said.

"I told Collette I was going to run things lean, so I don't think there'll be any problem. The boys are going to help out also. You know Jack would love that."

"I know he would," Cynthia said and gave her friend's hand a squeeze.

"I might need some extra help getting the place ready before the opening, though, so I was thinking I might offer Carrie a little work to check her out in case I might want to use her in the future," Betty said.

"That's a good idea. Then there's no commitment," Cynthia said. "By the way, Mom and Granny are visiting in a week and a half so they can see the baby and will still be here for your grand opening also. They're going to be thrilled."

"Oh, that's great. I can't wait to see them again. Now there's a couple of good taste-testers I could use."

"They're going to fly into Charlotte so they can see Pippa," Cynthia said. "I'll drive up there and bring them back here when we're done visiting. I hope Christopher can come with me also. We're going to stay in a hotel since Millie doesn't have enough room for all of us, nor does she need the stress of company. Her hands are full—in fact, they'll be full the rest of her life."

"You're right about that," Betty agreed with a chuckle.

"And I'm going to stay here, Betty, so maybe you can pick me up a couple of days and I can come help with something to do with the restaurant," Purvell informed her.

"I'll take you up on that," Betty said, patting Purvell's arm.

The women talked another twenty minutes before Cynthia said they needed to go home. She rounded up Christopher and they were on their way.

The sun had gone down, and no one spoke in the dark car. Her thoughts went to Millie and the baby, causing her heart to feel light. A week and a half until she got to hold that little doll again. Wait until her mom and Granny saw her, and Christopher too: he'd surely be wrapped around her little finger. Little Pippa had no idea how much love was coming her way, or maybe she did. Cynthia knew she would do anything for her.

❧

The events of the previous week were catching up with Cynthia, so the next day was spent taking it easy before she went back to work the next morning.

It had been a week since the baby was born and a few days more since Purvell's accident. What a week!

When Cynthia stepped through the doors of the ER the next morning, she was back in her element, so happy she did what she did for a living.

Before she knew it, her day was almost half over. After she finished charting, she pulled up the schedule to request the time off she needed to go to Millie's when her mom and Granny came. This meant she would have to work the next seven out of nine days in order to take the week off to be with them. It was worth it, but poor Purvell wouldn't see much of her.

Purvell was understanding about Cynthia having to work so much.

"This is a time for your family," Purvell said. "You don't need me hanging—or in this case, hobbling, around. I've several people who can get me out on occasion, so no worries. Betty, Daniel, and others, I'm sure, so go enjoy that baby."

"You're being way too kind, and I appreciate you more than you can imagine."

"It's no big deal," Purvell said, smiling.

"Listen, I'm really tired," Cynthia said. "If you don't mind, I'm going up to bed after I eat something. I'll be off on Thursday, so maybe we can go out to lunch and the grocery store. Get some things you like."

"I've got a better idea," Purvell said. "Maybe Daniel would take me to the grocery store. He still hasn't shown me his new house, so I'll get him to take me there before he brings me back here. Gives you a little break."

"Okay, but we'll still go to lunch on my day off."

"Definitely," Purvell said.

So, the week continued. Betty got her approval for her kitchen, and she picked Purvell up on Tuesday to taste-test at Heaven Sent. Brad Davies came by Heaven Sent to see how things were going while Purvell was there and invited her to see his office and talk real estate on Wednesday. On Thursday, Cynthia's day off, she and Purvell went to lunch at Mallery Cafe, and since Purvell was maneuvering so well, they went to some of the shops by the pier. While at lunch on Thursday, Purvell was very mysterious about what she was going to do on Friday, and Cynthia was too tired to pursue it. Cynthia guessed maybe she was getting together with Daniel and didn't want her to be thinking about what they were doing or talking about.

The truth was Cynthia didn't have much time to think during the day, but when she finally put her head on the pillow that night, Daniel was the first thought that popped in her head. What was he doing? Whom was he with? Where was he? Did he think about her? What would she say to him the next time she saw him? Would he even talk to her again? What was wrong with her? It went on and on.

While she lay in bed Thursday night, she remembered the vivid dreams she used to have. For some reason they only occurred occasionally now. Many times the dreams would help her sort things out, so in the morning her mind was at peace.

She closed her eyes and recalled a dream she'd had about Philip when she was staying with her mom on White Lake last summer. The dream once again began to play out in her mind as it did the first time.

There were rowboats all over the shore of White Lake. She saw friends and family around her, all still alive except one. Philip. He was smiling as everyone climbed in the boats and set off rowing to the center of the lake.

She motioned to him to get in with her, but he shook his head, blew her a kiss, threw the rope in, and shoved her off alone, waving. As she floated toward the others, she saw the boats around her were filled with mumbling, blurred people. In the middle of the floating boats was one lone person whom she couldn't make out, treading water.

She'd thought Philip was telling her it was time to move on, giving her the idea to scatter his ashes on White Lake. After employing Ian to send her the ashes, she'd scattered them around the inlet on the lake. She expected this would be the closure she needed and that her life would change. Now it seemed she was wrong.

To help clear her head, she took some deep breaths and slowly exhaled, then counted to one hundred and then back down to one, as her thoughts continued to swirl in her head. After about thirty more minutes of overthinking, she finally calmed down and slipped into sleep.

CHAPTER 24

When she heard the doorbell ring, Purvell looked to see who it was and opened the door.

"Hi. Where are we going today? Somewhere fun, I hope," she said with a flirty smile.

"How about shopping at St. Johns Town Center in Jacksonville? Do you think it might be too much for you? You don't want to overdo it with your leg," said her visitor.

"I think mall therapy is just what I need! I'll let you know if it's too much. You are so sweet. Let's go," she said.

He helped Purvell down the stairs and to the car, though she actually could have done it on her own. She liked the way he treated her. He was different than any other guy she had gone out with before.

"So, what have you been doing this week? This place must be boring to a busy New York girl like you," he said as they got into his car.

"Actually, I have a busy social life," she laughed. "Monday I didn't go anywhere. I did a little reading out on the deck and cooked a nice dinner for Cynthia and me—and of course, Christopher. He likes to eat."

"That's right, he lives with Cynthia."

"No, no. There's an apartment below her house he lives in," Purvell explained. "He decided to drop out of college and works two jobs over on Jekyll. At one time he was going to be a nurse, but now I'm not sure what he's going to do. A great kid, just trying to figure out where he fits in. We've all been there."

"Not me. I always knew what I wanted to do," he smiled. "From the time I was about twelve."

"Most of us aren't that focused," she said, patting his knee as he pulled the car onto Ocean Road. "I've not always been focused, but I've always been driven. In fact as a teenager, I worked in a little ladies' clothing shop called Jeffrey's in my hometown, Neenah, Wisconsin, as a salesperson. I liked selling, so business seemed to be obvious for me. After I graduated from college, I wanted to go somewhere exciting— and what could be more exciting than New York City? By dumb luck I got into real estate, and the rest is history."

"You must be focused to be the success you are."

"You're right, but I like to have fun also. I can't be all focus. Did you have much fun in college, or was it all work?" Purvell asked.

"I had some fun, but there were times I didn't think college would ever end," he said, flashing a handsome smile.

"Really? There were times I never wanted it to end," she said and laughed.

"So, tell me what else you did this week," he requested.

"A friend of Cynthia's and mine is opening a new restaurant on Frederica Road called Heaven Sent. Maybe you know her, Betty Franklin?"

"I do, and I knew her husband, Jack. Loved their barbeque. Such a shame what happened to Jack. Their place was a landmark on the island. I noticed they were building something on the property. So, what's it going to be?" he asked.

"A little shopping center," she answered. "Betty is opening a bakery and sandwich shop for breakfast and lunch. I believe the plan is to start the first weekend in May. She's having a little party the night before for her friends. Maybe I can get you an invite. She's going to do some catering also. I offered my services to help her get things ready, so she picked me up Tuesday morning and put me to work taste-testing. I quite enjoyed myself. While I was there, a Realtor named Brad Davies who helped Betty develop the property came by. We hit it off and he invited me to lunch the next day, then brought me by his office to meet his partner, Sherrye," Purvell shared with a slight smile on her lips.

"Really?" he asked with genuine interest. "What does that mean?"

"Oh, I don't know. I have some thinking to do," she teased.

"Purvell, I know we haven't known each other long, but I've never met anyone like you. If you said you were thinking of staying down here even part-time, I'd be a happy man. I'd like us get to know each other better."

"I feel the same way," she said and took his hand. "I really like it down here and need a change in my life."

"I wonder when you're going to tell your friend Cynthia we've been seeing each other? Why are you keeping it a secret?"

"I have my reasons. After I do my thinking, I'll tell her. Please don't ask me any more about it. I'll tell you in time." She gave his hand a reassuring squeeze.

"Okay, you know what's best, I guess. So, what store do you want to shop at first?"

"Let's start at one end and work our way to the other," she said, in typical Purvell fashion.

The day was the best that week. They covered a lot of ground, her leg feeling fine. When she got home, she would prop it up to rest. At lunch they had a glass or two of wine, enjoying each other's company.

Back at Cynthia's house, he made sure Purvell got inside safely, leaving her with a long lingering kiss—or two—before departing. *What a great day,* she thought, as she lifted her leg up to rest and lay back on the couch, closing her eyes. She was a little tired.

What she didn't want to say was how on Wednesday when she visited Brad's office, he'd shown her around as they exchanged business stories and accomplishments. Evidently Daniel had already told him all about her and given a strong endorsement. He told Brad about how long he'd been doing business with her, her sales skills, how well she'd run her business, her professionalism, and how she was the best agent he'd ever worked with. Brad asked her if she was possibly interested in becoming a partner of his team. He wanted to get more into commercial sales, and she could be a big asset. Daniel had mentioned maybe she was ready to make a change in her life and move down there.

Brad's offer sounded good, and she would give the proposition serious consideration, but she wanted to make the decision on her own with no interfering opinions of others. She'd made all her own decisions her whole life and wasn't going to change now.

What baffled her was how she felt about this man. She was falling for him and couldn't be happier. For the first time, she was allowing the prospect of love to play in a decision she was making. It was true, she was tired of being alone. Daniel had got her thinking about how her life could be different with the change he'd made moving down there. She'd told Brad to give her some time to think about his offer. Also she asked him not to mention it to anyone—not even Daniel. He agreed.

She heard a knock that could only mean it was Christopher. He waited a few seconds and came in.

"Hey, did you have a nice day?" he asked.

"Why yes, nothing special. How about you?"

"Not bad. I've been thinking more about how I need to get back to college, but don't tell Mom, okay? A guy has to have a few things he keeps to himself. She'll start getting all excited asking questions I don't want to answer yet."

"I understand. I don't tell her everything either," she said, smiling.

"Right ... So is that who I thought it was leaving here just now?"

Purvell was stunned. "I don't know what you're talking about," she said, feigning ignorance.

"Oh, you know who I'm talking about. It's the second time I've seen him around here. Does Mom know—or is that one of the things you don't tell her?"

She was busted by Christopher. What could she bribe him with? Money might work.

"I can tell by the look on your face there's more to the story, but I'll give you a break. My lips are sealed," Christopher laughed. "You crack me up," he said and walked into the kitchen. Purvell heard the refrigerator door open.

She felt like a caught teenager.

"Do you want to play a video game?" he asked when he came back with a plate of leftovers and bottle of Gatorade.

"Sure. So, can I ask you questions about you wanting to go back to college?"

"If I can ask you a few about your guest?" he bargained, raising an eyebrow.

Hmm, she thought. *Why not?* "Sure, but I get to go first," Purvell said, thinking she could maybe sidetrack him and avoid his questions. "What prompted this change of mind, if I may ask?"

"I've come to see an education will be the only way for me to live a decent life," he said, booting up the game console. "I mean, look at Daniel. When he was a kid, he was no different than me and now he can live anywhere he wants, has a great car, and an airplane. He's told me about how hard he's had to work his whole life, and I'm not afraid to work. That's why I want to talk to your boyfriend. I have some questions, and he might be able to answer them."

"He's not my boyfriend ...." Purvell interjected.

"Whatever you want to call him, I don't care. You've been acting goofy lately, so nice try. You're lucky Mom's so preoccupied with her life, she doesn't notice—but wait till Grandma and Granny get here," he said and started laughing.

He was right. But by then she'd have her decision made and would reveal her relationship. She was looking forward to Cynthia and Christopher being gone to Millie's next week so she could do some serious thinking.

"You're going with your mom next week, aren't you?" Purvell asked.

Laughing, Christopher said, "Yes. So, ask your boyfriend if he wouldn't mind getting together with me to talk before we go. Give him my number."

"I'll call him right now. I'm sure he's home," she said and dialed the number.

"Hi ... Yes, I had a great time today also ... Listen, I was wondering if you had time before next Wednesday to meet with Christopher, Cynthia's son? ... I'm not sure exactly, but he feels you may be able to give him some guidance about what he wants to do in college ... Just a second, and I'll ask him. Can you meet him Monday for lunch?" she asked Christopher.

"No problem," Christopher said. "How about 12:30 p.m.?"

"He says fine, how about 12:30? ... Great." Then she asked Christopher, "Is Sal's okay for pizza?"

"I love the place," Christopher responded.

"I'll text you his phone number ... Thank you again for today. Bye." Purvell hung up. "There, done. So, you won't say anything about my friend, right? I'll tell your mom when I'm ready, but I have some other things going on also that I'm waiting to come together."

"It's our secret. So, let's play some video games? I'll let you pick, or do you want to try something new?"

"Surprise me, kid," she said and slapped him on the back.

She wondered what Christopher had up his sleeve. Nothing would make Cynthia happier than him going back to college. The kid could do really well in business with the personality he had. He was a little bit like his dad, actually.

Purvell's thoughts then went back to her dilemma. What was she going to do? For the first time in her life, she knew she would make this decision with her heart, not her head. Ever since she'd arrived here, events had been pointing her in one direction. It was time to make a change and trust the forces around her to guide her to the right path.

CHAPTER 25

The Shoppes on St. Simons were nearing completion. Heaven Sent was done, and Betty was busy getting everything in shape. Daniel was proud of it. There were a few things to do in the other units yet, but today the Heaven Sent sign and the big sign with the name of the center were going up. Daniel could see Betty and some other people through the window of the restaurant as he parked his car.

When he opened the restaurant door, a bell tinkled, causing everyone inside to turn. The smell he walked into *was* heaven sent. Betty had started using her ovens.

"Daniel, you've perfect timing. Taste this," Betty commanded while Carrie stood behind her, holding a tray with various pastries. Shoving two delicacies in front of him, Betty continued, "Collette just made them, some cream, covered with chocolate and some lemon, dusted with powdered sugar. Try them and tell us what you think."

"Laddie, I've been here all morning and may need to be rolled out, I've eaten so much." It was Ian sitting at a table with Vernon.

"It's a tough job, Daniel, but someone has to do it," Vernon laughed, shoving one of the pastries in his mouth.

"We've been taste-testing today," Carrie informed Daniel. "Collette is an unbelievable baker. Did you know she went to a French pastry school?"

"No, I didn't," Daniel responded. "It seems I do have perfect timing," he said and he popped the lemon one in his mouth first. "Oh … yum. Give me a second and I'll try the other."

"I'm so excited about my signs going up today. What time will they be here?" Betty said, wiping her hands on her apron.

"Anytime in the next two hours. I'll take that chocolate one now, Betty," Daniel said, and he popped it into his mouth. "Holy cow. Okay, I like them both, but I'm partial to the chocolate."

"I think we'll do both. The muffins and pies will be out of the oven in five minutes," Betty said.

"I don't think I can eat another sweet, darlin'," Ian moaned from his corner, but Betty ignored him as she placed what Daniel had just tasted in front of him.

"I've so much to do, Daniel," Betty said. "I have all but one of the six units rented. Once we open, however, the word will get out about this place. It's a great location. You know Jack and I bought this property shortly after we were married. Jack always said it was a good investment, and he was right."

"He was right, but he helped make it a good investment with the success of the restaurant he built here. I hope that's one of the things I've taught your boys working with them on this project," Daniel said.

"They've learned a lot from you, Daniel. It's always, 'Daniel said this,' 'Daniel said that.' I'll forever be grateful for the day I met you," said Betty, and she gave Daniel a hug.

Collette came out of the kitchen with a tray of muffins. "Here's the muffins I want you to try. Oh hi, Daniel. We could use a fresh palate. These two have been great, but they might be in a sugar stupor by now," she said, nodding at Ian and Vernon.

"More like a coma," Ian said, letting out a little burp, then smiling sheepishly.

"Sure, I'll try some. Hey, maybe the guys who hang your sign today might even give you an opinion," Daniel said, and he took a muffin over to a table and sat down, Betty following him. "I'm sorry, Betty, but I won't be able to make your grand opening party. I have to go back to New York and help my nephew settle a few things and sign some papers," he added.

"That's okay. I forget sometimes you have another business to run. Just make sure you come by after you get back for lunch, you hear?"

"I'll be by," he said, then hesitated. "Hey, I have to ask you this ..." but before he could ask the question, Betty answered.

"I had Cynthia and Purvell over for dinner a little over a week ago. Cynthia is fine on the outside, but I think she has a struggle on the inside. Does it have to do with you?"

He laughed and turned a little red. "I hope so—in a good way. I know she has Millie's baby on her mind right now and Purvell's injury. I've put a little pressure on her. I think she's running from something, Betty, and I don't want it to be me."

"Everything will work out as it should, Daniel. I sense many positive forces around you. You are one of those people who help the rest of us make things happen. A catalyst, so to speak. Look back on your life and I think you'll see what I'm talking about." Betty took his hand and said, "Just keep living life to its fullest."

"Thanks, Betty. I'm grateful for the friendship I've found in you. It's more than business for me."

Betty smiled. "Now, try that muffin before Collette comes back with her buttermilk pie. Bet you never had a piece of that in New York. Hers is to die for."

"You're right, I haven't," he said, broke off the top of the muffin, and took a big bite. He instantly felt better. Betty *was* heaven sent.

❦

Christopher walked into Sal's Neighborhood Pizzeria and scanned the room. There he was, the guy he was meeting—Purvell's "boyfriend."

"Hi, Dr. Carroll," Christopher said, as he slid into the booth. "I appreciate you meeting me here."

"Listen, how about you just call me Max? Dr. Carroll seems so formal," he said, shaking Christopher's hand.

"Sure, I can do that."

"I bet you're looking forward to seeing your niece this week; you're going with your mom, aren't you?"

"Yeah, I can't wait to see her," Christopher said, smiling. "I don't really know much about babies, but I figure it can't be too hard. I don't think I'll be changing any diapers, just mostly playing with her. Can't wait to see my sister and her husband along with my grandma and great grandma who will be coming from Wisconsin. I haven't seen them since Christmas. Should be a fun week for us."

"Yes, it should," said Max. "A new baby in a family is very special. I have two children that are grown, both married, but no grandkids for me yet. I'm looking forward to the day I'm called Grandpa."

"You sound like my mom. She's a little crazy about Pippa—that's short for Philipa, her full name. My dad's name was Philip."

"What a nice way to remember him."

"Yeah, I guess," Christopher said, not convincing.

"So, let's order before we get to the reason you wanted to meet me here today. I'm easy when it comes to pizza. I like everything."

"Me too. How about a large with pepperoni, sausage, ham, and mushrooms?" Christopher suggested.

"Now you're talking," Max responded.

They placed their order and Christopher started.

"I don't know how much Purvell has told about me, but I'll start from the beginning. I've always admired my mom and her job as a nurse. So much that I decided my senior year in high school, I wanted to be a nurse. I started out in college and was happy, but then began to feel burned out. I decided I didn't want to be there, so I dropped out. Didn't tell my mom, but just did it. I mean, why waste the money?" Christopher stared at his hands as he laced his fingers.

"I'm sure it took a lot to make that decision on your own, knowing your mom might not be too happy with you. What did your mom do when you told her?"

"Oh, she wasn't happy with me at all. I did talk with my brother-in-law, Jimmy, about it, and he saw my point. She was mostly mad because I didn't talk to her about it first. She's had so much to deal with the past few years, I didn't want to add to it, but I guess my decision added to it anyway."

"In your mom's defense, she was paying for college," said Max.

"I know. She would've forced me to stay. I kind of took advantage of her situation," Christopher said, biting his lip. "Mom went away on vacation to England last July for two weeks. My uncle's wife, Ann, had a bad accident while she was there, causing my mom to stay and help out until Ann suddenly died at the end of December. Mom came back in January. I guess I should have told her, but I did what I thought was right at the time. So, I've been here since then, working at a golf course and the Jekyll Island Club."

"So, where do I fit in?" Max asked him.

"I realize I'll never get ahead if I don't go to college and I still want to stay somewhere in the medical field, I just don't know where. I'm kind of thinking of a physician's assistant, maybe? It's a reach, but up until my last semester, I was doing real well in school. I can do it. I was wondering what advice you could give me?" Christopher said hopefully.

"Wow. That's a big decision on your part. The first thing I would suggest is getting a job in the healthcare field, so you're sure that's what you want to do before you commit yourself to more schooling. The best job would be a certified nurse assistant, or CNA. There's several places you can take classes to get your CNA license. Then, I would suggest a job at the hospital. That should give you a good picture of what you're getting yourself into. After that if you think it's what you want, apply to PA school and see what happens. A nurse practitioner is also a good job, or a nurse anesthetist. When you get your CNA license, let me know and I'll help you get a job at the hospital," Max said.

"That would be awesome. I'll start checking out classes today," Christopher said, making a note on his phone.

"But before you do anything, I insist you talk to your mom. You should tell her you talked to me, okay?"

"Okay. I think I'll tell her my decision when we're driving up to Charlotte on Wednesday. She'll be so happy. Thanks, Max. I can't tell you how much this means to me."

Just then their pizza arrived, and they talked about sports and life on the island.

"Do you like to fish, Max?" asked Christopher. "You'll have to get together with me and a couple of my friends. They're your age, not mine, but they're just about the best friends I've ever had. Ian Roberts and Daniel Benton. They would like you."

"I like to fish but don't get much opportunity. I'll give you my number and you can call me sometime. So, I have one question to ask you if you don't mind," Max said, his tone becoming more serious. "I don't want to ask your mom. How did your dad die? Had he been sick?"

"I don't mind at all. He died of a thing called Brugada syndrome. His dad and grandfather both died the same way, but they didn't know what it was back then. It's hereditary in males, so I've been tested, but thank God I don't have it. He died from it the day he and my mom moved here from Atlanta about two-and-a-half years ago. He came to your hospital in fact," said Christopher as he took a bite of pizza.

"I see," Max said with a funny look on his face.

"There's even more to it, but I don't talk about it. It's in the past, and Mom does the best she can. She's my hero for not only working in the same hospital Dad died in, but now in the same ER."

"Yes," was all Max said.

Max gave Christopher his phone number and they parted. Before Max started his car to leave, he sat for a few minutes. As Christopher told the story of his father's death, Max began to remember the night Philip had come into the ER. He could remember telling Cynthia that her husband was dead. He'd seen so many people, he didn't always remember them, but as Christopher spoke, he remembered. Cynthia had looked different that night, but it was her. What a strong woman to work in the same department connected to such a terrible memory. He wasn't sure he could do it.

He called Purvell.

"Hi, can I stop by?" he asked. "Can you go for a ride with me? ... Okay, I'll be there in about five or ten minutes."

Purvell was waiting when he pulled in. They drove down to the pier. "I'll park here close to the pier so you don't have to go far," he said. They went down to the end where there were some benches to sit on.

"Is everything okay with Christopher?" she asked.

"Oh, yes, he's fine. He wants to go back to college and study to be a PA. I admire his determination. He's a nice kid. Even invited me to go fishing with a couple of friends of his. Ian and Daniel."

"I'm familiar with both of them," Purvell said. "I've done business with Daniel for more years than I can remember in New York. He's living down here now and going back to New York when he needs to. Don't you dare repeat this, but he and Cynthia have a thing for each other. It's a long story, but I introduced them and wish they would just get together."

"What's he doing down here?"

"Decided to make a change in his life. Developing properties and repurposing buildings. He's the one who kind of got me thinking about moving here myself." She paused and took his hand. "And meeting you has helped," she said, smiling. Max pulled her hand up and kissed it.

The afternoon was warm, but the breeze from the water kept them comfortable.

"I love this," Purvell said. "Do you know there's still snow some places in New York? Does it ever snow here?"

"It has, but rarely. It gets cold in the winter, but it's basically pleasant. I've always lived in the South."

"Not me. Went from Wisconsin to New York. Maybe if I'd visited this place when I was young, I would have stayed here. I'm tired of the cold, really."

"I like to hear that," said Max, and he put his arm around her. "Did you know I was the doctor who pronounced Cynthia's husband dead and conveyed the news to her?" he asked, shaking his head.

Purvell sat up and looked at him. "I did and I didn't mention it, because Cynthia decided to keep it to herself. Who told you? Not Christopher?"

"He did, but not intentionally. I asked him today how his dad died, and it all came back to me when he told me. Cynthia is one tough cookie."

"She wanted to go back to the ICU, but there weren't any positions—only in the ER, and she needed the job."

"I don't mind telling you, she's a very good nurse and one I don't question when she gives her opinion. She knows her stuff and has a gift for sensing what the patient needs. I love those kinds of nurses because they make my job easier," Max said.

"I'm not surprised," said Purvell. "She always said she was called to be a nurse. We were roommates all through college, and I can tell you she threw herself into it."

"You better not tell her I know," he said, using his arm to pull her close to him. "How's she going to feel about you dating me?"

"I'm not really sure. One step at a time."

Max looked at his watch. "It's getting late; I need to run by the hospital. When do you see the doctor again?"

"Next Friday. I might graduate to a boot I can walk in if all looks well. I can't wait," said Purvell.

"I imagine it's hard to depend on everyone else to get you around. Soon you'll be free again," he said, and they got up and walked back to the car.

The woman sitting to the left of them laughed to herself. She was wearing a hat and sunglasses, so Purvell never noticed who it was.

Connie Dixon got more than she'd planned when she decided to sit on the pier for a while and enjoy the day. Vernon had to go to work after they'd left Betty's restaurant, but Connie had decided to take her own car and do a little shopping before going home. It was amazing what she learned about these people and their lives without even trying. But how to use it to her advantage? Daniel had all the money, and he was in love with Cynthia.

Connie walked back to her car when she knew Purvell and her boyfriend were gone, not paying much attention to her surroundings. She was going over and over her options in her mind. She needed to make a move so she could get the hell out of here. Sometime after Betty's grand opening, she would get the job done.

Connie was so preoccupied, she didn't notice the two men in the car next to her pull out and begin to follow her off St. Simons Island, through Brunswick, over the bridge, and onto Jekyll Island to the street where she lived with Vernon.

"That's her; I'm sure of it," said Dean, the guy driving the car.

"I don't know. We need more proof before we can make a move on her," said Ricky, the passenger.

"You're right. We don't need to make any mistakes. And if we have to kill her, we don't want it to be the wrong person."

"We can be patient. I mean, look how long it's taken us to find her. All that time looking for her in Atlanta and she was hiding in this little paradise. Kind of smart on her part, really. Good thing you found that list of her clients so we could narrow it down," Ricky said.

"Yeah, that guy who lived over on St. Simons owed her a lot of money from gambling," said Dean as they turned off Connie and Vernon's street. "I found out he's dead, but she must have an angle to be here. Good thing I used to date her, so I know the way she thinks. I don't want her to see me, so I'm going to disguise myself before our next move. Let's get a place to stay and we can check her out a little bit more tomorrow. She looks kinda different, so let's be absolutely sure it's her."

"Sounds good. I'm tired—and hungry," Ricky said. "And I need a drink."

They got a room at a hotel on the water, ordered room service, and planned their next move.

CHAPTER 26

To say she was exhausted didn't even touch the way Cynthia felt, but it was worth working all those days to have the next week off. She did a little packing over the weekend and finished the rest of it after work on Tuesday, so she was ready to go Wednesday morning.

"Purvell, are you sure you're going to be fine?" Cynthia asked as she prepared to leave.

"Yes, Cynthia. You go and enjoy Pippa and your family. I've plenty of people who want to help me out. I'll admit I'm going to miss Christopher, though, and his video games. Maybe Daniel will come over and play some with me."

"Have you seen Daniel lately?" Cynthia couldn't resist asking.

"No, but I've talked to him. He was going up to Savannah in his plane, something about a job he's doing. You know, maybe next time I visit, we can go to Savannah. I heard how nice it is," Purvell suggested.

"I love Savannah. Philip and I went there once. Beautiful and full of history. We'll go for sure. Another place I want to go is Cumberland Island, down by St. Marys. Daniel flew over the island when he took Christopher and me up in his plane last month. There's so many places around here I've never visited but have wanted to."

"The next trip, and I promise to be more careful," Purvell said as she hugged her friend. "You have a safe drive and don't worry at all about me."

"I will only a little," said Cynthia. "Bye, and call me every day."

"Yes, ma'am," Purvell responded.

After they put the last suitcase in the trunk, Cynthia handed Christopher the keys. "You drive, sweetheart. I'm so tired I think I may try and nap on the way if you don't mind."

"No problem, Mom," he said, and they were off.

Grace and Granny would arrive in Charlotte before Cynthia and Christopher, but Jimmy was handling the pick up at the airport. Cynthia couldn't wait to see them.

The movement of the car was soothing, lulling her to sleep before the Savannah exit. Just before they reached Columbia, she woke up.

"Whoa, you weren't lying when you said you were tired. You were even snoring," Christopher informed his mom.

"I don't believe you. I never snore," Cynthia replied.

"Ah, yeah you do. I'm getting my phone out next time so I can video you," he said and laughed.

"Not while you're driving," his mother replied. "Where are we?"

"Columbia, South Carolina. I've been waiting for you to wake up because I'm starving. Where do you want to stop?"

"Whereever you want. I really needed that nap. Thank you so much for driving. I don't enjoy doing it that much. I miss your dad when it comes to driving on long trips."

"And I love it. I'll drive back too," Christopher volunteered. "I liked the car trips we went on as a family. We always had so much fun," he said, and then he hesitated. "… Do you mind if I ask you something? You may not want to answer me, but ... do you still miss Dad a lot? Is that why you don't want to date Daniel? Because I think Dad would be okay about it. He would want to see you happy."

Cynthia was taken aback by Christopher's direct question. She didn't have an answer for him. "I can't talk about it, Christopher," she said. "Please understand."

He leaned over and took her hand, much like his father used to do, as she felt a little twinge in her heart.

"Whatever you say, Mom." He squeezed her hand tenderly before he let it go. "I'm going to pull off here for something to eat."

As soon as they finished eating, they got back on the road. Millie called to see how much longer they would be. Her mom and Granny were already there safe and sound, taking turns holding Pippa.

When they pulled in the driveway, it was almost 3:30 p.m.

"We can get our stuff out later," Cynthia told Christopher. "I want to see that baby," she said and she was off.

Pippa was sleeping in Granny's arms. It couldn't have been a more beautiful sight.

"She's even cuter than a few weeks ago," Cynthia spoke in a whisper.

"Here, Millie," Granny said. "Why don't you slip her in the bassinet so we can all visit. I want to hug these two." Millie took the baby gently, and Granny got up to hug Cynthia and Christopher. Grace and Jimmy got their hugs in as well.

"How was your trip, dear?" Grace asked.

"Mom slept through most of it, Grandma," Christopher answered before Cynthia could. "She's been working a lot so she could get this next week off."

"I hope you didn't overdo it, Cynthia," her mom responded.

"No, but the nap helped. I'll be able to rest while I'm here. Now, how was your flight?"

"We spent last night in Milwaukee with Arthur and left from Mitchell Field on a direct flight here. Kind of nice to spend a little bit of time with him also," Granny informed them.

"You ladies sure don't have any trouble getting around airports," Jimmy said. "I offered to come inside, but they said no, they would meet me out at the curb, and sure enough, there they were."

"Well, Granny and I have been traveling for years, Jimmy. It's like an adventure for us. We do appreciate your concern though, don't we, Granny?" Grace responded.

"Yes, we do, Jimmy. It shows you love us, and you can't have too much of that," Granny added.

"Well, thanks," Jimmy said, rather awkwardly.

"When will Pippa wake up so I can play with her?" Christopher wanted to know.

"She sleeps more than she's awake right now, and when she's awake she wants to eat and then soon goes back to sleep," Millie said.

"Is that normal?" Christopher asked, and they all laughed except him.

"For a baby only a few weeks old? Yes," Millie said.

"I had no idea," Christopher replied, and they all laughed again.

Maybe Cynthia should have explained newborns to Christopher. She figured she better tell him that Millie would be breastfeeding too, in case Millie wasn't shy.

"Pippa will sleep a couple of hours if we're lucky, and after I feed her, you can hold her," Millie said.

"I've never held a baby before," Christopher admitted.

"Me neither until she came along," Jimmy shared, "but now I'm a natural. You'll have no problem. It's like holding a football."

"Really? I've got this then," Christopher said.

"Our neighbor Karen Horn had her daughter visiting from Green Bay last summer with her baby," said Granny. "Her daughter came in the house with the child and forgot to close the door of her van. Later on she noticed the door was open and on her car key she has a button to close the door without having to go outside."

"I know, Granny. Isn't that a convenient feature to have with children?" Cynthia said.

"Oh, it is, but what Karen's daughter didn't know was a squirrel had hopped in the van before she closed the door and ended up spending the night inside. Next day Karen and her daughter decided to go into town for a few things, and when the door was opened, that poor squirrel flew out. When they looked inside, they found the critter had pooped everywhere and got under the dash to gnaw the wire going to the radio. They spent the rest of the day cleaning the van out and never went into town."

"It really happened," Grace assured. "We walked down to see it."

"If we ever get a van, Millie, make sure you close the doors. We have so many squirrels around here, I don't want to take any chances," Jimmy said and laughed.

The talk then centered around babies and Pippa, which was no surprise. Great Great Granny, Great Grandma, and Grandma gave advice to Millie and Jimmy, talking about when they'd had children until they heard a squawking cry from the other room. They all jumped up and ran in to watch Pippa wake up.

"She's beautiful, Millie," Cynthia said.

"I think she looks like you did as a baby, Cynthia," Granny said.

"I kind of see Millie," said Grace.

"I think she's beautiful too, but how can you tell she looks like anybody?" Christopher asked, and the women gave him one of those looks he was far too familiar with.

They all took turns holding the baby and snapping a few pictures before Pippa was soon sound asleep again.

Cynthia loved watching the baby as her face made uncontrollable smiles and frowns while she dozed. What could she be dreaming of?

"So, Mom, what did you decide Pippa will call you?" Millie asked.

"I don't know. Have you any ideas?" Cynthia responded.

"Yes, how about 'Cici'?" Millie suggested.

Cynthia thought about is. Jimmy's mom was going to be "Mimi" so "Cici" sounded good. "I like it. 'Cici' it is."

Granny and Grace took over the kitchen. After a day of traveling, one would have thought they needed to rest, but they'd had Jimmy stop at the grocery store after leaving the airport so they could pick up what they wanted to cook for their supper. They were roasting two chickens with mashed potatoes, gravy, carrots, and green beans.

"Mom," Cynthia said, "you don't have to do all this. We could've ordered takeout from somewhere."

"Granny and I have been waiting for this," Grace said, dismissing her concern. "We have a plan. When we make a meal while we're here, we want to make extra so we can freeze some dinners for Millie to use after we've left. Our way of helping out."

"That's so sweet and thoughtful of you," Cynthia said and gave both women hugs. "Let me know what I can do to help. What a great idea."

❦

"It's amazing how we forget what it was like having a newborn," Cynthia said to her mom. They were cleaning up the kitchen after dinner. "When I look back, that newborn stage seems to be such a small part. I know Millie doesn't feel that way right now, because it's all so overwhelming, but I think she's doing well."

"I think it's because Jimmy is such a helpful husband. Why, in my day it was sink or swim. The dads weren't even allowed in the delivery room, and now they even cut the baby's cord. Your father would have been passed out cold on the floor if he had to do that," Grace told her daughter, laughing.

"You're right, he probably would have been. I remember Philip afterwards saying he became a little faint briefly, but when he heard that first cry, he rallied. I feel so blessed to have been able to bring two souls into this world and now to see Pippa. Life is amazing," Cynthia said, as she searched for lids to fit the plastic food containers she'd just filled.

"Just imagine how Granny must feel to look at all of us. To be her age and know we all came from her. Yes, life *is* amazing," Grace affirmed.

"I was wondering if there is anything special you and Granny want to do when you're at my place?"

"Of course we want to see Betty and that darling Ian and his new wife," said Grace. "Maybe they could come over for dinner one night. I looked at that fancy hotel on Jekyll Island one day online and saw they served a Victorian tea at four o'clock every day. Maybe we could do that before Purvell goes back to New York. I've never had a Victorian tea before and think it might be fun."

"I agree, it would be," said Cynthia. "Purvell will love it, and maybe Betty could tear herself away from the restaurant preparations and join us."

"Oh, that would be great. Listen, speaking of Purvell, how's that girl doing? The slower pace of the island must be driving her crazy."

"No, she's doing surprisingly well. I've gotten the feeling she's getting tired of the fast pace of living and looking for a change." Cynthia didn't want to say it was Daniel's move that had Purvell thinking about a change—it was best not to open that can of worms. Her mother was unaware Daniel was living permanently on Jekyll Island, as far as Cynthia knew.

"Wouldn't that be lovely? You know Granny and I haven't given up yet on that child finding a husband. What a wonderful companion she would have made for some man, or for that matter still would. Does she have any prospects at the moment?"

"None at the moment, I'm afraid. I think she's happy with her life, Mom." Granny and Grace had always been concerned about Purvell's lack of a husband.

"Well, I suppose," Grace responded.

Granny came in the kitchen. "When you're done, Christopher wants to tell us something."

Cynthia remembered the last time she was at Millie's and Christopher wanted to tell her he had dropped out of college. *Now what?*

"We're finished, Granny. Just getting caught up a bit. We'll be right in," Cynthia said.

They went into the family room, where everyone was gathered, and sat down.

"So, what do you want to tell us, Christopher?" Grace asked.

Christopher took a deep breath before he spoke. "You all know I decided to take some time off from school because I wasn't sure what I wanted to do. I was doing what I thought I was supposed to do, but not sure it was what I really wanted. I've done a lot of thinking, and I feel like maybe after Dad died I should have taken some time off. We all went through several major life changes as a family then, and I think it all caught up with me after Mom went to England last year. I wondered if I was doing the right thing and knew I had to get away from school to make sure. I don't know if this makes sense to all of you, but it does to me. Anyway, I've had the chance to talk to people who are successful, wondering how they knew what was the right path for them, and have found there is no simple answer."

The room was silent while Christopher spoke; he sounded like a man, not a kid. It was obvious to Cynthia she had been absent for him because of her own unresolved feelings. She felt like she'd let him down.

"I've decided to get a job as a nurse's aide at the hospital where Mom works and see how I really like it. Then I'm going to apply to a physician's assistant program. I'm determined to do this and hope I can count on all your support," he said and then smiled sheepishly.

After a short pause, Cynthia was the first to speak. "I'm so proud of you, son," her voice cracked. "You'll do wonderfully. I'll do whatever you need for support. I can even help you get a job at the hospital."

"Thanks, Mom, but Max is going to help me."

"Who's Max?" she asked.

"Dr. Carroll. He told me to call him Max. I met with him to ask about PA school, and he's the one who suggested I come to work at the hospital as a nurse's aide to expose myself to what it might be like before I jump into anything."

"How nice. I'll tell him thank you next time I see him."

They were all excited for Christopher and happy he was making a decision to go back to school.

Cynthia was curious about Christopher and Dr. Carroll, or she should say, "Max." She wondered when they might have gotten together and why Christopher hadn't talked to her first.

She wasn't going to ask him now but later, maybe when they were home. Right now she was thrilled with his decision.

❦

As is always the case, their visit went quickly.

The Monday before they left, Millie and Jimmy took Pippa for a checkup to find out what they already knew: she was perfect.

One afternoon Cynthia, Grace, Granny, and Christopher took Pippa for a walk in her stroller to give Millie and Jimmy a break and some time to be alone.

Christopher spent Saturday and Sunday at UNC Charlotte, where he'd previously attended school, to hang out with a few of the friends he'd made while there.

On Tuesday before Cynthia, Christopher, Grace, and Granny all left for St. Simons Island, the new little family stood in the driveway waving good-bye, Millie tearful, causing Cynthia and Grace to fight back their own tears.

"Now, Millie," Granny said, "you know we'll be back here to visit, but I want you to bring that little tike to White Lake next summer when she's toddling around. You all can come like you used to do, and maybe now that Arthur's back, he can come also."

"That's a great idea, Granny, or maybe we all can go to Mom's house," said Millie.

"That works," Granny said. "And remember, we fixed enough meals for you in your freezer to help out on those difficult days. It'll be almost like having us here." Granny gave Millie and Jimmy kisses and then put her hand on Pippa's head. "What a privilege to meet you, sweet darling. You have made my life complete," she said and kissed the top of her head.

That did it, a few tears trailed down Cynthia's face as she got into the car to head back to St. Simons.

CHAPTER 27

*D*ean looked at himself in the mirror. "I don't think even my mother would recognize me. What do you think?"

Ricky had made himself comfortable in the living room of the suite they were staying in on Jekyll Island, intent on watching one of those shows where they restore old cars, so he didn't hear Dean.

"Hey, idiot, are you listening to me?" asked Dean.

"What? I'm trying to watch something here," Ricky said, rather annoyed, and turned to Dean.

"So, what do you think?" Dean repeated, turning back to admire himself in the mirror.

"Oh, yeah. I guess it's a good look for you. I thought you looked fine before."

"You dumbass. This is my disguise so Connie doesn't recognize me while we check her out. I said I didn't think even my mom would recognize me. What do you think?"

Ricky tore himself away again. It was a commercial. "Yeah, I would probably walk right by you. I like the fake ponytail hanging from the back of the hat. The earring makes you look like a pirate, and the shades scream Tom Cruise," he said with a snicker.

Dean went over to Ricky and smacked the back of his head.

Ricky grabbed his head and sneered. "Why'd you do that?"

"Because. Turn the damn TV off so we can make our plans."

"I thought we weren't sure it was her?" Ricky responded.

"Oh, I'm very sure it's her. We just need to figure out what she's up to. We'll go back to the place she went to yesterday and watch till she leaves, then follow her, you know, to get an idea of what's going on."

"You seem pretty determined, like you want to get even or something."

"Other than the fact our boss, Mr. Thornberry, wants the money she owes him, I wouldn't mind seeing her suffer," said the tall guy.

"Aww. What'd she do, break your heart?" Ricky asked, laughing.

"Just shut your mouth. You make me sick. When we're done with this, I'm working solo from now on. I don't need stupid-ass people like you dragging me down."

"If you say so," Ricky laughed and got up to get ready for their stakeout.

After they grabbed something to eat, they headed over to where they thought Connie lived to wait for her to make a move.

At about 10:45 a.m., Connie's car pulled out of the driveway, and they followed at a safe distance. She didn't go far before turning down the road to the north pier on the island. After parking, she got out and entered the bait shop.

"I guess she must like to fish," Ricky said.

Dean ignored him and parked a safe distance away then said, "I want you to go in and pretend you're just looking around, but see what she's doing. I'm going to wait here. Don't disappoint me, okay?"

Ricky went inside the bait shop. He guessed it was a normal bait shop. He wasn't sure, however, since he'd never fished a day in his life. He saw Connie talking to a guy in the back, but before he could wander that way, some kid asked him if he needed help. He said "no" and proceeded on his mission, getting close enough to hear what they were saying.

"Do you know what time?" the guy asked her. "If you don't, Ian's on the pier fishing; you can ask him."

"I thought Cynthia might come also," Connie said.

"You sure seem to be interested in her and what she does a lot."

"She seems nice, and she's friends with Ian and Betty. You know I hate it when you criticize me," Connie said.

"I only made a speculation. There was no criticism, Carrie."

Ricky noticed the guy Connie was talking to called her "Carrie." Maybe she wasn't who Dean thought after all.

"I'm going to find Ian," she said and quickly turned to walk away.

Connie proceeded out the door, and Ricky followed as smoothly as he could at a safe distance while she headed down the pier.

There's a lot of people fishing for a weekday, he thought, but what did he know? Connie headed down the left arm of the pier to a man with several poles set up. *That must be Ian,* Ricky thought. He was able to get close enough to hear their conversation while pretending to enjoy the view.

"Do you know what time the band will be at Bennie's Red Barn on Friday?" Connie asked.

"I think they start around eight o'clock, but we're having dinner there beforehand, so let's say we meet you lot about 6:30 p.m. That way we can get a good table," Ian said.

"Are Cynthia and Daniel coming?" she asked.

"I would be careful using those two names in the same sentence, lass," Ian chuckled. "Cynthia has company, but I think we may see Daniel. Why do you ask?"

"Just wondering. So, who's visiting Cynthia?" Connie prodded.

"Her mum and great grandmum from Wisconsin. Lovely ladies, I must say. Can cook like angels," Ian said, closing his eyes with a smile on his face.

"Maybe they'd like to come also. Is that friend of hers still here? I bet she would enjoy it," Connie said.

"You may be right. I was going to stop by tomorrow to see them. I'll ask. Lovely women they are."

"Well, say 'hi' to Collette for me. See you this weekend," Connie said, and she was headed back down the pier so quickly, Ricky couldn't keep up.

He was expecting Dean to berate him for not keeping up with her when he got in the car, but it wasn't the case.

"A guy she was talking to in the shop called her 'Carrie.' Maybe it's not her," Ricky told Dean.

"Oh, that was her," Dean said excitedly. "We got 'er. She's going to be sorry when I turn her ass in."

"Geez, you do have a vendetta against this chick."

"I don't, I'm just doing my job. Let's grab something to eat at that Red Bug Pizza I saw back there so you can tell me what you heard and saw."

❧

Daniel's phone rang.

"Hi, Daniel. What're you doing for lunch today?" It was Purvell.

"I thought Cynthia was coming back today?"

"Not until evening. They left this morning and are stopping at the outlet mall outside of Savannah, so I don't expect them back until late. I thought maybe you could take me to lunch and then show me your new home today. How does that sound?"

"Should be doable. I'll pick you up at 11:30 a.m. I have some business with Brad Davies, and then I'll be by."

True to his word, Daniel was there by eleven thirty that morning.

"How much help do you need getting down the stairs?" he asked her.

"Absolutely none. I've become an expert on getting around. I feel I'm healing well, but until Friday when I see the doctor again, I'll have this cast on. I'm counting on getting something a little less cumbersome then, since I've been such a good girl," Purvell said, hobbling her way down the stairs.

"I hope you do also. That boot has to be annoying. I thought we'd go over on Jekyll to have lunch at The Wharf. It's by the club on the pier, and I'm pretty sure you'll like it," he said.

"I can't wait. Am I dressed properly?" Purvell asked. She was wearing a black skirt that hit just above her knee and a silky, sleeveless blouse in pastel shades.

"You always are, my dear." He shook his head and laughed.

On the way Daniel asked, "So, how's Cynthia been?"

"Very busy with the baby being born and me underfoot. And now with her mom and Granny coming, she has a full house. I know what you want to ask, but she hasn't talked about you at all," Purvell said, and bit her lip.

Daniel looked over at her. "Thanks for being honest. You do put in a good word for me now and then, I hope?"

"Every chance I get," Purvell responded.

Purvell was most impressed when they arrived at their destination.

"What a beautiful view," she said after being seated at their table in The Wharf.

"I think the best one is from the turret on the hotel over there," Daniel said, and he tossed his head that way.

"I haven't been to the hotel yet."

"You'll love it. All those multimillionaires from New York we've heard about in the late 1800s came and stayed on this beautiful island as a refuge. They thought they were roughing it and called the homes they lived in 'cottages,'" Daniel shared. "Hey, do you think you're up to maybe going over to the hotel when we're done?"

"Yeah, I would love that. How was your meeting with Brad this morning?" Purvell asked. "I got to meet him two weeks ago when he came by Heaven Sent while I was helping Betty out. The next day I visited his office."

"You know, he's looking for another partner?"

Purvell hesitated. *Should she tell him?* "I thought you might have had something to do with that," she said. "He asked me to join the partnership. I was going to keep it to myself, but actually could use someone to talk to."

"I only told him he should meet you. It was his decision to make the offer—a good decision, I might add. So, are you going to take it?"

"I'm leaning toward 'yes'. You started me thinking about a change in my life with your move. I love it here. Cynthia's here, you're here, a job is here ..." she hesitated.

"What is it?" Daniel asked when Purvell didn't go on.

"Well. I met someone I kind of like; mind you, it's only been a few weeks, but we've really hit it off."

"Wow, I had no idea," he said, giving her a playful jab to the shoulder. "You do look very happy, Purvell. Relaxed too. Does Cynthia know about all of this?"

"No, none of it," Purvell said, scrunching her face. "Like I said, she's been busy and we haven't had much time to talk. I'll tell her this week."

"So, who's the guy?" Daniel asked.

"I'm not divulging that little piece of info just yet," she said. "Lunch has been wonderful. So, how about we check out the hotel?" she suggested, changing the subject.

Daniel and Purvell went over to the hotel to look around before getting into the car to drive by the "cottages" of the late 1800s. He drew her attention to some other highlights on the route to his home.

"Here's where I keep my airplane," Daniel said, pointing left as they traveled down Riverview Drive.

"What's that?" Purvell asked, looking at a weathered building with only its walls standing.

"Oh, that's Horton House. It was built in the mid-1700s by William Horton, who was a military aide to James Oglethorpe. You should see how this house looks in the evening. Creepy. You won't catch me going there at night," he laughed. "You'll have to brush up on Southern history if you're going to live here and sell real estate, you know."

They continued onto Beachview Drive. "And on the left here is the North Pier, where I go fishing with Ian and Christopher," Daniel explained, "and to the right is the campground Ian manages. Over there is Driftwood Beach, where Ian and Collette had their wedding ceremony. My place is just down the road. There's still more on the lower southern part of the island we can see another time. Past my place is a shopping area called Beach Village, some hotels, a convention center, camps for kids, and a marina."

"I can see why you love it here," Purvell said. "I'm surprised it's not overdeveloped and commercialized. How do they manage to prevent it?"

"The state of Georgia owns the island and is committed to keeping it like this. There's only a certain percentage they'll develop. I hope it never changes. Well, here's The Cottages where I live, much different than the 'cottages' I showed you by the hotel," Daniel said as he pulled in the entrance, down a road, and into his driveway.

"What time do you need to be back?" Daniel asked.

"I don't expect them until late, maybe eight o'clock or so, but I left a note that I was with you. Why?"

"I'm meeting a client at five, so I'll have you back before then," said Daniel.

"Sounds good. Now give me the tour of this beautiful place," Purvell said, and they went in the front door.

❦

Cynthia came in the door and called to Purvell. "We're back!" There was no answer. She turned to her mom. "I bet she's out on the deck," she said and headed that way when she saw the note.

> *Went to lunch and spending the afternoon with*
> *Daniel. Didn't think you would be home until late.*
> *—Purvell*

Right now Cynthia wanted to avoid telling the rest of them Purvell was with Daniel. "Here's a note from Purvell. She'll be back soon," she said, and she stuffed the paper in her pocket.

"It's nice she can get out and about, even with a bum leg," Grace said.

"You have no idea, Grandma," Christopher said as he walked in carrying a suitcase. "She has a posse to entertain her, me included. It's no surprise the woman is in sales—you can't say 'no' to her."

"Oh, you exaggerate, Christopher," Grace said.

Christopher looked at his mom and took a deep breath, shook his head, and went back to the car for more luggage.

"Where are you putting us, dear?" It was Granny.

"I have Purvell down here in the study bedroom, so you and Mom can have your pick of either room upstairs."

"Come on, Grace," Granny said to her daughter. "I'd like the one facing the ocean if you don't mind. I love the sound of the waves coming in to shore. Soothing and hypnotic."

"That's fine with me, mother," Grace responded, and they both headed upstairs talking about going for a walk and unpacking their suitcases later.

"They both sure are an inspiration," Cynthia said to Christopher.

"Yeah, let's hope we got their genes," Christopher said and started transporting suitcases upstairs. "This is just like work at the hotel. I'm not going to miss it when I start working at the hospital," he laughed.

As she watched him head upstairs, Cynthia felt a swell of pride inside; she saw a man before her. How had she missed it before? And then she thought, everyone, even Christopher, was moving forward while she was in a limbo, not moving anywhere.

"We decided to head to the beach," her mother said, startling her, and she jumped. "Oh, I'm sorry, Cynthia. I thought you heard us coming down the stairs. I didn't mean to surprise you like that."

"Why don't you come with us?" Granny suggested.

"I think I'm going to put my stuff away and make a list of a few things I need at the store," Cynthia said. "You can add what you want when you come in from your walk."

"We won't be too long," said Grace. "Just want to stretch our legs a bit after being in the car so long. Wait till you're our age, right Granny? We have to stay limber. I can't wait to get my toes in the sand."

"You got that right, Grace." Granny said, and the two headed out the door to the deck and stairs leading to the beach.

Cynthia went into the kitchen for a glass of water, when she heard a car and looked out the window. Sure enough, it was Daniel's car. Good thing her mom and Granny were still on the beach. Christopher was out in the driveway shooting some hoops and started talking to them. He pointed to the front door and all three headed that way, and then the back deck door opened and Grace and Granny walked through.

"Hello," Purvell called out as she walked through the door with Christopher and Daniel behind her.

"Purvell!" Grace exclaimed as both older women headed straight for her with open arms. They hadn't yet spotted Daniel. "You poor thing. How's that leg doing? You better sit down, dear," Grace insisted.

"I don't need to sit down; in fact I think I'm about ready to get rid of this cast," said Purvell. "I'll find out on Friday. Do you work this Friday, Cynthia?"

"Hello, ladies," said Daniel, silencing the whole group.

"Young man, what are you doing here?" Granny asked and then looked to Cynthia with a crooked smile and then back to Daniel.

"I live here now," Daniel responded.

"Here?" Grace asked, looking at Cynthia and around the house, then back at Daniel with shock on her face.

Both Cynthia and Daniel answered at the same time, "No! Not *here!*"

Cynthia was so flustered. "Daniel has a home on Jekyll Island. Unknown to me, he moved here in January."

"That's right," Daniel concurred. "I've fallen in love with … this area, and after much thought, I decided to be kind of semi-retired. I've started a construction business; in fact I've helped Betty Franklin and her sons build the new retail space on their property. I'm not as semi-retired as I thought I would be, but I'm having a good time," he explained and flashed a handsome smile.

"I see," Granny said, and that was all.

"Where are our manners? Come in and sit down, Daniel," Grace said.

"Well, for a minute or two. I have a meeting not far from here at five o'clock," said Daniel, and he sat down while the older ladies reminisced about the holidays and how much they'd enjoyed Daniel and Purvell's visit. Just then, the doorbell rang. It was Ian and Collette.

"I heard two lovely lasses from the north were coming for a visit, and here you be. Welcome to island time," Ian said as only he could.

"Young man, we're so happy to see you," Granny said, coming forward to hug Ian and then Collette, and taking a hand from each of them in hers. "Congratulations on your wedding and best wishes for a happy life."

"Thank you," Collette said. "So nice to see you both again."

"How did you know we were here?" Grace asked.

"I didn't know if you would be here yet, so I thought I would take a chance. I also wanted to finally meet Purvell in person. We've only talked on the phone," Ian responded.

"Here I am," Purvell said, "the woman who drove you crazy last summer," she said, and she raised her right hand. Ian gave her a hug.

"Well, it wasn't that bad," he said as he pulled away.

"That's not what you told me," Christopher interjected, and they all laughed.

Ian gave Christopher a look and continued. "We want you all to come out on Saturday night to Bennie's Red Barn for some music and dancing. Some lads who fish on the pier have a little band performing that night. They asked if I would come and bring some of my friends," he said, gesturing to everyone.

"I want to go," said Purvell.

"I'll go," Daniel said. "What time?"

"We want to have dinner before, so 'bout 6:30 p.m. would be lovely. How about you ladies?" Ian asked the other women.

"We just got home, Ian, so why don't you let us get back to you. Let's say tomorrow," Cynthia said.

"Sounds fine, darlin', I'll be waiting. Vernon and Carrie are coming also. We should have a grand time."

"Listen, I have to take off for my meeting," Daniel said. "So happy to see you Grace and Granny. Maybe one day while you're here I can take you over to Jekyll Island to see my new place," he added, and he turned to Cynthia, "I'd like to show it to you also."

Her eyes connected with his and she said, "Okay."

"I'm going to leave with you, Daniel," Ian said. "Ladies, always a pleasure. Purvell, you look just like I thought you would," he said, and she chuckled. He gave a bow and they were gone.

"How nice," said Granny. "I love Englishmen. They could say anything and it sounds polite," she said, and they all laughed. "In fact," Granny continued, "we had a French chef at the Walden Falls Diner who was English, by the name of Bertrand Smyth-Ashworth, when you were a little girl, Grace. Do you remember? He ended up in our area after marrying a local girl by the name of Mathelda Graunke. They met in Milwaukee while Mathelda was helping her sister out after the birth of her seventh child. He was the French pastry chef at the Pfister Hotel at the time. They met in a bar one night when Mathelda was out with a few girls she had made friends with at church. Bertie, as she called him, went to culinary school at Le Cordon Bleu in France before he moved to the United States with dreams of becoming a famous chef. I don't think it turned out like he thought, but he *was* famous in Walden Falls. He offered cooking classes in his home for us women in town. I learned a lot from that fella. They ended up moving back to Milwaukee, and I heard he opened a bakery."

"I don't remember him, Mother. I must have been too young," Grace said.

"Like I said, you were a little girl. Ian's the only other Englishman I know." Granny then turned her attention to Cynthia. "Why don't you and Purvell go Saturday night and don't worry about us, right Grace? I insist."

"That's right. Sitting out on the deck here, watching the world go by is what I'd like to do," Grace said, agreeing with her mother.

"I don't want to leave you alone," Cynthia said.

"We're here for over a month, dear. We insist." So it was final. They were going out Saturday night.

"I'm going to get my clothes unpacked," Grace said and went for her purse that was sitting on an end table. She pulled out a credit card handed it to Christopher. "Sweetheart, I'm putting you in charge of ordering us some takeout pizza for supper. We've all had a long day, and pizza sounds good. Surprise us, okay?"

"Okay, Grandma," he said, and he pulled out his phone to get his favorite pizza place's number.

"Good idea, Mom," said Cynthia. "It'll give us all a chance to get our things put away and relax. I have to work in the morning, so I'll want to get to bed early."

Grace and Granny went upstairs and left Cynthia alone with Purvell.

"That didn't go so bad with Daniel, did it?" Purvell said. "We had a really nice day together. I think you two should put things behind you and move forward. Forget the past. Saturday night might be a good start."

There it was, Cynthia thought. *Move forward.* Easier said than done.

"We'll see," was all she said.

"I hope Friday you can go to my doctor appointment with me. Maybe we can stop for lunch together just the two of us since I'll be leaving soon. What do you say?" Purvell asked.

"Sure," Cynthia said, mustering up some enthusiasm. "I hate we haven't had a proper visit."

"It's been a fine visit. I haven't relaxed this much in a long time. Can't wait to tell you at lunch about all the fun I've been having while you've been gone."

CHAPTER 28

The next morning while driving to work, Cynthia thought about how good it had been to see Daniel. But there was still something in her way. She could think of only one person she could talk to who might understand, and that was Betty. She had to see her before Saturday night.

The hospital was as it was before she left. That would never change. Soon she was into the flow of things, and any thoughts of her problems were pushed back when the sick and injured people started coming in.

"Cynthia, glad you're back," said Dr. Carroll. "We missed you."

"Thanks, Dr. Carroll. If we ever have a few minutes today, I'd like to talk to you."

"Well, that's funny, because I want to talk to you also. We'll see how the day goes and squeeze it in somewhere," he said.

It was about 3:00 p.m. before they had a moment to talk.

"What a day," Dr. Carroll said. "I had three guys from a construction site who were hurt when a cable snapped. Bad injuries, but I think they'll be okay."

"My day has been a broken arm, food poisoning, abdominal pain, and chest pains," Cynthia shared.

"Yeah. One thing about working in the ER, no day is ever the same, don't you agree?" he asked, shaking his head.

"Yes, I do. In fact, that's what I liked about working in the ICU, the variation in a day."

"Why don't we step in this examining room to talk," Dr. Carroll suggested, and Cynthia followed him in.

Cynthia started, "I wanted to thank you for your interest in my son, Christopher. He's been struggling to find his place, and I'm so happy he reached out to you for advice. It's good to see him excited about a career path finally, and offering to help him get a job here is above and beyond. I'm very appreciative."

"He's a great kid, Cynthia. He even invited me to go fishing with a couple of his friends. We had a great talk that day. I'm more than happy to help a young adult find their way," he said, smiling.

"I have to remind myself sometimes that he is a young adult. I feel since his dad died I haven't been there to guide him as I should," Cynthia said, and she looked down.

"And that's why I wanted to talk to you," Dr. Carroll said, and Cynthia looked up, puzzled. He took a breath and spoke. "I'm sorry I didn't remember you from the night your husband died." Cynthia was shocked. "Why didn't you tell me I was the doctor attending your husband that night right here in this ER? I'm even the one who told you he had died. I remember that night, but you looked much different, so I'm sure it's why I didn't recognize you. I can't imagine how hard it must have been to start working here and continue. How do you do it?" he asked gently.

Cynthia sat down in a chair, stunned. This was the last thing she thought he was going to say. Everything came crashing in, just like when Dr. Carroll had told her that night. They had been in a room very similar to this one.

"Cynthia, I'm sorry if I've upset you; it wasn't my intention. I only wanted you to know I knew."

"So, I guess Christopher told you," she said, very calm.

"He did only because I asked how his dad died. He meant no harm by telling me—only answered my question. He also told me how much he admired you for being able to work here. You've got a great kid, Cynthia."

"Yes, I do," she answered.

"Listen, we have a full staff right now and things have slowed down. Why don't you take the rest of the day off? I've upset you, I can tell, and I feel bad."

"No, I'm fine," she said, but she wasn't. She had done so well ignoring the fact that she had a history here, but now that someone knew, it was hard to ignore the reality: Philip had died here. "Maybe I will go," she changed her mind. "Please, don't tell anyone, Dr. Carroll," she added, her eyes glassy.

"I would never, and please only call me Dr. Carroll around the other staff. From now on, I'm Max to you."

"Yes. Sure, Max," she said and smiled weakly.

After retrieving her things from her locker, Cynthia went to her car. There was only one place she wanted to be right now, so she headed on the causeway to St. Simons Island, not to home but down Frederica Road until she saw the small parking area and tabby stone pillars. The Wesley Memorial Garden was the only place she wanted to be, and she hoped she would be alone.

Springtime was budding as Cynthia walked into the enclosed area and sat on one of the stone benches. After closing her eyes, she emptied every thought from her head for as long as she could until life gradually entered in again. Although she loved all the people visiting her at the moment, she needed some alone time. Dr. Carroll—Max—

had opened up some wounds she hadn't wanted to face, and she was scared. She had been able to keep these feelings carefully contained, but now they were exposed.

Her thoughts went back to the park she'd enjoyed in England and she wished to put her hands on the conker tree she was so fond of. None of these trees called to her as it did. After a little while, she got up and walked the trail winding through the garden, taking her time, until she was back where she'd started, feeling slightly better and able to cope. It was time to go.

Cynthia was going to make some changes in her life; the biggest would be to move forward out of the stagnation she had become so comfortable with and follow what came from her heart. Saturday night would be a good start by going out with her friends. She hadn't gone out in a while. This would be fun. She needed to do something different and have a good time.

⚜

"I can't wait to hear the words 'your broken bones are healed' from the doctor," Purvell said that Friday on the way to the orthopedic doctor's office to whom Dr. Carroll had referred her.

"They're still going to want you to take it easy for a while and give you some exercises to get the strength back into your leg. There's more healing to be done since the ligaments get slack from being confined and supported in the cast you wore. You may have problems in the future if you don't properly introduce the unsupported ankle and leg into everyday life," Cynthia told her.

Purvell stared at her for several seconds with no expression and then said, "You medical people all sound the same."

"I'm just telling you as it is," Cynthia laughed.

"Okay, okay, I know," Purvell said, and she changed the subject. "I'm really looking forward to lunch with just the two of us. I can't believe how the past month has flown by since I've been here."

The doctor's report was good on Purvell's injury. It was just as Cynthia had told her. They gave her a boot to wear, allowing her to walk without crutches but still keep her injury protected, and she was released to go back to New York. She was to do daily exercises for the leg and ankle and walk around the house with a good supportive tennis shoe. No stilettos yet.

They decided on Barbara Jean's for lunch, where they were seated in a booth and given a basket of their famous breads.

"I love how cute this place is. I feel as if I'm in an old-time diner in Wisconsin. Even the ceiling screams diner," Purvell said.

"I like it also. Hey, let's splurge and get dessert today. They have this thing called 'chocolate stuff' that I can't even explain, you just have to try it."

"You don't have to talk me into it," Purvell agreed.

"I'm sure going to miss you when you leave. I've gotten used to coming home to your smiling face," Cynthia told her dear friend.

"You make me sound like your pet dog, Cynthia," Purvell laughed. "What if you could see me anytime you wanted?"

"What do you mean?" Cynthia asked, taken aback.

"Well, I've been offered a partnership with Brad Davies and Sherrye Gibson at their new real estate office, and I'm going to do it."

Cynthia was speechless. Did she hear right? Purvell laughed at her.

"I know I've taken you by surprise, but I decided I'm ready for a change. New York has been good to me, and I can go visit anytime. The weather is just so awesome here, and so are the people. People I love and a new job challenge, so why not?"

"I'm shocked but thrilled," Cynthia said, squeezing her friend's hand. "What about your business in New York? What will happen to it?"

"I hope my partner will want to buy me out, and if not, I'll look at it as an investment," said Purvell, beaming.

Cynthia was still in shock, letting what Purvell had said sink in.

"Daniel is the one who got me thinking about coming here," Purvell said. "I've been wanting some kind of change in my life, you know, different than what I've been doing for the past several decades," she said and laughed.

"This is great. Wow, tomorrow night we have something to celebrate, don't we?" Cynthia said.

"Yeah, we sure do! Broken bones healed and new job."

"So, what's your plan for making this happen? You've got your apartment to sell and find a place here, although you're welcome to stay with me as long as you want. Just like back in college." Cynthia was excited.

"I'll rent my apartment out in New York, not sell it. It's paid for and in a great location, so the rent will make a nice income for me. Not sure where I'd like to live here yet. I may take you up on your offer until I decide," said Purvell.

"Good, I would love to have you as long as it takes."

"Thanks," Purvell said and then looked down and then up again.

"What is it?" Cynthia asked.

Purvell looked at her with a slight smile on her face, deeply inhaled, and then out again, still pausing.

"*What?*" Cynthia said again.

"I have one more thing to tell you," Purvell said, and Cynthia raised an eyebrow. "You know how Dr. Carroll came over to check on me?"

"Yes."

"Well, he's been checking on me a lot. In fact, while you've been gone, he's not only been checking on me, but taking me out. We're kind of seeing each other. I like him, Cynthia. I've never gone out with a guy like him before and want to see where it goes. I know it's crazy to hear that from me, but whatever," she said and smiled.

Cynthia was shocked once more. "He's a very nice man, and I'm happy to hear all your news," Cynthia said, fighting back a sudden onset of tears.

"I've upset you. Why?" Purvell asked, concerned.

"They're tears of happiness for someone who deserves to find a guy like Dr. Carroll—actually, he told me to call him, 'Max.' I'm happy for you," Cynthia said, but really, she felt panicked.

"It's all new, so we'll see. You know that darn Christopher knew I was seeing Max for some time and never said anything. He blackmailed me into getting Max to meet with him. That kid of yours is something else. I love his drive. You know, I think he could do quite well in sales."

'Something else' is a good way to describe him," Cynthia said, wiping away a tear. "Christopher has decided to go back to school and become a physician's assistant. That's why he wanted to meet with Max. I'm grateful to Max for his guidance, and I told him so the other day. I also found out Christopher told Max he was the doctor who attended Philip the night he died. It's okay. It made me realize I have a few things to work out myself." She paused. "But I don't want to talk about *my* stuff. Let's order lunch and talk about your move."

Cynthia was excited about her friend living in the same place as she. It would be like old times, and wait until her mom and Granny heard.

Purvell told them that night at dinner.

"I can't believe it," Grace said. "You two girls together again. Maybe we better alert the local authorities," she joked. "You both had your escapades in college."

"But we're mature, responsible women now, Grace," Purvell said. "At least one of us."

"Ah, which one of us?" Cynthia asked.

"I can't say," Purvell teased. "But in all seriousness, I think this will be the best time of my life down here, not that New York hasn't been great, because it has, but this place feels like home. It's a new stage of my life. Oh, listen to me being sentimental," she said and wiped a little wet spot from the corner of her left eye, thinking no one noticed.

"Cynthia, next thing you know your mom and I will be relocating to St. Simons. Wouldn't that be something?" Granny said.

"I couldn't be happier at the prospect," Cynthia responded.

"Mother, we're going to stay put especially now Arthur's in Milwaukee. So many years we didn't get to see him while he was in England. He kind of needs us now, at least till he gets used to things. A new life, new job, new place to live, you know how it is, Cynthia," Grace said and looked at her daughter.

Cynthia was taken off-guard. Yes, she knew how it was, because she was still there. She answered her mother with only a nod of her head.

"When I go back to New York, I'll get the ball rolling," Purvell said. "I haven't told my parents yet, but I will once I get back. Now that my brothers are running the farm, maybe they'll both come visit me down here. It'll have to be during the winter, 'cause Dad could never handle the summer on St. Simons for a day," she said, and they all laughed.

"Where do you want to live?" Grace asked.

"I'm not sure, but I was talking to Brad and Sherrye about some cute townhomes being built. A brand new place built the way I want it would be fun, kind of like what Daniel did. I want to stay on St. Simons since my office will be here and I don't think being on the water matters, since I can always come see Cynthia," she laughed. "I have lots of options."

"Maybe you can find a Southern fella down here," Granny said with a sly look on her face.

Cynthia and Purvell looked at each other, both wondering the same thing. Did she know about Max? Granny frequently knew things before anyone else. Maybe Christopher had said something to tip her off.

"You know, Granny, I would like that," Purvell answered.

They were all so happy for Purvell and this big life change. It was a good thing, leading Cynthia to feel encouraged that she too would work out her life one of these days.

CHAPTER 29

"*M*an, it was pure luck you followed Connie into that bait shop and overheard her conversation about going out tonight," Dean said. "Since it's Saturday night, Bennie's will be so full of people, she'll never know we're there watching her."

"Yeah, this is going to be fun," Ricky laughed, slapping his beer gut.

The two had eaten dinner at Bennie's on Thursday, so they could check the place out.

"What we want to do is wait for the right moment when Connie's alone and we just happen to be there," Dean said. "I don't want any of her friends around to hear. We don't need anyone knowing, because then we wouldn't have anything to hang over her head."

"What're we going to do if she runs on us after we make our presence known?" Ricky asked.

"She won't run," Dean said, wagging a thin finger. "She's in over her head; otherwise she would've taken care of things by now. I'm going to strongly suggest we get together later to talk, and then we're going force her to accept our help," he laughed. "I'll point out how hard it must be working alone and how much easier it could be with us on board, but not for free, of course. Knowing Connie as I do, she probably has a little bonus added on the money she's extorting anyway. We're going to get a cut of that bonus too. No one will know but the three of us."

"Yeah, I like your thinking, Dean," said Ricky.

"Yeah," Dean said, sliding his fingers through his thinning hair, "but we're really only on *our* side." The two laughed.

"Hey, listen, I want to go take a nap so I'm at my best tonight. Should I wear something special do you think?" Ricky asked.

"What do you mean 'something special'? This ain't no fancy place," Dean yelled. "You saw it. Just wear jeans and a shirt. You don't want to stick out, but blend in. Do you have any common sense? Geez, when you talk like this I wonder if I should leave you here and go it alone. What the hell's the matter with you?" Dean asked, frowning at his partner.

"Hey, you don't have to get personal, I'm only asking a simple question. I think you're letting this woman get into your head. Think about that, Mr. Common A-hole. I'm taking my nap!" Ricky went into his room and slammed the door.

Dean couldn't wait to finish this job and get rid of him. The end of this partnership couldn't come soon enough.

❦

Cynthia was working in the ER with fog all around her, similar to the kind that rolled off the ocean whenever the temperature changed quickly. The air had a heavy, humid dampness to it. Occasionally there would be a flash of light and then a crack of thunder. As she walked, the fog cleared a path in front of her. She could see other people working here and there, not bothered by the fog or lightning, as if it weren't there. She saw Max down the hall with Purvell, but when she walked toward them, they disappeared into the fog. When she turned to go back the way she'd come, the fog cleared to expose a door that led to the room not used very often in the ER—the room they'd taken her to the night Philip died. She went in and Philip was sitting in the same chair Cynthia had sat in that night. There was a body covered head to toe on the table. "Do it before it's too late. You may not have much time," Philip said. There was a huge clap of thunder and she awoke with a start.

"Are you looking forward to this evening, sweetheart?" Grace asked as Cynthia entered the kitchen in the morning. Her mom was at the coffee maker, pouring herself a cup. "Can I pour one for you, also?"

"Thanks, that would be great," said Cynthia. "I had a weird dream last night that has me unsettled. I think going out tonight and a lighter schedule next week at work will probably be good for me. Do you know I've been so busy, I haven't gone running since before the baby was born? After this cup of coffee, I'm going out to the beach and do it."

"I think that's great, dear," said Grace. "You know how much I envy you being able to run like that. Why, in my day, girls were discouraged from physical activity. I think I might have enjoyed running myself, actually."

"Maybe you could try to run a little, Mom. Why not?"

"I'll stick to my walking. I like it just fine. I may come out there and walk while you run; how does that sound?"

"Sounds great," Cynthia said. She looked up at her mom after stirring some milk into her coffee. She was so happy her mom was still there for her. "You know, I appreciate you for always being so supportive of me. I don't know what I would've done without you the past several years."

"That's what a mother's for. You do the same for Millie and Christopher. I've watched you and think what a wonderful mother *you* are. I'm proud of you," Grace said, and she gave her daughter a hug. "Now go do your run and I'll come out and walk a cool-down mile with you."

"Great, I'll go change. Oh yeah, what are you and Granny going to do tonight?" Cynthia asked.

"Goodness, I forgot to tell you. Betty's coming by this afternoon and picking us up. We're going over to Heaven Sent for a grand tour. You know, see her ovens, menu, and sample some of what she's serving. She wants our opinion on a few things. Isn't that sweet of her?"

"Sounds right up your alley. So, Betty's not coming tonight? I kind of wanted to talk with her, but I'll catch her later. Wait till you see what she's created. You know Ian's wife, Collette, is her pastry chef. The people on this island are going to love it. Betty is one creative and talented lady," Cynthia said and headed upstairs with her coffee and a banana.

She slipped on her running clothes and, after digging around, found her running shoes hidden under some other shoes. It felt good as she slipped them on her feet and tied the laces.

Before she headed out the door to the beach, she hollered, "I'm leaving, Mom."

Grace answered from the kitchen, "Okay, dear, I'm heading out soon myself."

Once Cynthia hit the beach, the rest of the world was forgotten. The ocean breeze blew in her face, whipping her ponytail back and forth. She always started out with the wind in her face because she appreciated that little push at her back when she turned around and headed home.

As always when she ran, a pack of gulls followed until they figured out she had no food for them, a few still tagging along just in case. The sky was cloudless today, and the sun was warm but comfortable. Soon it would be very warm at this time of day, resulting in her running at sunrise or after the sun went down on the other side of the island.

She relaxed and her mind began to wander.

That was one strange dream she'd had this morning. What did it mean, if anything?

After a while, she'd lost track of how much time had passed. Her poor mother must be wondering where she was, so she turned around and headed back, but couldn't stop thinking about the dream. She eventually saw her mother ahead, waving.

"Dear, I was getting worried about you. I thought maybe you were trying to run around the whole island!" Grace teased.

"No, I just lose track of time occasionally when I run. Maybe I should set a timer. I start thinking too much sometimes and don't know where I am."

"I know. I do the same when I walk. Today I was thinking about little Pippa. You know, next week she'll be a month old. I was wondering, do you think Millie and Jimmy would feel comfortable traveling with her? It would be so nice for them to come down here for a few days before we leave. Do you think we should ask them, or is that too much?"

Cynthia knew she would love nothing more than to see Millie and Pippa. Millie had called and texted a picture of Pippa every day. The baby was already changing and Cynthia would love to see the little doll in person.

"What a great idea. It wouldn't hurt to ask. I'll see if she's up to making a trip. I remember the first trips with my newborns. Yikes," said Cynthia.

"Oh, I know, and back in my day we didn't have all the helpful baby paraphernalia the mothers have today. Why, we didn't even have car seats. Now, mind you, our cars were much bigger then, but I put my baby bassinette in the back seat area and laid you in it. When Arthur came along, we pushed it over a bit and you sat next to him with no seat belt. How did we ever manage?" she said, and they laughed.

"I know," said Cynthia. "I have a feeling Millie and Jimmy will have all the new stuff." They laughed again. "I'll ask Millie when I talk to her. You know, she calls every day with a new question, but I'm happy she does. It's funny how some of the things she asks me I know I went through, but I barely remember them. So I tell her what I think and to relax because it'll pass, and sure enough the next day she has something new to ask me."

"Yes, I remember another young mother who did that with me, and I'm sure Granny will say the same. I guess this has gone on for generations. Keeps us all connected as women," Grace said, and she took her daughter's hand.

They finished their walk and found Granny and Purvell on the deck.

"Hope you enjoyed your walk. I was wondering when you'd be back. Thought maybe the two of you got snatched by a shark or something," Granny said. "Purvell and I have been having a nice visit here on the deck."

"No, we're safe and sound," Grace said. "It's just beautiful out there today. Do you even have sharks around here, Cynthia?"

"We must, although I don't hear much about them. I know Christopher and Ian talk about catching small ones when they fish."

"I love Shark Week on TV," Granny said. "I saw this story about how a group of dolphins circled around some people who were swimming in the ocean somewhere, suddenly slapping their tales against the water. The people couldn't believe what was happening, and then they saw it—a great white shark. They started swimming to shore, and the dolphins kept their circle around them till they reached land safely. Saved their lives. Isn't that amazing?" she asked, shaking her head.

"I know we have dolphins around here, but great white sharks probably not, or I would've heard of them. Tell you what, ask Ian next time you see him or his friend Vernon who runs the bait shop over on Jekyll. They'll know," Cynthia said.

"I'm going to do that," Granny said.

"Granny was telling me you're going over to Heaven Sent with Betty this afternoon. When is she picking you up?" Purvell asked.

"At about three o'clock after Granny's nap," Grace said. "We're going to eat dinner at the restaurant and visit. I've never known anyone who owned a restaurant before, you know, as a friend. It's so impressive how Betty has made lemonade out of her lemons. Such a strong, determined woman."

Betty was making the best of her situation for sure.

"It's a lovely place," Purvell said. "Cynthia, have you seen the finished restaurant?"

"No. I only saw it under construction. I'll have to be surprised next Friday, I guess."

After visiting awhile, they all went in, and after lunch, Granny took her nap while Purvell showed Grace how to play some of the video games she had been learning from Christopher. Cynthia went upstairs to read, she said, but she wanted to rest herself. The past weeks since Pippa's birth had been busy, and she was tired. A little power nap was what she needed before going out tonight.

❦

"Your mom and Granny sure do make me smile," Purvell said as they were on their way to Bennie's. "Do you think we'll be like them when we're old? I mean, they really don't seem old to me actually. I want to be like that."

"Yeah, I know what you mean. I think because they keep busy, have a great attitude, and neither are afraid of change, they don't seem their age. They look at life as an adventure," said Cynthia, and then she began wondering what her life would be like as an older woman.

"Cynthia? *Cynthia?*" Purvell asked, shaking her arm.

"What? I'm sorry, just thinking of something. What did you say?" Cynthia responded.

"I said I'm going keep the two of them as my senior citizen role models."

"Me too," Cynthia said. "There's Bennie's." She pulled her car in and found a parking spot. "This is going to be fun. I never asked, but did you invite Max to come?"

"I mentioned it, but he was visiting his daughter this weekend, although he will be at Betty's party next Friday— as my date. I guess that means we better tell your mom and Granny about Max before then."

"What's this 'we' stuff? Besides, they'll be thrilled when you tell them."

"I guess they will," Purvell said and then said what Cynthia wanted to know. "I'm wondering if we'll see Daniel tonight. It would be a good opportunity for you two to make peace."

"I've been wondering if he's coming also. Just don't try to push things along, okay?" Cynthia said.

"Who, me?" Purvell laughed, and Cynthia gave her a sideways look. "Okay," Purvell responded with a warm smile.

They went in and found Ian. They were first to have dinner in the dining room and then move out to the patio area by the Treebar, where the band would be playing. Everyone said "hi." Along with Ian were Collette, Vernon, and Carrie—but no Daniel. Cynthia wanted to ask if he would be coming.

"Where's Daniel?" Purvell asked, reading Cynthia's mind again.

"He just called and said he may not make it, so to have dinner without him. Something about a new client," Ian said.

Cynthia was disappointed.

Dinner was fun, made even better by the beer and wine they drank. Cynthia was starting to feel more comfortable with Carrie also. She guessed Carrie was trying so hard to fit in she came across as pushy. Cynthia would give her more of a chance.

When they were finished with dinner, they moved out to the patio bar area, and pushed together two of the picnic tables to accommodate their group. The band started playing, and Ian and Vernon dragged Collette and Carrie onto the dance floor.

"I'm going to the ladies' room, Cynthia," Purvell said, and Cynthia was alone.

She looked around the patio, thinking the band was pretty good, and happy Ian invited them. Then there he was standing in the door way—Daniel. She waited a moment before she waved. When he saw her, a big smile came over his face, causing her heart to swell.

"Hi, where's everybody?" he asked when he reached the table.

"Purvell went to the ladies' room and everyone else is on the dance floor," Cynthia responded. "I thought maybe you weren't coming."

"I was afraid I may not be able to myself. I have a new client I'm restoring an old building for down in St. Marys. The meeting seemed to go on and on with him this afternoon. We were outside the whole time in the heat. I don't think I've ever sweat that much before in my life," he said and laughed. "By the time I got home, it was too late to make it here for dinner, so I got myself cleaned up, and here I am." He extended his arms out and smiled. *Here you are*, thought Cynthia.

Just then, Purvell came back.

"Hey, glad you made it. You missed a great dinner, Daniel," Purvell told him.

"Purvell, do you mind if we leave you alone?" Daniel asked, and before Purvell could answer, he stood up and took Cynthia's hand. "Let's go dance, Cynthia."

It was a slow song. Daniel put his hand on her hip, then, taking her right hand in his, placed it over his heart as he slid his arm further around her back, drawing her close to him. Cynthia let her head rest next to his and took a slow, deep breath. She could tell he had just shaved before he came; the skin on his cheek was smooth and comforting, and he smelled good. She closed her eyes and surrendered to his movements as he led her through the song, neither speaking a word. When the song finished, they reluctantly parted, his hand wavering a moment on her hip, not wanting to lose the connection.

"Thank you for the dance," she said and smiled.

"No, thank *you*," he responded. "How about another?"

"Sure," she said.

They silently danced the next several songs, and on the last one, she spoke.

"I don't like being at odds with you. I regret some of the things I said when you flew me to Charlotte. Honestly, I don't know why you've hung around."

"Shhh." Daniel put his finger against her lips. "I don't want to hear any more. Let's wipe the slate clean and forget the past. Start over. I said some things and you said some things, let's leave it there. Do you think you can?"

"I do," Cynthia said and met his eyes.

They went back to the table with all eyes on them. Ian was the first to speak.

"So happy you made it, mate. Do you need us to get you something to eat?"

"No," Daniel said with a laugh. "I knew I wasn't going to make it here for dinner, so I made myself a peanut butter and jelly sandwich before I left."

They all laughed, and Ian said, "A real gourmet you are, Daniel."

The rest of the evening was so enjoyable for them all. Daniel took Purvell and her less-encumbered leg to the dance floor for a slow dance and then Cynthia a few more times before it was time to go home.

"I have to stop in the ladies' room before we leave," Carrie, all smiles, said to Vernon. "I'll be back in a minute. This has been such a fun night," she added, surprising herself because she meant it.

On her way out of the ladies' room, a tall man stood in front of Carrie.

"Hi, Connie."

She thought she was going to pass out when she looked up and saw Dean. She found her voice after a moment. "You must have me mistaken for another person," she said and tried to go around him.

"You may have changed your appearance, Connie, but I'd know you anywhere. We can talk now, or maybe later is better for you. It's your choice. Here's my number. Oh, and don't try to run, because the way I look at it, you're gonna need my help to get yourself out of this situation you're in," Dean said, and he handed her a piece of paper.

Connie looked at him for a good length of time as she thought and then said, "I'll call you. Now leave me alone you son of a bitch," she hissed and then shoved past him on her way back to her friends.

"Come on, Vernon, let's go. Thank you, everyone, for such a nice evening," she said quickly and headed to the door, Vernon following at a distance.

The rest of them parted ways. They thanked Ian for organizing the get together and said they should do something like this again real soon.

Daniel walked Cynthia and Purvell to the car. Purvell got in on her side, but Cynthia lingered before opening her door.

"This was fun tonight," Daniel said. "I'll be in touch, okay."

"Okay. I guess I'll see you at Betty's on Friday."

"I actually have to fly up to New York on Thursday and will be gone for a week. Business. Maybe I can see you before I go?" he offered.

"I work Monday, Wednesday, and Thursday if that works, and if not I'll always be here when you get back," she said and smiled.

He leaned over and gave her a gentle kiss. She kissed back, "Good-night," he said.

"Good-night," she responded and got into the car.

"This night turned out better than I could imagine. It's about time," Purvell said.

"Hush," Cynthia said and started the car. She was happy it was dark, because she knew she was blushing. It was a good night and a good step forward for her.

⚜

Connie's head was spinning. How did Dean find her—or recognize her? She thought her makeover was pretty good, but still he'd found her. When he'd said her name, she felt all the blood drain from her body. What was she going to do?

"Carrie, what's wrong?" Vernon asked for the third time. She never heard the other two attempts.

"Ah, I don't feel good," she said, panicked.

"Are you sick? What's wrong? You seem to have been fine up until you went to the ladies' room," Vernon said.

"Yeah, I'm sick," she said, which wasn't a lie.

"Where are you sick? Is it your head or your stomach? Do you want me to stop somewhere before we get home so you can get some medicine? What can I do for you?"

His continuous questions were too much. One right after the other. She needed to think. She felt like she was going to throw up.

"Stop the car, Vernon. Right now!"

Vernon pulled off the road just before they drove onto the bridge. Connie opened the car door and vomited.

"Do you want me to turn around and go to the emergency room at the hospital?" Vernon asked. "Maybe you got food poisoning."

"What I want you to do is stop asking me questions. Don't say another word. I'm sick, that's it, leave me alone!" she screamed at him, tears running down her cheeks.

"Okay, but I'm concerned about you."

Through her tears Connie said, "Just get me home. I want to get home."

They drove the rest of the way without a word spoken, Connie staring out the car window and going over in her head what had just happened. She had been so careful, sure no one would find her.

Vernon spoke when they arrived home. "Can I help you inside, Carrie? You must be weak."

She didn't answer, but opened her door, becoming lightheaded when she rose. Vernon was right there to take her arm and guided her into the house to a chair.

"There, you just sit here for a minute and I'll get the bed ready."

When he came back, he took her arm again and guided her to the bed. She sat on the edge, and he helped her into her pajamas.

"Would you like to get cleaned up in the bathroom?" Vernon asked, placing a hand on her back.

She looked at him a few seconds and answered, "Yes, I think I can make it alone," and got up, heading in that direction.

"Tell you what, Carrie, I have to go to work in the morning, so why don't I sleep in the extra bedroom tonight so you get your rest? I'll get my stuff so I don't wake you up when I leave. How does that sound?"

She thought it sounded good. She wanted to be alone.

"Good," and she added, "Thank you, Vernon."

Connie stared at her face in the bathroom mirror, her makeup all smeared from crying. How did Dean recognize her? And then she remembered the phone number in her purse that he'd given her. Dean wanted to talk to her about the situation she was in. Could the guys from the gambling ring have hired him to find her since she still hadn't given them the money from Philip Lewis? It was possible. Dean had said something about helping her. She could use some help, but could she trust him? It seemed she might not have a choice.

After washing her face and brushing her teeth, Connie felt slightly better. Vernon had opened up the bed, pulling the covers aside so she could easily crawl between the sheets. He really was a nice guy. She would miss him when this was all over and she was gone; in fact she was going to miss all these people, even Cynthia. How could this have happened? Liking these people. *I must be getting soft,* she thought as she fell asleep.

CHAPTER 30

When Cynthia woke the next morning, it was ten o'clock; she couldn't remember the last time she'd slept that late. Her bed felt so good, she stayed there another forty-five minutes before finally getting up. When she came downstairs, the house was empty, but after looking out the window toward the beach, she saw her mother alone on the deck.

"Hey, Mom. Where is everyone?"

"Oh, Cynthia. I'm so happy you got some rest, dear. Christopher took Granny and Purvell out for brunch. They're going to bring us something back. Did you sleep well?"

"I did. I think I needed sleep more than I realized. I hate it that you stayed here for me, Mom. You could've gone and left me a note."

"Oh, it's no big deal for me. I rather enjoy the quiet out here. The waves going in and out, the birds looking for food, and the people strolling down the beach are enough entertainment for me this morning. Speaking of entertainment, did you have a good time last night?" Grace turned to her with a smile.

"I think we all had a good time and decided to do it again."

"I heard Daniel was there," Grace said, looking out at the beach, not Cynthia. "What's going on between the two of you, Cynthia?"

Cynthia didn't answer right away, and her mother waited. "I'm not sure. What has Purvell told you?"

"Nothing. I only know what you've told me and what I've gathered, which is not much. So, why don't you fill in the spaces for me?"

Again she didn't answer right away.

"I can't seem to let him in, Mom. I'm not sure why, because I do care about him." It was the first time she'd been honest and spoken aloud about her feelings for Daniel.

"Sweetheart, Philip was the love of your life and no one will ever replace him," said Grace. "Think of a wedding day as the beginning of a new extension of your life. You grow in that new part of life together, which becomes more than just two people who love each other. Over time, the love you feel for that person transcends what you felt on your wedding day. The love becomes the family and life you create. Look at little Pippa. The result keeps going. The only difference is Philip's gone, but you're still here."

"Yes, I keep telling myself that," Cynthia said.

"We have a part of our self that protects us. It's that little voice that can help us as well as cause us trouble. You know the same one that tells you 'I look fat in this' when you really look good." They both laughed at this common truth.

"That voice blinds us from reality at times," Grace continued. "Living in fear of change or hurt, the voice can prevent you from seeing anything unpleasant you may need to get past. Take some time to think about what I'm saying and I believe you'll find it makes sense. Cynthia, only you alone can decide if you're going to journey on the new road presented before you or stay where it's unchanged and appears safe."

Cynthia stared at the ocean waves, thoughtful for several moments before she spoke. "I have so much going through my head, Mom. My life is not at all as I had it planned."

"So what, Cynthia. The God of this vast universe has something great planned for you anyway. You're just not in on the plan. Trust and take each day at a time. You can't change the past and you can't predict the future. You can only live in the moment you're in."

Cynthia knew these words her mother spoke were true. A change wasn't going to happen overnight, but she was beginning to see a hairline crack in the bubble surrounding her.

"Thanks, Mom. You've given me a harsh truth I needed to hear."

Her mom got up out of the lounge chair she was in and came to Cynthia. Cynthia slid over so her mom could slide in and put her arms around her. "I love you and want to see you happy again." Cynthia buried her head in her mom's shoulder and cried like a little girl.

✤

Later that afternoon, Purvell and Cynthia were on the deck having a glass of wine.

"I'm going to tell them about Max today," Purvell said, referring to Grace and Granny.

"Good idea, since he's going to be at Betty's party with you on Friday," Cynthia laughed. "They'd be disappointed if they didn't know ahead of time."

"I wish Daniel were going to be there also. You two were kind of friendly last night, huh? I hope you noticed I didn't interfere at all, even though I wanted to," Purvell said with a sly look on her face. "Oh yeah, and what was up with Carrie right at the end? She looked like she had seen a ghost or something when she came back from the ladies' room. Took off without a word."

"I noticed that also. Maybe she and Vernon had a disagreement, although they seemed to be having a good time. I like her okay, but she's kind of different. Don't think we'll ever be best friends, but she's friends with Ian and Collette, so that's good enough for me. Maybe she felt sick? That would explain her urgency. We'll see her Friday, so maybe she'll mention it."

"Let's go in and see what your mom and Granny are doing," Purvell said.

They found the older ladies in the kitchen, baking some cookies.

"I would be so fat if I were around the two of you all the time from all your cooking and baking," Purvell said and grabbed three cookies before sitting in a chair. Cynthia sat next to her.

"So, I told you about my new job down here, but I have something else to share," Purvell said, addressing Grace and Granny. "While I've been here, I kind of met a guy. His name's Max. He's coming to Betty's party with me Friday so you'll get to meet him." Granny and Grace looked at each other, Granny with a smile and Grace straight-faced.

"What?" Purvell asked.

"Grace and I had a little bet and she lost," said Granny.

"You made a bet?" Purvell was surprised.

"I said I thought there was a man involved with your decision to move down here, and she didn't." Granny looked in Grace's direction. "I won."

"And what was the wager for this bet?" Purvell was curious now.

"A dollar," Grace laughed.

"You bet a dollar on whether I had a boyfriend down here. Do you do this often?" Purvell asked.

"All the time," Granny said, as she put another cookie sheet in the oven.

"Do you have any bets on me, Granny?" Cynthia asked, but Christopher walked in all excited, saving Granny from having to answer.

"Guess what?" Christopher said. "I got an email from a school Max told me about in Brunswick where I can get my CNA license in four weeks if I go full-time. I'm going to start classes the first of June. Is that awesome or what?"

"I'm so happy and proud of you, Christopher." Cynthia got up and hugged her son.

"You'll do great," Granny said with Grace and Purvell smiling behind her.

"I have to give them a deposit, Mom, to hold my spot, but I don't have the money. I hate to ask you, but ...."

"If the money's a problem, I'll write you a check," Grace said, looking from him to Cynthia.

"It's not a problem, Mom, but I appreciate the offer," said Cynthia. "Let me know how much and I'll transfer it to your checking account tonight. I have money set aside for your education, so don't be afraid to ask, okay?"

"Okay," Christopher said. "I'm going to give Max a call and tell him," he said, and he left the room.

"Is that *your* Max, Purvell? Is he the same one who has been helping Christopher?" Granny asked. She didn't miss a thing.

"One and the same," Purvell responded with a smile.

"He's actually head of the ER where I work," Cynthia said.

"I'm looking forward to meeting this fella," Granny said, raising her eyebrows.

"No more bets though, okay?" Purvell laughed.

Granny looked sternly at Purvell. "I'll be ninety-six years old in July, and I don't promise anything," she said, returning to her cookies.

The room was still dark and the house quiet when Connie woke up. *What time is it,* she thought, and rolled over to see. It was 2:00 p.m. according to the clock on the dresser. She had slept half the day away. Vernon wouldn't be home for a while, which was good, since she needed some time to be alone and think. Her stomach growled, so she got up, used the bathroom, and went into the kitchen.

There was a note on the counter from Vernon. *I hope you feel better. Don't worry about dinner, I'll pick something up.*

He was a nice guy. Too bad for him he'd gotten involved with her. Perhaps he could find a nice girl after she was gone.

Connie fixed a bowl of cereal because it was easy and she thought it might make her stomach feel better. As she ate one spoonful after another, she thought about what to do. How could she make this work to her advantage now that Dean was in the picture? Getting rid of him she knew would not be an option. Dean was a sorry excuse for a human being and would do anything to destroy her. They had been in a short-lived relationship several years ago, the details of which she wanted to forget. The old saying came to mind, keep your friends close and your enemies closer. That's what she would have to do right now.

She was so out of sorts, her brain wasn't working properly, and she thought maybe a shower could bring her back to life. The warm water ran over her body, and for a brief time, she forgot the turmoil her life was in, feeling slightly rebooted when she stepped out of the shower. She really did need some help to pull this off, but she had to come up with a plan before Dean tried to take over. After last night, she knew Daniel was where she would get the money. He was crazy about Cynthia, and she could tell he would do anything for her. She would have to share the extra $100,000 since Dean was surely going to have his hand out for a cut. She couldn't get a break.

When Connie got out of the shower, she wrapped her hair and then her body in towels, heading to the kitchen to make some coffee. The sun was coming through the sliding doors off the living room, so she sat in the light with her cup of coffee, staring out at the day in which she'd failed to be a participant.

Connie wanted to run away, but she had no money and the people from the gambling ring wouldn't stop trying to find her. God only knew what they would do to her when they did. No one would miss her. She hadn't had any contact with her family for years, and they'd never really cared about her anyway. When her new friends found out who she really was, they would hate her. Collette was the first real girlfriend Connie had ever had, and Vernon was kinder than any man had ever been to her before. He'd been so genuinely concerned about her the night before. She was going to miss him.

"Snap out of it!" Connie said aloud. Her attention needed to be focused on the business at hand. She'd better call Dean before Vernon got home and get an idea of what was going through Dean's head. She retrieved his number from the back of her sock drawer where she'd hid it last night, but then decided to get dressed first. *Get it together,* she thought. After putting her clothes on and combing her hair, she went back to the chair in the sun and dialed Dean's number. He answered.

"Hello?"

"Hello, Dean. It's Connie." Connie felt the bile come up her throat.

"Connie, long time no see. I love your makeover. You look great," Dean said with a laugh.

"Forget the BS, Dean, and let's get to why you're here. What do you want?"

"Don't waste any time, do you? You never did, as I recall," he said and his laugh made Connie feel sick. "You remember a little matter of $100,000 owed to Mr. Thornberry by a client of yours? Me and my partner, Ricky, are here to assist you in the accusation of those overdue funds. It was $100,000 originally, but I'm afraid I'm gonna have to charge interest, sweetheart. We're looking at $200,000."

"What? I think you mean 'acquisition,' Dean. And who's the Einstein that did that math, you?" Connie protested. "How do you figure that?"

"Tell you what. Why don't you report this to the Better Business Bureau?" Dean said and laughed until he fell into a fit of deep, raspy coughs. "I'm sure they'd love to hear that one."

"Drop dead. I hate your guts, you snake," Connie said.

"You don't have to like me, just work with me on this little transaction. Mr. Thornberry has waited long enough and ..."

"I'm working on a plan," Connie blurted, cutting him off, "but your appearance could blow the whole thing. How would Mr. Thornberry like that? Keep your nose out of my business and your ugly face out of my sight."

"That ain't going to happen, sweetheart. I'm going to help you so *you* don't screw up—and by the way, I want a cut. It's either that or I tell the guys where you are and let them handle it themselves. I think your best option is to work with me. Let's meet somewhere. Ricky and me have been spending a lot of time checking out this area. Have you heard of Epworth by the Sea?" he asked and laughed. "Probably not. It's a religious retreat center on St. Simons, and I know you wouldn't be caught dead around church folk."

"I'm hanging up right now."

"No, you won't," he said. "Meet me there tomorrow, say 11:00 a.m. Park by the little white church, then walk over to the water and sit on one of the benches. I'll find you."

"No. I can't meet until Tuesday."

"I said tomorrow," Dean demanded.

"You remember Nicole, one of the women you cheated on me with? Nicole with the husband who was a body builder who would smash beer cans on his forehead? I'm sure you remember how he wanted to kill you with his bare hands. He gave me his phone number and said to call if I ever came across your ugly face. I still have the number," Connie said, hoping the bluff would work.

"Fine," Dean said, sounding annoyed. "You better show up is all I have to say."

"I'll be there. Don't bother me before then, you hear?" she told him.

"Yeah, yeah, whatever. Oh, and nice house, sweetheart. I'll be keeping my eye on you and that little boyfriend of yours," he sneered and laughed his sick laugh.

Connie hung up.

The first step was done: now what? She had just two days to figure it out what she would do next.

CHAPTER 31

*M*onday when she was back at work, Cynthia asked one of the other nurses if Dr. Carroll was there and she was told he wouldn't be back until Wednesday. Cynthia wanted to thank him for being so kind to her the other day.

At about 11:00 a.m., she took a short break and noticed someone had called her. It was Daniel. She got a little excited and called him back right away.

"Hi, Cynthia. How's your day? Do you have a couple minutes to talk?" he asked.

"So far my day is good. Yeah, I have a few minutes. How's yours?" she smiled, wondering if he knew he'd just made her day by calling.

"I'm running around all over the place, but will mostly be at Betty's getting the final touches done for Friday. Hate I won't be there, but you can tell me all about it when I get back," he said.

"I'm so happy for Betty. She's quite the business woman."

"I agree, and her boys are going be a lot of help for her. They're both smart young men. I've enjoyed working with them on this project. Well, I called for a reason. I wanted to invite you over for dinner tomorrow night and show you my new house." He sounded excited.

"I don't think we have anything going on that I know of, but I'll have to check with Purvell, Mom, and Granny," Cynthia replied.

There was a pause. "I didn't mean everyone," he said, "I just meant you. I was hoping to see you tomorrow night, because I'm leaving to go to New York early Thursday morning. Thought it would be nice to see each other before I go. What do you think?"

"I would love to come over," she heard herself say before she'd even thought about it.

"Great." He sounded so happy. "I'm going to grill for you. I've gotten pretty good at it," he added with a little chuckle.

"So, what time should I come?"

"Since you have to work the next day, what do you think?"

"How about 6:30 p.m.?" she suggested.

"I can't wait," he said.

"Me too," she replied, feeling a little nervous. "Well, I better get back to work. I'll see you tomorrow night. Thanks for inviting me."

"Thanks for coming," he said. "Well, until then. Bye, Cynthia."

❧

She told Purvell, her mom, and Granny about Daniel's invitation when she got home from work. The three of them began talking among themselves at the same time with unbridled excitement, and Purvell asked what she would wear. Then her mom and Granny began speculating on what he might be grilling for dinner.

"Okay, that's enough," Cynthia told them. "You're making too big a deal out of this and I don't want to hear anymore. I'm tired from work, so good-night," she said and went up to bed. Before she could sleep, however, she asked herself a dozen times, *What am I going to wear?*

The next day she was off, so first thing when she got up, she went through her closet and picked out her clothes for that evening. After she felt good about her outfit, she got ready for the day and called Millie to see how things were going and to suggest they come visit.

"Oh hi, Mom," Millie said. "You've called at a good time; I just finished feeding Pippa. Jimmy's going to hold her awhile and then put her in her bassinet. What's new with you?"

"Oh, nothing much. Have you talked to Christopher?" Cynthia asked.

"Yes, he called and told us about starting CNA school and getting a job at the hospital where you work. That guy Max seems to be his new buddy."

"That guy Max also happens to be head of the ER and my boss. I guess he forgot to tell you that ... oh, and Purvell and Max are dating."

"*What?* I'm afraid motherhood has taken me out of the loop."

"That's not all," Cynthia added. "Purvell has decided to move to St. Simons Island. She's been offered a partnership with Brad Davies, the man who sold your dad and me this house and took care of renting it while I was gone. All this happened while I was in Charlotte after Pippa was born, so I know how you feel about being out of the loop."

Millie started laughing. "Sounds like you're taking it all in stride as usual."

"Thanks. The reason I called, other than to see how you all were, is that your grandma wondered if maybe it might be possible for you and Jimmy to drive down here with the baby. We all would love to see you before they go back to White Lake. What do you think?" she asked.

"We were actually talking about the same thing, but do you have room for us?"

"I thought of that. Purvell's broken bones have healed well, but the doctor wants to see her one more time before she leaves a week from this Saturday. I was thinking you could come the day after Purvell leaves and stay as long as you like. Grandma and Granny leave the following weekend, so that should give you a good amount of time to be with them," Cynthia proposed.

"I think it sounds good, but let me talk it over with Jimmy."

The rest of their phone conversation centered around Pippa and what she was doing now, along with Millie's current baby questions. Cynthia loved hearing every detail of her granddaughter's life and couldn't wait until she held the sweet little baby in her arms again. They said good-bye and Millie promised to text a picture the next time Pippa woke up.

Next, Cynthia called Betty.

"Hi, Betty. It seems like I haven't seen you in forever."

"I know; I've been so busy with Heaven Sent, and you've been busy with your family and work. I hope you're not calling to tell me I won't see you Friday at my opening party," said Betty.

"No, I wouldn't miss that. I was wondering if you had a little time to see me this morning? I can meet you anywhere."

"I'm at Heaven Sent, so come anytime you want."

"I appreciate you letting me come by."

"I would drop anything for you, Cynthia," Betty said. "You're like a sister to me."

"I feel the same about you," Cynthia said, smiling. "See you in an hour or so."

With that settled, Cynthia went downstairs to get some coffee and tell her mom and Granny the news about the baby's visit.

"I hate I won't see her," Purvell said, "but I understand. Besides, once I'm settled here she'll be seeing her Auntie Purvell every time she visits. I'm going to spoil her rotten."

"I can't wait to start buying her cute little dresses," Cynthia said. "I want to make sure she's the best-dressed little girl in Charlotte."

"And don't forget to get shoes to match. We have to train that little girl the right way," Purvell added, and they all laughed.

"Maybe we can run down to the mall in Jacksonville before they come, Cynthia, to get her wardrobe started," Grace suggested.

"Great idea, Mom. How about this weekend or next week one day? I'll check my work schedule."

"Can we stop at a toy store?" Granny asked. "I want to get her a baby doll to remember me by."

Cynthia got a lump in her throat and couldn't speak for a moment. The reality of Granny's age and the fact that she wouldn't see this precious little girl grow up put an ache in her chest.

"Of course, Granny. It'll be our first stop. And let's call the doll Hazel Pearl after you. I think it's a perfect name for a baby doll." Cynthia gave her Granny a hug and kiss. No one spoke, all thinking the same thing.

Grace broke the silence. "So, what's planned for today?"

"I hope you all don't mind, but I'd like to go out by myself to run a few errands," Cynthia said.

"Why, no, dear. Granny and I want to do a little baking this morning. We've been watching an English baking show on TV and want to make a Victoria sandwich cake today, inspired by the show."

"I love that show," Granny said. "They make things I never heard of. Lots of French pastries and interesting 'puddings' as they call them."

"And as always, I'm the taste-tester," Purvell said.

"Why don't you pick up something for lunch before you come home. Surprise us," said Grace.

"Sounds good. I'm going to grab my purse and keys and head on out," Cynthia said, and she was soon on her way.

Betty's shopping plaza had come a long way since Cynthia saw it last. Several signs were hung over the other shops that were also getting ready to open their doors, but the first sign you saw when you drove in was for Heaven Sent. The restaurant looked warm and inviting with its red, white, and blue striped awnings extending over the patio in front, where there were several wrought iron table and chairs arranged for people who wanted to sit outside.

Cynthia tapped on the door to be let in. A little bell tinkled as Betty opened it and greeted her.

"We have to lock the door because folks keep wanting to come in and eat," Betty told her. "I'm glad the word has gotten out and pray they'll come back this Saturday when we open for real."

"It all looks beautiful, Betty. You should be so proud."

"I've had lots of people helping me, like these two." She pointed to Collette and Carrie, whom Cynthia could see through the door leading to the kitchen. "And Brad, Daniel, and the boys. None of this would be happening without them."

"But you're the brains behind it all!" Cynthia said, and they laughed.

Collette came out of the kitchen.

"Hi, Cynthia, didn't know you were coming by," she said. "We're furiously getting ready for the party Friday and then our first day of business Saturday. I hope we're going to see you?"

"I wouldn't miss it. How's Carrie? She seemed as if something was wrong at the end of the evening when we were at Bennie's the other night."

Collette looked to the kitchen before she spoke and lowered her voice. "She hasn't said anything, but I noticed she's not her regular self. We all have those days."

"Yes, I guess we do," Cynthia responded.

"Cynthia and I are going over here to talk a bit," Betty said. "Would one of you mind heating up some water for a cup of tea and maybe a scone for us would be nice. What do you say, Cynthia?"

"Sounds perfect," she agreed, and the two went to sit at a table far from the kitchen.

"Now, what's going on?" Betty asked with those all-knowing eyes intent on Cynthia's face.

Cynthia didn't hesitate. "How is it you've been able to move forward so well since Jack died? I seem to go through the steps day to day, but then I go backwards."

"Does this have to do with Daniel?" Betty asked.

There was no fooling Betty. "Yes. He had some harsh words for me several weeks ago, and then after I talked with Mom, I realize I have a problem." She looked down at her hands and then back into Betty's face. Betty took her hand.

"He's a mighty nice guy, Cynthia, and he's crazy about you. Is there something about him you just don't care for?" Betty asked.

"No, I like him, but I still think about Philip and even have had some dreams involving him."

"We'll think about our husbands till the day we die. I know Philip had some added baggage you've had to deal with, but he's not here and you are. You now have to decide where your life goes. I can't say for sure what I'd do, since I haven't met someone like you have. You may be giving me this same talk one day, but I think you should take a chance and get to know him. He loves you, I can tell," Betty said and smiled warmly.

Just then, Carrie quietly appeared from around the corner with two cups of tea and a plate with some scones. "I brought an assortment of scones for you. Doing okay, Cynthia?"

"I'm fine, Carrie. I was wondering if you were okay this past Saturday night? I hope you weren't sick or anything. You seemed to rush out, and I thought you didn't look like you felt well."

"No, I was fine. Nothing's wrong. Can't imagine why you thought that," Carrie said with an uneasy laugh. "I've got to get back and help Collette," she added and was gone.

"I don't know about her," Betty said. "I get the feeling she needs some money. I've been having her help out here to get things ready, and I'm paying her in cash because she asked me to. She and Collette have become friends, but I just don't know. She's troubled in some way, and you know me, I'm always drawn to troubled souls."

"I know that first hand, but I understand what you're saying. She was definitely upset Saturday night. Purvell said her face looked like she saw a ghost. I don't know," Cynthia said.

She took a sip of her tea and continued, "Well, talking to you has helped me. Daniel's invited me to see his new house and fix me dinner tonight. I'm going to take it slow and get to know him because he *is* a nice man, and he's still hanging around after putting up with me and my indecision. He must care for me to do that," she said and laughed, as did Betty.

"Trust me, he does," Betty agreed.

Carrie came rushing out of the kitchen in a panic. "Betty, I have to run out for a little while, but I'll be back," she added and ran out the door.

"Like I said, there's something about that girl," Betty sighed. "Now I want to hear more about the baby."

They spent the next half hour visiting, and then Cynthia said she had to leave so she could pick up lunch to bring home.

"Nonsense," Betty said. "Collette, can you whip up a few sandwiches for Cynthia to take home? A little assortment?"

"Yes, ma'am, I sure can," she said, and in a few minutes, Collette came out carrying a brown-handled bag with the Heaven Sent logo printed on it. "Our first take out," Collette said and clapped her hands as Cynthia took the bag.

"Thank you, Betty. They will love this. Bye, Collette. See you ladies on Friday," Cynthia said.

"And have fun tonight, Cynthia. Life is for the living. You're such a vibrant woman. Don't waste what you have," Betty said to her friend and hugged her good-bye.

Cynthia was headed home when she was forced to take a detour down Demere Road toward Epworth by the Sea, a retreat center on the island. She decided to take a more scenic route home, rather than deal with the backed-up traffic and turned right on Sea Island Road, wanting a little more time by herself. That's when she saw Carrie pull out of the entrance leading to the retreat center. *That's odd,* she thought. She wondered what Carrie might be doing there. It was just like Betty said: there was something about that girl.

CHAPTER 32

Connie hadn't wanted to leave Heaven Sent to meet Dean and miss the opportunity to listen in on more of Betty and Cynthia's conversation. She wanted to hear anything she could about the details of Cynthia's relationship with Daniel.

Epworth by the Sea, where she was to meet Dean, was at the end of a long road. A sign indicating Lovely Lane Chapel was to the left. She couldn't miss the old-timey white church facing the water. Dean had told her to park by the chapel, then walk over to the water and sit on one of the benches; he would find her. She was sure Dean was there somewhere watching her every move. To think she used to like him. That was before she'd found out he had two other girlfriends besides her. He was a scumbag and a loser.

"Hi, Connie." It was Dean's annoying voice behind her.

Connie slowly stood and turned around. "Hi, Dean," she said, trying to sound calm. Then she looked at Ricky standing behind him. "Who's the chubby guy?"

"Hey, watch it," Ricky said. "This is all muscle."

"Right," Connie said and looked him up and down.

"This is my partner, Ricky," Dean said. Ricky smiled, but Connie ignored him.

"Let's get this over with. I have things to do."

Dean began, "We're here to assist you with the collection of the $200,000 owed Mr. Thornberry."

"I don't need assistance, especially from you. I'm leaving," Connie said, and she turned to walk away.

"I wouldn't do that, Connie." He hesitated and smiled. "If you walk away from here, my orders are to contact Mr. Thornberry's associates, and you're a dead woman by sundown."

Connie felt sick to her stomach like she had Saturday night when she first saw Dean. She knew they wouldn't hesitate to kill her.

"Okay, so you help me collect the $200,000 and I'm free to go. Is that it?"

"Pretty much," Dean said. "I figure you already have an idea of where you're gonna get the money, so why don't you tell me?"

What choice did she have? He would turn her in and never think twice about it.

She tried to swallow but her throat was dry. "One of the guys I was with the other night, Daniel Benton, is in love with Cynthia Lewis. She's the wife of Phil, the guy who owed the $100,000 from his gambling debt when he died. This Daniel Benton is a millionaire—maybe even billionaire. Guy's got his own plane and everything. I've done some checking up on him and he's got so much money, I don't think he'd miss $200,000."

"Nice job, Connie. But how were *you* gonna to get him to give *you* this money? Were you gonna just go up and ask him for it?" Dean asked, and his raspy cigarette cough started up as he laughed.

Connie rolled her eyes. "Cynthia's got several family members. All I've gotta do is make Daniel think one of them could get hurt if I don't get the money."

"Yeah, it's always convenient when they have family," Ricky said and laughed, attempting to be part of the planning. Dean gave him a sideways look as if to say "shut up."

"So, if the guy has that much money, I say let's tell him we want $500,000. That's $100,000 for each of us when all's said and done," Dean said, wringing his hands with a greedy look on his face.

"Wow, I didn't know you were capable of simple math, Dean," Connie said with a step toward him.

"Shut up. You haven't changed a bit. Same old mouthy bitch," Dean said and spat at her feet.

"But yet you're here working with me like the old days. Sure, we can ask for the $500,000," she said, sounding as confident as possible. *Is this guy crazy?* she thought.

"So, what was the first step of *your* plan, if I may ask?" Dean inquired.

"I was going to meet with Daniel and tell him how it is," she said.

Dean laughed in her face. "Seriously? Tell him how it is?" he continued to laugh, the cough starting again as he turned red in the face, trying to get back in control. *Maybe he'll choke and drop dead before my eyes,* Connie hoped.

"The first change in your plan is *I'm* going with you and *we* talk to him together. Ricky will wait in the car if we need to get away quickly," said Dean, catching his breath.

"Why do I always have to wait in the car, Dean? I'm tired of you yanking me around on a leash like I'm your dog," Ricky whined.

"Shut up," Dean said, squinting at Ricky. "The sooner we get this thing going, the sooner I'm rid of both of you." He looked from Ricky back to Connie, then pointed his finger at his chest and raised his voice. "*I'm* gonna call the shots. *I'm* gonna let *you* know when to call this Daniel Benton, and *I'm* gonna tell you where to set up a meeting," he said; then he pointed his finger angrily at Connie. "Keep your phone close. You can leave now and wait to hear from me."

Connie had her gun in her purse and thought about blowing Dean's brains out, but that would just get her in more trouble. All she wanted to do was get this over with, and as far away from here as possible. Maybe even leave the country and start over.

When she reached her car, she looked back to where they had been, but both men were gone. This meeting hadn't gone quite as she had planned. She would have to see it through with Dean in charge; otherwise she was sure he'd kill her.

"That Betty is one sweet girl," Granny said. "These sandwiches look delicious."

"Why did you stop by there, dear?" Grace asked.

"I was driving by and decided to see if anyone was at the restaurant. The place looks great," said Cynthia.

"That was nice, and look at these sandwiches," Grace said, taking in the scent of freshly made bread. "This smells wonderful. Let's eat."

They all chose a sandwich and sat at the kitchen table, talking about nothing in particular.

"Oh yeah, how did your cake turn out?" Cynthia asked.

"Well, take a look," Grace said and retrieved the cake.

"Beautiful, Mom." It was a yellow cake sandwiching butter cream frosting and strawberry jam between the two layers with a dusting of powder sugar on top. "Can we have some now?"

"We're going to have ours later, but I'm going send a piece for both you and Daniel to have tonight as your dessert," Grace said. She was very proud of her creation.

"Thank you. That's very thoughtful," Cynthia said, her mother beaming.

"And I have a surprise for you," Purvell said to Grace and Granny. "Max was coming by to take me out to dinner somewhere tonight. What do you say I invite him for dinner here instead so you can check him out?"

"I think that sounds like a splendid idea," Granny said. She loved meeting new people.

"But we were going to have leftovers tonight. That's not appropriate for a guest," Grace said to Granny.

"Trust me, your leftovers are better than what most people normally eat on a daily basis," Purvell told her. "Max is a casual guy and will love it."

"Good, we're settled then. Tell him to come by anytime he feels like it, but we're going to eat at six o'clock," Granny said with finality.

"Well, it looks like I'm overruled," Grace said.

Granny laughed.

❦

Although she knew the location of The Cottages where Daniel lived on Jekyll Island, Cynthia still put his address in her phone's GPS so she would be sure not to make a wrong turn. Her thoughts during the drive were entirely about the upcoming evening. *Relax and let be what will be,* she told herself as she approached the bridge.

The view from the bridge this time of day was like two colorful paintings. On one side was the wide expanse of the ocean in the distance and on the other, the sun sinking over the horizon to the west. She felt so small driving over the bridge.

When she was almost to The Cottages, she took several deep breaths. She decided she needed a little time to gather herself and pulled into the Convention Center parking lot for a moment. She looked at her eyes in the rearview mirror. This was silly: she was a grown woman acting like a teenage girl who had never gone out with a boy before. *Just relax and enjoy yourself. Let the evening unfold with no expectations.* A few more deep breaths and she continued to Daniel's.

His house was the third to the left on the street. The homes all looked very similar, yet each with a uniqueness to them. She picked up the container with the dessert her mom had made and a bottle of wine she had brought to have with dinner. Daniel must have been watching for her, because before she was parked, he was there to open her door.

"Hi, I was wondering if you'd gotten lost. Did you have a hard time finding my place?" he asked.

"No, not at all. I guess I misjudged the amount of time it would take to get here," Cynthia fibbed, not wanting to tell him she'd stopped a few minutes to get her act together.

"Well, come in," he said and led the way.

The house still had that new smell to it. He had a mix of leather and cloth furniture along with modern and traditional pieces in navy, light blue, and beige. His taste in furniture and color was appealing to her and had a homey feel.

"I love it," she said. "You have great taste and a good eye for color. I'm impressed."

"Wish I could take credit for it, but I hired a decorator," he laughed, looked down and then up again. "I told him what I liked and then he put it all together. He did good, because I feel very at home here. Let me show you the rest of the place before we go out to the porch."

"Okay, but let me give you this. A bottle of wine to have with dinner and dessert from Mom and Granny."

"Well, isn't that sweet of them? Can't wait to try it. Why don't you put our dessert and wine on the counter and then I'll give you the tour."

He took her upstairs first and then showed her the downstairs before opening the wine and heading out to the screened-in porch.

"I had to have a screened-in porch added because of those darn no-see-um bugs," Daniel said as they sat and enjoyed their wine. "You know the ones I'm talking about."

"I sure do. The most annoying things ever."

"I agree. They won't leave you alone. Since I've moved here, I love sitting on the porch with a beer at the end of the day, listening to the world. The ocean, animal, and bug noises, an occasional plane overhead—peacefulness. Such a difference from the noises of New York."

"I enjoy the sounds also," she said and felt the peace he was talking about. There was a lull of silence, not uncomfortable but companionable, as she looked at him and smiled. Then in an instant, a horn honked, several voices shouted back and forth, a car door slammed, and an engine revved. The moment was broken.

"Do you want another glass of wine?" he asked, getting up to go in the house.

"Sure. Let me come in for it," she said and followed him inside. They chitchatted as he poured her wine, but before going back out to the deck, he came in close and kissed her gently. "I hope you don't mind, but I had to do that," he said and smiled, lifting her chin toward his face.

"I don't mind," she said and kissed him back.

They returned to the porch and sat.

"When's the last time you talked to Christopher?" Cynthia asked.

"It's been a little while, why?"

"Much to my pleasure, he's going back to school," she said, smiling. "It's kind of crazy the way it's all come about. Christopher has become friends with Max Carroll, the doctor who I report to in the ER. I didn't even know they knew each other. He met with him to talk about becoming a physician's assistant. Max has been very encouraging and given Christopher good advice, so at this point Christopher is going to school to become a nurse's aide and see how he likes it before he applies to PA school. I'm grateful to Max for the interest he's taken in Christopher. He's even going to help him get a job at the hospital after he's done with his nurse's aide classes."

"That's wonderful. Christopher is a great kid. You and your husband did a good job raising him. So, how did he and Max meet if you didn't introduce him?" Daniel asked.

"Why, through Purvell, of course," Cynthia responded.

Daniel looked at her blankly. "Purvell? How would Purvell connect them?"

"Oh no. I thought you knew. For once, I'm not the one out of the loop. I don't feel bad telling you since I'm sure she's told you a few of my secrets."

He looked down into his wine glass and took a sip before looking up and saying, "Never." They both laughed.

"She's been dating Max. I just found out myself. This all happened while I was out of town when Millie had the baby. They first met in the ER the night of her accident. When I had to leave for Pippa's birth, Max offered to check in on Purvell for me, and it appears they hit it off."

"She did indicate there might be someone she was interested in, but not his name, when she told me about accepting a partnership with Brad … Now I may have spoken out of turn. You know she's moving down here, right?"

"Yes, and she's told Mom and Granny also, so everything's out in the open now," she said, and they both laughed again.

"I'm happy she's going to be moving down here. I enjoy her company and I like working with her. I know you're happy," said Daniel.

"Yes, it'll be nice," said Cynthia. "So, what are you grilling for me?"

"I picked up some perfectly marbled ribeye steaks, or at least the butcher said they were perfect, along with a salad and fresh baked bread."

"Wow, you bake bread?" Cynthia was impressed.

"It's the take-and-bake kind from the grocery store," he said and smiled.

"My favorite kind. Please let me come and help you," she offered.

"Okay, I never turn down help in the kitchen," he answered.

Cynthia put together the salad while Daniel got the steaks on the grill and popped the bread in the oven. She realized how much she missed having someone to do this with and remembered her mother saying, *You can only live in the moment you're in.*

She was loving this moment.

They ate on the porch by candlelight, finishing off the bottle of wine with their dinner. The dessert was a perfect ending. This was the best night Cynthia could remember in a long time, and if she were truthful, the best night since last year when Daniel rented her house and they first got to know one another. Sadly though, it was time for her to go home.

"It's getting late, Daniel, and it's time for me to leave. I've enjoyed tonight more than I can tell you."

"I feel the same way," he said as they walked inside from the deck. "Please thank your mother and Granny for dessert. It was wonderful," he said and took her in his arms, kissing her passionately. She reciprocated, feeling content. This continued for several minutes—maybe longer.

"I wish you would stay," he said as he pulled back and looked her in the eyes, brushing her hair from her face. At that moment, she knew she loved him. She also knew she had to take it slow. Last year things had moved too fast, and she didn't want to panic like she had then.

"I wish I could also, but I'm not ready yet. Can you understand? I just need some time to take it slowly."

"I do understand, but I still feel the same way about you," he said. "I told you last year when I found you on White Lake, 'I know you will love me'."

Now she knew it also.

They walked to the door, not uttering another word, smiled at each other before one last kiss, and she drove home with a smile on her face and an overflowing heart.

CHAPTER 33

Connie had a text message on her phone from Dean when she woke up Wednesday morning. *Meet me at Horton Pond 11 a.m.* Dread flowed through her body as she dressed. The pond was off the main road around Jekyll Island on the northeast side. It was secluded and not a place where you would fish, unless you were looking for turtles or alligators.

Her stomach was upset, so all she could manage was a cup of black coffee before she left. Last night she'd picked at her dinner, prompting Vernon to ask questions. She assured him everything was fine. It was really nice the way he was concerned. She'd never had anyone take notice of things like that before and wasn't sure how to respond to him.

Connie arrived at the pond five minutes before she was to meet Dean. He pulled up right on time with Ricky in tow. They made an awkward pair. Dean tall and skinny, and Ricky short and chubby. If it weren't for the situation, she would laugh.

"Ricky, you better go back and wait in the car," Dean told him.

"Why, Dean? I'm part of this little trio too. So, I have a say in what goes down," Ricky complained, sounding like a child.

Dean turned to look at him. "No, you don't, I do. And only me. So, you follow instructions, you hear? Now go wait in the car!" he yelled. Ricky scowled, then turn and went. Connie didn't utter a word.

"So, I want you to call Daniel Benton right now and tell him you need to talk about a business you want to start. Tell him you'll meet him tomorrow at that breakfast place on exit 38. My favorite thing to eat there is that pecan waffle." Dean seemed to lose himself momentarily, but then his miserable self came back. "Tell him you'll explain the details when you see him. Got it?" He waited for an answer.

Connie bit her lip and averted her eyes. Dean was such a pathetic excuse for a human being. "Got it," she replied, not letting her disgust show.

"So, what are you waiting for? Call."

She touched Daniel's number and he answered. "Hi, Daniel? This is Carrie ... You doing okay? Great ... Yeah, I was wondering if you could meet with me tomorrow? I just want to talk to you about a business I want to start. I figured you might be able to give me some good advice ... You are? Well, when will you be back? ... I see. Okay. So, can you give me a call when you're back? ... Hey, don't mention I called to Vernon if you see him, okay? This is an idea I have, and I just want some advice from you ... Yeah, have a safe trip. Bye," she said, and she hung up. "He's flying his plane to New York early in the morning and won't be back for a week."

"*What?* We have to wait a whole damn week?" Dean looked like he was going to burst a blood vessel in his head. Connie wished he would. He picked up some tree branches and started throwing them around like a two-year-old with a temper tantrum. When he was done, he headed toward the car, shouting a stream of curse words, continuing as he got into his car and he and Ricky drove away.

❦

No one was up yet when Cynthia left for the hospital the next morning, so she sat quietly with her thoughts and cup of coffee before leaving. Last night with Daniel had reminded Cynthia of this time last year when he'd rented her house. They'd spent many evenings enjoying each other's company on her deck, usually with a glass of wine. A whole year ago, and so much had happened.

Work was a struggle for her that Wednesday until the usual ebb and flow of emergency patients filled the waiting room. She finally caught up with Max at the end of the morning before they worked together on a critical patient.

"I have two things I want to talk to you about," she said as they walked down the hall together. "The first is to say thank you again for your interest in Christopher and your help getting him back on track."

"Thanks," Max said. "When I was a little older than Christopher, I had someone take an interest in me. I don't believe I ever would have become a doctor if it hadn't been for them. This is *my* way of saying thank you to them. Maybe Christopher will do the same for someone someday."

Cynthia got teary eyed and couldn't speak, but Max knew just how to handle it.

"Listen, I need your expertise with the patient in room 15A. I've never dealt with a situation like his before, but I bet you have in ICU." He got her attention and it was back to business in the ER. When they'd finished and determined the patient needed care their hospital wasn't able to provide, they had him transported him by helicopter to St. Vincent's Medical Center in Jacksonville.

Once the patient left, Cynthia turned to Max. "Remember I said I had two things to talk to you about? I wanted to ask how it went with my mom and Granny last night. Everyone was already in bed when I got home and not up yet when I left this morning. So, how was it?"

"I think I passed the test," Max laughed. "Your Granny has some interesting stories, and that's all I'll say." He winked, knocked on a door, and walked into the next patient's room.

When Cynthia got home, Purvell, Grace, and Granny were waiting for her. The questions came one after another.

So, how was dinner? ... What did he make? ... Did he like the dessert? ... Did you have a good time? ... When are you going to see him again? Her mother, Granny, and Purvell fired away.

Cynthia took a deep breath. "I had a very nice evening, he made steaks, we had wine, and we both enjoyed the dessert. Most of the night was spent talking about everything and anything, and I'm not sure when I'll see him again, but I'm sure I will." She paused and smiled. "So, now I want to hear about Max."

"He's a very nice man," her mother said. "Granny and I approve." She looked over at Purvell and smiled.

"You can marry him if you want, Purvell. You have my blessing," Granny said. "Nothing could make me happier than to see you married."

"Well thank you, Granny. You sound like my mother," Purvell responded. "I've only just started to get to know him, but I'll keep it in mind."

"I briefly talked to Max today about his dinner with you ladies last night. He mentioned Granny had some good stories," Cynthia said as if it were a question.

Grace and Purvell suppressed their grins.

"Oh, I told him some stories about our doctor who also was the veterinarian for all the farmers," Granny explained. "His office had a door on one side leading to an examining room for people and the other side, a door to an examining room for animals. He also made house calls for both. I know of him helping a difficult delivery of a calf in the morning and then delivering a child in the afternoon. You remember Dr. Springer, Grace, he delivered you."

"I do remember him vaguely. He gave me a shot," Grace said, smiling.

"He took your tonsils out also. Very multi-talented man and a blessing to our community," Granny said with admiration.

"I'm sure that story made an impression on Max, Granny," Cynthia said.

"I enjoyed getting to know him a little bit. I imagine he's a nice man to work with, Cynthia. Life is turning out nicely for you girls," her mother said with satisfaction.

Later when they were going upstairs to bed, Cynthia followed her mom into her room and sat down on the bed.

"I want to thank you, Mom, for being such an honest, positive force in my life," Cynthia said.

"Well, I've just done what every mother does, sweetheart. Nothing out of the ordinary."

"You're way too humble. You made me realize that I've been trapped in my grief and unable to see past it. I had no idea. I'll never forget Philip, but I've been allowing him to stand in the way of my happiness. It's about taking a chance."

"You know, realizing an obstacle is half the battle, dear. Come here," her mother opened her arms for a hug. "I love you. Now get to bed. You have work in the morning."

She didn't argue, because she was tired. "Good-night, Mom."

After Cynthia finished brushing her teeth, she took a moment to look at her refection. If half the battle was realizing her obstacle, like her mom had said, Cynthia hoped the other half would be less of a challenge.

❧

This is it, Betty Franklin thought as she walked through the door of Heaven Sent on Friday morning. She'd come in early to be by herself, needing some alone time in her restaurant before anyone else arrived. Soon her staff would be there preparing for the dry run she was having in the evening with her friends and family. Her restaurant, she never dreamed she would have done this in a million years.

Her theme colors were red, white, and blue because those were Jack's favorites. He might not have been here in body, but he was in spirit. She felt him beside her every day, although she didn't tell anyone that. They might think she was crazy.

She went into the kitchen and made a cup of tea, put a lemon rose scone on a little plate, and sat down at one of the round tables. "Well, Jack," she said aloud, "what do you think? Looks pretty nice if I must say so myself. And our boys helped," she hesitated, "couldn't have done it without them, so you kinda got what you wanted. A family business to pass on."

Tears were soon rolling down her cheeks. This didn't happen to her often, but she missed her husband so much, especially on a day like today. He was her soulmate, and she would never find another like him. After taking several deep breaths, she felt better and sat in the silence, not thinking anything when a car pulled up and parked. It was Carrie.

"Hi, Betty," Carrie said. "You okay?"

"Yes," Betty answered, coming back to the present. "Just thinking, that's all." Betty looked up and smiled at the girl, but she saw something in her face and felt a pain in her heart that made her smile fade away and ask, "Are you okay?"

Carrie looked uncomfortable all of a sudden. Something was just not right about that girl. She quickly responded, "I'm fine. I'm going to get started in the kitchen. Collette should be here soon," she said and went abruptly to the kitchen.

Betty couldn't put her finger on it; something unpleasant was following that girl she couldn't explain. She had thought about offering Carrie a permanent job, although what she'd felt cross her heart just now made her change her mind. She would keep her distance but also keep an eye on Carrie for the sake of Betty's friends.

❦

The parking lot was filled and the restaurant at fire code capacity. Betty was glowing, with Luke and John on either side of her when she asked for everyone's attention.

"I've asked all of you here because in some capacity, you have all meant something to me and my family over the years. Many of you were fans of Jack's Barbeque and are disappointed I didn't rebuild—but that was Jack's baby. I could never do it without him. This little place is *my* baby, and I pray you will all come to love it in the same way."

"We do already, Betty," shouted Ian, and everyone clapped.

Betty put up her hand. "Well, thank you, Ian. Just so you all know, Ian is married to Collette, my pastry chef." They all clapped again. "I want to thank my boys, Luke and John, along with Brad Davies and Daniel Benton for helping us put this shopping plaza together. Now make sure you tell all your friends—oh, and don't forget, we also cater." Everyone laughed. "Thank you all for coming, and enjoy yourself tonight."

The festivities began. Betty had several tables covered in cloths with drinks, sandwiches, salads, and desserts. There were about fifty people, so she had some extra tables brought in just for the evening. Cynthia, Grace, Granny, and Purvell fixed plates and found a table near the door. Ian and Vernon came over and asked to join them.

"Of course you can. I'm Granny, and what's your name, young man?" she asked.

"I'm Vernon Jones, ma'am," he said, and he tipped his head a bit. "It's a pleasure to meet you."

"Vernon runs the fishing bait shop down by the North Pier on Jekyll Island and dates Carrie," Ian said. "And here she is." Carrie walked up.

"Hi, everything okay?" she asked.

Cynthia spoke. "Carrie, I want you to meet my mom and Granny, who are visiting from Wisconsin. You already know Purvell."

"Hi, nice to meet you. Hi, Purvell," Carrie offered, and then she said nothing.

"Nice to meet you also," Grace said. "Are you working for Betty?"

"Just temporarily until she gets opened. I got to go," Carrie said, and she disappeared.

"Go get yourself something to eat before you sit down," Cynthia said to Ian and Vernon.

"Vernon, when you come back, I want to talk to you about the sharks in the area," Granny said.

"Sure, ma'am," Vernon responded and followed Ian to the tables of food. Cynthia looked at Granny and laughed to herself.

Shortly after that, Max walked in, and they introduced him to Ian and Vernon. Their party was complete.

The evening was very nice. The ladies enjoyed Ian and Vernon's fishing stories, and of course Granny threw in a few of her own. Max set up a future fishing date with both men, and Ian said he would see if Daniel and Christopher wanted to go, and maybe they could all charter a boat.

The place was packed. *If this is any indication of what Betty can expect in the future, she'll be a success,* Cynthia thought.

On the way home, Granny said, "It's too bad Daniel couldn't be here with us tonight. You said he went to New York, didn't you Cynthia? Can you imagine someone just jumping in their plane and flying somewhere? I sure have seen a lot in my lifetime."

"Yes, you have," Grace said to her mother. "Cynthia, what do you know about that Carrie? An odd child, I think."

"She is unique," Cynthia said.

Purvell snorted a laugh in the back seat and then said, "I think she leans toward the dramatic myself. This past Saturday when we were all at Bennie's, she was very pleasant and happy until right when we left and she came back from the ladies' room in a panic."

"Some people just need a little more of our love than others, and I think she's one of them. I hope you girls are nice to her," Grace said.

"Of course we are, Mom. We would never be hurtful," Cynthia said.

"I know, dear, but I had to say it. You know how mothers are."

And then out of the clear blue, Granny said, "Not only did I find out a few facts about sharks, but Jekyll Island has lots of alligators, and did you know they have a sea turtle center? I want to see that."

"I was thinking Monday we'd go to the club on Jekyll for tea at four o'clock, so maybe we can visit the turtle center before, Mother," Grace said to her.

"That would be splendid, Grace. Let's do it," Granny said.

"Turtles and Tea," Purvell said, "sounds like a song title."

"I'm so happy you're going to be back in my life again, Purvell. It's time for our second childhood to start," Cynthia said and laughed.

"I couldn't agree more, Cynthia," Purvell responded.

CHAPTER 34

" I can't wait to see the turtles," Granny said. "Vernon told me after they rehabilitate the injured turtles, they put a monitor on them before they're released back into their habitat. The monitor will keep track of where the turtles go. He said to ask if there might be a release today when we get there."

"Sounds like a cool thing to see," Purvell said.

"You don't think it might be too much for you to do all this, Purvell?" Grace asked with concern.

"I'm fine, Grace. Now that I've got this boot and the hang of it, nothing has stopped me. I've been doing a little walking around without it on when you and Granny have been napping and in my room. I'm good."

"You're one driven girl, Purvell," Granny said. "Reminds me of myself in my day. Nothing could stop me."

"I don't think time has changed you much, Granny," Cynthia said.

Much to their dismay, there was no turtle release that day, so they bought their tickets and went in.

Even though the center was geared for children and school groups, there was much for people of all ages to learn. They even watched a surgery being performed on a turtle whose flipper had been torn. They were told that after the turtle was healed, they would put her back in the ocean to live her life.

Behind the center was a tentlike building that housed a turtle about the size of Granny down to the little bitty ones Cynthia remembered having as a kid. It was feeding time, so the turtles were quite animated. All the turtles would eventually be released back into their habitats, as long as they were able to fend for themselves.

After stopping in the gift shop so Granny could get a T-shirt, they walked to the car.

"So, was it all you thought it was going to be, Granny?" Cynthia asked.

"Oh, that and more. Won't little Pippa love this when she's about two or three? I would love to see them release a turtle, wouldn't you?

"Next time you visit, we'll check to see when one will be released and come over here."

"Sounds good," said Granny with a wide grin.

"It's a little early for our tea, so let's take a drive around the island. I'll show you where Daniel and Ian live and some of the other fun stuff over here," said Cynthia, and they went for the drive.

⚜

Connie had received a text from Dean about mid-morning that Monday. He wanted to get together and talk further about what she was going to say to Daniel when he got back from New York. She was to meet Dean at 3:30 p.m. over by the Jekyll Island Club. She should park by The Wharf and start walking down the trail that led south on the island—he would find her.

It was 3:15 p.m. now, so she needed to be on her way.

Connie had thought of nothing else since she got Dean's text. What did he want now? Daniel would be back in two days, and if they were lucky, she could maybe get him to see her the day after.

Since it was a Monday, not many people were around. The parking lot had only a few cars in it. After locking her purse in the trunk, she put her keys in one pocket and phone in the other. She had decided to dress as if she were there for a walk or run. That way if she saw anyone who recognized her, they would assume she was there for the exercise.

The walk was rather nice. She had never done stuff like that before and decided when this thing with Dean was over and she was far away from here, she would start to exercise regularly. The good feeling didn't last long, as Dean came into sight about fifty feet down the path.

"Hello, Connie. Beautiful day isn't it?" Dean greeted her.

"Let's get this over with," she said. "What do you want?"

"A little time has passed since last we spoke, so I felt maybe a refresher on our plan was needed."

"Seriously, is that it?"

"What do you mean, 'is that it?' I think maybe this is more than an idiot like you can handle. I'm honestly concerned whether you can pull it off," Dean said, snickering and looking her up and down.

"Shut up. I can handle it. Where's your sidekick?"

"Never mind about him. He's an idiot like you." Then he remembered. "Oh yeah, I do have to give you credit for one thing. I've checked out that Daniel Benton. The guy's filthy rich. You wouldn't want to come on to him and see if we could get more money, would you?"

She stared at Dean with disgust. "No!" She felt vomit come up her throat. "Is that all?"

"That's all," he said, and reached toward her, running the back of his hand down her arm. "Maybe you and I can get together again … what do you think? For old time's sake?"

"Don't make me vomit," she said, hitting his hand away. "This is ridiculous; I'm out of here," she said, turned, and ran back to her car. She needed a drink. After retrieving her purse from the trunk, she headed toward the resort to get something at the bar.

❦

They had wanted Betty to join them for tea, but she had too much going on at the restaurant.

"Listen, you three go on in," Grace told them. "I want to use the ladies' room."

"We can wait," Cynthia said. "I'd rather go in together."

"Well, alright," her mom told her. "I won't be long," she said, and she went downstairs to where the ladies' room was located.

Next to the stairs was the entrance to the dining room and the open bar area, where there were several comfortable chairs and some tables off to the side. Cynthia, Purvell, and Granny sat down at one of the tables and waited for Grace to come back.

The three of them were talking when Cynthia looked up and saw Carrie over by the bar. *What is she doing here?* she wondered, and just then, Grace was back upstairs from the ladies' room, talking to Carrie.

"Hi, Carrie, remember me? I met you the other night at Betty's. I'm Cynthia's mom, Grace," she said with a little wave.

Carrie looked as if she may cry, and Cynthia thought she was maybe there for a drink.

"Listen, dear, the girls and I were going in here for afternoon tea. Why don't you join us? It's all my treat," Grace offered and pointed to the others.

Carrie looked over at Cynthia, Purvell, and Granny, prompting them each to give a little wave. She had a confused look on her face, so Cynthia got up and spoke to her. "Please, we'd love to have you join us. It should be fun."

"I don't want to intrude," Carrie said and started to leave.

"Nonsense," Granny said. "I always say, the more the merrier. Where we come from in Wisconsin, everyone is a friend and welcome. I've never met a stranger myself."

"Join us," Purvell said, "unless you have to be somewhere else?"

"I don't," Carrie said. "But I'm not really dressed for this."

"You look just fine, dear. Then it's settled," Grace said, and with that, she ushered Carrie along.

The tea was quite an experience. They first each chose a tea from a big wooden box or from containers with loose tea. The hostess recommended the peach-nectar white tea as a favorite. Once they chose their tea, they were seated at a table in the cheery sunroom off the Grand Dining Room. The hostess placed a large plate with a variety of finger sandwiches in triangle, square, and circle shapes on the table along with several smaller plates containing scones, French macarons, several bar cookies, and chocolate-dipped strawberries. Already on the table were various jellies, lemon curd, and crème fresh for the scones. It was lovely.

They talked about the grandmothers' current trip there, but mostly about home in Wisconsin. Cynthia's mom and Granny shared stories with Carrie about when Cynthia and Purvell were in college. Granny told several stories Cynthia had heard many times, but Carrie hadn't. That's why Granny liked meeting new people so much: she could tell her stories as if it were the first time.

It was getting late.

"This was really fun," Purvell said. "We'll have to do this once a week after I move here."

"You're moving here?" Carrie asked.

"Yes, I decided it's time to leave New York and live where it's warmer. I'll be working with a Realtor on St. Simons, so let me know if you want to buy a house."

"Selling already and you don't even have a Georgia license," Cynthia said.

"Oh my God, I forgot I have to take a test." After she got the shocked look of her face, she laughed. "I guess I'll have to get studying now."

"You all are so successful," Carrie said.

"Why, Carrie, you're a young woman. Decide on something and I'm sure that nice Vernon would be behind you all the way." Grace put her arm around Carrie and gave her a hug and a motherly smile.

"I've got to go," Carrie said. "This was one of the nicest things I've ever done," she said and looked in each of their faces. "Thank you," she said and quickly left.

The remaining four women were silent for a few moments, then Grace spoke.

"I think she's had a hard life. What do you think, Granny?"

"She's carrying something. I think if she sticks with Vernon, she'll be okay. Love can change people."

"I'm not sure what to think, but you two are always right. You can only do so much for a person though; some of it has to be done by them," Cynthia said, and with those words, she knew she was also talking about herself. Everything her mom had told her about Daniel suddenly made sense.

"I don't know; she's very complicated for being so young," Purvell said. "But I still would like to sell her a house."

Cynthia looked at her and said, "You're what Southerners would call a 'hot mess.'"

And with that, they left for home.

꩜

Carrie couldn't get out of the club fast enough. She ran across the front lawn to the parking lot and jumped in her hot car. She was suffocating from the heat, so she turned the car on and rolled down the windows. The tears started. After digging around in her purse, she found a pack of tissues.

What was she going to do? These people were so nice. She liked Cynthia and her friends and family. It was easier to go after the money when she'd hated all of them. When did this happen?

She didn't want to go through with Dean's plan, but if she didn't, he'd kill her. This was the price to pay for all the bad she'd done in the past. Punishment. She'd go through with it and then run far away and start a good life, like Cynthia's.

If she'd had a mother like Grace, how would her life have been different? She'd never know. More tears fell as she thought about how good it had felt when Grace put her arm around her. She wanted to rest her head on Grace's shoulder so badly. Cynthia didn't know how lucky she was.

CHAPTER 35

When the wheels of the airplane touched the Jekyll Island Airport tarmac Tuesday morning, Daniel let out a sigh. He had taken off from New York as soon as the sun rose to head back south. This is where he belonged now.

The Jekyll Island Airport had allowed him to leave his car while he was gone, so he grabbed his luggage out of the back of his plane and headed straight home. Everything was as he'd left it. Living alone, he didn't mess the place up much, but he still had someone come in to clean every other week. After he unpacked, Daniel decided to get caught up on some work, so he went to his office that was set up in one of the extra bedrooms. First thing he did was call Betty to see how things were going now that she was open.

"Betty, it's Daniel. I'm back and wanted to see how everything is and if I need to stop by."

"Glad you're back," said Betty. "I can only talk a minute, but yes everything is fine. The party Friday night went well. We did miss you."

"And how was your first day of business Saturday?"

"Better than I imagined it could be. It was all so exciting. I'm still riding on a high from all the people who came by to try our menu. I know everyone was curious about Heaven Sent, but my boys have told me we've got some online reviews indicating people love it. Time will tell."

"Yes, it will. I'm going to stop by for lunch soon. Just wanted to check and make sure all was good."

"It is. Just 'cause you're done with my restaurant doesn't mean you don't come see me, you hear? Why, after Cynthia's company leaves, I better see the two of you in here regularly. Have a good day and glad you're back."

"Thanks, Betty. See you soon," he smiled. It was the first time someone had referred to him and Cynthia as a couple.

Daniel's phone indicated an incoming call. He looked and it was Carrie. He had forgotten she'd called before he left to talk to him about business. He was tired and not up to talking to her yet, so he decided to ignore the call. He was sure she'd leave a message and he'd get back to her maybe tomorrow. There was too much he had to take care of right now with DB Properties.

Before he got started on his messages, he wanted to call Cynthia and see if she was home. Maybe he could take her to dinner. Her phone went to voicemail, so he left a message and then called Purvell.

"Hi, Daniel. Are you back?" she said, sounding chipper as ever.

"I am. Did I miss anything while I was gone?"

"No, just the party at Betty's restaurant. It was nice and lots of people."

"Well, good. How's Cynthia? I called her and I guess she must be working today," said Daniel.

"She is; in fact she's not off until Friday. We're all going out for lunch at Driftwood Bistro then since I'm going out with someone in the evening. I heard Cynthia told you about Max."

"Yes, I did hear something about him. I'm happy for you."

"Sorry I was so secretive with you about seeing someone, but I wanted to be sure."

"No apologies necessary."

"So, I leave Saturday morning, but I'll be back soon so you'll get a chance to meet him. You should come have lunch with us Friday."

"I'd love to, though I wish I could meet the guy and check him out."

"Trust me, Granny and Grace already have," said Purvell, and they both laughed.

"So, is your leg doing well? Are you going to be able to race around New York in true Purvell fashion when you're back?"

"I had my doctor's appointment yesterday, and as I suspected I'm very close to as good as new. I'll be wearing the boot for another week and then flats for a while, though. My mission when I get back to New York will be to find someone to run or buy my part of the business, rent my apartment, and then move. I want to be down here before the first snow in New York. Can I count on you for moral support?" she asked.

"Anytime. So, how about you call and let me know what time you ladies decide on having lunch Friday so I can see you?" Daniel suggested.

"I'd love it."

"Great. See you then. I've got to get back to work, so tell Cynthia to call me when she has a minute the next few days."

"You know, I'm happy to see things working out for you two."

"It appears to be. Time will tell. See you Friday."

"Bye, see you then," said Purvell, and they hung up.

Daniel's phone rang and it was Carrie again. He let it go to voicemail and went back to work.

❦

Connie was beside herself. She knew Dean would be calling her to see what Daniel had said about meeting them. Maybe Daniel wasn't back yet. She bet his phone had to be turned off to fly the plane, or maybe it just didn't work in the air. Yeah, that's what she'd tell Dean. She'd left a message for Daniel that he probably wouldn't get until he landed. To keep calling him would be annoying. He'd call back when he could.

"Hey, Carrie, what 'cha doing?" She jumped. It was Vernon. He was supposed to be at work.

"You scared me. What are you doing here? I thought you had to work all day," she said.

"Sorry, I wasn't feeling well. Maybe I've got what you had the other night."

Just then her phone rang; it was Dean. Now what should she do?

"Your phone's ringing; why don't you answer it?" Vernon asked.

"It's nobody. I don't recognize the number, so I don't answer those calls."

"But it might be important. You never know. Go ahead and answer," Vernon said, and he looked at her strangely. Did he know? Of course he didn't. He was a simple guy who owned a fishing shop.

"I don't want to. Now, if you're sick, go to bed. I'll make you some chicken noodle soup. You know, I don't think we have any, so I'll have to run down to The Jekyll Market and see if they have some." She grabbed her purse and headed for the door. "I'll be back," she said, and she was off.

Once Connie was down by the Convention Center, she pulled into their parking lot and called Dean.

"Listen, I've called Daniel twice and he didn't answer. He's supposed to be back today, but I don't know when. What if his plane went down and he's dead? What will we do then?" she said, a knot forming in her throat.

"Calm down, Connie. Get a grip on yourself. Geez, this is why I hate working with women. Which of Cynthia's friends would know if he was back?" asked Dean.

"Her friend Purvell, but I can't contact her. I barely know her." And then it hit her. "Betty might know. Bye," she said and called the number.

Heaven Sent was closed for the day, but she knew Betty and Collette would be there cleaning up and getting ready for tomorrow. Collette answered the phone.

"Hi, Collette," Connie said, as cool as she could.

"Hi, Carrie," Collette said.

"Wanted to know how things were going. Betty around?"

"No, she took off a few minutes ago," Collette informed her. "She's been working so hard, I told her to let me close up. Business has been real good. I guess the word's gotten out after the party Friday night. What did Vernon have to say about it?"

This was going nowhere. "He can't wait to come back again," she said, flatly. And then she had an idea. "It was too bad Daniel couldn't come, you know, him building this and everything."

"Yeah, he had to go to New York, but he's back," said Collette. "Betty talked to him this afternoon."

"Oh, great. Well, I just wanted to see how everything was. I've got to run now. I'll be in touch," said Connie, and she hung up.

Daniel was back but hadn't returned her call. At least she knew he was back.

As she thought about what to do next, she remembered she better come back with some soup for Vernon and maybe pick up a few other things, but she called Dean first.

"He's back, so I guess we just wait."

"That's all I've been doing, Connie, and I'm really close to losing it. Call me when you hear," Dean said, and he hung up.

⚜

Since he'd returned from New York, Daniel had been going nonstop. It was mid-afternoon on Thursday, and there was no end in sight. He had three projects going, and all three had problems, although that was typical in his business. Two projects were on St. Simons, and one was in Brunswick. On St. Simons, he was renovating a house and a restaurant, and in Brunswick, he was taking an old factory building in the vicinity of the downtown area and transforming it into an office building.

Before going to the next jobsite, he checked his phone for messages and saw one from Cynthia and the one from Carrie he hadn't returned. He would call Cynthia first and then Carrie. Cynthia didn't answer. They had been playing phone tag. He knew how tired she was after working several twelve-hour shifts in the ER—and then she had company, of course—so if he didn't talk to her tonight, he would see her at Purvell's going away lunch tomorrow. He called Carrie and she answered right away.

"Hi, Daniel. I was afraid you didn't get my message," she said.

"Sorry, I had so much to get caught up on with being away for a week," he said. "I'm a one-man show here with a bunch of subcontractors I use, but I love it that way. I may eventually have to hire some people, but for now this works. So, what can I do for you? You said something about a business, I think."

"Yes, I have an idea and wanted some advice from you since you have so much experience. I thought we might meet tomorrow. I want to act fast," she said, trying not to sound overly eager.

"Gee, I'm not sure about tomorrow," he said. "I already have a meeting with someone that will take up my morning and plans for lunch that might take up a good part of my afternoon. Maybe next week. Let me get my calendar out."

"I can't wait that long." Carrie was insistent. "How about Saturday?"

"I could do that," he said, though he wondered what was so important she couldn't wait until next week. Vernon sure had his hands full with this one and her drama. "I'm going to be at a job checking some work I've got going on in the downtown Brunswick area. There's a place called Daddy Cate's Coffees I like to go to. Let's say I meet you there at 10:00 a.m. after I check my job. If I'm a little late, don't worry, I'll be there. Does that work for you?" Daniel said, and he thought he heard Carrie sigh.

"Yes, that's great. Remember not to tell anyone, okay? I don't want anyone knowing until I have my ducks in a row," she said.

"Yeah, sure, I understand. That's the way I like to do business myself. You've got my curiosity now. See you at Daddy Cate's Saturday. Bye."

"Bye, Daniel, and thanks."

Strange woman, Daniel thought and went to the next job.

❦

"We're going to meet Daniel at ten o'clock Saturday morning at a place called Daddy Cate's in downtown Brunswick," Connie told Dean. Vernon was at work, so she had the house to herself. "I just got off the phone with him."

"I told you I wanted to go to that breakfast place I like," he yelled at her. "I've never heard of this other place. Can you get anything right?"

"Listen, you idiot, it was either this place on Saturday or wait until next week sometime. You want me to call him back?" Connie felt the heat in her ears, she was so angry with him.

"No, don't call him back. Ricky and I will go check it out tomorrow. I like to see the layout of a place before I do business," Dean told her. "Did he tell you what the hell took him so long to call us? I mean, it's already Thursday."

"I don't know, just be happy he called and we're going to get this over with. Is that it? Are you done?" Connie wanted this to be over.

"Maybe if we meet with him again it can be at the breakfast place. I had it in my mind we were going there," Dean said.

"Well, then you and Ricky take your sorry selves over there. Good-bye," she said and hung up.

Oh my God, she thought. The stress was getting to her. She couldn't eat or sleep. So much was going on right now, she couldn't keep it straight. Things were going to start moving faster. She better decide where she was going next, so she could leave fast once she had her money.

Then Connie thought about Vernon and how she was going to hurt him. She hadn't intended to like him and thought maybe she could let him in on her secret so he would run away with her. It would be nice to have some company and someone to make decisions with, but then, if he knew she'd been lying to him all along, it would hurt him more than if she just disappeared.

CHAPTER 36

"I never imagined when I decided to visit you that my whole life would change," Purvell told Cynthia as they went for a short walk Friday morning on the beach. "I'm excited about the change."

"Me too. You know I meant it when I said you could stay here with me. It'll take some pressure off till you find the perfect place, and I'd love to have your company. You know I have plenty of room," Cynthia said, patting her friend's back.

"I'm going to take you up on it. And just think—we can even double-date sometimes," Purvell laughed, "like the old days."

"Right now I wish I could get ahold of Daniel. I haven't talked to him since he got back. You don't think he changed his mind?" Cynthia said.

"You've got to be kidding me," Purvell stopped. "Look at me so I know you're listening. *No.* I talked to him the other day, and he's overwhelmed from being gone. You've been working the past three days, and he told me the two of you have been playing phone tag, but good news. He's coming to lunch today, so you'll see him then and can make plans for next week."

"We have been playing phone tag. You know Millie comes on Sunday and then Mom and Granny leave next Saturday, so I don't think we'll be able to get together till the following week. It's going to be weird not having any company after all of you leave. Just me and Christopher who I hardly see anyway," Cynthia said.

"Remember I'll be back before you know it, but until then, you and Daniel get the quality time you deserve. I'll probably come back and forth in the beginning anyway. Max is going to come up next month to see my world. Should be fun."

"I can't lie. I'm a little nervous about Daniel. For me, this is a big step. I really do like him—a lot."

Purvell laughed and shook her head slightly. "Oh, Cynthia, I know you do. Give it a chance. Life is for the living."

"You sound like Mom. She said the same thing," Cynthia said, with a smile.

"I'll take that as a compliment. Let's go in and get ready for our lunch."

Daniel was waiting for the ladies when they walked into Driftwood Bistro. "I've never seen such a beautiful group of ladies before," he said as he stood up.

"Hello, young man," Granny said. "I'm disappointed I haven't seen more of you on my visit. Are you going to come by before we leave next week Saturday?"

He looked at Cynthia and shrugged. "It's all up to her."

The hostess came and seated them.

Cynthia sat next to Daniel. "I'm so happy to finally catch up with you."

"I know. I've been thinking of you a lot. Maybe next week we can go out for lunch or dinner," Daniel suggested.

"Millie is coming on Sunday with the baby before Mom and Granny leave. I would love for you to come by while they're here and see our new family member."

"Okay, I'll do that," he said and squeezed her hand.

Lunch was very relaxed, with the women doing most of the talking. Daniel enjoyed every moment and was entertained by the stories and animation these four women possessed, although truth be told, he couldn't wait for the next time he could have Cynthia alone. When the check came, Daniel insisted lunch was on him.

Daniel gave Purvell a good-bye hug. "Have a safe trip back. I'm dying to meet this Max, Purvell. We'll double-date the next time you come down here."

Purvell looked at Cynthia and laughed. "Just like old times."

⚜

That night Max took Purvell to dinner in the Grand Dining Room at the Jekyll Island Club for dinner and dancing.

"I wish I didn't have to work tomorrow and I could take you to the airport," he said.

"Just make sure you're off so you can pick me up the next time I come down," she said.

He took her hand and pulled a rectangular box out from under the table. "This is for you."

"Max." Purvell was speechless as she untied the ribbon and lifted the lid. It was a beautiful silver link bracelet with diamonds, rubies, and sapphires. "It's beautiful. Here, will you put it on me?"

The bracelet sparkled from the candlelight on their table, but nothing sparkled more than Purvell's eyes. She knew she loved this man like she had never loved before. She was sure he felt the same.

"Thank you so much. This is so sweet. I'm going to wear it every day," she said, and she looked from the bracelet into his eyes.

"I've never met anyone like you before, Purvell, and I'm looking forward to what unfolds for us," Max said. "I thought I would spend the rest of my life alone, an old crotchety doctor, but now my future looks brighter because I met you. You've brought fun back into my life."

"I feel the same about you. I'm going to miss you," she said, her eyes beginning to tear a bit.

The band started up. After a few songs, Max asked Purvell to dance.

They spent the rest of the evening talking and dancing until it was time to go. Purvell had an early flight to catch the next day. Both regretted saying good-bye, so instead they gave each other a silent, passionate kiss when he brought her home.

The next morning Cynthia, Grace, and Granny took a very different Purvell to the airport in Jacksonville for her flight to New York.

Granny and Grace got out of the car to hug her.

"It was so wonderful to spend all this time with you, Purvell. Now you bring Max up to White Lake and see us, preferably in the summer since he's a Southern boy," Grace said.

"We love you like a daughter. I can't wait to come to yours and Max's wedding," Granny said with a wink.

"Granny, you are something else. We just met. Give us some time. You know I love you both," she said, and a tear rolled down her cheek.

Cynthia gave her friend a hug. "See you soon," she said, and Purvell disappeared through the automatic doors.

CHAPTER 37

Saturday morning, Daniel was still riding on a wave of happiness after seeing Cynthia, but he needed to keep his enthusiasm in check. That's what had gotten him in trouble the last time, so his intention was to step back and let things happen slowly. Right now all of Cynthia's family was visiting, but they would be going home in a week. He hoped he would be the one she would call on to fill the void after their departure.

After fixing a travel mug of coffee, he headed to downtown Brunswick and the old building he was repurposing into office space. It was the first time he'd used this particular subcontractor, so before Daniel went any further with the guy on other jobs, he wanted to see how good his work was. Being new to the area, Daniel still had to go through this trial and error, sorting out the good subcontractors from the not so good. Whenever he did find a good one, he made sure to pay them a little bit better so they always wanted to work for him.

Also on his agenda in Brunswick was to meet Carrie for coffee and talk about a business idea she had. Even though he really didn't want to meet with her, he was committed to giving advice to anyone who reached out to him. After all, he'd started from nothing and asked many people for guidance along the way, so he felt this was his way of paying it back. He only hoped her idea had some possibility.

Maybe when he was done with Carrie, he could swing by Heaven Sent for lunch. He might even call Cynthia and see if she, her mom, and Granny wanted to go also, or maybe he would get lucky and Cynthia would want to go alone with him.

Daniel was a happy man today.

Unfortunately, when he checked the building, he found the subcontractor hadn't done a very good job. The electrical work wasn't done to specs, and the job site was a mess. He'd pay the guy for the work done but find someone else to finish the job. Everything else looked good, and he felt confident he'd finish on the date he'd told his client.

Now to get his meeting with Carrie over with and then see about his idea for lunch.

❦

Saturday was always a busy day at the bait shop with Vernon up early and out the door by 7:30 a.m. Connie had also gotten up early; she was stressed out thinking about the meeting that morning with Daniel. *This could go real bad,* she thought, *what will Dean say?* Right now her main goal was to get this thing over with—without getting killed. Her stomach churned at the thought.

"Well, I'm leaving," Vernon said. "Doing anything special today?"

Oh, she thought, *just trying to extort a half-a-million dollars, that's all.*

"I thought I would do some cleaning and grocery shopping, maybe," she said. "And then I think I'll go for a walk on the beach."

She had decided she would go to Driftwood Beach after her morning meeting so she could sit on one of the trees washed ashore. The salt air and the sound of the water might possibly help her feel at peace.

"Hey. Let's go out to dinner tonight just the two of us. Anywhere you want," said Vernon, pulling her close.

"I still don't feel great, but we'll see." She turned away, but then slowly turned back to look at him. He was a goofy kind of guy; however, his kindness had touched her heart. Throughout her whole life, no one had ever cared about her the way he did. Not even her own family. She thought it was odd at first, but now after becoming part of this community on Jekyll Island, she realized this type of kindness was common. Cynthia and her family, Ian and Collette, Betty, even Daniel, who thought he was helping her start a business. There was nothing in it for any of them, and yet they were kind to her. "Thanks, Vernon," she said and meant it.

"For what, darling? I didn't do anything."

Her throat closed up and she couldn't speak, so she kissed him and went to get the only thing she could keep down in her stomach. Coffee.

<hr>

Dean wanted Connie to be fifteen minutes early, so she left her place at 9:15 a.m., giving herself enough time to get there. *Wait until Daniel finds out who I really am,* she thought. *He'll hate me.* That bothered her. It used to be she hated people like Daniel, but not anymore.

When she pulled up, she saw Dean's car with Ricky sitting inside. Dean treated him like crap, and she was ashamed she used to be like Dean.

She parked and went inside.

"Hi, Dean."

"Good, you're here. This is the plan. You sit here by yourself, and once Daniel sits down, I'll come over and do the talking from that point on. Keep your pie hole shut. Do you get it?"

She said nothing, looking at him with disgust.

"I'm going over here to sit and wait," Dean said, taking a seat where he could keep an eye on her. And they waited.

Connie had never hated anyone more than Dean at the moment.

At 10:03 a.m., Daniel Benton walked in.

"Hi, Carrie," he said. "Sorry I'm a bit late. How's Vernon?"

"He's fine," Connie said.

"So, did you enjoy Betty's opening party? I hated to miss it, but there were some things I had to take care of out of town."

"It was great. I know how it is sometimes having things to take care of," she said flatly, eyeing Dean across the room.

"Are you okay?" he asked. "You seem a little, I don't know—different. Why don't you tell me about your business idea?"

"Hi, Mr. Benton," Dean interrupted. "You don't need to know who I am, just what I need from you," he said and sat down.

Daniel looked from the man to Connie, who looked down at the table, not wanting to make eye contact.

"I understand you're involved with a certain woman by the name of Cynthia Lewis," Dean said. "I wonder if you're aware of the fact her late husband was a big gambler?"

"Who are you?" he looked at the man and then Connie again, who was still looking down at the table.

"Let me explain more. This here," Dean pointed at Connie, "was Philip Lewis's bookie. Mr. Lewis died owing a good bit of money. Connie here, or I guess you know her by 'Carrie,' tried to collect it after his death with no luck. Unfortunately interest has kicked in, so the total debt has increased. We want our money and we think you might want to take care of it for your girlfriend."

"I'm aware of Philip's gambling problem," Daniel said with authority, "but how do I know what you've told me is true?"

"Oh, it's true," Dean laughed, then looked at Daniel straight in the eyes before he continued. "And if you don't pay soon, there may be some accidents. I understand Mrs. Lewis has a son and daughter, and then there's her mother and grandmother, along with a brother and niece—oh! And also a grandchild … little Pippa? You would be a fool not to believe me." He laughed. "See, I've done my homework, Mr. Benton, and this ain't no joke. Funny how accidents happen," Dean said and shook his head with a smirk on his face.

"What would you do? You're not saying you're going to kill someone, are you?" Daniel asked, his heart about to beat out of his chest.

"I never said that, did I? People do have accidents though, don't they? You never know when one might happen, usually when you least expect it," Dean said, squinting his eyes.

He is pure evil, Connie thought. She briefly looked at Daniel. His face was pale as if he might pass out.

"How much money are we talking?" Daniel asked.

Dean picked up a napkin from the table and pulled a pen from his pocket. He wrote down $500,000 and gave the napkin to Daniel.

"What? Philip owed this much?"

"I told you—interest. The people I work for don't take money owed them lightly. I've done some research on you also, Mr. Benton, and this is a drop in the bucket for you." Dean waved his hand. "So, Connie and I will go and let you think about it. You have Connie's number, so give her a call after you digest this a little—but don't wait too long.

My boss has waited long enough and he wants his money, understand? Oh, and don't you tell a soul about this, or there will be hell to pay. Good-bye, Mr. Benton."

Dean got up and walked to the door, turning to look at Connie, and bellowed at her, "Come on, Connie. It's time to go." Connie looked at Daniel for the first time since Dean had started talking. Tears were pooled along her bottom eyelids. Daniel gave her a look as if to ask, *why?* She got up, staring at the floor, and followed Dean out.

As soon as Connie backed out of the parking lot, she began to sob. She continued to sob through the streets of Brunswick until she reached the turn to go home, but instead of turning right and going to the beach as she'd planned, she turned left and took the causeway to St. Simons Island and then Frederica Road until she came to the small gravel parking area outside the Wesley Memorial Garden. No one was there, so she went in and sat by the cross.

What can I do to make this right? Connie thought silently as she sobbed. *I feel so alone. Is there anyone who can help me?* There were no answers. She sat with her eyes closed for a while and then looked off into nothing as if in a trance. The sound of a car pulling up prompted her to wipe her face on her sleeve and walk along the garden path until she could slip out unnoticed.

When she finally made it home, she crawled into bed feeling drained and fell asleep.

Stunned by what he had just heard, Daniel sat in Daddy Cate's with a cup of coffee for a while before he got up to leave. The waitress brought over the bill for the man and Carrie's—no, Connie's—coffee.

"Are you paying this?" the waitress asked Daniel. He looked up, still dazed by what had just been said to him.

"Sure, why not," he responded, as he pulled out his wallet and handed the girl a fifty dollar bill. He left without getting his change. The words the man had said echoed over and over in his head. He looked at the numbers scribbled on the napkin just in case he'd misread what was written. *$500,000.* There was no mistake.

His earlier idea about lunch at Betty's was forgotten as Daniel drove onto Jekyll Island. He didn't want to go home, but where to go? The North Pier was one of his favorite places on the island, so he headed that way and parked. He saw the bait shop and wondered if Vernon knew his girlfriend wasn't who she said she was.

The pier was busy with people fishing—after all, it was a Saturday. Daniel went down the right extension of the pier, where he sat on a bench and stared out over the ocean, thinking of what the possible outcomes could be if he did or didn't come up with the money; none of them were good.

After an hour, he came to a conclusion. He would have to give them the money. If he didn't, he could never face Cynthia again, knowing someone dear to her could be injured in any way because of his refusal when he'd had the means to prevent it. He would have to do this quietly and not breathe a word of it to anyone ever. He didn't care about the money, only the people who would be hurt if he didn't pay it. It was decided; now he had to come up with a plan to quietly do this.

It was mid-afternoon, and all Daniel had in his stomach was the coffee. He needed to eat something, so before he went home, he'd stop by Jekyll Market and get a sandwich.

As he walked off the pier, he saw Vernon coming toward him. There was no way to avoid saying "hi," so he went with it.

"Hey, Daniel. I don't see your fishing pole. Is Ian out here? He usually stops to say, 'hi,'" Vernon said.

"I just came to look today. Had some thinking to do," Daniel told him, forcing a normal conversation with the man.

"I know what you mean. A man has to do that on occasion," Vernon said and laughed. "I was thinking maybe sometime you and Cynthia could get together with Carrie and me for dinner, maybe in the next couple of weeks?"

Daniel didn't know what to say. "I'll have to check with Cynthia; she has company right now, and her schedule as a nurse can be unpredictable. I'm sorry, but I'm not feeling well, Vernon. I think I better run."

"Funny, but Carrie hasn't been feeling well either and I had a little something myself. I'm kind of worried about her. She's been sick ever since we went to Bennie's. Hey, you don't think there was some kind of virus the three of us could have picked up there, do you?"

Daniel looked into Vernon's face and said, "No, Vernon, I don't have what she has. I've got to go," he said, and headed to his car.

When Daniel got home, he changed and took the sandwich he'd picked up along with a beer into his office to start assessing the situation. With paper and pen in hand, he began writing down the facts to help him feel some control in the situation.

He figured the man and Connie were a part of a small-time gambling ring, since it had taken two-and-a-half years for them to pursue Philip's debt. It also crossed his mind that it was just the two of them extorting money from him. No matter what, the threat was real and he would take it seriously.

In New York he had a safe where along with some valuable coins, jewelry, a couple of antique guns, and important papers, he also had cash, $750,000, in hundreds, for an emergency. He'd have to fly to New York to get it though. All of Cynthia's family would be on St. Simons this week, making them far too accessible to the man and

Connie. He would feel much better if they were not in the area when he handed over the money. He would have to put Carrie—or Connie—and her partner off until they all went back home. Millie was leaving mid-week, and Grace and Granny were leaving Saturday. Daniel would have to come up with an idea on getting Christopher out of town. It meant next week Saturday was the earliest he could arrange to meet with Connie and her partner.

Just then, Daniel thought of something and went into his bedroom closet with a stool. There it was on the shelf in the corner where he'd left it locked in its case. His gun. He may need it but hoped he wouldn't. After putting it back on the shelf, he returned to his office and continued with his plan.

Tomorrow he would call Connie back and tell her he couldn't get that much money together overnight without suspicion, so he needed several days. They would probably know you can't just walk into a bank and ask for that much money without suspicion and reports being filled out. He would have to go to New York first, he would tell her, because that's where his banks were. Calling her tomorrow would also give him a night to think about a possible way out.

After getting another beer, Daniel went over his plan again and then put it aside. There was nothing more for him to do. His phone call with Connie tomorrow would dictate how the rest of the week would fall into place.

He felt anxious and needed to get out of his house. Not wanting to be alone, he called Ian.

"Hi, Daniel. What's new, my friend?"

"Do you think Collette would mind if we started up your fire pit tonight? I'll bring the beer."

Ian hesitated for several seconds. "I thought you and Cynthia were getting along grand these days?"

"We are. Just need some downtime tonight and couldn't think of any friend I would rather get drunk with than you," Daniel said, trying not to sigh too loudly.

"Well, in that case, I'm still at work right now but will be leaving at 6:30 p.m. Come by at 6:45 p.m. I'll get the wood started in the fire pit."

"I'll be there with the beer. Thanks, Ian."

"Anytime, mate."

It was Sunday morning, and Connie had been checking her phone for a call from Daniel since she got up. She thought he'd have called by now, but nothing. It was almost one o'clock. Dean would probably be harassing her if she didn't get a call from Daniel by the end of the day.

At about 2:15 p.m., Daniel's number showed on the screen of her silenced phone, so she told Vernon she wanted to go for a walk and headed out to return his call.

"Hi, Daniel." She didn't have to tell him who it was.

"I'll give you the money," he said as Connie's heart thudded in her chest. "Only problem is, I have to go to New York to get it. I have to be careful, since withdrawing all that at once could draw some attention. I don't think you want that. I'll have to go to a few different banks over several days where I have money to gather that much without suspicion."

She hadn't thought of that and apparently Dean hadn't either. "Fine. What's your time frame on this?"

"I can fly up there Tuesday morning and be back later in the week. It's the only way I can get that much cash together without raising suspicion."

"I'll pass the info on and get back to you." She hung up, called Dean, and filled him in.

"I hadn't thought about that," Dean said. "We sure don't want a bank flagging him for money laundering. This whole thing could backfire in our faces. Tell him there better not be any funny business. Tell him if I don't have the money soon, someone will pay for it."

Connie passed the information back to Daniel. She hated being the go between but was relieved it was almost over. This week, she'd make her get away plans.

CHAPTER 38

It was amazing how much stuff was needed for a tiny baby. Millie and Jimmy arrived on Sunday with their car packed as if they were staying a month instead of just a few days. In less than twenty-four hours, Cynthia's house was transformed into baby central. Granny was the most curious of the new "gadgets," as she called them. Pippa was definitely a lucky little girl.

After taking Purvell to the airport in Jacksonville the day before, Cynthia, Grace, and Granny had gone shopping for Pippa. Granny had found the perfect doll, while Cynthia and her mom went a little crazy buying clothes, making sure to buy some in bigger sizes so Pippa would always have something new to wear as she grew.

When Pippa woke up from her nap, Granny couldn't wait to give her the doll. Millie was touched.

"Why, Granny, this is her first doll. We'll keep it forever. I wonder what we should name her?" Millie said.

"We thought Hazel Pearl might be nice," Cynthia said and gave Millie a wink.

"That's the perfect name, Mom. Thank you, Granny, for something so thoughtful," Millie said, and Granny just beamed.

"Dear, Granny and I are fixing a special dinner tomorrow night since Christopher will be home also," Grace explained, "and we've also invited Betty and her boys, along with Ian, and Collette, thinking this would be a good way for them all to see the baby. Cynthia, did you invite Daniel?" Grace asked her.

"No, Mom, I haven't. I thought I might have heard from him by now, so I'll just give him a call later. I'm sure he'll want to come, so count him in on your plans," Cynthia told her.

The rest of the day was spent doting over Pippa when she was awake. Christopher lay on the floor, talking to her in funny voices while Pippa watched him intently. The baby was staying awake a little longer in between naps, so it made playing with her fun.

When Cynthia called Daniel to invite him to have dinner with her family, it went straight to his voicemail, so she left a message. Later, she missed his return call, but he left her an answer about dinner. He said, "no," he had to fly his plane to New York early Tuesday morning again and wasn't sure when he'd be back. She should say good-bye to her mom and Granny for him because he doubted he would see them before they left on Saturday. Also tell Millie and Jimmy "hi" and he would get his chance to hold Pippa during their next visit.

Cynthia understood but was rather disappointed he hadn't wanted to just swing by or talk with her before he left. She also wondered why he had to go back to New York so soon when he was there only last week. She went to call him back and see if he could just stop by, but then hesitated. He was obviously busy and would call when he got back.

Dinner was very nice. Cynthia wished she could do this more often.

Everyone took turns holding Pippa, marveling at how perfect she was.

"I wonder when one of the boys will get married and give me one of these?" Betty queried.

"Mom, please," John said, and everyone laughed.

"It's the best ever," Cynthia told her.

"We might as well tell them, love. Go ahead," Ian said to Collette.

"We're going to be having one of our own." Collette looked at Ian, all smiles. "Just found out. I have my first doctor's appointment this week."

"Wow, Ian," Christopher said, amazed, like he couldn't believe it. "You a father?"

"I know, lad. They'll let anyone become one," he winked, and they all laughed.

They all were full of the warmest congratulations.

"As long as we're telling good news," Jimmy said, "Millie and I have something to share."

Cynthia looked from Millie to Jimmy and back to Millie. "Another baby?"

"No!" Jimmy said quickly. "No, no, not yet. I've been given a big promotion with my job and they're going to move me."

Oh no, Cynthia thought. She couldn't stand to have them move far away.

"That's one reason we made this trip. I'm being transferred to Savannah. We're going to meet with a Realtor on the way back to look for a house. We'll be about an hour and a half away."

Cynthia jumped up and gave them both a hug.

"Oh, Jimmy, that's so great. Savannah is such a lovely city. How soon?" Cynthia asked, "Do you have to wait to sell your house?"

"They want me to start in a month. We're going to use our current house as an investment and rent it out. We hope to find a place we like right away, but if not, the company will put us up in a place for ninety days and we can continue to look."

Cynthia was thrilled.

Everyone was so happy to hear the good news, but none more than Cynthia. She began to see her world moving forward in a positive way and couldn't wait to see what happened next.

⚜

It was a slightly cloudy day, but that wasn't going to stop Daniel as he headed out for his eight-hour flight in his Cessna to New York. It was Tuesday morning—his plan was to come back late Thursday and lay low until the money exchange took place. He didn't care where or when it took place, as long as it was after Cynthia's family were far from the Jekyll Island area.

The money he needed was in a safe at his New York office and would take only a few minutes to retrieve, but the man and Connie didn't know that. The $500,000 was the only control he had in this transaction. Just maybe he would think of a way out of this before he came back.

So, Carrie was really Connie. He had always heard people who were trying to pass themselves off as someone else picked a name very similar to their real name.

When they'd met at Daddy Cate's, he didn't get the feeling she was fully committed in this. She hadn't participated at all in the conversation; the guy with her had called the shots and done all the talking. The whole time, she'd kept her eyes down, never looking at him. Daniel figured the guy must have something to hang over Connie's head, which made her the weakest link in this deal.

Try as he might, Daniel could think of nothing to change the outcome of all of this. In reality, he would pay a million dollars if it kept Cynthia and her family safe. By this time next week, their lives would be back to normal with no one but him knowing what had happened.

❧

"Millie's visit went so fast, Mom. I can't believe it's already Wednesday and you'll be leaving Saturday," Cynthia said, waving to Millie and Jimmy as they backed out of the driveway.

"But Cynthia, just think of how much closer they'll be now. You can run up there for the day when you need a baby fix," Grace said.

"I know, I can't believe it, and they can come down for a weekend. I couldn't be happier."

"I have to tell you," said Granny, "when I first met Jimmy, I wasn't sure that boy was ready to be married much less a father, but our Millie must have seen something in him not visible to the naked eye. He has turned out to be a good man. It's really a miracle."

"Just between us, Granny, I felt the same way," said Cynthia. "I worried about the kind of life Millie was going to have with him. I guess we could say he was a late bloomer." They laughed as they went back inside.

"Cynthia, you haven't mentioned much about Daniel. Is everything okay?" Grace asked as she closed the door.

"I guess so. I haven't heard from him since Monday, and that was just a message left in my voicemail. I think everything's okay, though. He did tell me he was going to

New York and wouldn't be back in time to say good-bye to you, so I'm not sure when I'll see him."

"That seems odd," said Grace. "I'm sure it's just business and once he gets back here, he'll tell you all about it. Now let's get something cold to drink and sit out on the deck. That little baby has tired me out."

"Me too," Granny said, "but she sure is a cute thing. I can't get enough of her."

Cynthia hugged her grandmother. "And we can't get enough of you, Granny. You both go out there and I'll fix us something to drink and a snack."

She pulled her phone out of her pocket after they both were outside and touched Daniel's phone number. It rang until the voicemail picked up. She decided to leave a message. "Hey, Daniel. Just hoping you're okay and wondering when you'll be back. … I miss you."

⚜

It was close to seven o'clock Thursday evening when Daniel landed at the Jekyll Island Airport. Behind his seat was a suitcase with his clothes and a backpack containing $500,000. A pretty expensive flight.

Before he unloaded his baggage, he put his plane in the hangar at the airport. One of the guys working there came out and spoke to him.

"Someone inside wants to talk to you. They've been waiting some time."

"Who is it?" Daniel asked, concerned it was Connie and her partner. "Is it a petite woman and a tall man?"

"No. Just go through that door," the man said with a shrug.

Daniel couldn't imagine who it was. He was relieved when he walked through the door. "Hi. That guy said you were waiting for me. What's up?"

"We need to talk," the person said.

"Right now? I just got back from a long flight and want to go home," Daniel said.

The person pulled out what looked like a wallet, but inside it held a badge that said "Federal Marshal."

"Right through here, Daniel," the person said, pointing the way through an open door.

Daniel followed without a word.

❦

Later, on his way home from the airport, Daniel called Christopher.

"Hey, Daniel, you're back! Mom will be so happy. I think she's really missed you. When are you coming by?" Christopher asked.

"Not anytime soon, I'm afraid. Are you working or at home?"

"I'm actually at the Wee Pub eating with friends. I just finished work. Why?"

"Stay there, I need to talk to you alone. It's important."

"Okay, I'll be here waiting." Daniel looked at his watch. It was already 9:00 p.m.

Daniel found Christopher with a couple of his friends. Christopher introduced them, and Daniel sat down. Shortly after, the friends left to go back to work and they were alone.

"So, what's up, Daniel?"

"I'm going to ask you to trust me. I want you to go away for the weekend somewhere. It's for a good reason, I just can't tell you why," he said, keeping his voice as steady as possible. "Do you trust me?"

"I do," Christopher said. "Like I would my dad."

Daniel got a lump in his throat and couldn't speak.

"I'll go up to Charlotte and hang out with some friends. I do that on occasion. You're kinda scaring me though, Daniel. Can't you give me a little more info?"

Daniel wanted to tell Christopher, but he knew it was best if he didn't. "Maybe I can someday, but not now."

Christopher sat staring at him for a good length of time before he spoke. "Okay, I'll go, I'd like to see my friends anyway."

"Thanks, son," he answered. "I'll be in touch; just don't tell your mom. Make sure you leave by Saturday morning."

⚜

The next day, Friday morning, Daniel called Connie.

"Are you back?" she asked before he could say a word.

"Come out to the Jekyll Island Airport—alone," Daniel told her.

"Why? Is this a trap? How can I trust you?" she asked.

"I'm far more trustworthy than that guy you're working with. Can you come without being followed?" Daniel asked.

"I don't know," she responded. "I can try."

"Then try. Someone at the airport will ask if you're Carrie when you get there; just say 'yes,'" he said and hung up.

Connie looked out her windows and didn't see Dean and Ricky's car, but that didn't mean anything. She decided to call Dean to see if she could find out where they were.

"Hey, I haven't heard from Daniel yet; do you want me to call him?"

"No, but if we don't hear anything by the end of Saturday, we'll maybe have to get ahold of that kid of Cynthia's and hold him hostage to show we mean business," Dean responded.

"I want nothing to do with anyone getting hurt, Dean," Connie said firmly. "Daniel will give us the money; just be patient, you fool. You go holding someone hostage and the authorities will be after us for kidnapping on top of everything else. I'm washing my hands of this whole thing and walking if you do a stupid thing like that. I can't wait until this is over. I need my money to get as far away from here—and you—as I can," she said. She was fuming and couldn't hold her tongue.

"I can assure you, the feeling is mutual. Ricky and I are going to see if we can find some babes on the beach," Dean said, and he laughed.

"Right. Good luck with that." Connie hung up.

Thirty minutes later, she was parking at the airport. A guy approached her car and asked if she was Carrie. She said "yes," and he took her in the airport building. A door opened and Daniel came out of a room to talk to her.

"Glad you could make it. You weren't followed, were you?"

"I'm sure I wasn't. Now what's this all about?" she demanded.

"Good. Someone wants to talk to you. Follow me," Daniel said and took her in the room.

When Connie saw the person, she stopped. "What's going on here? I'm leaving."

The person stood up and walked toward her. "Hi. Have a seat. I'm going to tell you a little story you might find interesting. I just ask you don't interrupt me until I'm done."

CHAPTER 39

Cynthia was on her way home to an empty house after dropping her mom and Granny at the airport. Even Christopher had left town, deciding to spend the weekend with his friends in Charlotte.

She thought she'd stop at Heaven Sent to see Betty before she went home, but when she stopped by, Betty wasn't there, nor Collette, so after a trip to the grocery store, she went home.

Still concerned about Daniel, she called him again, his phone going straight to voicemail. She hung up. In reality, some time alone would be good for her after all the company the last few months. A run, a light supper, a glass of wine, and a movie sounded good.

Just as she was getting ready to go out the door for a run, her phone rang and she saw it was the hospital ER number. It could only mean one thing. Someone had called in sick and they needed help.

"Hello."

"Hi. Cynthia?"

"Yes?" she said, trying not to sound annoyed.

"This is Peggy from the ER. I need your help. Mary Wilber just found out about a death in her family, so I was wondering if you could work her shift? I know it's late notice, but I'd be grateful."

"When do you need me?"

"She was scheduled 3:00 p.m. to 11:00 p.m. I know you usually work the day shift, but Dr. Carroll suggested I call you."

"He did? Well, I guess I'll have to thank him." They both laughed. "I'll come in. It might be a little after three, but I'll be there."

"Thanks. I really appreciate it," Peggy said.

"Sure, glad I can help."

Cynthia ate a snack and fixed some leftovers to take with her before going upstairs to change into her scrubs. By 2:30 p.m. she was ready to leave.

On the way to work, Daniel came to mind. Maybe she would hear from him yet today or tomorrow. If she didn't by Monday, she would see if Purvell could check his whereabouts. She was starting to become concerned.

Connie called Dean and Ricky.

"He's back and he's got the money."

"Awesome," Dean said. "About time."

"What's the next move?" Connie asked. "I need to know so I can make my plans to head out of town."

"I've got several ideas. Let me think about it and I'll call back," Dean said, sounding distracted. "We're going to meet with him tonight though for sure. The sooner we get this done and ourselves off this island, the better."

Dean hung up and said to Ricky, "It's show time. He's back with half-a-million dollars."

"So, what's the next step? I hate the way you've been keeping me in the dark like this," Ricky said.

"I wanted to wait until the last moment, in case Daniel Benton decides to be a hero."

"Do you think he would be stupid enough to do that?"

"Yeah, I do," Dean said. "He's got that goody-two-shoes all-American look about him. Makes me sick to see people like that. It's not natural."

Ricky was thoughtful and then said, "But I think there's an element of good in everyone."

Dean looked at him as if considering what he said. "What the hell are you talking about? You've been watching too much TV." Dean waved his hand and shook his head at Ricky. "I've just decided, we're meeting him ten thirty tonight at Horton House. You know that old shell of a house on the north side of the island? Nobody will be around there that late. It's too spooky-looking," he said with a laugh. "I'm going to have Connie meet Daniel at the pier and then drive him over there. We're going to be waiting across the street at the cemetery, so we can't be seen, and make sure the coast is clear before we grab the money and take off down the trail to where our car is. Then we'll split."

"What about Connie?" Ricky asked.

Dean rolled his eyes. Ricky was such an amateur. "She jumps in her car and leaves Daniel stranded. He can't follow, and by the time he gets help, we're gone."

"How will she get her cut of the money?" Ricky wanted to know.

"We'll catch up with her later," Dean said.

"But what if she can't get away?" Ricky continued.

So many questions. "The important thing is *we* get away with the money safe and sound. It's a brilliant plan," Dean told him.

"If you say so." Ricky didn't sound convinced.

"Hey, I'm hungry. Run down to that yogurt ice cream place and get us something. You know what I like," Dean said.

"I'm not your slave," Ricky yelled back. Then, after a few seconds, he picked up a room key and said, "I'm only going because I want some ice cream too." He slammed the door as he left the hotel room.

Dean sat down in one of the chairs and put his elbows on his knees and his head in his hands. He was happy to be alone for a time to get his thoughts together. This was not working out as he had planned. He had been entrusted by Mr. Thornberry to find Connie and work with her to get the money she'd never collected—or else. He had to succeed.

If he pulled this off, he could be proud of himself and finally get a promotion and some respect from the other guys he worked with. Right now they just treated him like a piece of crap. He had been sent on this job with no help except useless, stupid Ricky. And then he had to deal with that dumb bitch, Connie. She was only good for one thing in his opinion, but he'd burnt that bridge when he cheated on her.

He was going to think positive. He would be successful tonight, and soon he would be rid of Ricky and Connie and have his long-awaited moment to shine.

❦

It was seven o'clock Saturday evening and Daniel hadn't heard from Connie yet. He was getting anxious. *Maybe they want to wait until tomorrow,* he thought. He wanted to get it over with.

The Yankees were playing, so he turned on the TV to distract himself. At 8:00 p.m., Connie called.

"Hi, meet me in the North Pier parking lot at 10:25 p.m. sharp," she said.

"Okay. See you then," he said, feeling nervous like he never had before.

Daniel went upstairs to his bedroom closet with a stool and the key to his gun case. The only time he ever carried the gun in public was when he went to target practice, but tonight he wasn't going empty handed. After he unlocked the case, he took the gun out and held it in his hand for a moment before opening the chamber and loading it. He hoped he wouldn't have to use it but would if he had to.

He grabbed the book bag with the money and set it by the door, then went back to watch the game, his mind elsewhere.

✦

The clock in the ER said 9:30 p.m. Cynthia was tired. Evenings were not too different than days in the ER. Tonight they'd had a sick baby, a snake bite, an appendicitis attack, chest pains, food poisoning, and a home-improvement accident. Enough to make the time go by quickly. She finally got to speak to Max.

"I understand I can thank you for suggesting I fill in tonight," she said.

"I figured since all your company was gone, you might be lonely. I knew this would fill the void," he said and laughed.

"I *was* lonely," Cynthia admitted. "Hey, have you talked to Purvell?" she asked.

"Every day, why?"

"Has she mentioned seeing Daniel? He went up there on Tuesday and I haven't heard from him. I'm trying not to get concerned—but I am. I thought maybe he might have gotten together with her," she said.

"No, she didn't mention it. I'll ask next time we talk if you want?" he offered.

"That's okay, I'm going to call her tomorrow myself."

Just then, they heard an ambulance siren.

"I guess it's back to work," Max said and went down the hall.

There was a slight mist in the air, just enough for Daniel to run his wipers every so often. It only took a few minutes to reach the pier parking lot from his house. Connie's car was parked toward the back. It said 10:24 p.m. on his dashboard clock.

He parked next to her and rolled down his window as she did the same with her window on the passenger side.

"Are you ready for this?" Daniel asked before he got out.

"As ready as I'll ever be," Connie answered. "Get in and let's get it over with. Oh yeah, I'm supposed to make sure you don't have a gun. Do you?"

He smiled, but didn't answer. The bag of money and his gun were next to him. He slipped the gun into the back of his pants, grabbed the book bag, and got into Connie's car. "Let's go," he said.

Connie waited and then spoke before driving, "I'm not sure what you think of me, but I'm really not a bad person." She wouldn't look him in the eyes. "At one time I hated Cynthia and her life, but now that I've gotten to know all of you, I wish I'd never had to do this." She looked up at him, a single tear rolling down her cheek. "You're nice people, and I'm different for knowing you. Please tell everyone that," she said, and she looked down again.

He was surprised by her words. He'd always believed in giving second chances to people who wanted to change.

"Well, you're going to get your chance to live a new life. If you really want to change, you will, and soon you'll see the world around you change also. Remember that," he said, and he touched her shoulder. "So let's work together and close the door on this chapter, okay?"

"Okay," she said, turning from him to wipe her eyes. She put the car into drive.

After parking the car, Connie and Daniel got out and walked over to the remnants of Horton House. The mist had let up, the stars now providing a stunning backdrop behind the house. On any other night, Daniel would have taken time to enjoy the view above him.

"So, what next, Connie?" Daniel asked.

"Be patient and quiet. I'm not really sure myself," Connie said in a soft voice, but soon, Daniel's question was answered. Dean came out of the darkness with Ricky behind him.

"So, nice to see you again," Dean said as Ricky smiled and tipped his head.

"We're going to take a walk across the street over here to the family cemetery and down that path for some privacy in case someone drives by. Oh, and if you're thinking of any funny business, I have a gun with a silencer here in my pocket, and so does my associate." He laughed.

The cemetery was not as visible from the road, so once they were across the street, both Dean and Ricky pulled their guns out.

"Now, let's see what's in that bag," Dean insisted while Ricky hung back.

Daniel handed him the book bag. "It's all there. I'm a man of my word."

In his excitement, Dean fumbled as he unzipped the bag, but he finally got a good look at the money. He grinned from ear to ear.

"It looks as if our business is done. It's been a pleasure, but I'm sorry to say I can't leave any witnesses, Mr. Benton."

"Come on, Dean, let's just get out of here," Ricky said, shuffling his feet.

"You said nothing about killing someone, Dean," Connie said, her voice trembling. "Let him go. He won't tell anyone."

"I'm sick of looking at you and hearing your voice. This will shut you up!" Dean said, and in one fell swoop, he pointed the gun at Connie and shot her in the chest.

"Why did you do that, Dean?" Ricky shouted in a panic.

"Shut up or you're next," Dean shouted back.

Daniel slowly reached for his gun as the two argued, but Dean saw the movement out of the corner of his eye. Without hesitation, he shot Daniel, who fell to the ground. As he lay bleeding, Daniel saw the man he'd met at the airport emerge from the bushes along with other law enforcement officers, their guns pointed at Dean. Soon, they all faded to black.

***

"Cynthia!" It was Max, racing down the hall. "I just got a call; there's been a shooting on Jekyll Island. Two people are on the way here with gunshot wounds. I need your help."

"Of course. How long before they're here?"

"Not sure, but we're getting the rooms prepared. Get gowned up and ready."

The adrenaline was pumping as Cynthia put on a gown. Soon in the background she heard the ambulance approach the hospital, so she went back out to the hallway. Two gurneys came in, both individuals appearing nonresponsive.

Cynthia stayed back out of the way, allowing the EMS and patients to get through quickly, until Max came to her.

"I've got a team working on the patient in room 10," he said. "The gunshot wound is in the heart area. The other patient is in room 15 with a bullet entry in the leg and a head injury that appears to be from a fall. Surgery is prepping for both of them. I'm putting you in charge of the team for the patient in room 15. They both need to be ready to go as soon as we get the call from surgery. Come with me," he said and Max led the way.

Cynthia began directing her team but stopped when she saw the patient's face.

"Cynthia, what's wrong? We need to move!" Max said.

She looked at Max. "It's Daniel. Oh my God, it's Daniel." Her knees became weak and she wavered to a kneeling position.

"Amy, take over. Cynthia, you'll have to leave. Someone help her out of here," Max said, as he began to work on Daniel.

Cynthia crawled out the door and sat leaned against the wall, her knees pulled to her chest. That's when she thought she saw Vernon run down the hall. *What would he be doing here?* Her head spun.

She went to the nurses' station, where she could sit down and be out of the way. She felt dizzy. There were law enforcement people everywhere. What was Daniel involved in? She couldn't imagine. All she knew was she loved Daniel and didn't want to lose him.

After about an hour, Max came to find her. "I wanted to let you know Daniel is in surgery. He hit his head when he fell after taking a bullet to the leg. He's lost a lot of blood, and there's concern that the bullet may have hit his femoral artery. He'll probably need a transfusion. The bullet is still in his thigh, and he has a grade-two concussion. The woman who came in with him died. There was no way to save her."

"Max, do you have any idea what was going on?" Cynthia asked, bewildered.

"Not really. I'll see what I can find out. Right now, why don't you go to the surgery waiting room. I called up there and told the guy at the desk you were the next of kin, so check in with him when you get up there. Grab a blanket and pillow to take with you. It's going to be a long night, I'm afraid. I'll come find you when I finish up here."

"Thanks," she said and hugged him.

Before she could leave the ER, two men and a woman approached her with official-looking badges on their chests. One man held a phone to his ear.

"Just a minute," he said to the person on the phone. "Are you Cynthia Lewis?"

"Yes," she said, almost afraid to tell him.

"I'll call you back. I found her," he said into the phone and hung up. "I'm Special Agent McGee. I was wondering if I could have a minute or two of your time?"

"I think I would like to have someone with me. Could Dr. Max Carroll sit in? He's head of the ER."

They looked at each other and Special Agent McGee said, "Sure," and told the woman to find Dr. Carroll. When Max arrived, they were led to a room down the hall.

"Please, sit down," Agent McGee said, and he gestured to a chair.

"I would like to ask you a few questions that might help us out. How long have you known Daniel Benton?"

"I met him two-and-a-half years ago," she said, her voice wavering.

"Do you know a Connie Dickson?"

"Connie Dickson?—Is this about my late husband's gambling debt?"

"Right now I'm unable to answer questions, only ask, ma'am. If you could answer, please."

"Yes, I met her once," she said, and she hesitated. "She was my late husband's bookie."

"Did you ever pay her any money?"

"No, never. She came to my house once not long after my husband died, looking for money she said he owed. But I sent her away and told her I'd call the police if she ever showed up again."

"And you had no contact with her after that?" Agent McGee asked, taking notes.

"No, none whatsoever. Why are you asking all this?"

"Like I said, I'm not able to say at this time. Here's my card. You're free to go, but we request you not leave town for the next ten days in the event we need to ask more questions," he said and stood up.

They left the room and Max said, "In all my days in the ER, this one tops them all. What the heck is going on?"

"I don't know," said Cynthia, "but it keeps getting more and more curious. I'm sure you've gathered that my late husband had a gambling problem I didn't know about till after he died. Not sure what it has to do with this, but right now my focus is on Daniel. I'm going to the surgery waiting room," she said and left.

After letting the waiting room attendant know who she was waiting for, she made herself comfortable on a sofa and soon fell asleep. Her shift had ended hours ago.

She awoke to someone gently shaking her. It was Max. "Cynthia, the surgery's done." She sat up, a little dazed. "Daniel did well. He's stable and in a room. The bullet was safely removed from his thigh, and he should make a full recovery. He's under observation for the concussion. He's not going to be fully awake for a while, so I suggest you go home and rest."

"I don't want to leave until I can see him," she insisted, shaking her head.

"I'll take you to his room so you can see he's fine, but then go home and rest. The poor guy will be out of it for a while. He's being well taken care of and is going to need you more later when he's awake," Max told her.

She had told many family members of patients this same thing and knew he was right. "Okay," she said and followed Max.

Daniel looked so helpless when Cynthia saw him. She took his hand in hers and bent to his forehead, where she gave him a gentle kiss and began to cry.

"I love you, Daniel."

Max walked Cynthia to her car. She would go home and rest. Daniel was in good hands.

CHAPTER 40

Cynthia went back to the hospital mid-morning on Sunday to find Daniel sitting up in his hospital bed.

He held his arms out to her, and she gently went into them. No words were spoken as they held each other for several moments before Cynthia pulled back and asked the question that had plagued her since she'd first seen Daniel on the gurney in the ER.

"What happened? What was this all about, Daniel?"

"The Federal Marshals were in first thing this morning, asking me the same thing," he answered.

Daniel lay back and closed his eyes for a moment, leading Cynthia to believe he'd fallen asleep, but when he opened them, tears trailed down his cheeks. She let him take his time.

"I'll start at the beginning with what I know," he said. "Do you remember Connie Dickson, who came to your house wanting money Philip owed her?"

Cynthia was confused. How did he know Connie's name? "Why, yes, I'll never forget her."

"Carrie was Connie Dickson."

"I don't understand. How could that be? Carrie didn't look anything like the woman who came to my house that day," Cynthia said, her face pale.

Connie was under pressure from the gambling organization she worked for to get the money Philip owed at the time of his death. After the day she visited you, she went underground for a period of time, out of fear from the gambling ring. She changed her appearance. She had planned on coming back to pressure you again, except you went to England and stayed for six months, messing up her time frame, so she had no choice but to wait for you. Her original plan was to work alone, get the money, then go somewhere and start over—away from the gambling organization. This backfired when a guy by the name of Dean got involved. He and his partner, Ricky, worked for the same organization she did. The only thing Dean didn't know was Ricky had been working undercover, so he passed all information on to the Federal Marshals." Daniel hesitated and laid his head back. "I'm getting ahead of myself now."

"I'm a little confused, Daniel." Cynthia's head was swimming. "How did *you* get involved with this?" she asked.

"They came to me for the money Philip owed Connie and Dean. They threatened your family, Cynthia. I guess they chose me because they knew I could pay it and that I would. Last week when I went to New York, I went to get the money to pay them off so they would leave you alone."

"How much money did they tell you Philip owed?" Cynthia asked.

Daniel closed his eyes and rested awhile.

"They wanted $500,000," he said.

"*What?* Philip owed them $100,000 according to Connie—or Carrie," Cynthia said, shocked. It was all so difficult to comprehend.

"Interest," was all Daniel said, and he rested again before continuing. "When I came back from New York, a Federal Marshall was waiting to talk to me who knew everything that was going on. He asked me to work with him to bust this case. I said I would."

"Why would you do that?" Cynthia asked.

"That Marshal was Vernon," Daniel answered. "He's been working undercover with the Federal Marshals for years. He graduated from the Federal Law Enforcement Training Center in Brunswick during his early twenties, when he was approached to work for them. Apparently he's helped crack a ton of crime rings, from drugs to gambling."

"I can't believe that sweet Vernon was a part of all this. And the fact that he and Carrie—Connie were involved. How in the world did that happen, I wonder?" Cynthia said.

"Vernon didn't know Connie had been involved with organized crime when he first met her. It was purely chance that they met," Daniel explained. "The Marshals were going to rush in as soon as Dean took possession of the money, but Dean shot Connie first, point blank, and then me, before they could move in and stop him."

Cynthia was stunned with what Daniel had just told her.

"So, how is Connie doing?" Daniel asked.

He didn't know. She waited a long while before she spoke.

"Connie died, Daniel. She didn't last long after she arrived at the hospital."

Daniel looked away and out the window. When he turned back, tears streamed down his cheeks. "And what about Vernon? The Marshalls had made a deal that if Connie helped us, she'd be granted amnesty. She and Vernon planned to go somewhere and start a new life together. Vernon was to be reassigned, and Connie was going with him."

"I don't know, but that explains why I saw him in the hospital last night. I'm sure he's long gone by now."

"Yes, he probably is," Daniel said.

"Daniel, I can't believe what you've done for me and my family. You put your own life in jeopardy to protect the ones I hold dear. There's nothing I can do to ever thank you enough," Cynthia said and sat on the side of the bed, taking his hand. She was overwhelmed by his selflessness.

"There is one thing you can do," he said, placing a hand on her cheek. "Tell me you love me and will never leave my side. I love you, Cynthia."

She looked at the man in front of her. The only man she had ever said those words to was Philip. She touched Daniel's hair and ran her hand down his bristled cheek. Last night when she saw him in the ER, she'd realized she loved him with all her heart. She couldn't bear the thought of losing him.

"I love you too, Daniel," she said and stopped to take a deep breath. "And I'll never leave your side."

CHAPTER 41

One year later.

rane Cottage, in the Jekyll Island Historic District, was the perfect venue for a wedding. The ceremony was to be held in the home's sunken garden on the side, with a cocktail hour overlooking the reflection pool in the front, then dinner and dancing in the courtyard behind the historic home. The day couldn't have been more perfect, with a blue sky full of fluffy white clouds.

It was 3:30 p.m.; the wedding starting at 4:00 p.m. sharp, so guests had begun to arrive. The bride was safely tucked away in one of the guest room suites with her mother and her only attendant.

Christopher was the lookout for them, popping his head in now and then to give a report on the activity they couldn't see.

"It's starting to fill up," Christopher told them. "You know, I used to get a chance to help out for weddings over here sometimes when I worked for the club."

The minister knocked on the door, wanting to know if everything was fine. They all assured him it was. There were ten minutes to go.

The bride wore a full-length, sophisticated blush-pink dress from a fancy shop in New York. The attendant wore a knee-length, soft floral pastel dress to complement the bride.

"Well, this is it. Mom, you better go so you can be seated," the bride said to her mother.

"I can't believe this day is finally here," her mother said, giving her a kiss before she left. Five minutes later, the bride and her attendant went to take their places.

The view from the back of the sunken garden was breathtaking. White chairs filled with guests sat in neat rows, and the garden setting couldn't have made a lovelier backdrop for the ceremony.

The music started and the attendant proceeded down to her place up front with the groom and his best man. The music changed, and then it was the bride's turn.

Purvell looked radiant as she and her father headed down the aisle to a smiling Max. When the minister asked, "Who gives this woman away in marriage?" Purvell's dad, Ronnie, got all choked up but came through with, "Jane and I do."

Cynthia looked around at the people in attendance. On the one side of the aisle was Purvell's whole family. They'd had to hire someone to attend to the farm so they could all attend the wedding. Max had asked his son to be his best man, the rest of his family filling the chairs on the other side of the aisle.

She scanned the crowd for Daniel. His eyes met hers and he smiled. She loved him more each day.

The ceremony wasn't long, and soon they were heading back down the aisle to celebrate the marriage of Dr. and Mrs. Maxwell Carroll.

As Cynthia followed them, she thought of her own wedding not that long ago. She and Daniel had gone a much more casual route.

Three months after the incident at Horton House, Daniel had asked Cynthia to marry him. She of course said, "yes." They'd decided not to wait and kept it simple. Daniel had come up with the idea of getting married on White Lake with just family and their closest friends.

The wedding had taken place in late September in front of the white birches that gave the lake its name. The ceremony was performed in the cleared area where Cynthia and her friends had played as kids, close to the water circled by the trees. Purvell was maid of honor, of course, and Ian, best man. After the minister pronounced them husband and wife, a wind blew just like the day she'd spread Philip's ashes on the lake. Was that his blessing? She believed it was.

The reception had been held at—where else? The Kelly Lake Motel ballroom. Their family and friends took up most of the motel rooms for the weekend. In addition to Cynthia's and Daniel's families, there were Purvell's parents, Collette, Betty, her boys, and Max. Cynthia couldn't have loved it more.

After their wedding, Daniel moved into Cynthia's house and they rented out his place on Jekyll Island—or went there sometimes themselves when they wanted a change of scenery. Cynthia stayed in the ER, coming to enjoy the work she did there, and enrolled in an online program for her master's in nursing. Daniel had begun to make a name for himself in the coastal area as a developer, with more work than he knew what to do with. Their life settled into a beautiful, uneventful ebb and flow.

Purvell had finally made the move to St. Simons Island by the end of the year, when Max asked her to marry him. Jane, Purvell's mother, was beside herself to finally have her only daughter getting married. Ronnie, her dad, had tried to convince Purvell to have the wedding up by them in Wisconsin, but Purvell told him he would finally have to come south.

After the wedding guests began to clear out of the garden and head to the reflection pool where cocktails and appetizers were being served, Cynthia found Daniel waiting for her off to the side and walked over to him.

"You look beautiful," he said as he smiled and gave her a kiss. She smiled back.

"We're going to have a few pictures taken, and then I'll meet you over by the reflection pool in the front," she said. "Find the kids and Mom, okay?"

A month after Cynthia's wedding, there had been a beautiful, unseasonably warm day on White Lake, the kind of day that had always been Granny's favorite. Granny had told Grace she was taking a cup of tea out on the porch that overlooked White Lake from Grace's cottage, to sit and watch the world go by. When Grace came out with her own cup of tea to visit with Granny, she'd found her fast asleep. Grace sat down, and after a period of time, went to wake Granny to come in, only to find she had passed away peacefully in a place she loved, on the kind of day she enjoyed. What more could anyone ask for?

The pictures were over, and Cynthia went to find her family. She saw Daniel in the distance with her mom, Christopher, Millie, Jimmy, and Pippa, who had just started walking the month before, along with Betty and her sons, Ian, Collette, and their baby boy, Alistair. Pippa was toddling around with the doll Granny had given her after she was born. Little Hazel Pearl was Pippa's constant companion.

As Cynthia approached, Pippa saw her and headed her way, excited. Cynthia picked the child up and lifted her in the air, Pippa squealing with happiness. She brought her down to her face and kissed her little fat cheeks, bringing on more squeals, then setting her loose to toddle around some more.

Everyone was focused on Pippa, except Grace, who came over to Cynthia.

"What a beautiful day. It's so good to see you two girls settled and happy. Only wish Granny were here to share in it. How she would have loved to be at Purvell's wedding, but I'm grateful she got to see you and Daniel marry before she left us. I miss her so much."

"So do I, Mom," Cynthia said, and took her mom's hand. "Why don't you think about spending the winters with us from now on? I don't like the thought of you being all alone that time of year."

"I think I will, sweetheart. Thank you for asking. Did you check with Daniel first?"

"It was his idea. He loves having you around, as do I. It's because of you I was able to see my way through to him."

"Me? Well, I don't know about that," her mom said.

"There were so many things I willingly allowed to cloud my way. Not anymore. You were right as always."

"Oh, sweetheart. It takes a whole lifetime to learn the lessons you need to learn, and I've had plenty of those lessons. You're almost there yourself," she teased.

Cynthia hugged her mom. "I love you, Mom."

"I love you too, sweetheart. You know I can't wait to see what life brings us next."

Cynthia looked at her children and Daniel and felt a swell of peace in her heart. "Me too, Mom. Me too."

ACKNOWLEDGMENTS

When I was about eight or nine years old, I overheard my parents talking about the book my grandmother had written. Their exchange centered around what in the world had possessed her to write a book, how she would ever get it published, how it couldn't be very good, and how much money it would cost. At that moment, the writing gene that was passed on to me from my grandmother must have been activated, because after eavesdropping on Mom and Dad's conversation, the first thing I thought was, I'm going to write a book too.

Grandma never did get her book published. I have the manually typed manuscript in the original cardboard dress box tied with a string. The book is a love story titled *Down in the Hollow* by Hazel Wells Amond (her pen name). Her real name was Hazel Pearl Gomber Amond. The book is long, 538 typed pages, and I'll admit I've read bits and pieces, but never the entire manuscript. The book was beautifully written in prose, which seems like a lot of work to me, but was very popular back in the day. At times I take a few pages out of the box and read what my grandmother so eloquently put on paper, finding inspiration in her words.

I also have some poetry she wrote and many prayers. My grandma had a gift.

She was not the kind of grandma who was hugging and kissing you all the time, but the kind who expected my two brothers and I to act like a young lady and gentlemen. Children were to be seen and not heard. When we had dinner with her, it was at the dining room table set with china and silver. She made the best roasted chicken, cookies, and cakes, but her baking forte was cake donuts. We were always given a brown paper bag filled with donut holes for our ride home after we visited. I remember her as being very beautiful, poised, and interesting. Not only did she play the baby grand piano in her parlor, as she called it, but she also did exquisite needle work and oil paintings, which my brothers and I have proudly hung in our homes. My grandfather's youngest sister once told me, when she was a young girl she remembered when my grandparents had courted and then their wedding. It was like a fairy tale to her and she wanted to be like my grandmother. I've always said if grandma had lived in the South she would have been considered a Southern belle.

So, with that being said I want to dedicate this book to her memory. I'm not only grateful for her inspiration, but for leading me to what has provided more personal satisfaction than anything I've ever done before in my life. Who would have ever imagined that the thought my parents' conversation put in my head decades ago would one day come to fruition?

I have many other individuals I'm also grateful for. First is my family, for their support. My daughters, Elizabeth and Julianne, who are my biggest fans, and my husband, Bill, who gives me the space I need to do this crazy writing thing. My brothers Drew and David have been a constant support along with my Aunt Lois and all my cousins, sisters-in-law, and so many friends, I don't have enough space for all your names. I'm a grateful woman and love you all.

A big thanks goes to my publisher, Mindy Kuhn and editor, Amy Ashby at Warren Publishing. Love working with you ladies.

I want to recognize all the Barnes and Noble Booksellers in the Charlotte, NC area. Zack James, Arboretum; Thom Hayes and Kemi Adetolu-Robbs, Birkdale Village; Roxie Risky, Carolina Place; and Cindy DeLuca and Matthew Lowe, Morrison. Thank you for opening your doors to me. I want to especially thank the staff of the Arboretum store for being the first to take a chance on a new author and always being so supportive.

Many thanks go to the ladies who chose to read my first book, *White Lake,* in the twenty-plus book clubs I've attended over the past two years. You have been an inspiration.

What an honor it's been for me to participate in The Fox Cities Book Festival for 2017 and 2018, speaking both years at my hometown library in Neenah, WI.

More than anything, I want to thank you for reading this, my second book. I have several more in my head waiting to come out, the next of which is *Life's Fortune.*

Please follow me on Facebook, Instagram, and at susanamondtodd.com.